Praise for *Whiteout*

"This is an impressive debut, rich in ideas and feeling, told in a voice all its own."
—*Publishers Weekly* (starred review)

"A strikingly assured, mature drama, engrossing and beautifully constructed . . . an estimable and highly auspicious debut."
—*Kirkus Reviews* (starred review)

"Considering how often (and badly) virtual reality is being used in the field, and the rather simplistic approach SF usually takes toward international politics, this debut novel should be inhaled quickly—for it is as invigorating as the fresh, frosty air enlivening Walker's Antarctic winter."
—*Locus*

"Tough, sexy, and smart—as smooth and savvy as the best thrillers, but peopled with real human beings, and carrying a real science fiction b   lker is a stylish and powerful new voi   s."

or of
zine

"A striking debu   character and vivid renditio   stinguish her as a new writer of spe   r cyberspace fans."
—*Booklist*

WHITEOUT

ALSO BY SAGE WALKER

Man in the Tree

SAGE

WALKER

WHITEOUT

A TOM DOHERTY ASSOCIATES BOOK
NEW YORK

WHITEOUT

A Tor Book
Published by Tom Doherty Associates
175 Fifth Avenue
New York, NY 10010

www.tor-forge.com

Tor® is a registered trademark of Macmillan Publishing Group, LLC.

ISBN 978-0-7653-8980-0

Our books may be purchased in bulk for promotional, educational, or business use. Please contact your local bookseller or the Macmillan Corporate and Premium Sales Department at 1-800-221-7945, extension 5442, or by e-mail at MacmillanSpecialMarkets@macmillan.com.

First Edition: April 1996
First Mass Market Edition: October 2017

Printed in the United States of America

0 9 8 7 6 5 4 3 2 1

For Hank,
who buoys up my dreams
with love, skill, and patience

I'd like to thank Norm Belew, Captain P. Burr Loomis (retired), USNR, and Bill Wells for Neat Stuff generously shared, and I salute the dauntless courage of the 1991 incarnation of the Very Small Array: Sally Gwylan, Pat McCraw, Karen McCue, Pati Nagle, Melinda Snodgrass, and Walter Jon Williams. Thank you, Brendan McFeely, for offering the right word at the right time. Special thanks go to Mary Rosenblum for helping build worlds and characters, and to Gardner Dozois for nudging.

WHITEOUT

PROLOGUE

This third night, not a true night, for there could be no true nights in the December summer, the changing weather of the Drake Passage gave them what they needed, squall and sleet in the dark of the moon, and seas that boiled and tossed but were as calm as these Antarctic waters would ever be in a storm.

Mihalis said he could take the Zodiac out, and he did, slipping the inflatable boat over the side of the trawler and into the blowing needles of ice. His words, whatever they were, were lost in the howl of the wind.

Psyche waited. Nikos, the brother of Mihalis, waited silent beside her in the cabin.

Mus, the boy from Naxos, was too young and too restless for waiting. He tightened the drawstring of his parka around his face and went out into the storm. Psyche watched him slip on the frozen deck and catch his balance like a cat. He stood gripping the rails with his mittened hands, looking into white nothing.

The wind increased. It roared sounds that were almost words; it whined through the rigging with a sound of giant wasps. The wind drove ice before it, rime that grew in minutes into spikes of wild white hair that coated the lines, the rails, the windward shoulder of the boy. Mus stared out into the storm as if he could see the Tanaka ship that Mihalis planned to cripple, or Mihalis himself coming back across the water. The ice scattered the dim light and made the boy's thickly bundled shape look like a flat paper cutout. Psyche thought of calling him in, but Mus would watch for icebergs as well as for Mihalis, and it was the face of Mus that would freeze, not hers.

Psyche let the *Sirena* turn into the wind. The *Sirena* sent out false codes that made her seem to be a Tanaka ship. Mihalis had copied the chip the Tanaka woman gave him, thinking he might use the codes again someday. The fool. For all Psyche knew, the radios now marked them as Korean, or, worse, as a boat out of Chile. Mihalis trusted too much.

Mihalis had been gone too long.

The sonar was turned off, its red display dark before her, but she could sense the sweetness of the water beneath them, could feel that it was thick with buggy little krill and the larger fish that ate them. In any other time she could imagine, they would circle away from the storm, let it move past, and come back to this spot, where she knew they could load their nets as soon as they were spread.

Dull orange, a wash of light came up from the dark, a false, terrible dawn. The glare turned the frozen spindrift on the lines into dragon's teeth stained with the colors of flame. The shadow of the boy from Naxos became a black giant ghost that scrambled across the deck.

Mus slammed the cabin door behind him as Psyche hit the throttle. The trawler's engines rumbled as the *Sirena* turned toward the dark where the light had vanished. Terror waited there, possibilities of death.

The radio, tuned to search, chattered static and nothing else. The readouts still marked the *Sirena* with a false ID. Psyche jerked the foreign woman's little chip out of its slot and threw it against a bulkhead. It skittered across the tilting deck and came to rest by her feet. The *Sirena* ran silent, anonymous, a dark and dangerous shape on anyone's radar.

They searched for a long, long time, Psyche and the brother of Mihalis and the boy from Naxos, with their torches strobing futile circles into the sleet. They bellowed with the ship's horns and with their voices, sounds that vanished in the roar of the storm.

They found ice, only ice, brash, and floes tossed by the sea.

Eventually, the squall forced them away.

ONE

Snow fell in Taos.

Signy pulled pine splits from the woodpile on the portal, an armload, a hundred bucks a cord and going fast. Tiny snowflakes found the sliver of exposed skin where her parka and her gloves did not meet. Melting, the flakes burned a pattern, a secret little snow message on the tender skin of her wrist. She didn't have the patience to try to read it.

Signy hooked her foot around the edge of the door, levered it open, carried her wood inside, and shoved her butt against the door. The door slammed with a satisfying bang.

Shelter, warmth, security, the old adobe house provided it generously, but only if the house was supplied with constant infusions of money, lots of money, and this morning it seemed that nobody she loved cared about that.

One hundred dollars a cord, Signy stacked her wood by the corner fireplace. The fire burned busily, money up the chimney, gone.

A spider scrambled from beneath a stick and ran for cover. It wasn't a black widow. Signy let it go, wondering what the hell it found to eat in a dry woodpile where the temperatures dropped below zero at night.

"Signy?"

Pilar's voice, damn it, from the holo stage in the center of the studio. Signy kept her back to the stage and fed a log to the fire.

"You're back," Signy said. She shrugged out of her parka and laid it on the *banco* next to the logs, still not looking behind her.

"Signy, I'm sorry."

Edges' corporate funds were down to almost nil: Thank you, Pilar. Pilar was sorry.

"Is Jared there?" Pilar asked.

That did it. Looking for Jared, was she?

Signy stamped across the room, flung herself into the rolling chair at her console, and keyed up full resolution on the holo stage. Pilar had blown all of Edges' money, and Pilar's response? Guilt? Contrition? None of that. Pilar wanted Jared; he would give her comfort and hugs. There, there, he'd say, and fix the pain. Let Jared make everything *feel* better, right!

"Jared is up skiing," Signy said.

A presence built of bytes and photons, Pilar, life-sized, immediate, stood isolated at center stage. Mist sparkled on her long, Hispanic-black hair. The strap of a carry-on dented the padding in the shoulder of her jacket, this one printed within a geometry of primary colors: whites, blacks, bright oranges, and blues. Mayan-looking, new, probably expensive.

Signy pulled her headset over her eyes, giving herself a full surround of Pilar's setting. Pilar was at home in Seattle, yes, in the studio there, with its bay window and its polished wood floors.

"You're angry," Pilar said.

"Damned straight I'm angry! Pilar, we're *broke!* What the hell happened?"

"I told you. I felt I was getting stale. I wanted the presence and stress a live audience gives. The feedback. It's different from virtual, from studio sessions and replays."

Pilar shrugged the carry-on off her shoulder, a dancer even in that simple gesture; so graceful. Pilar, the performance artist, performing now for Signy. Just once, Signy wished, would you please just turn it *off?*

"And I played to empty theaters. Nobody wants *live* anymore; nobody wants acoustic; they want scent and touch, the whole shtick, sensory jolts and virtual icicles down their backs. That's what they want. Or anyway, that's what they want from *me*."

Pilar retreated to a wall, braced her back against it, and slid down to sit cross-legged on the floor, theatrical dejection in every motion of those trained muscles. Signy wanted to thump her, hard.

"Look, I'm sorry your artistic sensibilities got wounded, but did you *once* look at what this caper cost us? Even *once*, Pilar?"

"No."

"No." The debits had just kept coming in from Pilar's draws on Edges' corporate credit accounts; lighting, a new guitarist at studio rates, different costumes when the first ones didn't suit. Then the road crew, the fees for interstate use, because shipping all the gear by airfreight seemed too expensive at the time. But Pilar hadn't bothered to figure in the cost of *feeding* the roadies.

"You must hate me," Pilar said.

Signy took a deep breath. "Listen, Pilar. Just listen for a minute. We have enough money to cover one more month's mortgage payments on the houses in Taos and Seattle. And that's all we've got." Paul's house in New Hampshire was a family legacy of his and paid for a hundred years ago, thank goodness. "We have one more payment coming in from that bit we did for Gulf Coast Intersystems, the tweak on their negotiations with the Arian people for fuel canisters. It's a small payment. That's it. I don't have *time* to hate you right now. I've got to dig around for a contract for us, or Edges goes poof!"

Signy wondered, even as the words came flying out, what the hell she was doing. Having a temper tantrum, obviously, and she knew she would feel guilty later, sick at her loss of control, contrite.

"Why didn't you stop me?" Pilar asked.

Pilar really did look hurt. Wounded. Worried, even. Oh, damn that face of hers, perfect wedge of cheekbone, big dark eyes, her aristocratic Hispanic-Anglo features.

"Damn it, Pilar! The charges that damn near broke us came in all in the same day, and you were off-line. Out of the net. Taking that little recreation break with your new guitarist, weren't you?"

Mendez was tasty, granted. If I'd been Pilar, Signy thought, I would have stolen a few hours in that Scottsdale hotel, the one with the good security that Paul and I couldn't break through.

We had fun trying, Paul and I, but if we can't get some work real fast, the fun's over. I can't let this group be destroyed, not without a fight, certainly not because Pilar-fucking-Videla gets urges for artistic flings. "You're a grown-up, Pilar. It's not my job to *stop* you. It isn't Paul's job, either."

"Look, I said I'm sorry." Pilar stood up and reached down for her carry-on. Tears stood in Pilar's eyes. "You're over the edge, Signy. We'll talk about this later."

"Pilar—"

Pilar dissolved, damn it, just vanished, all the feeds to Seattle blanked out, and Pilar's dramatic exit did not help Signy's temper at all. Signy tried an access sequence to the Seattle house, another, but the codes were tricky. She kept herself away from the emergency override, unwilling to break the unwritten rule that said, Don't use emergency overrides unless it's an emergency; we all need privacy sometimes.

Signy slapped at the keyboard and folded her arms against her chest. Pilar didn't always act like a grown-up? How about Signy Thomas? Mature, reasonable Signy Thomas, terrified of losing the group, family, whatever, called Edges. Pilar and Janine. Signy and Jared. Paul. All they were to each other, strength, support, synergy; they couldn't *lose* each other, damn it! Afraid of that loss,

Signy had tried to hide her fear in anger, and the obvious target had been Pilar.

Signy typed a message for Seattle.

[Signy] Apologies. Contrition. I love you.

She sent it. The message would sit there until Pilar decided to respond, and that could be days; sometimes when Pilar got upset she vanished to the streets and didn't come back until she'd settled whatever demons were after her. She'd done it before.

Janine might help, but Signy hadn't seen her in the Seattle house. Janine had gone off to visit her folks while Pilar was out on the road, but Janine was due back—

Signy pulled up the file where Edges posted itineraries, when they remembered. Janine was due back sometime today.

Paul's Call Me light blinked awake on Signy's console. He was up early, for Paul. In New Hampshire, it was noon.

Paul wanted something. Okay, she'd talk to him.

[Signy] What is it, Paul?

[Paul] A contract.

[Signy] We'll take it.

She got up and walked toward the kitchen, hoping this morning's coffee hadn't gone too stale.

Paul's voice came through the speaker above the sink. "Just like that? Don't you think you should hear what it is before we sign on?"

"Just take it, Paul. I don't care if it's with the *Mafia*, for pity's sake. We need the money."

Signy poured herself a cold cup of coffee and stuck it in the nuke.

"Calm down, Signy."

Listening, was he, while she yelled at Pilar? Oh, Paul!

"I'll try," Signy said.

"Drink your coffee," Paul said.

The coffee tasted bitter, old. Signy sipped at it anyway,

forced it down over the lump in her throat. "Go ahead, Paul. Tell me about the job."

"The contract is with a company called Tanaka," Paul said. "Come in the studio and we'll look at it."

TWO

Settling her coffee cup on her desk in the big room in Taos, the studio with its paired desks and monitors, hers, Jared's, set low to give a heads-up view of the holo stage. Signy expected documents, charts, Paul's voice in overlay.

"Full interface, please," Paul said.

Done some work on this, had he? Signy pulled on her headset and accepted the illusion of Paul Maury's world.

Colors and white noise blurred and then cleared before Signy's eyes, as if she blinked away a wash of tears. Paul smiled at her, his face in close focus because his face was where she had entered virtual, winter-pale skin, the black feather of an eyebrow, heavy lashes. Signy backed away. Paul wore a maroon turtleneck and rumpled tweed slacks and ragg wool socks. One of his socks was patched with duct tape.

Paul was lean elegance, but you couldn't take him anywhere. Signy didn't try. She wiggled her back against the familiar Queen Anne chair that had formed behind her, the feel of its burgundy leather a fiction produced by tiny pressure shifts in the skinthin she wore.

Paul had set up the library in his New Hampshire house for this, the room he favored for conversation, a familiar and polished construct. Paul sat in his leather chair by the fireplace. Reflections of firelight picked out random gleams of gold on the shadowed wall of books behind him.

"The richest waters on Earth," Paul said.

He fashioned a globe in his hands, a blue-white Earth that he hugged in his lap as if it were a child. He turned it upside down and his fingers sank in the clouds he had imaged over the Sahara.

"The Southern Sea."

A true master of illusion, Paul had fashioned the little world he held in his hands with great care. The Great American Desert stretched up toward Canada. The Sahara-Sahel blotted most of the African continent; California's floating archipelago thrust its tiny islands out into the Pacific. Paul had even built a minuscule model in bas-relief of man-made Los Angeles, anchored in the shallows of Catalina Bay. Antarctica, now on top of the globe, glowed white in a dark green sea, and its tiny mountains pebbled the globe's smooth surface.

"You've worked on this. How long did it take?" Signy asked.

"The globe? I had it filed somewhere."

Not the globe. The job offer, Signy started to say.

"The proposal came in last night. It's interesting, Signy." Paul put his finger on a minuscule orange and black barber pole that marked the South Pole. It was out of scale. "It's for some work in Antarctica."

"Antarctica?" Signy asked.

"Well, in Lisbon. The Antarctic Treaty Commission is meeting in Lisbon this year."

"Lisbon. Right."

"Both places, actually. Tanaka is a Japan-based company that turns krill biomass into usable protein," Paul said. "Tanaka, our prospective employer, wants us to help sell some changes in the Antarctic Treaty."

"International law? Paul, do we know anyone with that sort of expertise?"

"It's accessible. The project breaks down into bits I think we can handle," Paul said.

"I think I've heard that before," Signy said. She got out of her imaged chair and walked to the fireplace. She rested her hand against the mantel, where Paul had created the sensation of dust on polished mahoghany, gritty against her palm. Paul was no housekeeper. Even his virtuals were dusty.

"No, really. We can do this." Paul looked at the Earth model he held in his hands. He squeezed the globe down to grapefruit size and put it on the table beside him. Signy watched the veins rise and tighten in the backs of his hands.

"What do they want us to do? Opinion shaping? Media work?" Signy asked.

Edges sold both. Sometimes phrases that an ad agency could work with, sometimes information tailored for the ears of an official who could could sway a political decision; Edges fitted answers to problems, many kinds of problems.

"We'll be finding phraseology for Tanaka's legal staff to sell in Lisbon. That's the job, basically."

"What phraseology, Paul?" Signy asked.

"Tanaka would like to see limits set on the krill harvest. Tanaka didn't come up with the proposal; a bunch of scientist types did. Tanaka likes the concept and so does a majority of the voting members of the Treaty Commission. All we have to do is keep a favorable climate for the proposal."

"What do we have to do?" Signy asked. If the job was doable, if Pilar wasn't too ticked off, maybe Edges was still in business.

"We are to convince the Antarctic Treaty Commission's members to go for yearly, variable take-out quotas on krill, tonnages based on some theories set up by marine biologists," Paul said. "The fishing fleets are worried about depleting the take. There's considerable support for limits, at least in the countries that aren't starving. We'll have to make sure the members don't get distracted by other proposals if they come up, and that the majority remains a majority, at least until the votes are in."

Janine could help handle the biology; Janine was trained as an environmental engineer. She'd know if the figures on the biomass made sense. Signy wondered if Janine was home yet; if she'd gone to soothe Pilar. Janine could settle Pilar down if anyone could.

"Paul, hold, would you? I want to check something." Signy vanished the room and called up a scan of the Seattle house. Janine wasn't in it and Pilar hadn't picked up her message.

"Okay," Signy said. "I'm back."

Paul looked slightly miffed at Signy's interruption. "There are fifty-six delegates from fifty-six separate nations, each of them with different agendas, political needs, and personal foibles. Just steer an international commission the way we want it to go. Simple, wouldn't you think?"

"What about the Russians?" Signy asked.

"At the moment, they're for the plan," Paul said. "The Russians have been in the Antarctic business from the beginning. They still think they found the place first, actually."

"Simple, right," Signy said. "If we're lucky, and some lobby or the other doesn't get a flap going about something else. Seems like Tanaka has handed us something that sounds a little too easy, whoever Tanaka is. I never heard of them. And I thought the krill situation had been settled years ago."

"Think of krill as kilotons of edible, self-replicating protein," Paul said. "Think of it as an endangered food source, one that is diminishing. Tanaka has some concerns about the amount that's coming out of the water. They are willing to give up part of their share to keep the harvest in limits they think are safe. Enough for the whales, enough for profit, but not too much for safety. I like caution, Signy."

Cautious Paul Maury and his legalese, his deliberate

sense of time. Sometimes Signy thought Paul was determined to dot every *i* and cross every *t* on Earth.

"It's risky work," Paul said. "We've messed with lots of things, but we've never played with what's left of the world's food supply."

"Terms?" Signy asked.

"Oh, very good terms," Paul said. "Tanaka has diversified interests—circuits, manufacturing, shipping, and so on. He's agreed to pay expenses, of course, plus ten percent of the income from one year's harvest at the new limits; if we can get the new limits set for him. And residuals, but that's a complicated—"

Paul would run Tanaka's profit-and-loss statements for the last decade if she didn't stop him. "He?" Signy asked.

"One man, yes. Who seems to want to start a dynasty. Yoshiro Tanaka, that's his name," Paul said. "Signy, I don't know what we're getting into here; not precisely. The corporate structure is convoluted; there are blocks of data that have some unusual features. It might be an okay job but I'll need some time to fit these people together."

"They're listed on real stock exchanges, aren't they?" Signy asked.

"Oh, yes. Yes, indeed. Tanaka stock has been doing quite well over many years; solid, slow growth. The company is quite legitimate in that regard. Certainly."

"Take some earnest money and we'll sort them out later," Signy said. "We can always bail out if we don't like what we find." Take it. Tell them we'll do it, Paul, whatever it is they want done. "We're in a bind, Paul. We can't get too picky."

His image tented its fingers under its chin and stared at her. "I didn't know you were this upset."

"I'm upset. The prospect of starvation upsets me. I admit it," Signy said.

"All right, Signy. I'll sign us on."

Paul vanished his construct of the New Hampshire room, and Signy, in real time, stared at the Taos studio, where the fire had just about gone out.

Signy thought about letting the fire die, about closing the heat-sucking flue, leaving the heating to the furnace and the solar arrays. But credits were coming in. Edges had a job.

She built up the fire, a nice cheery fire for Jared when he came back down the mountain.

THREE

Signy heard Jared coming down the hall, a pad of snow-boots on the hardwood floor. He brought smells of snow and pine with him. A chill of clean air brushed against the back of Signy's neck, cold air that clung to Jared's clothes and brought some of the winter day inside.

"We have a job," Signy said.

"Good." Jared braced his gloved hands on the desk, trapping Signy where she sat working, and leaned down to kiss her. His cold lips brushed her cheek.

"Hey!" She ducked away from him. "How was the snow?"

"Superb." Shrugging out of his parka.

"There's a pot of *posolé* in the slow cooker," Signy said.

Jared went off toward the kitchen.

On Signy's monitor, a list of Antarctic species scrolled by. *Euphasia superba*, that was krill, the king bug, the basis of all the wealth. There were more kinds of penguins than Signy had ever thought about. Emperors, kings, macaronis.

"Macaronis?" Jared asked. He carried a bowl of *posolé* to his desk and sat down, his hands loaded with the bowl, a spoon, and a couple of rolled flour tortillas.

"Penguins," Signy said. She transferred the display to his monitor and windowed up Seattle. Still no Janine, and no Pilar. "We have a job."

"Is that why you look so worried?"

"I've pissed Pilar off," Signy said. "Seriously."

"How?" Jared asked.

"I told her she was a spendthrift. I told her she'd put our asses in a bind."

Jared smiled. Ah, so beautiful, Jared's face darkened with a day of snow and sun, a big man comfortable in his strength.

"Signy, my sweet, you'll never learn. You can't just blurt out truth like that and not hurt people's feelings," Jared said.

"Yeah. I threw a fit, I guess. Now Pilar's disappeared, and Janine isn't around."

Paul's crab sigil appeared on Signy's monitor.

[Paul] Pilar's at a cafe in the Pike Street Market. Janine's with her.

"Oh, great," Signy said. "Oh, damn it! Jared, I'll have to figure out what to say to her when she gets home. I mean, I'm sorry I blew up, but you're right, I was stating a rather obvious fact or two."

"You'll think of something," Jared said. "Now, what's this about a job?"

[Paul] Antarctic Treaty Commission work. Signy, we're going to need some new bits from there. Everything in the archives comes from the days before the tourist ban. Old. Dull.

"So I'm going to Antarctica?" Signy asked.

[Paul] No. Jared's going to Antarctica. Signy, you'll go to Houston.

"Antarctica?" Jared looked absolutely delighted at the idea.

"Houston?" Signy asked. "Paul, Houston is not my favorite place."

[Paul] Data sets, my dear.

A waft of steam from Jared's *posolé* drifted toward Signy's nose, the scent of simmered fat kernels of lime-washed corn, pork, green chiles, and oregano.

"Okay. I'll go. You can tell Pilar a trip to Houston is my penance for losing my temper."

[Paul] Silly.

Signy typed a message back to him.

[Signy] Out to lunch. Later.

Jared was already immersed in some project; addresses marched down his monitor screen. Signy went out to the kitchen and got her *posolé*. Munching a tortilla, she dumped the stale coffee and noodled around with a few dirty dishes.

Happy. Because Jared was home, because the Sangre de Cristos were pale red in the sunset light and there they were, snow-clad serene peaks in full view from the big window in the kitchen.

Jared's voice came from the studio, the timbre of it, just far enough away that Signy couldn't pick out individual words. Jared was talking to somebody but he wasn't sending the conversation to the kitchen speakers.

We'll be fine, Signy thought. Paul is an old maid. He'll nose around until he gets this Tanaka company dissected and laid out for inspection. Whatever he finds, we'll deal with it.

Signy heated a tortilla, spread sinful real butter on it, and sat down at the table, mesmerized by the look of the icy blue shadows marching east, by the colors fading away from the mountains.

[Signy] Apologies. Contrition. I love you.

The message glowed on Pilar's monitor in the Seattle house. Pilar, with Janine looking over her shoulder, read it and shrugged.

"I think she means it," Janine said.

Pilar tapped her keyboard and Signy's words disappeared.

"She shouldn't apologize. I was careless," Pilar said.

That's what a person said, wasn't it? Admit it and go on. Yeah, Pilar thought, I was careless. But would anyone have said it if we'd made megabucks from my tour?

Outside the bay window, fog hid the January world. Pilar shivered, missing, just for a moment, the Southwest, dry air, summer heat.

"Are you going to talk to her?" Janine asked.

Janine's blue eyes got so wide when she worried. She looked like one of those kewpie dolls that sometimes showed up in antique stores, except kewpie dolls had dimples and Janine didn't. A somewhat bedraggled kewpie doll, her blond hair dark with mist, her cheeks red from the wet breeze outside.

"Sure. In a minute." Pilar tapped idly at her keyboard, scrolling through some of the backlog of messages that had piled up for the past two weeks. A price for coming home.

"I'll make tea," Janine said.

Pilar read through chatter from friends, jumped past some routine stuff that shouldn't have gotten through the barriers she left in her mail. Maybe Paul could reset the guards.

A note from her agent, reporting some royalties on an old, make that ancient, song. That little piece went back ten whole years.

And then Paul and Signy, earlier today, talking about a job. Pilar skimmed through the conversation, keyed up the full virtual from Paul's studio when it began to get interesting.

Pilar heard the clunk of a mug on the desk near her hand.

"Janine, we've got work," Pilar said.

"Hoo!" Janine said. "That was fast."

Ignoring the noises Janine made settling at her own console, rustles and a couple of indrawn breaths, Pilar let her fingers play through controls. A phrase from a song she had started before the tour floated to her earphones. Not bad.

Let Signy wait, Pilar was thinking, but she found she'd pulled up the view from the kitchen cameras in Taos. The twilight softened the shapes of the massive vigas, the peeled logs that supported the ceiling, the primitive textures of adobe walls, old oiled wood.

Watching Signy watch the dark square of glass where the mountains had just faded into night. Broad shoulders, narrow hips, Signy always looked so strong. Signy blended into the colors around her, a woman camouflaged in a taupe skinthin, her hair the color of old oak. She was twisting a strand of it, just sitting there.

I love you. That's what Signy had left flashing on the screen.

Don't challenge me that way, Pilar thought. I—*need*—you, Janine and Paul and Jared, and you too, Signy, because you give me the space to play. Because I can do my stuff around you guys and you piss me off less than anybody else I ever knew. Love? I'm not sure I know what that means.

Pilar windowed Signy away and looked in at the Taos studio. Jared paced around the stage, talking to a travel agent.

Pilar sighed and sent her voice to the kitchen mike in Taos.

"I hear we're solvent," Pilar said.

Signy jumped and twisted around to blink up at the speaker over the sink.

"Pilar, I'm sorry—"

"Forget it." Pilar said. "It's okay, Signy."

That's done, Pilar thought. She exited Taos, pulled off her headset, and stretched out her muscles.

That's a beginning, Signy thought. Pilar still has some snit to get through, and I need to figure out better safeguards for her, I guess, so she can't hurt us, or hurt herself. Paul can fix up a system that gives Pilar access to funds but doesn't break us. We should have done it years ago. But at least Pilar's not off somewhere pouting. It's a beginning.

Signy grabbed a sweater from a peg in the hallway

and pulled it over her skinthin. The night was clear and the nights got really cold.

"I got a flight south," Jared said as Signy walked into the studio. "You have to have a job to go down there. No tourists. Tanaka could have fudged that, but it turns out there's an old buddy of mine working as a ship's doc for Tanaka. Saigo Kihara, the guy from the river trip. I'll do a locum tenens for him while I'm there."

"Hey! Fast work," Signy said.

"Yes. I'm leaving at five A.M."

"In the morning? Just like that?"

"Just like that," Jared said. "Paul says he's already talked to the Gulf Coast people in Houston. You get the lunch slot in two days. All you need to do is schedule your flights."

"Joy."

"Joy. I'll go pack."

Signy woke her screens and scheduled a flight to Houston.

That done, she looked in at New Hampshire. Paul was barriered behind his crab sigil, his "don't bother me" sign.

In Seattle, Pilar and Janine tossed word lists back and forth between their monitors. They were doing a sort of free-association contest, words that might or might not bring up emotional responses from people who worked at Gulf Coast Intersystems, a multinational group that conveniently happened to work in Houston, Texas, U.S.A. Pilar and Janine were on a roll, intent, laughing now and then, absorbed in what they were doing. Signy didn't interrupt them. And besides, Jared was leaving in a few short hours.

Time, however, could be very subjective. Very subjective. It's bedtime, Signy decided.

Signy lay bathed in Jared's heat, stretched out next to him. She felt as relaxed as an overfed housecat. She felt a little too warm, but she didn't want to move away from him.

"Just don't freeze anything important when you're down there chasing penguins," Signy said.

"I'll pick up a fur jockstrap first chance I get," Jared said.

"You do that." She was almost asleep. Jared wiggled up against the headboard, disturbing Signy's perfectly comfortable position, and settled a pillow behind his neck.

"I think I'd better tell you something," he said.

"Now what?" Signy moved one leg to the colder part of the bed. The chill felt okay.

"I know you don't like to be surprised when my long-lost loves call in."

"I certainly don't." She really didn't. As open as this relationship was, Signy never quite knew what to say—Oh, hello, nice to meet you; Jared *is* good in bed, isn't he?

"There's a girl I met in Canada. Her name is Susan. Susanna."

"I'll bet she hates her name."

"I don't know if she likes it or not. I never asked her."

"Uh-huh. What about this Susanna?" Signy asked.

"It seems she's living with my brother these days."

Well. Indeed. Signy wished she didn't feel hurt. She felt hurt. "Does Mark know about your, uh, involvement with her?"

"Sure. Anyway, Susan sent a video. A sort of Christmas letter, I guess. You might want to look at it. Since she's sort of family, and all that."

The hell she wanted to look at one more of Jared's prior lovers. Jared was free, but Signy would rather not know about it. She had affairs of her own, when she chose. It was just that she didn't choose, or hadn't for the past couple of years.

But she might, someday. She just might. "Did you introduce her to your brother?"

"I certainly did. I thought they would get along," Jared said.

"You just couldn't desert her, I guess."

"Maybe. Something like that."

Jared wasn't coming across as if this Susanna had been just a casual fling. Well, Jared had had a life before Signy met him, and that's just how things were.

Jared shifted in bed so he was looking directly at Signy's face, and he looked like he didn't want her to be angry. Okay. She would forgive him, any minute now.

"Do you have anything else to tell me before you leave?" Signy asked.

He frowned as if he were reviewing the past month. "I don't think so."

Damn him. "Tell me you'll miss me."

"I'll miss you." He looked so worried. He pulled her close and his lips were soft against her throat, and she wasn't that sleepy after all.

"Prove it," Signy said.

He did. Jared knew her so well, down to the last possible synapse of her multiorgasmic self.

Wonderful.

Jared left quietly, so quietly that Signy roused a little when she heard the muffled thump of the closing hallway door.

High above her, one of the vigas creaked in the predawn cold.

Signy was left in the solitude of kisses not taken, goodbyes missed, in a room so dark, the cold outside so terrible, the house so empty. All alone, everyone gone.

Alone, with Edges dissolving away from her. Signy *knew* Edges was lost, *knew* with the truthful clarity that comes before waking when reason displaces truth with facts.

They slipped away, all of them. Signy saw Jared with

a new lover, Pilar in the embrace of a less sedate group, one that wouldn't nag her about silly things like funds or remind her that she needed to sleep, sometimes. Pilar, with Janine following her, ever hopeful, ever ignored.

Paul? Paul would likely not even notice if everyone vanished. He'd just sit there in his study and vector out the future history of the African coalitions. But he'd forget to publish, and no one would ever know he'd been right.

Signy's arms ached. All through the night, she figured, she'd been trying to hold something that couldn't be held. She didn't want Edges to fall apart. That had happened to her once, a group dear to her, lost. And Paul was part of it.

Signy's Ph.D. in neurobiology and five years of hard work had given her a lab of her own at Genapt Technologies, where she coordinated the work of six researchers and their complement of techs. They had worked on aging in mammalian brains. Semistarvation increased life spans, that was a given. If lean animals were fed microdoses of growth hormone, the spans increased again by a significant amount. Signy's team fed small doses of pharmaceuticals to these geriatric marvels. Central nervous system stimulants produced remarkable learning curves in the youthful old rats. Excited, her team watched changes in oxygen use, neurotransmitter concentrations, the busy chemistry of vertebrate brains in real time. Their simulations taught them the colors of the brain at work in situations of anger, of fear, of fatigue. They had good times, good arguments; they battled among themselves and defended their own mental constructs of mental processes.

Signy had headed up the Atlanta lab until the takeover. Then Paul had appeared, Paul the outsider, the opposition.

In the cool light of the conference room, his tweeds had looked too heavy for March in the South. She stared at the fabric of his jacket, nubs of various wools and soft glossy fibers as well, maybe silk—while he calmly tore her world into shreds. Takeover, department cuts, alteration of research goals.

Signy tried to keep her voice calm. She tried to ask questions to give her some hope to take back to her team. They were hard workers and they had families to support. Jim had a new house and an old boat, his pride and joy. Sara supported her divorced daughter's kids. Damn it, these were lives in her care and it looked like there was nothing she could do, nothing, to keep them safe.

Paul Maury studied her face as if for clues that would tell him how to phrase his delivery; his brown eyes kept watching her for reactions as he made his speech to the wary group of Genapt execs. Signy tried to stay calm, while she felt sweat soak her armpits and the sides of her shirt. She wanted to take it off and throw it at this effete intruder.

Shifts in government funding, Paul said. New emphasis on foodstuffs research, less interest in neurologic disease, particularly in the aging.

Signy wished he would just shut the fuck up; she had the picture, okay?

She had survived the last minutes of her first meeting with Paul by thinking about escape. Her town house in a secured compound promised safety. The house could have been anywhere, anywhen, except that the bloom of wisteria and the white painted columns outside made it seem somewhat Southern. On her way out, Paul smiled.

"You care about your people," Paul said.

"Damned right I do."

"Will you come to dinner?"

Know your enemy, someone had said. Then he can't surprise you.

"I think I will do just that. Thank you."

Paul Maury, Harvard Law, Boston Brahmin, hid profound shyness with wry wit. She had not been offended that he seemed to expect that she would pay her half of the bill. There were no sexual moves on his part that first night. She wondered if he might be gay.

The negotiations continued through that Atlanta spring. A repeat invitation from Paul, that Signy show him the countryside, had pleased her. She didn't know this enemy quite well enough; he might still surprise her. They toured plantations and museums and walked through lush gardens in soft spring air; they searched antique shops. He was looking for a silver bowl, he said. For an old family place in New Hampshire. By some alchemy of understanding, they did not mention the company. Signy would have bribed him, with sex or money, but he didn't seem bribable.

She remembered the sepia light of dusty shops on Paul's thin face. Intent on the details of the chasings of antique jewelry, garnets and emeralds in baroque settings, he would ask, "Do you like this?" And he waited for Signy's approval, as if it mattered.

The spring night was unseasonably cool, cool enough for Paul's tweed jacket to feel comfortable on her shoulders when she asked to borrow it. It smelled good. So finally she asked him to bed. And found him shy, no pro, but gentle and willing to learn.

Two weeks, he told them in the boardroom the next morning. Two weeks to reapply for the jobs that will remain.

Signy clenched her jaw on rage. She managed to get up from her chair and out of the room without saying a word.

Her mother's voice had sounded in her memory just then. *We don't cry, Signy.* Outrage, however, was perfectly acceptable.

She had to walk Genapt's long bare hallway, under its

silent rows of cables and conduits; she had to go back to the lab. Jim waited, and Sara, and Signy had to tell them it was over. Behind her, Paul followed, keeping his distance. She looked back at him and watched his pace falter. He stopped and turned away.

But when she came back into the hallway, an hour later, he was there, leaning against the wall.

"Signy?" Paul kept his hands behind him, and his face was vulnerable if she chose to punch him. He looked scared. "Come and work with me."

"Damn Yankee." She'd grown up in Tucson but he was a damn Yankee, and even as she said it she knew her accusation was ridiculous.

"Yes," he said. "I suppose that's true."

He'd only been doing his job. The company that had hired him was based in Singapore. He was still a damn Yankee. "Come and work with me," he repeated. "Please?"

That was how we started. That was then. This is now, Signy told herself. I will *not* let us lose each other.

Am I still mad at Paul after all these years?

Wondering about it, she rolled over, hauled the down comforter up over her nose, and firmly sent herself back to sleep.

FOUR

Signy walked toward the dining room at Gulf Coast Intersystems with what she hoped looked like assurance. The familiar elastic tension of her dress-for-the-public skinthin felt reassuring, firm against her skin. She wore the taupe Lycra one, still new enough to look glossy. Her red silk jacket was loose and floaty and just slightly luxurious, but not too rich for this group, not offensively so.

"You're beautiful," Paul said.

The sensor resting on Signy's cheek itched, and she tapped at it. She wore a headband camera, but no goggles to give her a heads-up data display. For communication with Paul, who had promised to monitor, she had a speaker patch behind her ear and a throat mike taped in place, hidden beneath the skinthin's high turtleneck.

"Our shares of Gulf Coast Intersystems are down three this morning," Paul told her.

"Paul, why do you pick these particular times to give me news like this?" Signy whispered. "I'm walking into the damned dining room right this minute."

"I know," Paul said. **"But I thought you'd be interested."**

"Hmmph." Beyond the double doors, people circulated in the large room and wanderers checked the buffet with idle interest.

"Where's Jared?" Signy asked.

"I don't know. He hasn't called in since yesterday. Maybe he's stuck in Chile or something."

"Great," Signy said. She scanned the room, checking the setting. Tall windows draped in bitter green velvet opened to holos of an idealized harbor, complete with gulls.

Gulf Coast employees moved toward the buffet, where dishes were arrayed on ice or sheltered under heavy silver domes. The tables were draped with floral brocades and bouquets of hothouse red tulips. The setting seemed designed to recall memories of oil barons and opulence, so unlike Houston's desperate poverty now. Gulf Coast kept that poverty out with razor wire and walls of reinforced concrete faced in cosmetic fieldstone.

Wary of crowds, Signy stepped into the room, trying to ignore the part of her that feared strangers. Don't frown, she told herself. You're on duty. She set her expression to combine business with vulnerability. Jared had taught her to mold her body language, practicing reactions with her and a dozen virtual Signys. A dozen Signys, a dozen Jareds; the work had ended in a kaleidoscope of flesh and laughter, and they had made love while their multiple images cavorted around them. Signy let the memory reach her face, knowing it would lend a touch of lust to her expression and would brighten her eyes.

Jared was good at evoking lusty thoughts. Signy hadn't looked at the message from Jared's Susanna yet. Somehow, she just hadn't found time.

It occurred to Signy that she might be indulging in a little procrastination. Indeed. Okay, she'd look at the damned thing as soon as lunch was over.

At the buffet table, Signy picked up a handheld mike that she had placed just there, yesterday, and tested—maybe three times. She cleared her throat. The mike picked up the sound. Wups.

"Hello. My name is Signy Thomas. My company, Edges, is buying your lunch today. While you're eating, some words will sound through speakers that are placed

here and there throughout the room. This isn't sublimi-
nal stuff—you'll hear the words if you listen for them.

"We're collecting responses to terms concerning Antarctica. Edges plans to use your reaction sets to help us
optimize the use of Earth's largest wild fishery."

Some people had already started to talk again. That
was good.

"Please pass your cards through the counter at the
door as you leave. We are paying seventy-five dollars for
your information. Thank you." Signy turned to all corners of the room, made eye contact where she could (the
woman in the chartreuse coverall looked so tired),
smiled, and traced her way through the crowd. That tall
man, she had seen him—where? When? He was a redhead, and attractive in a rawhide sort of way. Signy
smiled at him, keeping eye contact for the benefit of her
cameras, and Paul's views of what they saw. "Who?" she
whispered.

**"I'm looking in the company files. Alan Camp-
bell,"** Paul said. **"Engineer. Astronaut, ex. He helped
build the Station."**

"Hello," Campbell said.

"Nice to see you again, Mr. Campbell. If you'll pardon
me? Biz." Signy continued out the door and upstairs to
the control booth and sat down with a sigh of relief.

She wasn't alone. Her companion, sitting in a rolling
chair next to her, wore black cottons that contrasted un-
favorably with his dead-white skin. He was pudgy. He
wore a full skin-thin under his cottons, and padded headphones over his ears.

"Hello. I'm Jimmy."

"Jimmy?"

"Jimmy McKenna. Temp contract with Gulf Coast."

Which meant Signy couldn't kick him out. She didn't
need any help in here, for pity's sake. And she didn't appreciate a Gulf Coast observer. What did Gulf Coast
think she was going to do? Broadcast "fuck your boss"

all over the room? "Hello," Signy said, while Paul's voice said, **"Jimmy McKenna. Not at all what I expected. He pitched us to Tanaka, or so Tanaka says. Thank him for us, when you get a minute, would you?"**

"I'm Signy." Jimmy's soft features made it hard to judge his age. She'd thought eighteen at first. He could be thirty.

Behind the bank of monitors, one-way glass gave a discreet view of the dining room. Signy peered down at the crowd. There was a nice trickle of repeat visitors at the buffet. That was reassuring. The caterers must be as good as their fees said they were.

"Signy. That's a nice placement," Jimmy said. He nodded his head toward a monitor that graphed the position of Signy's mikes. "I've tried a few setups in the room before. You found all the dead spots."

"Thank you." Signy keyed in Pilar's and Janine's stash of replicated conversations and fed them to speakers directed at random tables, matching their volume to the level of the room's chatter. She listened to scattered voices; her hands flew over the studio's consoles. Ghost voices fed themselves to the diners, voices that seemed to come from the next table, from across the room. From various tables, she heard some of the key words come into conversations: COCAINE, IVORY, KRILL, SALA-MANDER. Signy smiled. There were other words, other phrases: TOXIN, which was blunted from overuse but a good monitor of precisely that parameter; WHITE, as a simple adjective. At the exec tables, others words played, ERMINE, SANDALWOOD. Some of the conversations in play spoke of appetites, of flavors.

Later, she and Paul would pair responses to the words. Negative connotations were easier to correlate than positives; positives often had to be inferred. SALA-MANDER.

". . . and Costa Rica still maintains some pristine areas

of rain forest," someone said. "Of course, 'pristine' is a relative term."

Signy let herself relax for a moment. RAIN FOREST, all the key words were in circulation. Signy feathered up the volume of her recorded phrases to match the rise in talk as people finished their meals. Some began to leave, not too fast, not too slow. The program synched with the volume of conversations and faded in good order. Signy risked a few spot checks. So far, so good.

"That's it, then," Jimmy McKenna said.

His voice startled her. Signy had managed to forget he was in the room.

"Yes. That's it."

Jimmy spun his chair to face her. "I could help pick up the mikes. When everybody's cleared out."

"You don't have to do that."

"Ask him about the Tanaka contract," Paul said.

"My partner says you helped us get a contract with Tanaka."

Jimmy had started to get out of his chair. He sat back down.

"Yes. I did."

"Thank you."

Jimmy stared at her as if he wanted to memorize her face. He stared until Signy felt uncomfortable, so she asked, "Why did you recommend us?"

He didn't quite make eye contact. "Because you're good," he said. "You work with Pilar Videla, don't you?"

Ah-ha. A contract won on a little case of adulation. She would tell Pilar.

"Yes."

"She's wonderful."

"I'll tell her you said so."

Jimmy looked past Signy's shoulder to the door. "Campbell's here. I'll go get the mikes and pack them for you. Your cases are in the service hall, aren't they?"

"Yes, but . . ."

"I'd like to do it. Don't worry, I'll be careful." Jimmy dug for something in his hip pocket. "Would you take this? Please? It's a gift."

He handed over a flat white plastic chip case and left without a word, squeezing past Alan Campbell, who stood aside for him. Campbell carried a plate swathed in plastic wrap.

"Hi," Signy said. She couldn't think of any reason for Campbell to seek her out. Paul had arranged the paid luncheon but Edges had no other business scheduled with Gulf Coast. Not that she knew about, anyway.

"Alan Campbell. We met at a party when Gulf Coast got the booster contract. I didn't think you'd remember me."

"I had to get some help with your name," Signy said. "But I knew I'd seen you somewhere." Alan spoke with a soft cadence that wasn't Texan. "So that's where it was," Signy said.

"You were with a doctor fellow. We talked for a while."

"Jared. My partner, yes."

"You've met Jimmy?" Campbell asked.

"I think so," Signy said.

"Right. He's not much on conversation, but he's damned good with schematics. I brought you some lunch. Working a lunch hour, people don't usually get fed." Campbell put the plate down and pulled the plastic away. "Of course, if you've eaten . . ."

"I haven't," Signy said. She reached for a skewer of beef *saté* and bit into it. It was excellent.

Campbell sat down in Jimmy's vacated chair. He had a relaxed air about him, a competent presence. "Did you get what you needed?"

Signy forked up some pilaf. Alan reached in a pocket and pulled out a bottle of mineral water. Signy unscrewed the cap and took a long pull, icy cold. "I won't know until we've run some correlations," Signy said. She tried some of the veggies. They were nicely seasoned.

Alan waited while she ate. He seemed comfortable waiting, as if he had all the time in the world. Signy finished the *saté*, put the skewer down, licked sauce from her fingers, and tried to pull the studio headset away from her ears. A lead snagged in her hair and she tugged at it.

"Got it," Alan said. He untangled the wire, deft and gentle, and there were scattered freckles on the backs of his hands. His wrist brushed against her cheek as he lifted the headphones away, and his touch was soft.

"Thank you. Mr. Campbell?"

"Alan."

"Alan, is this a business meeting?"

He grinned. His eyes were hazel, and the corners of his eyes crinkled when he smiled. "No. And nobody sent me to entertain you, if you were wondering. I happened to notice that your plane doesn't leave until morning. I happened to notice you are in town alone. So I came to get acquainted."

Alan Campbell had helped build the Station, and small though it was, it was the *only* space station. He was lean and relaxing to be around and not at all like Jared. Some choice pheromones seemed to be floating around this little cubicle. Perhaps.

"All you've done is watch me eat," Signy said. She looked at the monitors. All the data had been dumped to temporary storage in the guest suite the company had assigned to her. Signy closed down the boards and got up. Alan rose when she did.

"That's right. So I hardly think we're acquainted at all yet. I plan on taking the night off, if you'd like some company," Alan said.

"I'd like some company." If she left the Gulf Coast compound, she'd have to ask a guard to go with her. Mall cruising didn't appeal, nor did dinner on a tray in her room.

"Why don't I come by about seven?"

"Okay." Signy watched him walk away, and she approved of his walk.

"He's from Colorado," her ear speaker told her. Signy had forgotten Paul was on-line. **"Divorced, one child. Methodical, perfectionistic, and he has a temper."** Paul was methodical and perfectionistic, and Signy put up with *him* somehow. Colorado, she could believe. Alan Campbell walked the corridor with lanky ease, as if it were a high country prairie.

Late in the afternoon, Signy sent a backup of the day's work to Seattle.

"Catch," Signy muttered.

"Got it." Janine answered real-time from Seattle, and sent a view of her face to Signy's monitor. Behind Janine, Pilar worked with a light pen in the corner of the studio. Stripes of neon colors danced on the walls, Pilar choreographing something or the other.

"That's pretty," Signy said. "Pilar's stuff. Not the stuff I just sent you."

"You look worried," Janine said. Amber light from Pilar's pen strobed across Janine's face.

"Do I? Maybe it's this Tanaka business. Paul says he can't sort them out, and it worries him."

"Maybe you miss Jared." Janine frowned at the monitor.

"Janine, you are *so* perceptive. How would you like to meet yet another of Jared's women?" Signy set up the chip Jared had given her and readied it to show.

"Sure," Janine said. "I guess."

The picture that formed on the flatscreen was grainy and badly framed.

"Hello, Jared," a smiling girl said. Susanna, if this was Susanna, was a Native American, tall, with very good cheekbones and a classic nose. Her smile was wonderful. She stood by a stone fireplace in a room with peeled log walls. The logs were huge. She wore jeans and boots and a navy blue wool shirt. "I'd say 'Season's Greetings,' but we were gone for the holidays. And you know Mark never remembers holidays anyway until the last minute. He's fine."

Cut: to Jared's brother's face, a view taken in outdoor light with a background of prairie sky. Mark looked much like Jared, but he had grown a full beard since Signy had seen him last. He made a "go away" motion toward the camera.

Cut: Susanna again, the cabin interior. The cuts were amateurish, at best. Signy wondered who had held the camera. "Mark's business is doing well."

In the background, Mark's voice called, "Sue? Sue?"

"We hope you'll come and visit. I gotta go now."

And that was that.

"Mark is Jared's brother?" Janine asked.

"Uh-huh," Signy said. "The girl's name is Susanna. She's Mark's live-in now."

"Mark looks like Jared. Sort of," Janine said.

Pilar's hawk sigil appeared on the screen, a discreet reminder that she was listening in.

"Pilar, did you see that?" Signy asked.

"The girl? Sure. She's pretty. Signy, are you jealous?" Pilar asked.

"I shouldn't be. I shouldn't be at all. Jared sleeps with you, with Janine, with me, and that's fine. What gets to me, I guess, is that I start wondering what was *wrong* with this young thing that Jared figured he could fix. I mean, I wish he would stop bringing home stray kittens."

"He didn't bring her home," Janine said.

"No. He took her to his brother. That's different?"

"Yes," Pilar said. "I think it is. Do you want to *marry* him, Signy?"

"No." Marriage negated part of a woman's identity. Signy couldn't imagine herself as "Mrs." anybody. Marriage was still the best institution for the protection of children, granted, but Signy didn't plan to have children. She feared she would do nothing else but mother, if she had a child.

"But you want him to change." Pilar, visible over Janine's shoulder, put her light pen down.

"No," Signy said. "No, I don't want that. Not at all. I don't want him to change a single hair on his infuriating head."

Pilar laughed at that and walked out of the Seattle studio, off screen.

"I'll start work on what you sent, Signy," Janine said.

"Oh, noble person," Signy said.

"That's me." Janine flipped away, back to her lists.

In the anonymous visitor's suite in Houston, Signy blinked at the empty flatscreen. The interchange with Pilar had been—comfortable, everyday, business as usual.

It couldn't be this easy, Signy thought, but Paul's crab sigil blinked on the screen and Signy began the business of sorting through the day's work with him, looking for all sorts of pairings.

From credit-card listings, Paul had pulled records of family size, income, political leanings, and consumer records. He matched those with frequencies of the words Signy's mikes had fed the test population today along with their lunch. There was nothing arcane about symbol correlation. It just took some big hunks of bytes to sort through it.

Intent, they worked, saying little except for monosyllables and grunts, flashing correlations back and forth, tossing some aside. They were fast at this, Paul and Signy; part of their speed was practice effect. They knew each other's signals.

IVORY. Signy froze the screen. The wild elephants were gone, their habitats now pathetic deserts, but people reacted to ivory with nostalgia, with longing, with an odd mix of guilt and desire. Antique ivory commanded outrageous prices.

"Slowing down, Signy?" Paul asked.

Signy's shoulders ached. She was woolgathering. How long had they been at this? The room was getting dark. It was time to quit.

"I'm afraid so," Signy said. "Enough. I'm off-line until morning."

"Are you planning a romantic interlude?"

"Hah. Maybe I am. Goodnight, Paul."

"Enjoy."

The feeling of a pinched heel, unobtrusive but there since noon, became suddenly unbearable. Signy shucked out of her skinthin and her boots and rubbed at the sore spot. The skin-thin landed in a corner, its recording chips still tucked inside. Her legs ached when she got up to pull the skinthin's chips out of their little pockets. She fed the chips to the console and sent their information to New Hampshire.

"Alan Campbell is here," the room told her.

"Shit," Signy said. She tossed the chips in the direction of the discarded skinthin. "What time is it?"

"Nineteen-twelve."

"Oh, damn. I mean, tell him to come in."

Her sense of balance was out of kilter, and she staggered to the bathroom and grabbed a towel. Working portable links could never be as engrossing as working in virtual, but even small screens held magic and could keep her unaware of the rest of the world. Her eyes saw ghosts of numerical progressions and chaos geometries. Jared was forever fussing at her to remember to move and stretch while she worked. She never remembered.

A little sound made her turn. She pulled the towel up over her breasts. Alan Campbell stood at the suite's small bar, working on easing the cork out of a bottle of Veuve-Cliquot.

"Some people work too hard," Alan said.

"Oh, I'm sorry. I planned to set an alarm. I guess I forgot." Signy accepted a tulip of champagne with one hand and held her towel with the other. "Thanks." Tiny smooth bubbles flooded her mouth with tastes of silk and summer. The champagne was very good. Signy smiled at him. "There is no other taste like good champagne, not in the entire world," she said.

Alan sampled his glass and lifted it in salute. "I'll be damned. It's a decent bottle," he said.

"It's lovely. I'll get a quick shower and then we'll go from there."

"There isn't any rush. We don't roll up the sidewalks for another two hours."

"I won't rush, then," Signy said. She sipped at her glass again, still standing with her towel wrapped over most of her. She wondered if the window reflected her naked back to Alan's eyes, for he looked at the window and smiled.

Now, she didn't know him at all. He worked here, in this enclosed community, and had for years. If he turned out to be a total kook, all she had to do was yell. She knew damned well that Security monitored the guest suites.

"I could soap your back," Alan said.

"You'll get wet." Signy hoped.

"I like to get wet," he said.

Signy picked up her champagne glass and the ice bucket. Her towel fell and she stepped over it on her way to the shower.

Alan followed her. His jeans joined her skinthin in the corner. Fatigue and champagne mixed in wondrous ways. Signy let any shreds of hesitation wash away in steam and scented soap and accepted, invited, Alan's deft skills at the gentle art of seduction. He took care of the condom, when it came time for that, without fuss or bother. He had freckles on his shoulders. His eyelashes were pale at the tips and his skin was the delicate skin of a true redhead, so fine to touch. He had a scar on the long finger of his left hand. It was ugly. She didn't ask him how he got it; people hated to be asked that sort of thing over and over. But Signy wondered.

After a time, hunger intruded. "Would you like to go to dinner?" Alan asked.

"I'd like to stay here." Cradled in the crook of his arm and watching his hand rest on her belly, she felt no desire to leave. She stroked the back of Alan's hand and let her touch linger on the faint ridge of the scar that circled his long finger.

Alan pulled his hand away. "Cart service," he asked the room. A mike was live in here; Gulf Coast could have recorded the bedroom acrobatics. What the hell, Signy decided. We were good. Alan ordered more champagne, and a servocart brought up a tray. They pulled cushions to a low table and sat facing each other. They ate shrimp from the Gulf's filtered seawater farms (guaranteed to be within federal standards for toxin concentration, and expensive), with little side dishes of spiced sauces, Cajun-inspired and Houston-modified. There was a selection of fruit for nibbling. Signy tasted a raspberry and leaned across the tray to feed one to Alan. He took the fruit in his teeth and nipped at her finger.

"Ouch!" Signy said.

Alan kissed her finger and fitted his left hand against hers, palm to palm. "Try this," he said. He ran his thumb and forefinger down the knuckle side of their mated fingers.

Signy copied his gesture. Slight differences in the temperatures and textures of his skin and hers created the sensation of numbness. "I remember the game," she said. "It's called Dead Man's Finger."

"That's how the scar feels," Alan said. "There wasn't any way to do microsurgery in orbit. So that part of my touch is always numb."

"Tell me," she said. "Tell me about how it is up there."

"In a little while."

Later, in drifts of musing, postcoital conversation, Alan told her of the silence and the cold, and the way the Earth looks from far away, blue-white and still and so very precious. There were hesitations in his speech at times, long silences. There was, in him, a knowledge of total dependence on others for each breath, for heat and light enough to permit survival. He carried memories of a violation of trust, memories of ice crystals and dying cells puffing silently away from a broken glove. Alan was a man who loved life and found it fragile.

And, Signy noted pleasantly, he did not snore.

FIVE

Half-dazed with restless airplane sleep, his ears numbed by the roar and whicker of helo blades, Jared endured yet another leg of travel. He had climbed into the helo in Punta Arenas at 10 A.M. local. His hindbrain insisted that he was awake in the middle of the night. His eyes disagreed and reported light suitable to a summer afternoon. Helo, not chopper; the term was different "down on the ice." Jared shifted his weight, trying to find a more comfortable position in the seat-belt harness, in the confinement of layers of unfamiliar clothing. A bright yellow flotation suit covered his parka, and the hood stayed bunched at the back of his neck, no matter how he fiddled with it.

The pilot had watched him struggle into the bulky coverall, not helping, just grinning under his handlebar mustache. A generic caballero named Cordova, he came complete with swagger, but he had flown for years and he was still alive. That implied some degree of skill and caution. Or at least luck.

"Not that you will be alive in these waters past one minute," Cordova had said. "But your corpse will float. Perhaps someone would haul it in."

The helo cast its tiny shadow on a glittering sea where rounded tiles of pancake ice formed a mosaic that stretched from horizon to horizon. Darkest blue tinged with green; Signy would have a name for the color. Something like a duck, Jared remembered. Teal, he remembered suddenly.

Signy knew so many things. She knew the precise location of the spot on his back that always itched when
he got tired, and the exact friction required to make it
go away. Jared tried to rub the spot against the back of
his seat. Damn. Didn't work.

Signy was probably still pissed about that business
with Susanna. But if he hadn't told her, sooner or later
Mark would say something, or Susanna would show up
in Taos. Jared didn't want Signy to be surprised when
that happened, or to think that he'd been hiding a long
and complicated relationship from her. It hadn't been
like that at all.

"I hope your ship does not run into trouble." Cordova
spoke into his mike. His eyes were on the horizon somewhere. "One of this Tanaka fleet's ships is lost, so I have
heard."

"Lost?" Jared asked.

"A small one. It happens." Cordova raised one shoulder in a small shrug.

"When was it lost?" Jared knew he should have called
home before he left Punta Arenas, but the paper shuf-
fling in the customs offices, the availability of a pilot, the
hunger for destination, had distracted him. He felt uneasy,
for no good reason. Nobody seemed to know enough, this
time. But Edges always went in with a few unknowns to
think about.

"Two days ago. Perhaps three, or four. The ship may
have had some help in becoming lost," Cordova said.
"There are many arguments about what is taken from
these waters."

Record this? Get on-line to home? Yeah. Jared should
have been recording in Punta Arenas, and Paul would
fuss at him, but Paul wasn't the one getting groggy from
too many hours of commercial flying. Jared unzipped his
duffel.

"Do you need something?" Cordova asked.

"Camera," Jared said. The pilot's tension suggested

that he might have thought Jared was reaching for a gun. "Just a camera." Jared kept his motions slow and calm while he pulled off the padded earphones that fed him the helicopter's radio inputs. He lifted a tangle of wires and lenses from the duffel, tapped the sensor patch in place on the corner of his left eyelid, and settled the lenses of his forehead.

"That is a fancy rig." Cordova yelled loud enough to be heard above the cabin noise.

"Thank you. It comes with the job," Jared shouted. He hooked a lead into the collar of his skinthin and powered up the recorders. He settled the helo's padded headphones over his ears and heard Cordova's voice, at normal volume again, ask, "This recorder is running?"

"It is."

"I am being recorded?"

"Only when I look at you. If we show your face, you get royalties."

"That would make me very unhappy," Cordova said. "Do not show my face, okay?"

"Okay." Now was not a good time to ask why. Cordova operated a charter service out of Punta Arenas. One of the guys who ran tourists up and down the coast had recommended him, and suggested that Cordova's availability was negotiable. It was, and the price was high. Jared had no desire to offend him. The sea looked empty, and very, very cold. They flew on, under a flat hazy sky that seemed close and low.

"Ah, we have a destination in sight," Cordova said. He tilted the helo on its right side. "See?"

Beneath Jared's right shoulder a tiny black ship made its way through geometric tiles of ice.

"Romeo Papa requesting permission to land," Cordova said.

Jared's headset fed him a flat Japanglish voice, a deck officer on the *Siranui Maru*.

"Romeo Papa incoming, we ask you hold at your

present altitude. We have a distress beacon in range on our present heading. Source unknown. Do you see anything from up there?"

"I see a pod of Bryde's whales at your stern, but nothing else. We will take a look," Cordova said. He circled the helo. As it turned its nose toward where its tail had just been, Jared saw the whales, pale outlines beneath the clear water. They were blunt-nosed, and their tails tapered and flared like the tails of cartoon mermaids. The ice, gray-white pancakes set edge to edge, spun against an immense horizon in a pattern of frozen intricacy that stretched away forever. Janine, were she watching, would get seasick.

"Got it." Cordova tilted the helo again, left this time. Jared stretched forward and saw an orange dot, ahead of the ship and probably hidden from her watchers by the shifting ice. "On your port side," Cordova said. "About two kilometers ahead. You'll be right on it if you hold your course."

"Roger, Romeo Papa."

"Shall I overfly?" Cordova asked.

"Negative, Romeo Papa. Come on down. Not to waste fuel."

"Roger."

The *Siranui*, Tanaka's mother harvester, traveled arrow straight, seeming oblivious of the shifting ice around her and trailed by the barest wake. She was huge, unlovely, and reassuringly substantial. Giant hatches on her deck were dogged tight. Electronic gear bristled from her superstructure, metal sensors that watched the sea and the approaching helo. She stayed steady on her course to let them come down. Birds wheeled across the ship's wake, black-and-white cape pigeons, the white airfoil shape of an albatross that seemed suspended, effortless, over the water. The helo sank toward a yellow X on the deck. Toy figures like children in snowsuits grew man-sized as the helo landed.

"We have the craft in sight," the deck reported.

The whine of the helo's rotors faded, replaced by the throbbing hum of the ship's diesels. Jared duckwalked beneath the helo's blades into sharp air that tasted of brine and chilled the windward side of his face.

Saigo Kihara's smile welcomed Jared aboard. The doc windmilled an arm in a "come forward" motion. Kihara held a square case of shiny black metal, CPR stenciled on its side in blocky white letters. Crewmen were headed toward the bow, and Kihara turned and trotted along behind them.

Sea legs, Jared remembered as his right foot came down on a deck tilting up. Kihara let Jared catch up with him. He had streaks of gray in his hair, new since Jared had seen him last.

"They've got a lifeboat in sight," Kihara said. "But I don't think there's much for us to do about it."

The diesels pounded a different rhythm, slowing the ship. The cold of the steel rail seeped through Jared's gloves. He bellied up to it and leaned over to watch a man in a black dry suit scuttle down the ship's ladder toward a scuffed orange inflatable. The raft bobbed empty against the ship's waterline, circling a fixed point as if held in place by something heavy. The crewman stepped into frozen slush, ankle deep in the raft. He rocked for balance, then stretched for the raft's slack bowline and clipped it to the ship's ladder.

"Ah, very bad!" the crewman yelled. "One helper, please." He fought to untangle dark blue fabric from the webbing on the raft's bumper, a sleeve, a human hand in a sleeve that began to sink as the fabric came free. The crewman grabbed the hand and held on tight. A second man went down the ladder.

"Send down a line!" someone called. Kneeling in the raft, the two men struggled with a corpse, bulky in soaked layers of clothing. They heaved the body into the inflatable. The crewmen passed a line beneath the limp arms and across the dead man's chest, working in haste and barehanded. "Bring him up," one of them shouted.

Hauled sloshing from the raft, the figure spun in its harness, swaying and bumping against the ship's hull. A boot fell away and splashed short of the raft. A hanged man, Jared thought, an execution. The man's head was tilted back on his neck and his dead white face stared toward the sky, Caucasian features, a black mustache. The crew let down the hoist and the dripping corpse sank to the deck.

Kihara had his kit open. The metal chest was filled with precisely arranged emergency supplies, endotracheal tubes, a breather bag, vials of medications.

"No," Kihara said.

Jared nodded agreement. He looked up at a wall of crewmen who circled the corpse, wary but curious. Japanese faces, mostly, but Jared saw a blond woman, a man with a brown beard, a mix of races.

"He's quite dead," Jared said. "There's nothing to be done."

The faces relaxed a little and some of them backed away.

"We will take the body to sick bay," Kihara said.

Cordova came trotting up to the circle of watchers. "Dr. Kihara?" he asked. "You are my return passenger?"

"Yes," Kihara said.

"We should leave soon. A storm is coming in."

"I'm packed," Kihara said. "Perhaps if you would help carry?"

"I . . ." Cordova looked around the deck, and he didn't look happy. A crewman arrived with a gurney. "I think my assistance is not needed. I will unload my passenger's luggage," Cordova said.

Rolled in a tarp, one of the dead man's knees stayed flexed as if he tried to climb an impossible staircase. Jared locked the wheels on the gurney and helped shift the rigid burden onto it. A lift took them down into the ship, and Kihara led the way, pulling the gurney through anonymous passageways, beneath mazes of pipes and ductwork, past unadorned metal bulkheads common to any working ship. The bulkheads were spotless, sanded smooth under their coats of tan paint.

The ship's small sick bay was warmer than the passageways had been. The room held a familiar clutter of equipment and a standard mix of astringent smells. Jared pushed the gurney inside and helped shift the body to a table.

Cordova dropped Jared's duffel at the sick-bay door and backed away.

"Coffee, pilot?" someone called from the passageway. Cordova accepted with an effusive burst of Spanish. Kihara pushed Jared's duffel aside with his foot and closed the door.

"We'll do a surface exam only," Kihara said. "The forensic procedures can wait for the authorities, whoever they turn out to be."

"Right," Jared said. He waited while Kihara pulled a postmortem form to his sick-bay screen, waited while Kihara pronounced the time and date in a flat, careful voice and gave his name, his degree, the location, and circumstances of the exam.

"Estimated time of death?" the screen asked.

"I'm no pathologist," Kihara said. "Jared, any ideas?"

"In this cold? In salt water? Hell, no." And why was the man alone in that raft? Was this poor sod an explorer, a lost fisherman, a saboteur? Tell me when the Tanaka ship went down and I'll make a guess, or I'll let Paul guess for you. Jared looked at the indicator lights that circled his wrist. Paul wasn't on-line.

"We are unable to estimate the time of death. And, screen, please note that I am assisted by Dr. Jared Balchen."

"Noted," the screen said.

"Kihara, I need to access the ship," Jared said.

"Eh? Oh, sure."

Jared hooked his transmitter into the ship's power, off the battery pack, and set it for real-time recording. He could dump the suit's storage later.

Kihara took exam gloves from a box on the counter and offered the box to Jared. His hands secure behind familiar powdered barriers of thin polymer, Jared folded the crackling blue tarp away from the still white face. The body smelled faintly of death, strongly of the sea.

Jared stared at the dead man's face, its contours and textures fascinating in their utter immobility. Why is it, he wondered, that dead faces, even more than photographs, permit, no, *demand*, such scrutiny? Ice formed lenses in the space between black thick eyebrows and gaunt cheekbones; its clarity brought out the contours of the half-closed bluish lids and the frozen black eyelashes. Part of the left eyelid was missing, gnawed away by some predator. The irises were brown. Mid-thirties, the man looked to have been. Salt crystals had dried on one sleeve of the man's sodden dark blue parka. His right hand was oddly twisted, the hand that had been tangled in the safety strap on the raft's inflatable bumper.

Above the rasp of Kihara's breath, and his own, Jared heard water dripping, falling onto scrubbed white tile. Kihara cut away layers of sodden coverall, sliced through a padded red and black flannel shirt, through a thermal undersuit. White skin wrinkled across the man's chest; a scant web of black hair curled across the indentation of his sternum.

"Help me roll him," Kihara said. In a hip pocket, Kihara found a stiff leather wallet and pried it open, retrieving a credit card that he carried to a sink and washed and dried carefully. Kihara went to his desk and called the bridge. "Mihalis Skylochori is his name," he said. "We have ID."

"We'll send someone to get it."

"Yes, thank you."

Kihara followed the screen's prompting and gave what answers were available from the exam. There wasn't much to report. No marks or scars, except for the deformity in the right hand, no apparent external trauma other than that.

"The right hand is twisted," Kihara said. "Jared, are there fractures?"

Jared explored, gently, the textures of Skylochori's fingers, the contours of his palm. Jagged edges grated beneath the tendons on the back of the hand. "Closed fractures are palpated in the third, fourth, and fifth metacarpals. I don't find any others." Frozen and thawed in salt ice, the skin had gathered into ridges and felt like wax. Ice coated each of the blue-tinged nails.

There were no other signs of trauma. Kihara got out a body bag. Accidental drowning was the obvious answer for Skylochori's death; nothing suggested otherwise. So why, Jared wondered, were the hairs rising on the back of his neck? Kihara was calm and businesslike about this; death could not be a stranger here in this violent sea. Something else felt wrong. Sleep disturbance, climate change, an awareness of stresses at home, any of those things could be feeding Jared's perceptions of danger. Stop it, he told himself, and brought his attention back to the task at hand. Jared helped Kihara load the corpse and the clothing into the bag and zip it shut.

Wax. A phrase nudged at Jared's memory, a Latin phrase used to describe catatonia in the living.

Kihara went back to the sink and Jared waited his turn, wanting hot water and soap to wash away the cold salt-soaked feel of dead flesh.

"Your pilot is anxious to leave," the screen reported.

"Acknowledged." Kihara shrugged and turned to Jared. "It seems I must hurry away," Kihara said. "The sick bay is standard, so are the complaints. There is little I could show you and nothing I could teach you if I were to stay."

"Do you have an assistant who knows the routines?"

"Her name is Anna de Brum. She's good. Sick call is at 0800 and Anna will stay with you." Kihara pulled a small red duffel from a cabinet. Packed and ready to go, was he? Kihara's anticipation of shore leave made Jared wonder what delights awaited him in Punta Arenas.

"Is there anyone I should watch out for?" Jared asked. A chronic patient, a ship's officer with problems?

"No. The *Siranui* runs with efficiency. The tours are short; people don't stay on long enough to get really crazy. It's not a bad ship." Kihara's readiness to leave was a palpable thing, but it seemed to be all anticipation, not a desire to escape. "I thank you again for your offer," Kihara said. "You could have worked your assignment here and not taken on my duties as well. Though they are usually scant. This is a young and healthy crew, by and large."

"I'll be here anyway," Jared said. "And I still owe you for Coppermine." Saigo Kihara had signed on, five years back, for a wilderness tour Jared was running. Kihara had waited on the river, nursing a man with a hot appendix, while Jared raced a raft to the nearest town and sent back an air ambulance.

"You gave me back my expenses," Kihara said.

"Actually, I didn't. The Texan did. Out of what he paid me."

Kihara smiled but he was moving fast.

"Saigo, old friend, do you have cabin fever?" Jared asked.

Kihara dried his hands and moved away from the sink. "I have a cure for cabin fever. It is to leave the ship whenever an old friend offers the opportunity."

Jared thumped the body bag, lightly. "Where does this go?"

"Until the bridge decides what to do with it, it goes to cold storage. On a harvester, there is little problem with that."

Cerea flexibilitas. Waxy flexibility, Jared remembered. Someone knocked at the door. Kihara turned to answer it. Jared picked up the dead man's credit card, reached into the bulky flotation suit that he still wore, and zipped the card across a sensor at his belt. Kihara opened the door and Jared put the card back down and shrugged out of the shoulders of the flotation suit in a continuation of the first motion. A stocky young woman, frank curiosity on her flat Polynesian features, looked at the zippered black body bag while she made a small bow to Kihara. "Your pilot wishes to leave," the woman said. "And the captain has sent me to bring the ID card."

Jared kicked the flotation suit down toward his ankles, stepped out of it, and handed it to Kihara. "You'll need this," he said. "Cordova insists."

"Thank you," Kihara said. He retrieved the ID card from the desk, handed it to the woman, and draped the flotation suit over one shoulder.

A click sounded in the speaker behind Jared's right ear.

"Anna de Brum is a Marshallese Islander; she has some impressive degrees in marine biology," Janine told him.

"That's all the ID the man had?" Pilar asked. Paul's voice came in right after hers. **"This is a transfer card, a discreet one. Account with Warburg-Paribas. Bloody Swiss security, we may not get much—"**

Jared tapped his left wrist twice with his right forefinger to shut them up while Kihara introduced Anna. Four pips were embedded in the wristband of the skinthin, indicators that glowed to mark Jared's unseen listeners. Three of them were lighted: Paul, Janine, Pilar. Not Signy.

Jared's new corpsman—Anna—called for someone to take the body into storage.

"Come with us," Kihara said. "And then Anna will show you to my quarters. Yours, for a week."

Wind howled outside. Cordova lifted the helo from a tilting deck as soon as Kihara climbed aboard, and turned sharply away from a solid wall of cloud. Snow gusted in front of the storm and the decks emptied, every

human headed below to relative safety. The temperature
had dropped to well below freezing. The birds had vanished, and the pancake ice as well, replaced by a charcoal sea, white-capped. Mountains of ice, silent bergs
with shattered peaks and looming valleys, traveled their
inscrutable courses. The sight of them chilled something
inside Jared, chilled the warm soft middle of him, where
a vulnerable small beast whimpered tales of giant's teeth,
of danger, of cold.

The storm reached them and the horizon vanished. A
solid wall of snow, a whiteout, hid the icebergs in an instant, unseen now, treacherous and waiting.

The ship has sonar, Jared told himself, and radar.
The ship knows how to dodge. Except icebergs are the
same density as seawater, more or less. They must use
some other system to stay out of the way. I hope.

"Paul?" Jared spoke to the wind, to the mike taped to
his neck. "I'm spooked. Find *out* about that dead guy,
would you?"

**"What's the problem? What's bugging you,
Jared?"** Janine answered, not Paul.

"I don't know."

"You're tense all over," Janine said. **"I'm getting
the willies just from monitoring your muscle tone."**

"Relax, intrepid explorer," Paul said. **"We need
the money you're making us. Get spooked on the
next job, okay?"**

"Yeah, right." Fatigue, cold, ship-crushing ice monsters,
and howling winds; they were plausible reasons, all of
them, for his discomfort. Still—

A hatch creaked open behind him.

"Come inside," Anna de Brum shouted. "It's midnight."

Jared struggled uphill toward her. There is no man-
overboard drill in Antarctic waters, he remembered.
Where, in this half-lit sphere of wind and snow, where
was night?

SIX

Late in the day, tired from the flight back from Houston, Signy shuffled toward the house at Taos through a light, fresh snowfall. The dry winter air gave her a few minutes of false energy. She contemplated shoveling the walks and didn't.

In the bedroom, she dropped the equipment bag and her duffel in the corner, a platform for her parka. She shrugged out of her red silk jacket and rolled it into a loose bundle to send to the cleaners.

Something hard in the inseam pocket thumped against the dresser. Susanna's chip, and Jimmy McKenna's gift. Signy had forgotten about that little puzzler. What whim had caused that quiet boy to give her this?

In the studio, Signy sat at her console for a little while, looking at the pale soft-plastered walls and the ashes she'd left in the fireplace. She felt tired, but it was an honest, pleasant tired, an aftermath of hard work and physical pleasure. Her body sent her the tiny sweet discomforts that resulted from enthusiastic sex. To be alone in the house was unusual and it felt good. Signy stretched and smiled.

Sex with Jared was a good and wonderful thing, always. Sex with Alan had, as promised, carried the spice of the unexpected, the delightful uncertainties of someone different. If work brought Alan back into her real-time space, yes, she would find another taste of that complex man worthwhile. If not? She'd had a good night. Signy hoped Alan had. Simple pleasures were a gift not to be rejected, or denied, or analyzed to death.

The Tanaka contract waited. Some of the delegates had already set up their territories in Lisbon, beginning the process of feeling each other out, testing each other for agreements and oppositions, looking for ways to build coalitions, blocs, alliances. There wasn't much time for Edges to catch up and get ready to help Tanaka do its own modeling and nudging.

Why did everyone in the whole damned world want everything yesterday? The Antarctic Treaty Commission met every thirty years. So Tanaka had given them less than a month to get a complex job ready. It figured. Signy punched keys and woke the system.

"What's happening?" she asked.

She got typescript, not a voice.

[Paul] Signy, scan Jared the minute you get in.

Followed by Jared's current address in a subdirectory of a ship called the *Siranui*.

Signy found him. Jared lay on his back, in bed, most likely, sending no visuals. Jared slept well, or so she could hope. Signy fast-scanned his suit's transmissions for the past hour. Jared had hooked his right arm around something solid. The sensors showed a flex and release at his elbow, a pattern that might reflect sleep responses to a tilting bed.

[Signy] Paul, Jared's asleep. Talk to me.

The intimate space behind her headset became Paul in his study, slouched in his leather chair, with his laptop perched on his knees. A lock of his black hair fell across his forehead, a forehead that was higher than it used to be.

"Oh, sure," Paul said. "Jared's dead man has been a real problem. Have you looked at the exam?"

"Dead man? Paul, I just walked in the door."

"Well, catch up with us, Signy, my sweet. There's a problem with Skylochori."

"With what?"

"The dead man." Janine's voice answered. The screen split and Janine appeared next to Paul, Janine in the Seattle studio, backlighted by the tall bay window where sometimes Mount Rainier could be seen.

Talking to them both in the same setting was easier on Signy's sense of *rightness*, so she switched Janine back to the New Hampshire study, to Paul's familiar and convenient macros of a room that Signy knew well, and liked. Janine wore bulky gray sweats and hadn't bothered with makeup.

No "Hi, how are you?" from either of them. No "How was your trip?" They were wrapped up in their work, and real time meant so little to either of them. "The dead man," Signy said. "Okay."

She left them and entered:

—a sick bay. Brought to her hands, to her muscles, Signy accessed Jared's familiar body language and saw his views, unedited, of a small white room and a still white face.

Jared seemed relaxed and calm. His interested distance from problems like this amazed her, still, annoyed her, sometimes. Just biz, to him. Death, pain, human misery—just biz. Signy let Jared's suit's transmissions feed to hers, accepting the simple signals of tensions at knee and wrist that told of Jared's motions, the complex sensors that gave her his touch, the crisp finish of the nylon that wrapped the corpse and the strange feel of a cold and broken hand. Jared's tension levels increased while he was doing the post mortem, but he didn't seem all that spooked. No more than anyone would be, exploring an everyday death at sea.

Signy dipped in and out of Jared's evening and picked up his increase in alertness when he met Anna de Brum. Scanning through Jared's journey to the deck, to watch Kihara leave, Signy felt Jared's fascination with and fear of the icebergs, acute sensations. Because Jared had felt a primitive terror, Signy did. It wasn't like Jared to fear anything. But the ice had moved so silently, been so massive.

"Signy?" Paul asked, an intrusive voice that seemed to

come from overhead. "Can you get an output from the bridge? Maybe they're looking for this guy."

"I'll try." Signy transferred her awareness away from Jared's sleep and brought herself back to real time in the Taos house. She fed the output from the *Siranui*'s bridge to a speaker and listened in for a while, but all she heard was chatter, mostly in Japanese, interspersed with occasional pidgin comments about a storm. She set a capture on the word Skylochori, left the audio pickups awake in Jared's cabin, and switched back to the New Hampshire studio.

"Hello," Paul said.

Janine looked up and smiled. "I'm glad you're back. How was the trip?"

"Fine, thanks."

"What's Jared doing now?" Janine asked.

"He's sleeping," Signy said. "You can pick him up if you want; he fell asleep with his skinthin on," Signy said.

"He didn't upload his trip yet," Janine said. "What we got is just the autopsy. You'd better look at it, Signy."

"I did already." Post mortems always made her feel like a perverted voyeur. Signy didn't like watching them.

Paul, in his warm, safe, American room, stayed intent on his flatscreen, where columns of pounds and yen scrolled past with dizzying rapidity.

"Paul, you act like this guy was murdered or something," Signy said.

"I don't know," Paul said. "But Tanaka lost a ship three days ago, or so the Internet says. Tanaka hasn't made much flap about it. They haven't called for a search, nothing like that. Now there's a drowned man and the Tanaka mother harvester just happens to pick him up. I'm interested."

"So I see. I'll check the bridge again, Paul." Signy listened to the *Siranui*'s bridge for a while, and heard a story, in English, about a sailor and a woman in Christchurch with remarkable and highly unlikely attributes.

"Nothing," Signy said.

"Odd." Paul stared at his flatscreen.

Janine's image lay sprawled on a cushion on Paul's worn China trade carpet, her elbows guarding a reader screen.

"Janine, what are you doing?" Signy asked.

"Looking through this treaty stuff," Janine said. "You've read it?"

"I've skimmed it," Signy said.

"I'm looking at documentation on the Antarctic Accord of 1991. Strange, strange."

"Where's Pilar?" Signy asked.

"Out. Walking, I guess." Janine dropped her head and began to read again.

And Paul hunted for Skylochori. Warburg-Paribas security gave him nothing, he reported. Nothing about the size of the man's account, or when or where deposits had been made. Paul tried hotel registries, starting at Chile's Teniente Rodolfo Marsh station, southernmost of public hostels, and circled outward, placing little red question marks on the South Polar map as he went from destination to destination. Ushuaia, in Argentina, Punta Arenas, in Chile. The question marks buzzed like bees as he left them. Paul's queries jumped across the map to New Zealand's South Island, where he searched hotels and job-call rosters in Christchurch. *Nada.*

Paul would be at his search for days if nothing distracted him. Signy sent a black patent high-heeled shoe to his display and tapped it impatiently. "Get off it," Signy said. "We'll hear what the ship finds out about this Skylochori sooner or later. And we're not working for him, whoever he was."

Paul transformed the shoe into a pink and blue nursery butterfly and fluttered it out of his way. "Ushuaia," he said. "Skylochori, debit for three cases of Henessey XO brandy. My, it's expensive."

Signy closed her eyes. Jared's view of sick bay came to

haunt her, the sound of water dripping from a dead man's hand. For distraction, she pulled up dossiers on Tanaka's execs in the company's offices in San Diego and Honolulu, profiles that she might need to know. They seemed a dull bunch, by and large.

"The treaty negotiations were so *polite*," Janine said.

"Yeah," Signy said. "I've looked through some stuff on them. It was easy to be noble, I guess, when there wasn't anything down there to want."

But now there was.

The ice at the end of the world had a strange history, due to get stranger. The hard-won and ridiculous balance of interests that had produced the Antarctic Treaty had changed in the past thirty years. Sentiment for banning mankind entirely from the white desert was rising. The seas, though, with their protein riches, inspired complex parameters of greed and confusion.

"Old solutions," Janine reported, "the weirdest set of gentleman's agreements you're ever likely to run across."

At the height of the cold war, the U. S. and Russia had agreed to set aside territorial claims in Antarctica and share information that they gleaned from scientific research in the International Geophysical Year of 1957. When Britain and Argentina were shooting at each other in the Falklands, their representatives came to the conference table each day and discussed wildlife protection on the continent. When Chile made territorial claims and had a pregnant woman deliver a child on "their" part of Antarctica, the bombastics were politely ignored. The place inspired strange courtesies; Signy had read that mutual survival was all that counted there. Usually.

"I'm beginning to believe that our client thinks he wants something that won't work," Janine said. "Any quota system that involves portioning out the harvest by nation, for God's sake, is going to get the diplomats up on their soapboxes. There's got to be a better way. I just haven't found it yet."

"Does anyone know how flexible our client is?" Signy asked.

"No," Janine said.

"I guess I'll start trying to find out," Signy said.

"I'll get on it." Janine stuck her tongue out at the screen and faded away from the New Hampshire floor.

Paul kept manipulating the smattering of information he had on the man named Skylochori.

"Are you still at that?" Signy asked him.

"Maybe Jared's on to something," Paul said. "Skull-duggery at sea, or somebody's secrets."

"You're woolgathering, Paul. This is just a contract, not a study in conspiracy theory."

"But Jared's instincts are good, Lioness."

If Signy fussed about Jared, Paul would defend him. If they both got on his case, Janine would become Jared's champion. Pilar seemed, always, to ignore all the inter-actions, to exist in her own little space, and tonight Pilar was out walking. Thinking of music? Of sculpture? Whatever, all of them would tiptoe around Pilar's definition of personal territory, would inconvenience themselves to make sure she had it.

"There's something funny about this Skylochori's purchase, I think." Paul pointed at something on his New Hampshire screen, but he forgot to send views of whatever he was looking at. "Skylochori bought his brandy from a little shop that sells, uh-huh, Euro perfumes, tinned caviar . . ."

"Does this have anything to do with the contract, Paul?"

"Who knows?"

"Tanaka lost a ship. We don't know how often fishing ships go down, or what the procedures are when they do. Jared will probably find out and then we can quit worrying about it," Signy said.

"I'm sure he'll do just that," Paul said. "He's an in-quisitive soul, our Jared."

It's just a contract, Signy told herself. We needed it, we

took it, we'll work it out. Paul's just anxious because we don't know all that much about Tanaka yet.

Paul kept on noodling with maps, vocal about it, and unaware he was making any noise at all. Signy ignored him and looked at her capture file on the *Siranui* for any mention of Skylochori. The file was blank.

Janine reappeared on Paul's carpet. "Our client is a visionary, by his own standards," Janine said.

Janine held a brown bread and cheese sandwich in one hand and grabbed salted peanuts with the other. Signy remembered she was hungry, herself.

"He's a tad unconventional," Janine said. "Yoshiro-san's company started out in manufacturing, which is what he learned from Daddy. Yoshiro is a lesser son. On his own, he's wrested power away from his older brothers. He's gotten religion about the sea, it seems. Figured from way back that it would be the primary food source for humanity. He's been keeping fishing operations going at scant profit to get long-term rights."

"So he's flexible," Signy said.

"Not necessarily. He could be as stubborn as a mule if he thinks we're calling it wrong." Janine licked salt from her fingers. She picked up a glass of some bright red drink and sipped at it.

"Interesting," Paul said. "The store at Ushuaia has sold eight hundred cases of brandy in the past nine months. And it has purchased—thirty."

"So they smuggle," Signy said.

"I think you are right, Miss Thomas. The question is, *what* do they smuggle?" Paul's face dissolved, replaced by the stylized crab sigil Paul used when he wanted to be left alone. The crab clicked its claws in Signy's direction and scuttled away into infinity.

SEVEN

Kihara's alarm beeped in the little cabin. Jared rolled over and slapped at it, feeling the tug of his skinthin against his arm. He'd fallen asleep in it. The skinthin still held a cache of stuff from the trip, recordings of the helo's landing, the tethered lifeboat with its unfortunate sea anchor.

Jared located Kihara's coffeemaker and started it brewing. He diddled with the cabin console until he got the upload function working, peeled out of his skinthin, dumped the suit's information to New Hampshire, and ran his shower hot and long.

Not late, though he felt as if he were, Jared traced the maze of the ship's passageways toward sick bay. Flat bright light came through the portholes, a restless brightness that implied noon. He knew the constant light disturbed some people. It disturbed *him*. He felt as if he had overslept.

Anna de Brum frowned at his forehead lenses. Her eyes followed the lead wires that ran down his neck and vanished under the collar of his skinthin.

"Don't worry," Jared said. "I don't record any visits with patients." Well, the drowned man? The recordings went only to Edges, and private storage. "But this rig is complicated to get on, so it goes on first thing every morning." And sometimes, after several thousand travel miles, he slept in it, but he didn't tell her that. He'd changed into his spare after his shower.

"You are a human camera?" Anna asked.

"I suppose that's a good enough description," Jared said.

"Dr. Kihara told me that you would be recording much of what you see. But I didn't expect . . ."

"All this gear." Jared waved his hand toward his forehead.

"Yes."

"Do we have anyone scheduled?"

"No." Anna smiled at him. Her smile was warm and generous. He felt forgiven.

"But we have a patient waiting," Anna said.

Competent, deliberate in her motions, Anna made a courteous point of having him approve her treatment of the morning's visitor, a crewwoman, Japanese, a muscular specimen who kept her eyes downcast. She had a sprained wrist.

"From work?" Jared asked.

"No," the woman said. Her noninjured hand came up to hide her face in a practiced gesture of shyness. "Volleyball."

Anna's laugh diffused the woman's formal embarrassment. Jared checked the X ray and approved Anna's choice of medication and her application of a wrist splint. No other patients appeared. He examined supplies and chart formats, and learned, hands on, the arrangement of crash equipment, the locations of emergency medications.

While the agenda of establishing his role with Anna continued. No, I have no intention of disrupting your routines; yes, I will let you function at your considerable level of competence; no, I won't let you feel you're stuck with decisions that should be mine to make.

When he felt that Anna had finished checking him out, and that he was comfortable enough with the layout, he called the session to a halt. They had learned enough of each other's abilities to get through the next day, at least. "What's next?" Jared asked.

"We're finished here," Anna said. "Unless someone is hurt or needs us. And then I will be called."

"My other job here is to see things," Jared said. "Where do I go first?"

"The bridge says you can go where you like."

"And they probably said somebody's supposed to keep me out of trouble. Who's my chaperone?"

"I am." She said it with a grin.

"Then I'll follow you around," Jared said. "If you wouldn't mind. Just chase me away when you're tired of me."

Knowing, because he'd done this before, that the major stress of a ship's doc's job was boredom. Days and days of nothing to do. So you found things to keep busy; poker, gossip, plans for writing the Great American Novel. Anything.

"I do some biology research," Anna said. "I was going to pick up some specimens from the ship's freezer. It could be a sort of tour, I guess."

"After you," Jared said.

Jared followed Anna through a maze of near-empty passageways in this floating city of a ship. They came through a hatch and onto a catwalk that spanned the *Siranui*'s sea factory. Brightly lit, the working space below was as big as a modest college field house. A door slid open at one end and a wall of fish and water poured into a vat, bringing with it a clean briny smell and a rush of activity in the space below.

"Whoa!" Jared said.

Anna stopped on the catwalk and smiled at him. "A lot, isn't it? We can process one hundred and fifty tons every forty minutes," Anna said.

"That's a lot," Jared said. He was in range of the ship's power and he switched his suit's transmission to real time. On his wrist, Signy's light glowed; she was back from Houston, he guessed.

"Some of the factory ships are bigger. Tanaka is not such a big company."

The scene beneath him looked like something out of Escher, belts and corners and angles running every which way. The space was filled with machines, workers, and fish. Nobody spoke. The workers were dressed in masks, gloves, and slick green waterproof coveralls. They looked like a surgical team. There were sounds of machinery, but less noise than Jared might have expected.

"It's simple to follow," Anna said. "See, there, the size nets?"

Jared looked where she pointed. The fish fell through nets of varying sizes and were beheaded, one by one and at great speed, by workers who fed them to buzzing saws.

"Then they run through a filleting machine, and a skinner."

"What about krill?" Jared asked.

"That comes in in blocks, from different trawlers," Anna said. The fillets emerged on a belt and passed over a transparent sheet of plastic lit from beneath. A worker watched the pale fillets go by, and now and again flipped one from the line and into a waiting bucket. "Candlers," Anna said. "Looking for blood spots or parasites, or whatever."

"What happens to the discards?" Jared asked.

"They come to me," Anna said.

The approved fillets were packed into boxes and shuttled into a flash freezer. Above a half-filled box, one set of dark eyes looked up at Jared and Anna. Woman? Man? The look was not friendly. Woman, Jared decided. The hairs went up on the back of his neck at something those eyes told him. The woman looked down, her hands quick in the piles of fish.

"Are there many problems with the harvest?" Jared asked. "It seems like the competition is stiff out here."

"The ocean is large," Anna said. "What sort of problems do you mean?"

"Oh, fights and territory stuff."

"That's not my field," Anna said. She moved on across the catwalk and opened an insulated door that led into a walk-in freezer. Metal shelves, like library stacks, bulged with irregular plastic packages. Jared's breath frosted around him.

In bins and on racks, specimens waited their turns at investigation. All labeled, all marked with tags that listed date, species, time and location of collection. Jared found himself face-to-face with a dead crab-eater seal pup, packaged in shrinkwrap.

"My pilot said something about a ship that sank."

"Yes." Anna busied herself with sacks and labels.

"Do you know anything about it?"

"Very little." Anna looked up at him, her hand, holding a thick inkstick, motionless. She looked down again. "Very little."

In Taos, Signy watched him, Jared and the woman. Jared's eyes scanned the freezer, rows of frosted plastic sacks, a glimpse of half-hidden black.

"Jared?" Signy asked.

He wasn't listening. Look at the back shelves, she wanted to tell him. Look back there, please.

Jared and Anna traveled back across the catwalk and out into the *Siranui*'s passageways.

Signy replayed what Jared had glanced over. She froze the scene, magnified the image, and saw a zippered seam. It was a body bag; it was Skylochori. So that's where they put the corpse.

In Taos, it was morning. On the *Siranui*, it was Tokyo time, late yesterday. Ship's time was the captain's choice, but it no way matched McMurdo time, Greenwich plus twelve hours, or the Pole itself, Greenwich. Or so Paul had told her. Or was it the other way around?

[Signy] Paul?

Paul was at his desk in New Hampshire, and he answered her in an instant.

"Paul, they put Skylochori in the fish freezer."

"That seems reasonable."

"I don't like it. Jared's not getting any answers about the lost ship from Anna."

"I doubt it's a medic's problem. Let it go, Signy. Have you looked through Jared's trip yesterday?"

"Not yet," Signy said.

"There's some good visuals," Paul said.

Let it go, Signy. Where a fishing ship decided to stash corpses wasn't Signy's problem. Paul seemed to have decided not to worry about the lost ship. Good.

Signy set Jared's trip up in full surround, hovered above seascapes and magic glimpses of whales, and let herself soar beside the checkerboard of birds circling the *Siranui.*

Jared and Anna idled through the ship, a factory with a thin layer of ship designed around it, cabins and service areas tucked in wherever they happened to fit.

"Lunch?" Anna asked.

Hunger struck at Jared's stomach.

"Oh, yes," Jared said.

Signy looked in on Jared, on his view of Anna's back as she traversed a maze of black lacquered chairs, legs upended, clipped to Western-style tables. Three workers in dark blue padded coveralls huddled around one of the tables, half-hidden in a geometric forest of chair legs. The workers nursed small cups of tea, and none of them seemed to be talking. A uniformed ship's officer and a tall man with red hair—Alan? Alan Campbell, yes— stood at a coffee cart. The officer nodded to Jared and Anna, and the two men left.

What the hell was Alan Campbell doing on the *Siranui*? Signy ran the scene back again, for Jared hadn't focused on him. His attention had been on the coffee.

[Signy] Jared?

But he wasn't wearing goggles and he couldn't see a letter display.

"Jared?" Signy tried a mike, but he didn't answer.

Jared filled a thick ceramic mug with steaming coffee and took a scalding sip. It was true ship's coffee, industrial strength and almost overcooked. It was the real fuel of any ship, and Jared wondered if ship's cooks carried its secret from one mess to another. It was wonderful.

Hunger attacked him and no food seemed to be in sight. Dull steel urns of coffee and tea, packets of sugar and dried whitener, lemon slices; that's all he could see on the coffee cart. He wanted to tear into a packet of sugar and eat it, granular and sweet. Would Anna find that strange?

"I'm so hungry," Jared said.

A stainless-steel panel opened in the wall next to the cart. A small thin Japanese man smiled at Jared.

"Dr. Balchen?"

Jared nodded.

"Please sit. A food order has been left for you."

Jared looked at Anna. She unsnapped two chairs from a nearby table and sat. Jared tried to pay attention to his coffee. When had he had a real meal last? In Taos? No matter what the kitchen brought him, he would eat it. Mystery soup, pickled plums; he wouldn't care. Anything.

The door opened. Cook brought out a tray. On it was a mound of steaming white rice and four perfect over-easy eggs that smelled of butter. And a slab of ham, sweet-scented, brown-speckled crisp at the edges. And a pile of light, puffy biscuits, and pots of California jam.

Thank the man, grab fork, grab biscuit; Jared's priorities were, for the moment, confused. He picked up a biscuit, lifted his fork, moaned, "Ahh, mmm," in a small voice and crammed the biscuit in his mouth. It was a sourdough biscuit. It was tender and rich.

"You're welcome," Cook said. He darted into the gallery and reappeared in moments with a similar tray for Anna, garnished with a side dish of pickled veggies and a small bowl of smelly fish sauce. Cook turned to Jared. "You are from a different time zone. Dr. Kihara has designed your food to help with the time lag. Many carbos, much lipid."

"Saigo Kihara is a wonderful man," Jared mumbled around a mouthful of rice. "*You're* a wonderful cook."

Anna spooned fish sauce over her rice.

Well-being rose from Jared's belly, and warmth that drowned out all apprehension. The strange woman had looked up at him from the hold because he was strange, or because she was bored. She wasn't a terrorist spy. A ship sank? Well, ships sank. Shit happened. He spread strawberry jam on the last biscuit.

Cook's smile faded as he observed the rapid depletion of Jared's plate. "More is coming," he said. He disappeared behind his magic door again.

EIGHT

Signy's head felt stuffed with information on krill, protein conversions, and biomass specs. Their cold wet realities were somewhat warmed by the heat of the fireplace, and when she felt too soggy, she could look out at the white, clean angles of Taos Mountain. She worked until sunset had spilled its blood-red shadows on the Sangre de Cristos.

Jared had gone from his meal to his cabin, and fallen into a nap that had lasted until well into his night. He'd sent her a brief grumble that he was completely off schedule, and then headed again to the mess, which never shut down. The factory ran day and night, and Jared talked to some of the crew while he ate. He was back asleep in less than an hour.

Yet to be dealt with was the slight discomfort caused by Alan Campbell's presence on the ship. Alan hadn't shown up in Jared's vision again, but he would. The one-night stand had to be mentioned.

Or did it?

Campbell was there on some business or other, something he hadn't bothered to tell Signy about. But reviewing their conversations, Signy couldn't remember telling Alan that *she* had business in Antarctica, so why would Alan have brought up any plans *he* had there? If she'd given Alan Campbell any ideas about Antarctica, and she probably had, it was still no problem for Edges.

Let it alone, or not? Not, Signy decided, but rather than deal with the miniproblem right now, Signy, at dusk, went into town for groceries.

At the parking entrance, a row of patient women stood, holding signs: WILL WORK FOR FOOD.

They looked Indian, wrapped in their blankets, but they weren't. The Pueblo took care of its own, the village still an isolated shelter against time and the outside world. Taos Pueblo was a shared hallucination, Signy sometimes thought, a dream place, romanticized and ridiculous. But its existence, its endurance, remained an odd comfort in complex mythology of the mountains and the mesas.

WILL WORK FOR FOOD, and the women would, whether the work was housekeeping or carpentry, or sexual accommodation of any known variety. Signy stowed her small sack of groceries in the little electric runabout and drove past them, trying, as she always tried, to ignore their faces. But she never could.

The night was moonless and clear. Snow beneath her boots went scritch, scritch, as Signy carried her sacks into the house, into the welcoming shelter of thick adobe walls. It was warmer in Antarctica tonight than it was here.

The groceries were oddities that Signy liked to eat when no one else was around. She stashed peanut butter and fat black olives and packets of instant cereals in her personal little cabinet and put the veggies and the milk and eggs away.

Unfinished business remained in the studio, and its name was Campbell. On Jared's empty desk, the pudgy tech's gift chip lay in its case, a reminder of Houston. Signy slipped her headset on and picked up the chip, idly, to turn it in her hands. Its cover was unadorned white plastic, and the chip was not the brand that Paul usually ordered, by the gross, for the group to use.

Signy entered the workspace, Antarctica, another world.

The deck of a four-rigger materialized beneath her feet. Pilar and Paul sat side by side on deck chairs, cozy in thick blankets, watching a seascape whose horizons tilted, and tilted.

"Signy, what's that?" Pilar asked.

Signy held up the chip.

"This tech gave it to me in Houston. I forgot I brought it home."

"Have you looked at it?" Paul asked.

Signy shook her head at him.

"Use the isolate rig," Paul snapped.

"Of course, fearless leader," Signy said. Security, security. Paul feared viruses in their little playground. Half of what they did was sent around on AT&T lines; the raw stuff was usually a jumble, anyway, nothing that would look tempting to any paid hacker. And still, Paul purged the programs once a month; and he always found some little bug or other.

Signy rolled her chair away from the imaged ship's deck and took off her headset. She powered up a PC that sat by its lonesome in a corner. She patted it, the little *huerfano*, and brought up—

Music. No visuals, just music. An oboe sobbed over the eerie sounds of some stringed instrument she did not recognize.

"A cello played *col legno*," Pilar said.

With the wood of the bow. Lonely, cold, the music ached with desolation and longing.

"Damned good," Pilar said.

"Maybe he wrote it," Signy said.

"Who?" Pilar asked.

"Jimmy McKenna. He's desperately in love with you, Pilar, and he found the Tanaka contract for us." Signy stared at the blank screen of the *huerfano*, as if waiting for visuals to appear.

"Tanaka's staff told me they looked around the net for 'brilliant new groups.' McKenna sent in a list of our stuff. He said we weren't new," Paul said.

"New? Not us," Signy said.

"But he said we had Pilar Videla, and that was as good as they were going to find," Paul continued.

"Oh, joy. A loyal fan," Pilar said. She hummed along with the music's phrases, repeated one. "It's what I need," she said.

"Paul, could there be anything in it that would mess up our system?" Signy asked.

Behind Pilar, behind Paul, white canvas billowed and rigging creaked.

"Not from what we've just heard, and that's in tonight's data already. If Pilar wants to use it, and if it's okay, then it's okay. I guess." Paul tucked his chin under his blanket. "Come on up, Signy. I'll fix a chair for you."

He did. Signy switched herself onto the deck, into Pilar's vision of the helo's flight, the ice, the images of a vast and lonely sea.

Signy's head worked best in the morning. Pilar and Paul insisted they couldn't function until the day began to fade. Jared couldn't think straight until he had gotten up a sweat doing one odd thing or another, and some of those odd things were *very* enjoyable. Janine could work anytime, anywhere, she said, as long as her feet were warm.

"Where's Janine?" Signy asked.

"Here." Janine popped into view on deck. She scooted her chair closer to Pilar and tucked her feet under Pilar's blanket.

"You can put your real feet in my lap, babe. I don't mind," Pilar said.

Then, "Shit! They're cold."

"Sorry," Janine said.

Watching, all of them, Jared's Antarctica, his arrival, the views of the raft with its faded letters and its sad cargo. Each of them framing their own images, important or trivial. Overlaying transparencies of their individual visions into malleable storage of tonight's real-time view of a day gone past.

As they worked, each set of inputs shifting in focus, in

interest, certain things were emphasized, others ignored. Shadows deepened, images strengthened in line and depth. Light glared across pancake ice, glowed beneath the streamlined shape of Bryde's whales. Myriad colors of blue. Birds scattered in a black and white. . . .

"That's close," Pilar said. She stared at something invisible above Janine's head. Janine wiggled her toes on Pilar's lap and Pilar resumed kneading them, automatic response.

"Break?" Signy asked.

An iceberg appeared at the horizon, pulled from Jared's walk on the icy deck before the storm.

"No," Pilar said. "Not yet." Pilar counted out some silent cadence, her lips moving and her attention somewhere totally not in this space.

Signy closed her eyes and waited. Her mind ran through some of her afternoon's reading; she saw tedious treaty language and polysyllabic descriptions of the reproductive cycles of krill. The critters shrank when they got low on food and built themselves smaller shells, an unusual thing for a crustacean to do. Antarctic creatures were mostly unusual. One fish swam around happy without having any oxygen-carrying pigment in its blood, getting what it needed from the cold water without need of hemoglobin. Predators and prey intertwined in unique ways. Krill populations were keyed to penguins; count penguins and decide how much to catch.

Signy opened her eyes at the sound of Jared's indrawn breath.

He appeared on the deck behind them, a blocky silhouette with no features.

"I can't get much detail from this little rig in Kihara's cabin," Jared said. "I'm sorry I'm just a blob, but that's all you're going to get."

"You woke up," Signy said.

"Maybe. It's three in the goddamned morning. Go ahead, Pilar. I'm just watching."

Signy transferred her awareness to Jared's recorded body language, while all of them followed Anna around the *Siranui*.

From long familiarity with Jared's muscular signatures, Signy accepted Jared's awareness of earth-mother Anna. Or was it Signy's desire for stolid warmth, *her* need to touch Anna's firm smooth skin?

Immersed in a new place, its sounds and colors and textures, all of them. Signy sensed no activity in the shadowed virtual figures on the deck beside her; she heard no restless click of keyboards. We're all a frigging bunch of voyeurs, she thought. Worse than that. We're so different, but we're alike in the pursuit of orgasmic moments of epiphany, realization. Devoted to the "Aha!" moment, the gestalt of what we distill for and from each other, the indrawn breath that is closure and opening. Called by so many names, that feeling. The moment of awakening. We're addicted to the search for images and symbols that give us a brain rush. We're brain-rush junkies.

"I've got something," Pilar said. "Be back in a minute."

"We're getting some beautiful stuff here," Janine said. "But so far it's tourism. Besides which, I think all we may need is going to be words, words that will translate from English treaty language into Japanese with some degree of grace. And that, I'll tell you right now, will be tough." Janine's voice trailed away.

"We need more than that," Jared said. "We need to know what the ins and outs are of this company we're working for. I tell you, I get a feeling of—a glass wall, or something, between what we've been asked to do and the reality that's down here. I'm uneasy."

"Are you uneasy working for inscrutable Asian bosses?" Paul asked; Paul, who had too much of New England Brahminism in his childhood and would spend his life overcompensating for it.

"No," Jared said. "It's wuzzy stuff. I feel like we're being set up for something. That dead guy, for instance. Everybody's so *quiet* about him."

"You're in a high-risk environment," Janine said. "Death on the job is a routine occurrence down there. In any fishing fleet, as best as I can tell."

"I feel—eyes. Eyes on me. Yes, there's time displacement and air and sea that are different—I hope I'm showing you *how* different this place feels. But—"

He seemed so afraid. Signy closed her eyes and concentrated on the inputs from Jared's skinthin. He sat very still, ready for fast action. He was in Kihara's cabin, he had told them, but his body said he didn't trust the locks on the door, that he tensed for invaders who might break into the cabin at any moment.

"It's just a week," Paul said. "You can get what we need in a week, and then your medic friend comes back and you can get out of there." Paul did not deny Jared's uneasiness, he just put it in a business perspective. "We need the money, you know."

Yes, the money. Signy noticed that Pilar had vanished from the virtual of the ship's deck, busy in some other work. Yes, the money. What do we do if this contract doesn't work out? Jared gets a locum tenens and works himself into a contract offer, pushing pills for money. He hates that. Do I follow him? Do I start the round of interviews, looking for a company that could use a slightly rusty neurobiologist? I wouldn't tailor street drugs; it's not something I could live with. And anyway, Jared wouldn't put up with that for five minutes. I'd have to go solo and stay away from them all. I would become a dangerous person to know. Oh, shit.

Pilar reappeared and sank into her deck chair. She had missed the interchange or chosen to ignore it. "Try this," Pilar said. "Oh, try this for size." And Pilar built:

—a looming presence of ice that floated in a silent sea. Jimmy's music breathed against the water. An albatross hung motionless in the air. The checkered black-and-white wings of cape pigeons wove intricate script against a stormy horizon, peripheral messages in an unknown language. The music ached with the rhythmic peace of ocean swells.

The four-rigger rocked against blue nothing as Pilar finished.

"Forty-six seconds," Paul said. "The computer says the eye-movement coordinates are spectacular. Pilar Videla, if we need a net spot, you just made one. What it sells I ain't quite sure yet, but whatever it is, I'm sold."

"You're not a typical audience, fearless leader," Pilar said.

"I am, I am. I promise you I am. Seas and dead men, they are food for my soul. Signy, has the bridge found out anything about Skylochori?"

So Paul wasn't going to dismiss Jared's fears, not entirely.

"Checking," Signy said.

Signy shifted the focus of her headset and left the cold and friendly deck, to see instead:

Banks of monitors. The ship's bridge output came rolling by, Signy's demons searching across its transmissions; Skylochori, Rescue, Red Cross, the words for death and drowning and shipwreck in English, in Spanish, in phonetic Japanese.

Pilar played, again, McKenna's counterpoint of woodwind and strings, and Signy remembered Jared's fascination with the corpse in the sea, the faded orange of the tilted life raft.

The *Siranui* had made no calls to Search and Rescue at McMurdo. The verbal log there was full of terse comments in aviation-speak, in a mix of regional U.S. accents.

"No," Signy told the others. "They have not mentioned this death. As far as I can tell."

She slipped back into the virtual.

—above the *Siranui*'s deck, Skylochori's body swayed

in its harness. A waft of chilled salt air struck Signy's cheek and brought the scent of soaked human hair. The keyboard's feel intruded, a presence beneath her hands that didn't belong there; cold, waxy. Damn. Signy wiped her fingers on her Lycraed thighs and felt a woolly ship's blanket under her hands, soft and thick.

"Damn!" Signy whispered.

"What is it?" Jared asked, from somewhere far away.

The texture of the fabric under Signy's hands changed from wool to crisp nylon. She felt Jared's warm hand touch Skylochori's cold fingers, the chill of leathery, salt-soaked flesh. The sobbing, low sound of the cello roared in her ears.

Signy heard herself whimper and choked back the sound.

"Signy?" Paul asked.

"Take that corpse *away!*" Signy tore the headset away from her face and stared at her netted hands.

"What corpse?" Janine asked.

The holo stage became a blur of transparent color; all images shattered.

"Signy, there's no corpses here," Janine said.

The stage in Taos was white and empty.

"I saw a replay of Jared's exam," Signy said. "You didn't?"

"No way, Signy." The empty stage blurred with colors, Paul seeking something. "Oops, oops, we've got a scrambler sequence in here, on everything Jared has sent from the *Siranui.*"

But the music still played. Signy closed her eyes, and saw ovals of ice that glazed the ridges of each blue fingernail into manicured perfection; the hand lying slack, cradled in crackling nylon. "God damn it, Pilar, turn that off!"

"Jared, what the hell are you doing?" Paul asked.

The music stopped.

"I'm doing nothing but sitting here in the dark," Jared said.

"It's the *music*," Paul said. "Something in the sequences. Clever as hell, actually. Signy, come back in here with us. It's okay, really. We'll fix it."

Signy lifted the headset back over her face.

So familiar:

—Paul in his study, with Pilar and Janine sitting beside him, and a dark octagon, Jared, on the floor by their feet.

"I guess I left the sensory inputs on when I looked through the logs," Signy said. "That's when I got the overlay. I felt wax all over the keyboard. Creepy." Paul's imaged fireplace burned bright, and the flames formed mysterious little patterns.

"You've got your own weird little montage," Pilar said. "I wonder if this guy McKenna *meant* to do it."

"It couldn't be McKenna," Paul said. "Unless he's a genius. This little sequence is tied into the *Siranui*'s transmissions. I'll need to dump all of tonight's stuff, Pilar. Sorry."

"I can rebuild it," Pilar said. "Hey, Signy? You back with us?"

"I'm okay," Signy said. "Really." She stared at Paul's fire. The ghost of a hand lay flaccid on a flaming sea and sank away in moments.

"Really?" Jared asked. "Signy, sweet, we're here. Don't get twitchy on us, okay?"

Jared's voice came to her, concerned, no longer fearful, since Signy was. Jared the comforter.

"I'm okay. I'm fine," Signy said. Sinking transparent into the flaming water, the hand's shape as innocent as a fallen leaf.

It was an afterimage. Her eyes were tired, the hand was just an afterimage from her own fears. Wasn't it?

"I'm going looking for McKenna," Paul said.

"Why?" Janine asked.

"So I can congratulate him. Before I crush him to virtual pulp."

"I'll help," Pilar said.

Paul had started to destroy his study, methodically stripping everything away, down to a basic carrier signal that brought ghost voices to Signy's ears, and no visuals at all.

"Signy?" Jared asked.

"I'm here."

"It's time for sick call. I've got to go to work. Call in as soon as Paul gets us back up and running, okay?"

"Okay," Signy said.

Jared would have sensed, if anyone did, how frightened she had been. In reality more than real, in sensations brought to the edge of overload, even death was a possibility. Some had died in the nets, where nightmares could get up and walk around and put their virtual claws around virtual necks.

A wild program had scrambled what happened tonight, that was all that had happened; a hacker, maybe, looking for something and finding a bunch of people watching the ocean. Big deal. But there were possibilities of synergy, of feedback loops, of emphasis laid in unconsciously by multiple inputs to a set of images that could go from order into chaos, from pleasure into pain. That edge, that point of balance, was the magic, was what they always sought.

Tonight, though, was pure accident, was a strange little tech's game or mistake or whatever. The sensory inputs were just scrambled into that weird set of terrors. They weren't designed by anyone, not by Jared's fears, the ones he couldn't put names to, not by Pilar's guilt, if Pilar still felt guilt.

We're always so damned careful, Signy told herself. We don't let damaging things happen. We watch out for each other. Don't we?

NINE

Signy paced through the empty house, stared at the dishes in the sink, heated cold coffee in the microwave, and went back to the studio.

The console waited. The sooner Signy got back on the damned thing, the less likely it was that she would freeze up and not be able to do it. She listened to audios that told her that Paul was running a reduction of the scrambler sequence, that told her Pilar worked at the synthesizer. Janine began rebuilding Pilar's iceberg sequence, working from Jared's raw transmissions.

Paul got his study reformatted and up and running again, with Pilar and Janine in it, all back to normal. But it wasn't.

Signy picked up her headset and slipped it on. "I'm going on break for a while," she said.

Pilar looked up from her synthesizer and nodded, her face blank, intent on whatever she was feeding into her headphones. Paul and Janine didn't seem to hear Signy at all.

Signy tiptoed away and settled herself on the *banco* in the bedroom. She sat by the fireplace and stroked her mother's blanket, purchased from Taos Pueblo years ago. Woven from strips of rabbit fur, it was dense and thick on Signy's fingers. Yeah, regression had its uses, and curling up under a blanket was regression in the purest sense.

The blanket had traveled from Taos to Atlanta with Signy's mother, and to Tucson, where a six-year-old Signy had found it in a box of old things and adopted it as her own. When Edges bought the house by the river, the blanket had come back to Taos. Its colors matched the colors of the mesas, and the rabbits outside were surely distant cousins to the sacrificed ones whose fur comforted her hands now.

Rabbit stew had become a staple in Taos, and not from gastronomic preference, either. There had been three cases of tularemia in Taos County in the past year. Signy pushed aside the guilt of the groceries she'd just bought, pushed away the memory of the six women blanketed in the snow outside the grocery store, still waiting late on a cold winter's night. She couldn't feed them all.

Paul's voice, Janine's voice, drifted into the bedroom.

"I think I see a way out of national quotas," Janine said. "If I could just talk Tanaka into it."

"Tanaka's legal department is good. Let's just go with what they want," Paul said. "They've spent mega to get the wording; they think the population quota system for permits will control overfishing problems. You've got a group of cautious nations involved in the takeout if this goes through; they don't want to blow what safety we have in this leaky food bucket," Paul said.

"No. There's something better. It's a permit system the North Atlantic group worked out, based on bids, not nations, and they're right. Tanaka's wrong." Janine's voice continued, a murmur that rose and fell. Signy wondered whether they continued their talk to soothe her, whether they waited for her to return to them.

Signy had told them she was tired, and she was. Paul and Janine kept talking because they didn't want to leave her alone and scared. But Signy *was* alone, and she feared the synthetic comfort of the virtuals. Always, the spaces where she worked were places of safety, of refuge. Signy had known their dangers, but overloads had been a fantasy to her, something that happened to the careless, the daring. Signy was neither.

She *liked* controlled reality, where emotions could be edited away. Uncomfortable things like starvation and poisoned food and tough relationships didn't have to exist there. Except that tonight, a monster presence had slipped into her safe space and frightened her. A result of Jared's fears, or her own, a virus, a hacker, whatever; she'd been *invaded*.

In this group, in these past calm years when they had just worked and loved and fought, Signy hadn't had to deal with anyone or anything that came uninvited to her world. She'd lost some layers on a skin that had been, for most of her life, thick enough. She'd trusted her world, and trust was always, always, a mistake, damn it.

Paul and Janine weren't *here* in this empty house, in this cold night. They hadn't been affected, hadn't felt the damned sensations crawling along Signy's skin. They could sympathize, and they did, but their concern was an abstract thing, a response of intellectual empathy. Their voices were just voices.

And Jared? Jared was in sick bay in a ship on a frozen sea, thousands of miles away. Signy wanted him to be here, right here, warm and real, a distraction to take away her fears of the dark. She needed to leave a message for him. She needed to bring up Alan Campbell.

There was no mysterious hand in the fireplace flames. Signy was not near her keyboard and it was not coated with wax. Nobody else saw that stuff. Maybe she had scrambled her own inputs.

Sure. Like hell she had. The whole episode had a mistake, a glitch, that's all.

In the studio, Pilar's voice asked, "Hey, you guys going to be up much longer?"

"Maybe an hour," Janine said.

"We're out of coffee," Pilar grumbled.

"I'll go get some," Janine said. "As soon as I finish this one bit . . ."

And then Janine said something that made Paul laugh. I'll go back in in a minute, Signy told herself.

She stared at the rumpled, empty bed.

The voices from the studio quieted. Signy held on to her security blanket and went back in.

Paul's reconstructed study was empty. Embers glowed in the New Hampshire fireplace.

Signy sat down and screened the messages waiting for Jared.

[Pilar] Could you get some visuals from under the sea? Go diving, maybe? Please, Jared, I need more than ice to look at.

[Paul] Signy says nobody's trying to find out about the dead man. This intrigues me.

I have to tell Jared something about Alan, Signy decided. I want to tell him I need him here, with me, that I'm afraid for him. That I'm afraid, too.

[Signy] I fucked Alan Campbell last week. See if you can find out why he's in Antarctica.

Not quite right.

[Signy] Alan Campbell is on the *Siranui*. He works for Gulf Coast Intersystems. Any connection with what we're doing?

Which avoided the problem.

[Signy] Add: tell him hello.

Idiot. It was no big deal. How could she phrase this, damn it? Her eyes wandered around the dusky shadows of Paul's study.

The silver bowl Paul had bought in Atlanta rested on a table near closed drapes of amber velvet. Sometimes he floated roses in it in the summer.

Signy remembered how it was, living with Paul in the old New England farmhouse. How it was when Paul brought Jared home, this neat guy who ran the wilderness tour Paul hadn't wanted to go on, not really. You need to sweat some, Signy had told him, and Paul had gone to sweat, and come back with Jared.

Before the weekend ended, Paul had asked Jared if he'd like a new job.

"It's a mosaic company that we're starting, an interactive

group of ideas and personalities that we want to build, a collection of disparate talents that can define answers and then come up with questions for people to ask about them. We want to work with the psychology of attractions, with the science of spin-doctoring, with virtual realities that can compact and condense amounts of information that would have staggered us in our childhoods."

In a weekend, that quickly, Signy had sensed what Jared's intense sense of life could add to what she and Paul were trying to do. Jared's acute senses, his intense absorption in whatever he was doing made everything he did seem important.

"Yes, we'll sell ideas, even products," Paul said. "But there will be an integrity in it, and that integrity will come from knowledge of the subject."

Jared had listened to all of this. He let Paul wind down, thought about the offer for a while, and said, "Yes."

"Yes, what?" Paul had asked.

"Yes, I'll work with you," Jared said.

"Why?"

"I could use the money. You could use a keeper."

The three of them had lived in the New Hampshire house for a while, and sometimes they had shared a bed.

Signy stared at the list of messages waiting for Jared's attention. Just say what needs to be said, Signy decided. Jared will ask any questions he wants to ask. I'll talk to him in a few hours, anyway.

[Signy] There's a guy on the ship I met in Houston. Alan Campbell, works for Gulf Coast Intersystems. He's the tall redhead that was in the mess yesterday. Can you find out why he's there? By the way, I slept with him.

Signy slept hard and woke early. She wandered into the studio with her second cup of coffee and pulled up the floating raft, intending to exorcise her memories of it. Its orange fabric was faded with salt or sun. It had been hauled on the *Siranui*'s deck and shoved aside while Jared looked down at the dead sailor. The faded black lettering on its side puzzled her. Signy traced what curves she could, overlaid them, upped the contrast, and tried again.

She made another pot of coffee. Later, she'd get breakfast and a bath. Just after she finished this one series.

The tracings she made of the lines looked like Japanese calligraphy. Useless to her; Signy's internal neural programming could complete the curve of an S, add the crossbars of an incomplete I, but Signy didn't read Japanese. Maybe Paul had a program that would do it.

There were other marks below the Japanese. In a line. She searched out English letters, found them—O. O or zero, B, or P.

OBU.

Anything else was total guesswork. And Jared had powered up his skinthin rig.

Signy tried audio.

"Jared?" she asked. But Jared was recording only; Signy couldn't talk to him until he chose to listen.

Across from him at a table, Anna de Brum spooned up the last traces of something tan and creamy from a glass dish. Anna wore a ginger yellow coverall and she had a bright red blossom behind her right ear. Dressing up for Jared, Signy figured. Anna laid down her spoon and moved the empty dish to the side of her tray.

"What are your plans for this afternoon?" Jared asked.

"I am planning to dissect some squid and weigh their ovaries," Anna said. "Want to help?"

"No. What I'd really like to do is go diving."

"Do you like that? Scuba diving?" Anna asked.

"Indeed I do," Jared said.

Anna frowned. "I am so sorry," Anna said. "But I have

limitations on how many excuses I can make to go under. The ship's divers will only go out if a net is tangled or some equipment malfunctions. And they would not like to take responsibility for you, I think. You could hitch a ride on one of the trawlers if there's a short run scheduled. But all they do is fish, usually." Anna looked at him over her the rim of her coffee mug. "You could take a nap."

"Marshallese sleep on and off all day, don't they?"

"On the atolls, yes," Anna said. "Work a little, eat a little, sleep a little. Dream a lot."

And they fear demons in the night, Signy had read, and will not sleep in the open. They sleep in stuffy rooms with the doors closed while Pacific winds cool the nights outside. They're doing okay on food, so we hear. Sometimes they have mostly fish and coconuts, but at least they have fish, and coconuts.

"I guess I'll go back to quarters and check in with my friends up north," Jared said.

"I'll be in the bio lab," Anna said.

The corridors Jared traveled held overhead mazes of conduits, like the hallway in Atlanta. Signy watched Jared pull a small monitor close to the unmade bunk in Kihara's cabin. Signy loved the look of the tight muscles of his ass, oh yes, but she reveled in the smooth motions of his shoulders, the precision of his sure touch. Jared's grace was never that of excess effort.

He stretched out on the bunk's rumpled off-white comforter, on mink brown sheets with a black stripe. Signals from his skinthin sent the feel of a ridge of bedding. He shrugged the comforter into a more comfortable contour. Signy and Jared were matched perfectly in height, something that had always delighted her; they met nose to nose and toe to toe.

Jared stuffed a pillow behind his neck and pulled up the message list.

Signy punched into ship's comp and activated the mike on Kihara's monitor. "Jared?"

"Hey." Jared's eyes were already scanning the screened messages; Signy saw the square letters through the cameras on his forehead.

"Oh," Jared said. He looked a little startled, a little quizzical.

Signy sent her face to Kihara's screen. She hadn't combed her hair yet. She ran her fingers through it and tossed a loose curl behind her shoulder.

Signy watched Jared's face through Kihara's monitor cameras, and she saw her own face as Jared saw it on the flat screen of the little monitor. Signy's face was square and her jaw always looked too determined to suit her. If she liked anything about her looks at all, she liked her eyes, true hazel, and not half bad if she remembered to wear mascara. But watching her own face was disorienting. Signy windowed her view of Kihara's monitor to the left, so she would not be distracted by the motion of her own lips; she hated to watch herself talk.

"Tell Pilar I don't get to dive today," Jared said.

Signy watched him closely, his pale gray eyes, the motions of his lips. Knowing her own face so distant on the flatscreen, unable to send him touch or smell. As if I am a memory to him, she thought, as if we speak across time. His afternoon is my morning. He has lived this day and I'm just starting it.

I hate time.

Jared was thinking about something. He had that look.

"Pilar, now. You know, it occurs to me that we drive her into these messes," Jared said. "That we always have. What we do is, we push Pilar out somewhere on a limb, and then we haul ass and get her out of trouble."

No, Signy thought. We don't. Yes, we do.

"That's ugly, Jared."

"People are ugly."

"Then we should stop."

"Maybe not. Maybe not. Think about it."

Signy thought about it. What Jared said made sense. Edges had leapfrogged their way into an affluence that a younger Signy would have found frightening. A lot of their success came from Pilar's tangential sense of creativity; Edges made her dreams real.

"I don't think knowing it would change Pilar's . . . structure," Signy said.

"I like her structure just fine, myself," Jared said.

"Yeah," Signy said. And I enjoyed Alan's, as I've enjoyed other "structures" now and again. That's how we are, isn't it? "Paul wants some numbers on tonnes of catch. I think I can pull them from ship's comp but if you aren't doing anything today—"

"I don't know yet." Jared was not fond of statistics.

"You'll find something, it sounds like. I like Anna."

"So do I."

Who's going to bring up Alan? Me, probably, Signy decided. "I pulled your views of the life raft last night and I'm trying to rebuild the lettering on it. OBU, OPU, something. And Paul is wondering if anybody's ever going to take that corpse out of the freezer."

"I'll ask Anna if she's heard anything. We signed Sky-lochori out of the sick-bay records, so it's bridge business. I may not hear about it. It still has an *unusual* feel to it, though." Jared pulled the pillow from behind his neck, punched it, and settled back again. His thighs felt heavy to him, to Signy as she/he let them rest on the bed.

"I'm getting weird, I guess," Jared said. "The light, maybe, no day and night. I feel like a house officer again. But it's only been a couple of days since this guy died. And I don't know the ship's policies on notifying families of sailors lost at sea."

"If there is a family," Signy said.

"Right. Now, about this Campbell?"

Signy heard herself speaking fast, with undertones of apology that she wished weren't there. "Just if you run into him. I don't know. Either he's looking to build something for Tanaka or he's looking for something in the tech Tanaka is using."

"I don't remember seeing any redheads."

"You were in the early stages of a feeding frenzy. I'll show you."

Signy sent views of the short Japanese officer and Alan beside him.

"He's a bony sucker," Jared said. As if he wondered at Signy's taste. "I've seen him before, I think."

"He's with Gulf Coast Intersystems," Signy said. "We met him at a party."

"I'll talk to him," Jared said. "If he's still here. Are you going to stay in the studio for a while?"

"Most of the day," Signy said.

"Stay with me, if you'd like. I'll go see what I can find."

"I'll check in and out. Jared?"

He smiled at her. "Right here, pet." With a halted motion of his arms, as if he would hug her.

"Right here, *there*." Signy wasn't going to tell him how scared she'd been when the virtuals got away from her, or tell him he was right to want to run like hell from whatever fears haunted him, for all fears seemed foolish in the warmth they could make together. This was just a job that needed doing, and Jared's uneasiness, Signy's terrors, were midnight vapors, best ignored until they vanished of their own improbability. Signy looked at Kihara's screen and saw that she had put on an "everything's fine" smile.

"Go to work, woman," Jared said. "I need this screen to pull up the ship's duty log."

"That means I have to look through lists of dead fish for Paul, not you."

"That's right."

Jared's face vanished.

Light snow fell on the blanketed figures outside the store. Signy parked her runabout and walked to where they stood. One finger over her lips to hush, if she could, the thanks she by no means wanted, she handed each one of them a fifty.

Back home, Signy combed her hair and put on mascara. She brought a mug of hot chocolate into the studio.

Newly constructed and presumably virus free, black-and-white birds wheeled over gray ocean swells, meshed in the rhythms of Pilar's music. They brought with them a sense of wonder, a feeling of the effortless power of tides and time.

TEN

Because it was the lonely time, when night people could be found, Pilar went looking for someone named Jimmy McKenna, knowing that wouldn't be the name he used. Privacies came in many strange forms in the net. What Pilar needed to find was someone who knew Jimmy's Name and would be willing to tell her his address.

Gulf Coast? The last place to look.

Music? Beethoven's Fifth Synchrony, BFS, hadn't heard of him, or so he said.

The Frisco Freak?

[Freak] No way, hon. Pilar, we're going to run a thing Thursday night at Infinity Warehouse. You wanna come down and do some fleshtime? Just for the old Freak, maybe?

[Pilar] $$$???

[Freak] Well, of course there's no *money* in it, am I the Freak or what?

Whiteline scored for her.

[Whiteline] Yeah, Jimmy the Mac. Let me tell you, Empress, this is a shy dude and he just keeps pulling every byte of yours off the net. But he checks in with me alla time and somehow he manages to ask if I've heard from you. So have I?

[Pilar] So you've heard from me, Whiteline. Like I want his ass soonest, okay?

[Whiteline] I figure ten minutes.

But it didn't happen in ten minutes. Pilar slept well into the morning, and dreamed of brick alleys that never dead-ended and never opened onto streets. It was a maze in a kid's book, she knew it, and if she could just get *up* high enough to look down, she could see where Out was.

The bricks were old, their faces dulled with years into that funny baked-bean color. It was Boston; it was where she'd been taken after the double funeral, both her parents in caskets heaped with flowers. Drunk driver, drunk driver, only this time Papa was the drunk driver. Pilar still remembered him, and security, and laughter, when she smelled bourbon. Odd that she liked the way it smelled, even now.

Pilar had sketched those brick walls, over and over. Sitting in Auntie Beatrice's bay window that looked out on Beacon Street, where little old ladies in cloned minks rode their bicycles to market and the light always seemed to come through a thin lens of gray oil.

Pilar woke to a Seattle fog, and she woke charged, ready to work. On the holo stage, she set—

A background of faded moiré velvet the color of tobacco, rumpled over cracked, stained marble. A stalk of dried mullein just there, its heavy head the shape of a candle flame. Tossed, a handful of freshwater pearls.

Pilar tilted her head and looked at what she'd done. The sound, the sound, yes.

It took her, for some inexplicable reason, several tries to find what she needed. In Symphony Hall in Boston, not the shrilling tune-up before a performance, but the time between movements of a string quartet. The first violin playing open fifths, quietly, to check the tuning, and somewhere, one cough, and then several. She took the sound, multiplied the tracks, and dulled them down to pianissimo. Then upped the echo again. A scent track? She tried a whiff of sandalwood. No.

Janine, scrubbed and polished, waited at the doorway when Pilar looked up.

"The florist is here," Janine said.

"Oh, yeah. I ordered some tulips for you. When's your interview with Tanaka?"

"Tonight. His tomorrow. Pilar, you going to eat today?"

"Later. Later."

Janine sighed and left. Pilar enjoyed, in some perverse way, Janine's concern. But pet, she wanted to tell her, I am not an anorexic. Or rather, I would be, but I have this thing about hot fudge sundaes. Pilar looked again at the tobacco velvet, at all the dry, soft textures.

"This sucks!" she yelled, and stood up in the middle of scattered virtual pearls. Trash it?

Pilar kicked a few pearls with her imaged foot and left them that way. She went into the kitchen and nuked up last night's twice-cooked pork and rice and ate it all, with three glasses of orange juice and a vitamin pill. Then she fixed the tulips for Janine, went back to the studio to store the pearls and velvet, and just sat, for a while, looking out the window to where Rainier probably was.

Signy, looking in, saw Pilar at rest, her profile dark against the pearly light from the window, one arm draped over her bent knee and her midnight hair pulled forward over one shoulder.

Pilar looked as if she had posed for a life class. Signy saved the image to storage and hunted for Jared on the *Siranui*.

She found Jared in a poker game. And didn't bother him.

Signy worked her way through the Houston data, looking for correlations that might overlay Pilar's iceberg scene. There were no telltale spikes in the graphics to give her a sure feel for emotional undertones. Rage, in the Houston population, was a dull thing, worn down by years and years of less and less. The world didn't whimper anymore, it just . . . dwindled. The Great Plains aquifers were dead, the West surviving on rainfall and caution. The seas, the biologists said, were graying. Their creatures were duller, less exuberant than in times past. Times past.

Signy lost herself, for a pleasant while, in Jared's views of the sea. The world looked pretty healthy there.

[Paul] It's time, Signy.

Seascapes vanished, replaced by Paul, dressed for Kobe's morning business hours. Paul wore money clothes. He had spruced up, close-shaven enough that he looked scraped and oiled, in a carefully knotted foulard, a blinding white shirt, a British tailor's charcoal suit. On the Seattle screen, Janine sat all proper in a pale gray business tunic. Her hands rested on Pilar's scrubbed birch table. Janine and Paul both had their notebooks propped beside them; Signy would be able to add silent comments while they talked. A mass of forced pink tulips stood on an oak sideboard behind Janine. They were very Dutch-looking tulips, loosely bundled in markedly non-Asian profusion.

"Okay?" Paul asked.

"You're gorgeous," Signy said. Grubby Signy. As soon as they finished this little conference, Signy figured she would shower, or maybe soak in the hot tub.

"Listen with us," Paul said. "Cut in if you need to."

"You're meeting with a company shyster," Signy said. "Not Tanaka himself. But the finery looks nice." And you're both as scared as I am. God, kids, don't blow it.

"Kazuyuki Itano," Janine said. "That's as close as we're likely to get to the center, for now."

Signy windowed up Itano's dossier. A Stanford graduate, he'd spent years in Tanaka's San Diego offices and now worked out of the home office in Kobe. Itano ran the fisheries for Tanaka and he would shepherd Tanaka's position at Antarctic Commission meetings in Lisbon.

"I may consult you while Itano is on-line," Paul said. "I want him to meet all of us, so he'll know we're not offing a junior on him if he talks to you."

"Show my face and I'll kill you," Signy said. "Other than that, fine."

A young man with a round face and glasses answered Paul's call. He wore a regulation dark business suit and looked too young to be a Stanford graduate. "Mr. Itano will speak with you now," he said. Roundeyes was a secretary, Signy realized.

Itano came onscreen, seated behind an expanse of glossy rosewood. The wall behind him was a windowless expanse of polished limestone rich with marine fossils. Kazuyuki Itano had white sideburns and a narrow European style nose.

Signy figured the sideburns were cosmetic.

"Mr. Maury, Dr. Hull," Itano began a ritual round of greetings in unaccented West Coast English. Good, Signy thought, he won't argue Janine's input, even if she is a gaijin blonde. "I have read your negotiating proposals, Mr. Maury. Your suggestion that the French-speaking delegations would find a reexamination of the tourist ban to be 'inflammatory' is intriguing."

"They will become upset. It would be good for a distraction, if you need one. Remind people, again, that only the affluent could afford to travel to Antarctica thirty years ago, and they were banned. Now, such travel would be limited to the filthy rich. Such people fund research, after all."

"Research is integral to Tanaka's interests," Itano said. He looked at something over Paul's head and seemed to change the subject. "We are pleased to learn that the nephew of the U.S. negotiator is graduating the Scripps Institute."

"I have heard that the young man is considering a position with Pacific Biosystems," Paul said.

"Is he?" Itano asked.

And said young man just might receive an offer from Tanaka, at rather a more favorable salary, if Signy was reading Itano's expression right. There was nothing ominous in such a move. We'll be okay, Signy thought.

"You have approved the advertisement in the *Economist?*" Ad*vertizment*, Paul said, dropping into British pronounciation.

Signy smiled.

"Your copy looked attractive to the type of recruit we seek," Itano said. "Our British PR agency approved the copy as written. Have you recommendations for other media exposure?"

"We have concerns about that," Paul said. "This is delicate—it may be that public awareness of the renewal date for the Antarctic treaty may reopen the discussion about mineral rights. If no blather is heard, then the old environmental guidelines may stand as is, and the public will likely remain unaware that mineral extraction is only temporarily forbidden under the terms of the treaty. The guidelines could be brought up for review again. A company who promised extravagant safety procedures might find sympathetic listeners in the Commission. The oil reserves are considerable, we know, and copper? Its availability may be greater than we think. There is always the possibility that 'objective' estimates made in the eighties and nineties were slanted to appear less, rather than more, in quantity."

"Thirty years ago, no one wanted the continent disturbed," Itano said. "Tanaka's opinion has not changed. Leave it alone, at any cost."

"My information is that mining the continent would be economically ridiculous, even now," Janine said.

Itano frowned in Janine's direction. Then, perhaps because the screen on the front of his desk was feeding him Janine's academic credentials, he looked directly at Dr. Janine Hull's face and nodded agreement.

Economically ridiculous now, Signy thought, economically feasible when all else became scarce. The Alaskan oil fields are still pumping. We'll need Antarctic oil and copper someday, but not yet. The restrictions keep the issue quiet, but not closed. Damned parasites, us humans. Still, some of us must live.

"If someone stirs up the Greens, if someone makes them aware that mineral extraction is still a possibility in Antarctica, they may decide to take on the cause of the poor fishes again," Janine said. "They would package the issues together; they would try to stop the mining, forever, stop fishing, forever."

So far, so good. Itano looked interested.

Pilar had framed Janine and her wide blue eyes in front of massed pink flowers, so European. Way to go, Pilar, Signy cheered. If you can't hide it, flaunt it. She wondered if Itano thought that Janine's rose and ivory coloring was pretty, or just strange.

Itano tented his fingers as if he were praying. "Maximum sustainable harvest is necessary. Many would starve without the sea harvest," he said. "I emphasize: sustainable. We have no intention of depleting the Antarctic, Dr. Hull."

"So we have heard," Janine said. "Mr. Itano, I am concerned about the proposed quota system. Giving the most fish to nations with the most people may not be the optimal way to maintain the safety of the biomass in the Southern Ocean."

"Nothing else has been proposed." Itano pulled his hands beneath his desk and out of sight.

[Signy] He's tensing up, Janine. Paul, you answer.

"A system was used in Arctic waters, briefly, twenty years ago," Paul said. "Permits went to the highest bidders. Not by nation; any fleet could bid. The fleets who could get the fish out the most efficiently paid percentages of profits to a UN fund. The UN spent the money on benthic research and allocated some to protein distribution."

[Signy] Janine, it's *Paul* who makes Itano tighten up. You take him, girl. He's warming to you.

"The agreement didn't last," Janine said. "Countries with no fisheries invoked the Law of the Sea agreement; 'sea resouces are the common heritage of mankind,' and all that. Several landlocked countries threatened to claim their share of the catch. The fishermen got upset and delivered some of the disputed share to a protesting country's embassy. A couple of truckloads of fresh fish can make quite a mess on a hot day."

Itano returned Janine's smile. "The Sardine Solution. Yes."

"You seriously suggest we propose opening such a can of . . . worms . . . again?" Itano asked.

"I seriously do." Janine's eyes were as big as saucers, as innocent as bluebells. "But I would not suggest that protests be met in the same way."

"Our time is limited," Itano said. "You are suggesting that we change our proposed strategy entirely."

"Our best recommendation, Mr. Itano."

Itano's hands pushed against the edge of the desk. "Difficult," he said.

"Possible. Possible, Mr. Itano." Janine's voice stayed low and she began to use a slower, more deliberate cadence. "For a company willing to maintain a long-term view."

[Signy] I can't be sure he will catch the change in emphasis, but give it a try.

Itano let his elbows rest on the desk and cupped his palms in front of him, as if he kept guard on some invisible object on the table, something that might scurry away. Paul crossed his arms and waited.

"Tanaka reported a catch of one hundred thousand tonnes of krill last season. Of *Nototheniops larseni*, of

Champsocephalus gunnari, and related bony fishes; fifty thousand tonnes. Tanaka's fleet is by no means the largest in Antarctic waters." Janine's tongue had no problems with the fishy names. Itano stayed intent on her words; Janine continued. "Other fleets report their catches to the Antarctic authorities on an honor system. The catch is variable by year, and a decrease in reported catches has been occurring each year for the past four years. This is considered alarming in some quarters. Arbitrary restrictions on all catches are being considered."

"You have done your homework, Dr. Hull. Have you calculated the changes attributed to decreasing salinity at the Antarctic upwelling? Ice-cap melt is increasing, but some researchers maintain that the productivity will increase, not decrease, because of it. We may be just seeing an adjustment in speciation, not a true decrease."

"Parameters are still in question," Janine said. "In many areas. Isn't that what people say when they don't know what's really happening, but they're afraid they're wrong?"

"The decreases cause us concern," Itano said. "We might like to manage the harvest differently. I am scheduled to arrive in Lisbon tomorrow. Time prevents us, unfortunately, from discussing the changes we would like to make."

Security concerns, Signy thought, prevent us . . . but Itano wasn't insisting that Edges go ahead and sell the proposed treaty language.

"But if you could come to Lisbon . . ."

[Signy] Aha! Your fish is nibbling the bait. You knew he might ask. I think you should go, Janine.

". . . we could perhaps discuss this further," Itano said.

"I—would be honored." Janine didn't look honored, she looked not very happy at all.

[Signy] Smile, damn it.

Smiles and bows finished the discussion. Itano's secretary followed Itano's goodbyes with promises of travel arrangements and guest housing for Janine. The secretary's round face vanished, and Signy waited for Janine's response.

"You did it, Janine. Itano's responses were negative to my comments, pretty much, from the few tension parameters I could read of him," Paul said.

"You're Harvard. He's Stanford. What did you expect?" Signy asked, voice this time, since the conference was over. Relief relaxed her shoulders. Relief was a comfortable, warm feeling. The contract, which had seemed so tenuous, felt real, felt doable.

"More friction than I got, actually. You've got to do it for us. Fleshtime, my dear Ms. Hull," Paul told Janine. "It is said that blue-eyed blondes get the highest prices in the better houses in Tokyo."

"Really?" Janine asked. "Paul, you are so low."

"Just information. Just information."

"We're on an open line, Paul," Signy said. Just this once, she was happy to catch him in a relative security goof.

Paul vanished.

Janine cut away into a carrier wave. Signy stretched and got up and sat down again. She looked in on Jared. He had finished his game, and he sat in Kihara's cabin, working at the flat-screen. Signy started to download some of the meeting to him, but then she figured Jared could just as well ask her for it. He would want a precis, anyway, and Signy didn't want to do one just now.

The Seattle cameras responded to motion, and Signy saw Janine at the doorway of the studio. Janine looked in at Pilar, who seemed unaware of her.

"I thought it went pretty well," Signy said.

"It seemed to," Janine said. "Is there anything to see in Lisbon in January?"

Signy had expected outrage, not resignation. "Oh, babe. I don't know."

Janine's formal tunic contrasted with the clutter, the

room's cameras showing unadorned Seattle walls, and Pilar in a paint-stained caftan, fingering her way through a box filled with wrinkled tubes of acrylic pigments.

"You're through?" Pilar asked. "I'll use the tulips, then."

"Yeah, I'm through." Janine pulled the tunic's high collar open and rubbed at her neck. "I'm going to Lisbon."

"Yeah." Pilar squeezed a blob of cadmium yellow on her palette and frowned at it.

"You going to paint tulips?" Janine started for the door, to get the tulips, Signy figured. She waited on Pilar's every whim, and Signy hated that she did.

Janine didn't leave; she sat down on a battered tapestry cushion and stared up at Pilar.

"Maybe. You know those knitted hats the sailors wear on the *Siranui*? I think they'd sell in L.A.," Pilar said.

"They're ugly." Janine frowned and picked at something on her cushion.

"That's why they would sell," Pilar said.

Signy pulled her headset off. The Taos house sat warm against the winter cold. She added a couple of logs to the corner fireplace and nudged them into place. Why didn't Pilar act pleased, or happy, or give some sort of human response? We all worked on this, sweated through this conference, and now Pilar chooses to ignore Janine, who needs a few strokes. Damn her for an insensitive . . .

Loud and insistent, Signy heard a siren whoop on the *Siranui*. The noise alarmed her, hit a deep vein of fear that she'd shoved aside. Running back to her station, she realized she was primed for this, that she had been waiting, all through Itano's call, waiting for something ominous to surface. Her headset felt sweat-slick when she pulled it on. Signy disappeared the Seattle inputs and scrambled to find Jared's signature in the *Siranui*'s virtual architecture. An accident? A medical alert? Jared was not in sick bay, but Signy hadn't expected to find him there. In Kihara's cabin, she found the familiar sense of Jared's body, awakening. Signy punched the volume control and heard Alan Campbell's voice.

". . . distress signal coming from a submersible."

"Anna's got the crash kit. I'll be right up," Jared said. He swiveled away from the cabin flatscreen.

Jared's body language felt alert, not alarmed, but he was tense enough to startle Signy as she felt him get to the cabin door and head for the lift.

Seen through Jared's cameras, the *Siranui*'s deck took shape before her, Alan's freckled neck visible for a moment above his collar, glimpses of Jared's feet in bulky moonboots. Crew members in bulky parkas pushed a helo into position for takeoff. The deck's granular black surface was rimed with ice, slippery, and Signy felt herself jerk as Jared skidded.

Anna's hand caught his elbow in a grip as strong and sure as a longshoreman's.

"Thanks!" Jared shouted above the helo's engines.

"Move it!" Anna yelled.

ELEVEN

Warm in contrast to the deck's intrusive cold, the helo's windows clouded with their breath. The pilot wiped his gloved hand back and forth across the front windscreen in short, measured arcs. The line of black hair above his ear was cut with surgical precision, and he looked no older than twenty-five. Anna pulled down jump seats, a row of three on the cabin's right side, and sat in the rearward one. She motioned Campbell and Jared to their places and harnessed herself to the seat.

Jared fought with a buckle but got it fastened. Campbell seemed to have no trouble working in his gloves, but Jared's seemed far too bulky and he stripped them off. The copilot held his cupped hands over his headphones, listening to instructions obscured by the helo's roar. His curly brown beard moved as he answered some comment.

The helo was set up for rescue operations. A pair of stretchers hugged the left wall of the cabin; supplies and oxy lines were Velcroed to the tan padding of the bulkheads. Jared looked over the space, locating equipment so he could reach it if he needed it, and giving visuals for Edges to sort through later. The back of the helo looked like the inside of an angular cornucopia, and Jared wondered what Pilar would do with that idea if he told her about it. Anna strapped the crash kit into place. The helo lifted away from the deck and turned left.

"Signy?" Jared asked. If she had managed to patch into the helo's nav system, she might hear him. Nothing.

Well, okay; Signy, or Paul, would get access to his transmissions or they wouldn't. No big deal. "I'll put a save on this, in case you want it," Jared said to no one.

Anna noticed his lips moving. She pointed to a padded headset clipped to the bulkhead above him. Jared pulled down the phones and fitted them over his ears. Alan Campbell copied his motions. Chatter from the *Siranui*'s bridge came in loud, voices directing the helo toward coordinates north and west of the ship's location.

"We are still getting transmissions from the *Gojiro*," a clipped voice said. "Voice contact is garbled. There are three crewmen listed on board and they report injury of some sort. The *Kasumi* is heading for the submersible's location."

The copilot turned back to look at his passengers. In front of him, ranks of instruments glowed green in hazy twilight. "Hi. I'm Trent." Last name? First name? Jared couldn't tell. "Welcome aboard. Your pilot today is Mr. Uchida, and we're tracking the *Kasumi*. We anticipate a pleasant flight of about one hour." Trent's accent was Midwestern. "If you want, I'll put you on intercom so you can talk to each other."

"Yeah," Campbell said. Jared nodded.

"*Gojiro?*" Jared asked.

"That's the sub that's in trouble," Trent said. "Your hostess today . . ."

"Shut up, Trent," Anna said. "No cabin service. I have my limits." Anna yawned, folded her arms, and leaned back against her harness. An outsider, a visitor, Jared felt suddenly alone. What intimacy, what interactions bridged these two? They teased each other with easy familiarity, and Jared assumed a history from that observation. What they were to each other might be something unfamiliar, hostile or dear or strange. Jared used the conventions of assumption; he imagined these two as friends or lovers. What assumptions did he make of this Campbell?

"What's the *Kasumi?*" Jared asked.

"She's a traveler." The copilot did not turn around again. The pilot hadn't said a word yet. "The *Kasumi* is fair-sized," Trent said. "She carries the fleet's three-man subs, both of them. She may have sent the second one down after the one that's in trouble."

"The *Gojiro* is down?" Campbell asked. "What's the other one called?"

"*Smogu*," the pilot said. He made a quick motion with the corner of his lip, a half smile.

"Has McMurdo Search and Rescue been called out?" Jared asked.

"No," Trent said.

"Expensive." Anna stared across the cabin, seemingly fascinated by the accordion folds in a length of translucent blue respirator tubing. "The fleet must pay expenses to lift a search-and-rescue operation and we know where this sub is."

"But if someone's closer . . ." Campbell said.

"No one's closer." Trent wiped condensation from the righthand window. The defrosters had kicked in and the front screens were clear. Jared could see hazy sky that looked brighter now than it had when the helo left the *Siranui*'s deck. The rear section of the helo had no windows. Jared's view of the outside world was limited to squares of clouded sky and the shadowed backs of the two airmen. Sorry about the visuals, kids, he thought. And the noise. "Nothing's happening," Jared whispered. "I'm turning us off for a while."

"Huh?" Alan asked.

"Oh. I'm talking to my suit."

"Oh, right. I'm used to seeing masks when people are recording. The headbands work as well as the masks?"

"I'm not using facial sensations, so I can get by with it, yeah." Jared turned his head, bringing the curve of the plastic sensor that rested against his cheek into Campbell's view.

"It looks better than those ski-mask outfits," Campbell

said. "I met a woman last week in Houston who wore a rig like yours."

"Yeah," Jared said. "She told me." *How was it for you? What did Signy see that had her in bed with you so fast? And what did you learn from her?*

"Signy?" Alan asked. "You work with her. She told me."

"She's a partner." *I live with her, Campbell, and I'm going to give you every chance I can think of to fuck up this conversation.*

"She's one of the most intriguing women I've ever met."

Not bad. A neutral comment on the positive side. Not bad, Campbell, and also cautious. "Signy was surprised to see you here," Jared said.

"See me?"

"Yeah. What I record gets home real fast." *Home, I said. Did you pick it up?*

Campbell leaned back in his chair. Snug in her harness, Anna had tucked her chin down and gone to sleep.

"She mentioned she was doing a job for Tanaka. I looked up the company and looked at the specs on their submersibles. Keeping vacuum out, keeping water out; there are similarities."

"Keeping air in," Jared said.

"Yeah, it just could be that I think we build a better scrubber system than the ones they're using now." Campbell grinned.

"So that's why you're here?"

"That's why I'm here. Maybe we'll get some work for Houston out of this. Thank her for me, will you?"

"I'll do that," Jared said.

Signy saw Jared's gloved hand reach for a grip beside the helo's door and then he disappeared in static. She switched to the bridge speakers and heard chatter about a ship named *Kasumi* and tried hooking in to it, but no go.

[Signy] Paul?

He didn't answer. "I don't fucking like this," Signy said. She hooked into Seattle and said it again.

"It's Jared's job." Pilar looked up from her console and ran her forefinger across her nose, smearing it with mint green acrylic as she did so. "Rescues and stuff."

"Yeah. But."

"But what, Lioness?"

Pilar wasn't worried about Jared, no. She was at her screens and working frantically with the *Siranui*'s programs.

"What are you doing?" Signy asked.

"I'm trying to get a different address for a trawler called the *Kasumi*," Pilar said.

"Any luck?"

"No better than yours." Pilar leaned back and folded her arms. "Signy, I found McKenna."

"Distract me, go ahead. Where did you find him?"

"In Seattle. While you were talking to Japan."

"And?"

"And he swears there was nothing on that chip but music, and it isn't his. Something he heard on the net, he says, and he copied for me."

"Do you believe him?"

"Believe, hell. I don't have a feel for him. He's just print on a screen. He says there's no way that a music sequence could do what I told him got done, and he wants to talk to me."

Another address for the *Kasumi*; Signy hadn't thought of that angle. Maybe, maybe somebody was tracing Alan. Key in Gulf Coast and ask them; it might be worth a try. She opened a channel to them, and half-heard Pilar say—

"So okay, I said, and he's coming over here."

"Yeah," Signy said. Then, "*What?*"

"We can't really kill him."

"Tell that to Paul," Signy said. "I'm going to try to trace Jared through the Gulf Coast net."

The New Hampshire screen came alive.

[Paul] I have contact. Will monitor. Jared is in the helo and he just turned us off. Nothing happening.

"Well, fine, then," Pilar said.

"Paul, can you send his stuff through to me?" Signy asked.

Paul sent his face and voice to the screens in Taos. He'd stripped out of the suit and tie and replaced them with thermals and an Aran sweater. "Yeah, sure, if anything gets interesting. Signy, you're too anxious about all this. It's just a job, you know."

"The hell," Signy said. Paul would watch Jared, she knew that. But Signy had felt something close to terror in Jared's lurching slip on the deck. He sent tensions and body uncertainties that were new to her, a cellular fear, as if some big predator breathed down his neck. "There's something wrong in that fleet, Paul. I want to pull us out. Get Jared out of there."

"Bullshit," Pilar said. "The major thing *wrong* is that if we don't get this one together, we go tits up. My fault, of course. Don't get on my case, Signy, and then blame it on Jared's case of the willies." Above the loose neckline of her caftan, the sharp angle of Pilar's collarbone stood out, high relief on shadow. Pilar lifted her hand toward her throat. It was shaking.

"No!" Signy said. "Pilar, baby, don't think like that. We're fine. We're going to be fine." Signy reached for Pilar's image, in a foolish and empty gesture of a hug.

Pilar's face vanished, replaced by a virtual crab that held a stylized Pilar in its lap.

[Paul] What Signy said. Love, warmth, pat, pat.

Pilar grinned at them. "Jared does it better," she said. "But okay, I got it. We'll be fine."

[Paul] Busy, my sweets. Later.

He popped away, off-line from them, for whatever reason.

Jared does it better. That is so true, Signy thought. If Jared were here, he would tease Janine, and Pilar would join in, and Janine wouldn't be so uncomfortable going off by herself. If Jared were *here*, he wouldn't be flying off to a stupid disaster at sea. . . .

Stop it, just stop it, Signy told herself. Rescues and drama, fast action like this, is what Jared likes. Flying a rescue mission across a frozen ocean probably is safer than working those "free" clinics where Jared goes and comes back so grim. Where over and over, the primary diagnosis is followed by "Secondary to CM&MTE," chronic malnutrition and multiple toxin exposure.

Jared had listed the possibilities for her once, scrolled them by in block letters over static medical photos of the dying, until Signy held her hands over her eyes and asked him to stop.

"People have to eat," Jared had said. "They damned sure have to drink water, no matter what's in it. And they have to live somewhere. That's how it is, Lioness."

Signy pushed away from the consoles and stood up and stretched, just like Jared was forever telling her to do. Find a distraction, don't get weird.

Shower? But Jared might call in. The hot tub was out of the question. Taos time, it was midnight. Signy pulled her headset back on and went looking for Janine, who would, if asked, give Pilar the hug, in fleshtime, that she so obviously needed.

The Seattle cameras found Janine standing at the front door. The porch light traced stained-glass diamonds on the entry floor, and the door chimes left dissonant harmonics in the air.

"Whozit?" Janine asked.

Signy switched to the porch scanner.

Jimmy McKenna, seen in profile, wore a camo parka

over a skinthin that might once have been military green. Intent and pale, his head looked too large for him and he hunched into his parka as if he were half-frozen. He carried a scuffed black duffel that bulged with irregular shapes.

He looked like he'd come to camp for a week. Lots of luck, Signy thought.

Jimmy found the camera's eye tucked beneath a porch beam, and looked up at it to answer Janine.

"Jimmy McKenna." He held up the duffel as if he expected it to be scanned.

Signy was, in fact, in the process of doing just that. There wasn't much metal in it. Maybe he had a bomb in there, but nothing looked like a gun or a knife.

"Pilar said I could stop by."

"Come in, then," Janine said.

"The bag's okay, I think," Signy said.

"Yeah. I looked." Janine swung the door open, and Jimmy got two steps inside and stopped. Pilar stood at the end of the hall, her paint-smeared white caftan swaying as she turned. The hall camera showed her back, her weight of black hair braided loose and heavy, and Jimmy's face, apparently mesmerized at the sight of her. Janine waited for McKenna to clear the door so she could shut it. Finally, she pushed at his shoulder and he moved one step forward.

"I brought you some music," Jimmy said.

"Did you, now?" Pilar smiled at him.

Janine tugged at the door and Jimmy moved out of the way when it bumped him. Pilar turned toward the virtual room and Jimmy followed her down the hall. Signy's view of the room showed it bare of any constructs, its projectors and consoles unadorned. Pilar's easel stood near the window.

Jimmy walked to the painting and whistled. He held his duffel in his left hand and his shoulders tilted toward its weight.

"Don't touch," Pilar said. "It's still wet, that's A, and it isn't finished, that's B."

The windowsill held the fat pottery jar of pink tulips. Jimmy looked at them and turned back to the painting.

"It's beautiful," Jimmy said. Still staring at the painting, he let his duffel slide to the floor. Pilar stood behind him, her head tilted as she watched the tech's absorption in her abstraction of pinks and earth colors.

"Were you working?" Jimmy asked. "I don't want to keep you from working." He reached out and brushed a fingertip across the silky skin of one of the tulips.

"You brought your gear?" Pilar asked. Jimmy nodded. "Are you going to show us how you crashed our system?"

[Signy] He'd better. Watch him, Paul.

[Paul] Watching.

"No," Jimmy said. "Oh, no. It wasn't like that. I told you I just got that music off the net. Oh, shit. Did you really get messed over?"

"We're up again," Pilar said.

Jimmy sat on the floor by his duffel and looked up at her with a relieved expression on his white, white face. "That's good," he said. "I brought some stuff to try to help out, if you weren't."

"Wizard, are you?" Pilar asked.

"I am. I really am."

"Let's test that. Get your act together and help me with something, then. I'm trying to get a texture thing going, and it isn't working."

Jimmy dropped to his knees and grabbed for the duffel's zipper with such haste that he jammed it. Pilar knelt to help him.

Janine brought in mugs of tea and found the two of them head-to-head on the floor, fighting with the zipper. She set the mugs down next to the battered tapestry cushions and left the room without saying a word.

So Janine's hurt. And I'm a voyeur, Signy told herself. She zoomed in on Pilar's dark slender fingers butting

Jimmy's pale hands away from the jammed zipper. Pilar giggled.

Tell them you're watching. Signy spoke to the room's speakers, full volume. "Pilar, you can't be serious."

Jimmy looked up. "Who are you?" he asked. He turned his head from side to side, searching for the speaker's location.

"I'm Signy."

"Oh. Hi."

"Indeed, I am completely serious," Pilar said. "I want to see what this guy can do, and Paul wants to see what he did, if he did it. There's no contract work accessible right now," Pilar said. "Sure, I'll let him in."

Override? Trust this stranger? Is there anything he could want, could learn from playing with Pilar's art that could harm us? Not bloody likely, Signy decided. But Paul would know.

[Signy] Paul, are you going to let him do this?

[Paul] Let him go for it. I'll transfer every move of his to storage, and he won't bring us down again. I'm interested, Signy.

[Signy] I don't like this. Get him the hell out of here.

[Paul] Don't be hysterical, darling.

Jimmy got us the Tanaka contract, Signy remembered. Because he said we were good. So okay, he wants to work with Pilar; he wants to see what we do. If Paul kept him barriered in real time, the kid wasn't likely to get any sabotage going. Not past Paul. And so far, Edges had stored reams of scientific articles on Antarctica that were public-access stuff anyway. And a post mortem on a dead sailor.

So let McKenna play, so that Paul could analyze just how he played. Let Jimmy carry away whatever he could find. It wasn't the raw data that made Edges work, it was assembly. Therefore—luck to him.

[Signy] Paul, has Jared checked in yet?

[Paul] No.

Signy watched Seattle, where Pilar claimed possession of the duffel. She pulled at the zipper, gently, and it opened on a clutter of equipment. Jimmy stripped off his parka and kicked it away. He pulled mask and gloves from the duffel, the usual finishes to the anonymous frogman costume of the virtual player. His skinthin was covered with spliced-in additions, patches of brown fabric adhered onto new circuitry, a welter of contacts on trigger points on his forearms, the locations of the muscles of his back—not pretty, but damned efficient-looking.

"Bring up what you've got," Jimmy said. "I'll noodle my way in; I'm compatible with almost any system."

And that, Signy decided, was for some odd reason one of the silliest come-ons she had ever heard. Signy reached for a focus control and got a whiff of sweat smell. Hers. Any minute now, she would get up and climb into the shower.

"I'm after the texture of oiled wool," Pilar said, "but I keep getting it too greasy."

"Umm," Jimmy said. He got his gloves operative, and Signy felt a swollen oval of contact where Jimmy's left thumb and index finger touched each other. Giant input, as if his hands spanned the room, jarring. Hesitance ruled his touch, his fingertips ached with cold, hot straps of tension bound the muscles in his shoulders. Pain burned razor hot in the area where his two fingers contacted each other, his pickups set too high for this sensitive system of theirs, and Signy felt a "gotcha" sense of unworthy satisfaction. Our rig's tighter than your rig, she did not say.

Jimmy toned down his sensory parameters. His fingers were not clumsy on the controls of his skinthin; he brought his touch and motion into something approaching human standards of comfort. He began to relax as Pilar brought up her construct, a simple tangle of blue-black yarn. "I don't think I've ever picked up oiled wool on purpose," he said.

Pilar drew out a strand from the tangle and held it between two fingers, prickly soft, midnight dark. She ran her fingers down its length. "Think lanolin," she said. "Think lambs, and resistance to rain, and wool holding heat when it's wet."

"This?" Jimmy asked. And changed the touch, just a little.

"That's it!" Pilar snapped her fingers. The sound made a sharp little crack.

Jimmy palmed a chip into Pilar's console and Signy drew in a breath, expecting the entire system to blow, expecting Paul's outrage at spending weeks resetting everything in the room, in the house. Nothing happened for a moment, and she found she had closed her eyes. Nothing reached her for a moment but the transmitted nudges of Jimmy's touch on controls. His fingers had warmed. Signy looked at Seattle through Pilar's eyes, and felt her friend's amusement at her awestruck visitor. Pilar liked him. Jimmy was harmless enough to look at, and his body language was that of—a deserted puppy. Hating him was going to be a hell of a lot of work.

"Try this," Jimmy said.

A swath of cashmere hovered like a magic carpet, yards and yards of it, murky dark, with the texture of the petals of pink tulips. It swirled and tossed in the air, and drifts of blossoms rose and tumbled slowly down to settle on the surface of the fabric.

Fast, fast work, to change whatever construct he had brought with him, to meld in the colors and textures of the objects in the room; tulips, clean glass panes, Pilar's imaged yarns. Oh, Jimmy, you are good.

Pilar clapped her hands and laughed.

[Janine] Signy, don't worry. I'll keep track of them.

"Thanks, babe," Signy said. Janine would watch them, of course she would.

Signy yawned. She was getting tired. Record the interchange with McKenna? Absolutely. If Pilar wanted to screen her away, Pilar could. Signy set the systems to monitor and store for replay and lifted her headset away from her face. The volume controls on any possible transmission from Jared were set loud enough that she would hear him. She had to rest.

The real room, the fleshtime room in Taos, looked strangely flat, its surfaces dull and contrived. The house half a continent away seemed much more substantial. Signy's skin remembered the touch of petal-soft wool. She stretched, and the muscles in her shoulders ached, dull and distant compared with her memories of the enhanced burning pain in Jimmy's fingers. Paul would wait for word from Jared. Janine would monitor Jimmy and Pilar, and if she sat here much longer she would grow to the chair. She felt stiff all over, and her eyes were beginning to see spots where spots weren't.

The reality of her discomfort woke her to a recurrent problem. Eat first or shower first? And she knew, on her way to stare into the refrigerator, that she was going to eat peanut butter on buttered toast, and ignore all the good stuff that waited to be cooked. Again.

Signy licked melted butter from her fingers while she wandered toward the shower. Hot water and soap worked their usual magic. She gave herself permission for the luxury of fatigue, and stretched out on the couch. She could see the doorway to the studio from here, but she wasn't *in* it. This was a *break*, after all. She burrowed into a down sleeping bag, a reject of Jared's. It had a red flannel lining printed with ducks, and he hated it.

A recitation played in her mind, the numbers as clear as if she read them: phytoplankton and microplankton, 6,400 million tonnes; 33 million seals weighing 7 million tonnes; 500 thousand whales weighing 9 million tonnes. Maybe more whales than that; the numbers were a decade old.

Jared was flying over that sea, right now. Or maybe he had reached the ship, and done whatever he needed to do there. Jared was getting acquainted with Alan Campbell. They would probably like each other. Jared was competent and skilled and a survivor. What was Signy worried about?

The sea was cold. And its riches fed—at least 75 million penguins and seabirds weighing at least 400 million tonnes. Anywhere from 100 million to 700 million tonnes of krill. Seven hundred million tonnes seemed a fair bet, since seabirds, whales, fish, squid, and "other predators" ate about 500 million tons of krill a year. More or less.

Other predators. Right. Big naked predators. This one had just sacrificed a batch of seeds, of reproductive marvels that could make new peanut plants, and now those little peanut embryos would never grow up and fix a single gram of nitrogen. Ever.

What's our share? Man never lived down on the ice; no humans ever figured into the balance of krill and whale, not until well into the nineteenth century. And then we trashed the Kerguelen fur seals, and the whales. Almost trashed them, anyway. They're back, the whales. The fur seals have filled their niche again and they are as mean as sharp nails. Good for them.

What's our share?

Would a penguin like peanut butter?

"Signy?"

She woke in the dark. Janine's voice, plaintive, called from the studio speaker. "Signy, you awake?"

"I am now." God, what time was it? The glowing numbers on her watch said 4:06. Maybe she was trying to fit Jared's schedule, waking up startled and hyper at this hour, but she felt alert. Signy hoped to find a status light that said she could talk to Jared. She would get up and go look any minute now, but it was so warm under the sleeping bag.

"Come help me pack," Janine said. "I've got to leave soon and I can't think."

"Okay, babe. Be right there."

Signy pulled the comforter over her shoulders and went into the studio. No Jared; the screen reserved for him was empty. Out of habit, Signy brought up the Seattle studio:

A Van Eyck fantasy, black-and-white tiled floor, high ceilings, walls of rough ecru plaster.

Signy liked it.

Precisely carved screens of pierced wood stood near a money-changer's desk where a quill pen wavered in a barely perceptible waft of air. Dull light outlined old coins and the scrolled arms of a tilted balance scale. Blue-black cashmere covered a low couch padded with thick downy cushions, and drifts of pink petals over-laid Pilar's golden skin, Jimmy's white back.

They sat knee to knee, motionless. A narrow mullioned window opened to an infinity of inky black and focused the sounds of a madrigal sung by inhuman voices. Its harmonies were modal, thick with parallel fifths and scored with innocent disregard of major/minor shifts.

"Wups," Signy said. But they couldn't have heard her. Signy's screens still listened to the *Siranui*'s bridge, silent for the moment. Jared's name had not been mentioned while she slept; no message lights blinked.

"I'm in my room," Janine said.

Signy switched to the camera there, to bright light and a view of Janine's compulsively spare bedroom. Every object in it looked ruthlessly clean; even the sueded nap on the bright yellow overstuffed chair seemed freshly brushed. Janine stared into her closet and sighed.

"Has anybody heard from Jared?" Signy asked.

"He hasn't called in."

"Pilar and Jimmy are having quite the visit," Signy said.

"Yeah. They screwing yet?"

A tricky business, sex in skinthins. Fleshtime sensations of fabric on fabric tended to intrude at the damndest times. Genital sensors tended to be off-putting, as well. Skinthins that permitted genital access were streetwear only for exhibitionists; that was one thing. Their ports were as obvious, to the most casual dabbler in virtuals, as the mating swellings of a chimpanzee.

There was quite a market in odd devices, anyway, perineal muscle monitors and stimulators, dildos with cameras. One pink view of vaginal mucosa in a sexual flush looked much like another, to Signy. But everybody, almost everybody, tried virtual copulation at least once. The trick was, who controlled what? The devices led to strange dominance games or exotic mutual masturbation, most of the time.

"No," Signy said. "They're just sitting around listening to music."

Janine pulled a maroon nylon carry-on out of the depths of her closet. She lifted jackets from their hangers and folded them into neat squares. An extra skinthin and makeup got tossed in, and the bag still sagged in nearly empty folds. Janine's portable equipment would fill it up when she got a chance at the virtual room. Janine zipped the bag closed and sat on the bed next to it.

"You'll make sure she keeps working?" Janine asked.

"I'll nudge her. I'll try."

"There was that time Pilar went off to L.A. and stayed with the body shaper. . . ."

"She came back," Signy said. "It didn't take her long to figure that the guy carving up all that meat had his own problems with image."

"She gets so distracted, sometimes."

And Janine loved her. With all of Janine's searching for the perfect man she kept telling Signy she would find, someday, her absolute conviction that somewhere there existed a master of more than one kind of heavy machinery, and he was, of course, looking for a Janine to make him happy—Janine loved Pilar. And Pilar knew it and Janine didn't know it and that's just how things were, sometimes. And me, I confuse possession with love and Jared knows it and laughs, because that's how *he* is.

"Pilar's oblivious, Janine. Just go in and pick up your portables. They'll never notice. Are you taking your toothbrush?"

Janine, sitting cross-legged, leaned forward, unzipped the carry-on, and looked inside. "Damn," she said.

"You can get one in Lisbon, I'm sure."

But Janine was already out the door and marching down the hall, chanting, "shampoo, razor, moisturizer, hairbrush," like a distracted robot.

TWELVE

The white-noise irritant of the rotors seeped through his padded headphones, a pervasive hypnotic hum. Jared's companions lapsed into silence. Anna slept. Campbell watched the bulkheads as if they were scribed with some arcane message.

Jared startled awake at a change in the rotor's pitch and knew he'd been drowsing in Stage One sleep. If someone had asked him, Jared would have said he wasn't sleeping at all.

A slight g-shift signaled descent. Anna woke on the instant, woke as a cat wakes, alert in one blink. The cabin tilted down and left. Jared saw a slice of horizon and a black outline of a ship, the *Kasumi*, a trawler. Out-sized winches at her stern loomed above a slick curved ramp that led into a sheltered enclosure. The pilot lined up the helo to match the deck's angle, diving for the deck at a speed that would have made Janine wince. Beyond the blocky silhouette of Trent's shoulders, winches, rotating dish antennae, and ice-coated ladders rose and fell as if they were attached to a roller coaster.

"They don't seem to be in a flap," Trent said. "One sub is in her berth."

"Where?" Jared asked.

"You can't see her. She's behind those aft doors."

The ship lurched over a swell. On deck, a crewman signaled with flourescent orange paddles, and Uchida brought the helo down, mating its computer to the landing indicators on the deck, so that they matched the ship's tilt and came down with a barest hiss of skids on the exact, precise center of the landing pad's X.

"The computer scores again," Trent said.

"Only when you know how to use it," Uchida said.

Trent grinned as he climbed out. He pulled his lips closed over his teeth when he hit the outside air. Icy wind swirled into the open door and they hustled out of the helo, single-filing toward the crewman's beckoning motions; this way, this way, toward a sealed hatch. Jared's bare fingers went numb in an instant, and he shoved his hands into his pockets, deep against wadded gloves that were a reminder of carelessness. Anna, last in line, carried the crash cart. Both of her gloved hands were locked on its handle to support the weight. I should have carried it, Jared thought. But she was last out; taking it would have slowed us down. She can handle it.

The crewman closed the hatch behind Anna. Gusts of frigid air swirled inside the passageway and competed with eddies of warmth that struck Jared's face and neck like blows. The passageway was narrow, with beige tile floors and scuffed tan paint on the bulkheads. Rows of fluorescent lights made the place look as bleak as a school hallway.

A ship's officer waited well beyond the range of the cold air that came in with their arrival. Short, Japanese, in padded black coveralls with gold stripes on the cuffs, he seemed as still as a mannequin. Uchida bowed to him and he came to life and bowed in return. He and Uchida spat rapid bursts of Japanese at each other. A complex of smells floated in the warm moist air; brine, a trace of a floral disinfectant, wet wool. Jared's nose began to run and he sniffed.

Anna put the crash kit down on the dull scoured tile. Her olive skin looked green in the fluorescent lighting; her face was expressionless. Jared backed away from the interchange of incomphrensible greetings. Anna shrugged her shoulders and rolled her head back on her neck, stretching out her muscles. Jared, on a guess, switched his skinthin controls to the same frequency the *Siranui* used. Maybe somebody could pick up the signals.

"What's going on?" Jared asked Anna.

"The sub is not here." Anna kept her eyes on the interchange and interspersed her comments sotto voce into the flow of Japanese. "The sub is fine. The *Gojiro*'s crew is wondering why the hell their support ship took off ten kilometers in the wrong direction. They will surface and wait for the *Kasumi* to return to them. They want their supper and it will be late."

A not-so-missing sub, a rescue call that didn't need to happen. This sort of glitch did not compute. What did compute was that Jared felt singled out, cut from the pack, isolated. Or maybe Campbell was the object of all this. Or Campbell had arranged this little side trip, so he could play with new toys. Or, more likely, Jared told himself, he was imagining trouble where there wasn't any.

The officer stood on tiptoe to see past Trent's and Campbell's shoulders, the motion of a man trying to watch a parade. "Dr. Balchen?" he asked.

"Yes?"

Campbell and Trent moved aside for him, shifting positions in the narrow passageway. Trent's beard had frosted on the journey across the deck, and he swiped beads of moisture away from his mustache with a practiced, seemingly automatic motion.

"I am Captain Ito. We have no emergency, it seems. We are very sorry."

Now what, Jared wondered, do I say to that? That I am disappointed that there are no nice messy wounds for me to treat?

Signy? Paul? Anybody home? The listener telltale on his wrist was blank. "I'm glad no one is hurt," Jared said.

"An unusual problem with the ship's electronics." Ito kept his eyes at the level of Jared's collar. Black, black eyes that seemed to have no pupils, and that, Jared thought, is what we once called "inscrutable." Captain Ito had a sprinkling of gray hairs above his ears. "We received the wrong coordinates for the sub's location, and a clear distress signal. The sonar also."

The sonar also what? And someone "inscrutable" wouldn't tell a stranger this right off the bat. But I'm crew, Jared remembered. That's why I'm here.

"We are investigating our systems. This will be settled very soon."

"Glitches happen," Jared said. Glitches happen and the last one had scared the hell out of Signy. That business with the hand had spooked her, and that, Paul had said, was something in the *Siranui*'s system. He wished that Signy were on-line right now. She wasn't. Jared wanted company. He looked behind him, searching for Anna. She emerged from a door marked HEAD and took up her post by the crash kit.

"You may return to the *Siranui*, of course," Captain Ito said. "But if you stayed with us, we could arrange routine exams for our crew in the morning. This would save a trip to the *Siranui* for them. If this is convenient for you."

Ask the real boss, Jared figured. The real boss of any sick bay is always the corpsman. Medics come and go, corpsmen run the show. "Anna?" Jared asked.

"If we clear with *Siranui*, I don't see a problem. Samuelson's the corpsman here, when he isn't fishing. He can walk you through sick bay; he's good help. I'll go back, of course."

"Fine, then," Jared said.

Ito bowed, a quick duck of his head. Jared copied the motion, aware that the rituals and courtesies of how far to bend were mysteries to him, and sources of amused tolerance or irritation to bystanders. Did he outrank this man or was he subordinate? Where did medics belong in this little ship's hierarchy?

"This way, then," Ito said. "We will call." He led them forward and up a ladder to the bridge, a glassed-in bubble crowded with monitors and displays. Matte black cabinetry circled the space. It looked like an air-traffic control room, not a ship's bridge. A ship's wheel was conspicuously absent. Joystick controls, maybe. An Asian woman, thick-waisted in her tight black coverall, sat in a swivel chair. She smiled as the group entered.

The sea outside was the color of watered grape juice. The woman's white teeth looked purple in the deep twilight. A full moon, too big, and squashed from top to bottom like an imperfect melon, hung low on the horizon. It looked dusty and dry. Close by, a small island with a black line of beach seemed to float in the sea, a tethered iceberg of an island. Pale boulders littered the shoreline. One of them shifted and became the snaky-necked silhouette of a huge elephant seal.

Ito spoke to the woman and she nodded and chattered into a mike.

Depth gauges, a pinging sonar, graphics of the seafloor— Jared recognized some displays. An arc traced through afterimages on one screen, scribed out amoeboid shapes that Jared figured might be schools of fish. Behind his ear, welcome as rain, he heard the tiny beep of someone calling in.

"Where the fuck are you?" Paul asked.

"Hello, Paul," Jared whispered, "I'm glad you're awake," while he triple-tapped his wrist to signal that he couldn't talk here.

"The *Siranui* approves your stay," Ito said. He looked at the pilot and Uchida straightened into a parade-rest stance, his hands behind his back.

Uchida smiled, bowed, and turned for the ladder, Trent and Anna close behind him.

"Mr. Campbell," Captain Ito said, "we hear that you have interest in our subs. We are glad that you will not increase your knowledge of escape techniques today."

"So am I," Campbell said.

"I have no one free to act as your guide on this watch, many apologies. Until then, gentlemen, please observe what you like. If you will not be offended at the lack of an escort, of course."

"Not at all," Jared said. "Thank you." And realized, as he spoke, that he was answering for Campbell as well. Campbell did not seem offended.

"When you are ready to see your quarters, please return to the bridge. Someone will escort you at that time." Ito's attention was on one of the monitor screens. The Asian woman tapped at a keyboard as she watched the screen's display.

Jared smiled, said thanks, and ducked at speed down the ladder. He caught sight of Trent and Uchida on their way down the passageway, and Anna's departing back, her solid strides closing the distance to the men. Uchida and Trent seemed in haste to return. Jared caught Anna's arm and reached for the crash kit's handle, its weight heavy against his palm. "Is this really okay with you?" he asked.

"Sure." She smiled. Something in her smile, the lift of her head, was so like Susan. Susanna, who had hiked alone into Yellowknife in the rain, who had left her boyfriend on the trail after an argument about cooking. She never wanted to see him again. Susanna's laugh had disarmed him, and her blunt honesty. She had been too young, but persistent. They had shared a quick affair of instant chemistry. Well, Mark would take good care of her.

Anna's eyes stayed on the flecked tile of the passageway. "I'll take sick call in the morning," she said. "And if you're needed, someone will come and get you."

Trent and Uchida fiddled with parkas and gloves. Trent stopped near the hatch and looked back at Anna. She pulled up her parka hood and reached for the case.

"I'll bring it out," Jared said. And tomorrow when I get back, I'll go through what's in here and toss out half of it. This sucker is overloaded.

"No need," Anna said. Trent spun the wheel to open the hatch, and Uchida ducked into the wall of impossibly cold air. Anna followed him, murmuring something toward Trent that made him laugh, a laugh that cut short as the hatch closed behind them. I could learn to miss Anna, Jared thought. When I get back, I'll see if I'm reading her signals right. Signy won't mind if we have a little friendly sex. Signy won't mind at all.

Enclosed in metal, Jared stared at the hatch and suddenly missed windows, windows that opened. Someone had scratched "E. I." in the gray enamel of the metal door. He found himself halfway down the corridor, seeking the warmth of the ship's belly in unconscious tropism. Campbell came down the ladder from the bridge. He nodded toward Jared, but he looked at each landmark in the passageway: hatches, red-enameled fire extinguishers in their glass-fronted cases, the locations of handholds. As if he memorized the ship's interior, its possible dangers and routes of escape. The two of them were alone in the passageway. Jared heard Paul's voice, patched through the ship's system to his ear speaker.

"Signy's asleep," Paul said. **"Janine's en route to Kobe. Can you talk yet?"**

Jared tapped his wrist, and Campbell's eyes noticed the gesture, a lift of eyebrows, no questions.

Jared felt a sudden awareness of the sensations he sent to Paul, as if he received input from someone else wearing a skin-thin and sending impulses to him—apprehension in his muscle tone, slight hunger, fatigue that he'd managed to suppress signaled in the grittiness behind his eyelids, his rapid blinks. And as Campbell came near, Jared felt the hairs on the back of his neck prickle and rise. If Campbell had an agenda, he wanted to know it. He planned to stay near Alan Campbell, to see what he wanted here. Paul is watching, Jared thought, and Signy sleeps. North America sleeps January sleep, winter solid, and I am alone a world away, on a restless ocean with my lover's lover. In the company of strangers.

"Want to see a baby sub?" Campbell tilted his head toward a hatch.

"Sure," Jared said.

Jared followed Campbell down a steel ladder, echoes of waves and the thrum of the ladder under their weight implying a cavern of large size. This feels like San Francisco, Jared thought. These struts look like the supports of some huge bridge; we are inside it. Around that bulkhead, I can imagine that there would be ships in the harbor far, far below us; we may fall.

The image vanished as they walked out on metal gridwork beneath a high flat expanse of corrugated steel that dripped condensation. The space was a square cavern. Giant doors opened toward the ship's stern. The light was dim, subterranean. The ship's engines rumbled, deep engine noise transmitted through water, an oddly reassuring sound. Campbell found a switch, and harsh floods lighted the space with mercury glare. Suspended like an egg in a spider's web, a tiny sub hung above them, cheery yellow and the shape of a goldfish. It had a grin painted where its mouth would be.

"It's so little," Jared said. It looked like a toy.

"It's a three-man sub," Campbell said. "A titanium sphere with holes in it, ports for air and communications. The sphere won't ever crush, but the ports could."

Campbell walked around beneath the sub, his head tilted back and his hands locked behind him in a "don't touch" position. A kid in a candy store. He found a ladder that led to a platform that collared the sub's top hatch, and grinned.

"You're going up there?" Jared asked.

"I'm going in," Campbell said.

"He's going to get your ass in trouble," Paul hissed.

"They said take a tour," Jared whispered. Campbell was already easing his feet into the hatch, accordion-folding his long legs down into the depths of the sub, and Jared stepped down behind him. Campbell guided his feet as Jared lowered himself into the cramped space, aware, as he sank into a couch that was hard against his back, aware of deep blackness, crushing pressures, death by suffocation. The inside of the sphere was ranked with instruments, dimly lighted with indicator pips, the inside of a Christmas ornament. The sub's shell cut off all exterior sounds. Jared heard himself breathing.

"Close quarters," Campbell muttered. They were knee to knee in the cramped space.

"Close." Jared's voice threatened to quaver if he tried to say more.

"If you ever got a leak in here, the water would jet through like a laser. Take off heads, legs, with better efficiency than a sword. You wouldn't die of drowning, at least. Even if you didn't get hit, your blood would boil from the pressure. Just like that." Campbell snapped his fingers.

Jared imagined the little space cut through with razor-sharp death, imagined the rise of salty blood-soaked water. He could not hear Paul. Paul's access light on Jared's wrist had gone dark; Jared's sensations transmitted to no one through the sub's thick metal. Jared hit the "record and save" button, for what Paul would make of the spherical array of instruments and the knee-to-knee intimacy was a fascinating thing to contemplate. So tiny. If Jared stood (and he very much wanted to stand), his head would be outside the baby sub and he would look like a chick in a broken egg; his breath would murk around him like a cloud and the cold fresh air would be so welcome on his face, this once.

Jesus, I'm claustrophobic, Jared realized.

"I'm getting up," Jared said. "Watch your head." He found the hatch rim with his fingers and stood up. Into a black, empty nothing. Someone had turned out the lights.

Working by touch alone, he lifted his body out of the sub, dim light from the sub outlining his waist as he cleared the hatch. His hands gripped the metal catwalk, cold sharp mesh under his fingers. He hauled himself to its security and lay there, panting, watching the circular patch of light that marked the sub's open hatch. "Campbell?" Jared hadn't meant to yell, but he heard echoes coming back to him from the dark hollows of the hold.

"Yo?" Muffled, from the depths of the sub.

"The lights are out up here."

"Oh."

"I can get back to the switch by the door. I think," Jared said.

"Wait a minute. Let me look here. Let's see, I don't want to power up this little baby by mistake. Fan, depth gauge, a joystick for attitude and prop pitch . . ."

He's talking for Ground Control, Jared realized. Campbell is telling them, or me, in this case, what he's doing that they can't see. Jared felt the ship list, riding a swell. He had one hand on the sub's slick side and he clutched at the catwalk with the other, belly flat on the metal grid. The sub swayed gently in its harnesses.

"The frigging switches aren't where you'd think—gotcha," Campbell said.

Twin beams of light stabbed into the dark hold, swaying against the walls as the sub swayed. The ship's engines went silent, making the slap of water against the hull sound loud as gunshots. Jared pulled himself to his feet and grabbed a line that hung above the sub's collar. He didn't want Campbell to find him clinging to the catwalk like a terrified baby, and light and upright posture gave him back a semblance of self-control.

Campbell's head emerged from the hatch. "We've stopped?" he asked.

"Yeah," Jared said. "Campbell, if we're picking up a

sub and loading it, wouldn't you think that some crew would be down here? Getting the berth ready, or something?"

"I'd think so." Campbell swung a long leg out of the hatch and reached up to find a handhold.

"I'll get the bay lights," Jared said. His moonboots beneath him gave him no sensation of contact with the catwalk, and he wished he could take them off and feel the grip of metal on his feet. He reached the switch and the bay lights came on, reassuring and harsh.

"I'm going up on deck," Jared said. "Maybe there's some action."

"Fine," Campbell said. "I'll close down the sub. No reason to run out the batteries, I guess."

Jared climbed the stairs toward a glowing Exit sign. The wheel on the hatch was cold and he remembered, this time, to get his gloves on. He wanted a brief look around, and he knew Campbell would take a little while to finish up below. Campbell seemed interested in the tech, yeah, but that didn't mean he'd sent a false alarm from anywhere. The whole interlude began to look like nothing more ominous than the captain had reported. And the visuals—should be good enough to please even Pilar.

Outside, Jared found himself on open deck, on a narrow walkway between the ship's bulk and the metal rail. The sky was still purplish, a deep twilight color, and the sea looked black and oily. He saw no one, heard nothing. The ship rocked, listless, under no power. Jared turned left, heading for the stern.

Something hit the back of his right knee and he tipped toward the rail. He raised his arms to try to find balance. Mistake, he thought, for the silvery gleam of a huge gaff came up and under his left arm, lifting him up and over the rail. The water is a long way down, Jared thought, surprised. Distantly, far, far away, he heard a feminine, high-pitched wail, and realized it was Paul, but he'd never heard Paul sound exactly like that.

Jared hit the water with his right arm outstretched, the wall of wet striking the right side of his face, numb even before the water closed, briefly, over his head. Remembering—a naked man immersed in water at minus 1.9 degrees C will lose his breathing reflex in five seconds. Jared flailed his arms and found the surface and pulled in as deep a breath as his lungs would hold.

But he wasn't naked. He had at least a minute, maybe three. A bubble of air rose up from beneath the clothing on his back and puffed up the shoulders of his parka. He pushed with his arms, fighting the numb cold in them and the air cushion of the parka's padded sleeves, and braced himself to scream.

Insectoid, black, a goggled face rose inches from his own. Diver? Jared wondered. How? It's so cold here. The black gleam of goggles, a rubber caricature of a human head. A gloved hand reached for his collar and he remembered: don't fight. He tried to relax while he felt himself pulled forward, the pain of burning ice flooding in around his neck and down his chest.

The rubber head tilted in the water, as if questioning something. And jerked his collar, hard, pulling him down, again, into the black water, into the darkness.

THIRTEEN

Signy!" Paul's voice screamed, hoarse and choked, a tortured scream that pulled Signy out of sleep and into a dead run toward the studio.

"Signy! My God! Get in here; get here now!"

From a solid, stonewalled sleep that seemed to have lasted only minutes.

"I'm coming. I'm coming, damn it!" Signy turned the corner into the hallway. The floor was cold on her bare feet.

The image of Paul's face filled the holo stage, in a projection so large that Signy waded through black stubble on his chin, each whisker as thick as her forearm. She was naked, her skinthin tossed on the bed behind her before she slept, so she was spared the expected sensation of the slick moisture of Paul's lip sliding across her face and down her shoulder as she entered the image of his skin. She reached through the inner corner of Paul's eyelid and grabbed for the room's controls.

"So cold," Paul whimpered. "Goddamned son of a bitch! Bad. Very bad."

"Paul, make sense! What the fuck is going on?" Signy snapped the words at him over dread that rose from her gut and a sudden sure inner vision of how Jared's face would look, relaxed in death.

Injured, or dead, someone had to be, or Paul would not have woken her like this. Paul's enraged face looked intact and Signy couldn't see anything else of him. Jared, then. Oh, my God, Jared. Signy pulled on her goggles and Paul's image shrunk to something human-sized.

"Jared," Paul gasped. "He was right. We wouldn't listen. Damn it, Signy, they've drowned the son of a bitch!"

"When? How?"

"He went overboard. I can't pick up anything, anything."

"Show me." Signy sat down, her fingers chilled and the keyboard cold. The fabric on the chair felt like ice. Signy moved Paul's image to the flatscreen in front of her and left the holo stage blank. "No, don't. He's in the water?"

"Damn it, yes!"

"When did this happen?"

"Now. Just now."

The clock on Signy's console read 0520. She shuddered with the hypothermia of disrupted sleep.

"Did anybody see him go over?" Signy tucked her hands into her armpits for the warmth and then untucked her right hand and hit the room's thermostat.

"I don't think so. I don't know," Paul said.

"Does the ship *know?*" Signy asked. She had to get a blanket. Jared drowned? No. Signy's heartbeat thudded in her ears, slow, loud, and she felt the muscles in her shoulders and belly begin to shiver in unwilled spasms, her body protecting itself from cold and fear. Jared drowned? Dead? No. She had to think, to keep him alive. Think!

"The ship?" Paul asked.

"Wake up, man! Call the *Kasumi*. It's a ship; it has a phone." Paul's face was so baffled. "Oh, shit, I'll do it. If we're lucky, they'll be pulling him out of the water about now, and if we're really lucky, he's still alive." Signy pulled Tanaka's information files to her screen and wondered how the hell the *Kasumi* would be listed. Stupid, she chided herself, as she punched in Tanaka Company's main number, 81 plus a string of digits, an international call that would get the offices in Kobe, for God's sake. Would the secretary speak English?

"Oh, God, Paul. Talk to them. I can't."

Signy switched his audio inputs to feed through to the open line. The call went out voice-only but she stared at the blank monitor screen as if a face would form from its blinking cursor.

"Tanaka Company," a young male voice said.

"There's a man overboard the *Kasumi*," Paul yelled. "Tell them!"

"Excuse me?" the voice asked.

"A man overboard. Tell the *Kasumi*."

"Emergency?"

Not so good with English, this kid. Codes, international codes, what was it you said? "Mayday!" Signy yelled. "We need contact with the *Kasumi*, a ship, a *Maru*. It belongs to Tanaka and it's in Antarctica. Mayday! Now!"

"Very good, sir," the voice said.

"Now!" Paul shouted.

A series of clicks and pauses went on forever.

"*Siranui*," a bored voice said.

"This is Paul Maury, of Edges. Jared Balchen just fell off the *Kasumi*. Stop the engines, do whatever you do. Do it fast. He's going to drown."

"Man overboard?" the voice asked.

"Yes, damn it!"

"You are calling on satellite-to-ship line. Is this a joke?"

"God damn it, no!"

"I will check with *Kasumi*," the voice said.

The studio filled with the white silence of a line on hold.

"I've g-got to get a blanket," Signy said.

Signy ran for the bedroom. Paul's face, seen in the unenhanced holo that he had just sent, was pale, haggard. When had he gotten so thin? Signy grabbed up Jared's down sleeping bag and her skinthin and heard *Siranui*'s bridge as she reached the hallway again, voices in Japanese that sounded like static.

"What do they say?" Signy slammed into her chair, draped the sleeping bag over her shoulders and rolled the skinthin up over her foot.

"Hush," Paul said.

"Caller?" a voice asked.

"I'm here," Paul said.

"*Kasumi* will call lifeboat drill. They will check."

"I *saw* him! Paul screamed.

Signy fought the tangle of fabric and jammed her leg into the skinthin. I should have rolled the son of a bitch up right, she thought. I'll never get this thing on. She twisted the heel around so it approximately fit on the back of her leg and then pulled the suit off and began to roll the legs down to try again.

"Lifeboat drill," the voice replied.

"Bastard!" Paul shouted.

"Excuse me?" the voice replied.

"Not nice," another voice said, and the line went on hold again.

Signy had the skinthin pulled up to her knees. She stood up, shrugged the suit up across her middle, and stuck her hands through the arms. A fold of Lycra caught at her elbow and she pulled at it, hard, and sat down fast, already reaching for her keyboard again, for the Tanaka directory. There had to be another line into the ship, had to be.

In the net, her skinthin feeding her the familiar sensations of dry, emotionless, unscented corporate lists, Signy scrolled her way past lists of departments, acronyms with unknown meanings, ranks of names listed with extension numbers first. Numbers. She found the 81 numbers and scanned through them, looking for anything familiar, anything at all.

"Have you heard Jared mention anyone's name on the *Kasumi?*" Signy asked.

"I can't remember," Paul said. "There's a captain. Jared met him. He recorded some hours and I watched—"

"There isn't *time* to go back and find his name. Damn."

"Caller?" the phone asked.

"Paul Maury here."

Signy looked away from the lists and to the flatscreen where Paul's face glared at his unseen caller.

"You have Captain Ito on the *Kasumi*," the phone said.

"Mr. Maury?" a different voice asked.

"Yes."

"We are calling a lifeboat drill. The stations are beginning to report in. You will listen, yes?"

"Yes. Oh, yes."

"Dr. Balchen did not have an assigned lifeboat station. This may take a few minutes."

Voices babbled in the background.

"I *saw* him fall," Paul said. "I *saw* him."

"Pardon me. Just a moment, please," Ito said.

"Sir, begging your pardon." In the background, Alan Campbell's Western drawl was unmistakable. "Do you have any idea where Dr. Balchen might be?"

Signy clenched her fists and shoved them, hard, against her mouth. It was true, then. It had happened. She rocked back and forth on her chair, tried to stop doing it, and couldn't. Red numbers on the clock face blinked from 0526 to 0527.

She pulled her fists away from her face and tried to relax them. Hands, fingers, the dextrous markers of human skills, and she couldn't remember how to make them work. Signy stared at her right index finger until it uncurled. Then she reached for the keyboard and punched in the familiar codes to wake the Seattle house.

"No one is reported missing in the crew," Captain Ito's voice said. "But Dr. Balchen has not appeared at any station."

"You will look for him?" Paul asked.

"We have looked in the water. We will search the ship

and retrace our last hour's course. Yes." Perhaps there was sympathy in the man's voice, perhaps only fatigue.

"Thank you," Paul said.

"You will get information from the *Siranui*," Ito said. "We will report everything to them. I am transferring your call there now."

"Wait!" Paul yelled.

Ito was gone.

A view of the Seattle studio blinked into place on Signy's screen.

"Signy, what the hell is going on?" Janine leaned against the door of the Seattle studio, her face lighted from the hall, the room behind her dark except for the tiny points of ready lights. In her good travel jacket with her duffel over her shoulder, she stood swaying back and forth like a sleepwalker. "Jared's lost," Signy said. "Wake Pilar."

"*Siranui*," the phone said.

"I'll get her." Janine paused at the doorway. "Jimmy's with her."

"Don't bring him," Signy said.

In the background, Paul argued with an officer on the *Siranui*. "Hang the expense," Paul said. "We're paying. Just leave the line open, okay?"

Janine nodded and left the room. Signy turned up the lights in Seattle, on the bare studio where the night was still black beyond the undraped window.

Paul and the *Siranui* continued to debate the wisdom and the costs of an extended ship-to-shore call. "At least give me a direct number," Paul said. "Please." He paused, listening. "Yes, I tell you, I watched him go overboard."

Paul's voice had lost its quaver and had gone to tones of formal outrage. He'd be quoting statutes at them any minute now, and Signy relaxed a little. Paul's consciousness was back on-line.

Splitscreen, Paul on one side, in Seattle:

—Pilar frowned as the room's light hit her eyes. She had tossed on her stained caftan and she pulled the black length of her hair free of its collar. Behind her, fiddling with the sensors on his skinthin, Jimmy McKenna padded into the room.

Abomination, this intruder in this place. "Company biz, Pilar." Signy's words hissed; the muscles in her mouth felt stiff. "God damn it, Janine, I told you not to bring him."

"I didn't *bring* him." Janine spun around toward Jimmy and looked ready to tackle him. Pilar stepped between the two of them on her way toward her keyboard in a move that was perhaps unplanned, but Pilar never made an unplanned move.

"Signy, you've been listening to the *Siranui* since Jared got there," Paul said. "Are we still hooked in?"

Paul's voice was a distraction Signy didn't, at the moment, want. "We only get what the *Siranui* transmits," Signy told him. "I don't have a bug on the bridge, just a capture on outgoing transmissions."

"Then we need the line," Paul said.

Signy looked at the Seattle crew: Jimmy, who had no business here, Pilar blinking at the bright lights, her eyes soft with sleep or, Signy figured, recent sex.

"Pilar, get him the fuck *out* of here."

Jimmy raised his head and looked at Signy's image on the flatscreen. "You need me," Jimmy said simply. He bent his head again and calmly continued adjusting his skinthin against his chest.

Janine backed away from McKenna. Janine tucked her head down like a bull about to charge.

"Jared's drowned?" Pilar asked.

Pilar's eyes had a way of going from brown to amber when she was very, very up on drugs or when she was stoned on her work. Her eyes glowed amber now, a hawk's eyes focused on prey.

"I don't know. Paul saw him go overboard. The ship is looking for him. Why do we need you, Jimmy? Tell me fast or get the hell out of here."

"I can get into Tanaka's private lines to the *Siranui*," Jimmy said.

"Can you?" Signy asked.

"Yeah," Jimmy said.

"Oh, hell. Just *do* it, then." Signy heard no objections from anyone. Jimmy's loyalties, wherever they might lie, were unimportant for the moment.

There was no talk from the *Siranui*. Jared's body would be rigid from the slushy salt cold by now, his flesh gone as waxy as Skylochori's dead hand. Food for busy crabs, sinking in the water, Jared's dark hair swirling in the currents as he sank.

Jimmy sat down at Pilar's station and hooked his leads into the system. Signy picked up a sudden wave of Jimmy's body signals, a slow man, warm and comfortable in his flesh, sleepy, but waking now toward a bemused pleasure in anticipation of an absorbing task. This was only work to him, just an off-hours call to midly interesting job. Didn't he care? Jared, my love, doesn't anyone care?

Jimmy pulled up a room that filled the space in Seattle and the holo stage in Taos, a solid image that washed over Pilar and Janine, leaving them blurred ghosts, unsuited as they were. Signy sat in that space, her flatscreens small squares in its reality. Brass fittings outlined the circle of a porthole high on a cabin wall. The cabin was shadowed. It looked warm; its polished teak fittings reflected the glowing lights of a bank of monitors and a desktop holo stage. A cabinet bunk was made up with puffy celadon comforters that had the soft sheen of raw silk.

"Where the hell are we?" Signy asked.

"On the *Siranui*," Jimmy said. "That's all I know. Hang on a minute."

The room lurched out of focus and twisted on its axis. Indefinite swirls of black and amber became a view through a fish-eye lens that looked down at cluttered desktops, a bird's-eye view of heads of black hair and the backs of hands busy at keyboards.

"Here's the *Siranui*'s control room," Jimmy said. "The camera's hung in an overhead light. Anybody speak Japanese?"

"Fuck, no," Pilar said, her disembodied voice harsh. "Record what they're saying. Save it all. I'll get somebody I know; there's this guy in L.A. Let me at your console, Janine."

"You'll need a suit," Signy said.

"I'm getting them!" Janine called, followed by the sounds of footsteps on an unseen floor. A door slammed.

On Signy's flatscreen, one of the officers on the *Siranui*'s bridge talked quietly into a telephone headset. Talked to Paul, and told him that he would try to get in touch with Mr. Campbell, as soon as there was a line available. Two other officers seemed intent on their monitor screens. Another chattered intermittently into a mike, in tones that sounded excited and not at all approving. He sat rigid in his chair and he had pulled away from the screen.

The officer looked like he was alarmed, but Signy couldn't read his Asian body language well enough to be sure of it.

"He's talking about the *Gojiro*," Paul said. "That's one of the subs from the *Kasumi*. Damn, I'd like to talk to Campbell."

"We need contact with someone down there. There's that woman," Signy said. "Anna. The med tech."

"Hush!" Paul said. "The *Siranui*—"

Signy windowed up a view of Paul, hunched over his phone.

"Yes," Paul said. He waited. "You will have Mr. Campbell call us as soon as possible. I understand."

Paul turned away from his console to watch his own stage in New Hampshire. Washes of color, reflected from Paul's view of the *Siranui*'s bridge, bronzed his cheekbones and deepened the hollows under his eyes. "The *Kasumi* got another call from its sub. They are leaving the area and going after it. There has been no sighting of anything in the water. Anything at all."

Signy remembered swimming in the Sea of Cortez, in placid water that was just barely cool. Even in a sheltered cove, the rocking of the quiet waters had made the yacht dip up and down, away from her sight at times. The world had become a totality of walls of water and sky, immensely lonely. And she'd been safe in that water, safe and comfortable, with the deck and help just yards away. Not lost in frozen twilight.

The *Kasumi* had given up. There had been nothing to see; she knew it.

Over. Gone. What should she be feeling? What response should she have?

She had to pee. Her overwhelming concern, in this moment that she would remember for years, for the rest of her life, was that she had to pee.

"Somebody try to call up Anna de Brum," Signy said. "Send a repeat to her on the sick-bay monitor. Here." Signy opened the codes for that address. "I'll be right back."

Signy stumbled out of the room and down the hallway. The dawn light was cloudy gray and bitter cold. Her mind raced and halted in infuriating ways. Janine should be leaving for the airport in less than an hour; Janine couldn't stay in Seattle and she wouldn't want to leave. Janine had to get to Lisbon, whether she wanted to go or not.

Signy sat on the commode, the comfort of an emptied bladder bringing with it a wave of fatigue. She yawned, hiccuped, and yawned again. How much sleep had she had since yesterday? Maybe three hours, maybe less. She pulled the skinthin back on and splashed water on her face.

Could anything they had seen be trusted? None of

them knew, firsthand, what conditions were on that water. It might have been bright in the sea; no true night ever darkened it at this time of the year. How could Jared drown in the light?

Jared was so strong. There may have been some way for him to survive.

I've killed him, Signy thought. I've killed him for money.

But Paul had watched, and Paul thought Jared might be alive. They had to look at what Paul's eyes had seen— Signy wasn't sure she was ready for that, but they had to do it, soon. Her dark warm Jared. Signy wanted to touch his skin, now, smell his sweat. She would always want that.

Jimmy had shrunk the bridge camera's view back to fit a console screen when Signy returned to the room. The Taos stage was filled with views of the Seattle studio in real time, and Signy picked up Pilar's sensations, her thin flesh tense with concentration.

"He ain't asleep. Don't give me that shit," Pilar said. "Get his ass on-line." Then her voice went silky. "Toshiki? Whiteline? Sweet ronin man, I have a little job for you."

Janine, suited and with her coat thrown over her shoulders, paced behind Pilar and Jimmy. Janine had no task and no console access at the moment.

"Sure," Pilar told Whiteline, whoever the hell he was. "I'll send the man over in ten minutes. You can't work sleepy, I know that."

Pilar reached behind her and gripped Janine's waiting hand. "I got the son of a bitch," Pilar said. "But the blow is going to cost us a little. Whiteline doesn't work without it."

"He's a good translator?" Janine asked.

"The best. He's a poet in Japanese *and* English," Pilar said.

"Then fill his nose," Janine said. "Wire him any way

he wants." Janine drew her hand away and held Pilar's shoulders, as if to massage them.

"Jimmy, send that bridge download to Pilar's screen," Signy said. "Janine, shouldn't you be gone?"

"I have an hour. But I can't go to *Portugal*, Signy. Not now."

"You must. We need you there."

Paul's virtual hand squeezed Signy's shoulder and jerked her back to her console. "You have a call," Paul said.

"Huh?" Signy looked down at her empty flatscreen.

"Hello?" The voice was Alan Campbell's. "Signy?"

"I'm here."

"You worked with Jared, he told me." Alan was on a voice-only line.

"Alan, what happened?"

"We were looking at one of the subs. Jared left and said he was going on deck. The sirens raised hell and called a lifeboat drill, was the next thing I knew. And everybody yelling for Dr. Balchen. I thought somebody got hurt."

"I understand. What's happening now?"

"The *Kasumi* just picked up its other sub. Everybody's pretty busy with that."

"So you didn't see anything."

"No. I'm sorry."

"Could he be somewhere on the ship? Hidden somewhere?"

"There's lots of hidey-holes on any boat," Alan said. "I'll look, but didn't I hear that you guys watched him go overboard? Took the crew a minute to sort that one out, let me tell you. We're down here beaucoup miles from anywhere and some gaijin yahoo in New Hampshire tells the captain somebody just fell off his ship. But I'll look, Signy. I'll look for him, just in case."

"When are you going back to the *Siranui*?" Signy asked.

"Not for a few days, is the plan."

"Do you know the med tech that was working with Jared?"

"Anna? I've met her."

"Listen, we're going to try to keep in contact with her. If you see anything, if there's any news at all—"

"I'll talk to her on ship-to-ship. At least twice a day, Signy. Whether I have any news or not."

"Thank you," Signy said.

Silence.

Signy raised her eyes to a view of Seattle, where Pilar tapped her fingers against her console and nodded at something Whiteline was doing. Janine sat on the floor, pulled her knees up and tucked her head down, hiding her face.

"Can we see the sequence where Jared fell?" Jimmy asked. "There might be something helpful in it."

Janine uncurled and got on her feet again.

Just standing there, quiet, she was every inch the bar-room brawler who had once emptied an Alaskan bar of a population of half-drunk roughnecks in ten seconds flat. Janine had been holding a beer bottle packed with crushed ice, then. She held nothing at all now; thank goodness. "Wouldn't you think you're being just a touch voyeuristic?" Janine's voice dripped sarcasm. "Just a tad *involved* in something that's going to cause us pain? Is that how you get off, McKenna?"

But there was nothing else, at the moment, to be done. No other channels to open, not that anyone had managed to think of yet. "Leave him alone, Janine," Signy said. "Jimmy's right. Maybe we'll see something that might help."

Janine relaxed with a visible effort of will and pulled a chair up to sit next to Pilar.

Paul's voice murmured in the background, leaving a message for Anna, his words slow and deliberate, his voice thick with tension. Signy waited for him to finish.

"Paul?" Signy asked.

"Yes."

"Let's see it."

"Yes."

The watchers vanished into shadowy darkness. The world filled with Jared's view of his own hand, flicking lights on to show a metal catwalk beneath his feet.

"Where are we?" Pilar asked.

"We're in the hold of the *Kasumi*," Paul said.

Jared talked to Campbell. Jared's body language, sensed as a familiar blanket of grace and strength, enveloped Signy, enveloped them all.

A sound intruded in real time, Janine, who sobbed once and choked back the sound.

"Nothing's wrong, I kept saying. We need this job. I did this," Signy said.

"Shut up, Signy," Paul said.

Paul let the virtual run at normal speed. Jared climbed out of the hold and on to the deck, and Signy caught her breath at the sudden blow to the back of her knee, bit her lip as the side of the ship rose and she/Jared/Paul fell. Signy felt the enforced relaxation of Jared's muscles as a hand tugged at the inflated parka, and a slow sense of amazement and pain as Jared sank—

"That was murder," Janine said. "That thing that hit him. He *didn't* slip. Jared was never clumsy a day in his life."

"What was it?" Pilar asked.

"A gaff." Paul froze the image, silver bar descending. There was no sight of a human, no view of a hand, not in the quick glimpse Jared had caught. Paul faded the scene and let Seattle show again, puzzled faces blinking in the studio's bright yellow light.

"Who? Why?" Pilar asked. "It makes no sense."

"Skylochori," Signy said, the dead sailor's name rising out of a cascade of suspicions left unexamined, worries glossed over.

"You think that sailor was murdered?" Pilar asked.

"A theory," Paul said. "Let's assume that Skylochori may have been involved in sabotage against Tanaka. That Mihalis Skylochori was on, or not on, the missing Tanaka ship, or that he sank it. That someone didn't want to have Skylochori see what he was seeing."

"The missing ship was sabotaged? Could have been. Someone, some group, wanted it sunk. They don't want cameras in the deep south, maybe," Janine said. "They don't want us to publicize whatever we're publicizing. Jared kept trying to get information; nobody knew anything. . . ."

"That's nonsense," Pilar said. "Shit, we don't even know what we're going to try to sell. Murder Jared, because we might push this treaty? Because we might oppose it?"

"The gaff could have fallen," Janine said. "Come loose from somewhere."

"Bullshit." Pilar watched her flatscreen, tuned to a view of the *Siranui*'s bridge. No words scrolled across her screen. Pilar spoke for her throat mike, in low and urgent tones. "Whiteline, you awake, man?"

"For sure," he said.

"Just checking, hon."

"Move Jared's sequence back just a little," Jimmy said. "As he fell. I think I saw—go back, Paul."

Signy shut her eyes while Seattle disappeared and images scattered.

"There," Jimmy said.

—silver bar of metal in peripheral vision, lurch of lost balance, catlike, trying to recover, a slick dark sea with a black cylinder bobbing up once as the water rose above his/our eyes.

"It's a Zodiac," Paul said.

A Zodiac, a black inflatable boat, a standard for fast travel on treacherous water. There were thousands of Zodiacs in the seas, and they all looked the same.

Signy felt water rising, a strange crawling on her skin

that would translate as cold if the suit's sensors would feed in cold that severe, felt a sensation of strong fingers on the back of her/his neck, saw a slick oval silhouette of a goggled head glimpsed once.

A sharp downward tug, and startled muscles jerked as the water closed again over mouth, nostrils, eyes. Black quiet, with twitches of sensation as the suit monitored the pressure of currents against lax muscles.

Superimposed, Signy heard Pilar sobbing, quiet, hushed little sobs.

"Paul, you didn't tell us someone was out there," Janine whispered.

"I didn't see it the first time," Paul said.

"Go back to the woman," Signy said.

Paul stopped the recording. Signy felt her world vanish into an aching void, as empty of sensation as if she were suddenly enveloped in vacuum. She was never prepared to be cut off without warning, hated it. Paul hadn't slipped up and jerked her out of contact like that in a long time. This was not the best time to yell at him for startling her. Later, she would fuss at him, but not now.

"Why do you think it's a woman?" Paul asked.

Twilight colors and the dull metal of the ship's hull reappeared, and the fingers of sensation that would have been burning cold on Jared's face and neck.

"I think it's a woman," Signy said. "I don't know why."

"Someone turned him off," Jimmy said.

"What?" Pilar asked.

"Turned Jared off. I mean, everything stops there, right? If he were dead and still powered, the suit would keep feeding us body motion and wave tilt, wouldn't it?"

He's right, Signy thought. Jared drowned or didn't drown, but someone was with him, someone who knew enough about him and about our rigs to find the power switch and shut him down.

"It could be a short in the skinthin," Jimmy said. "I've never tried to dunk mine in salt water, myself."

"The suits handle it just fine. Ours do, anyway," Pilar said.

"Metal," Janine said. "If Jared got blocked by something thick enough. Like that titanium submarine that he climbed into before. If he were in that thing, we couldn't pick up his signals."

Dead or alive, Jared became reality again. His presence shifted from an abstract in Signy's mind and became palpable, weighted, precious, and human. His body, at least, existed for her. Unless his murderess had turned him off and let him sink.

I'll kill her. I'll kill her, Signy realized. The decision gave her a sensation of cold; pure, exhilarating. The woman is there, somewhere in that wilderness. I will find her and she will die.

The Taos house, filled with winter morning light, already held the silence of desertion. The clock said 6:03. There wasn't much time to pack, not if she planned to get on the shuttle. Signy hoped she could find her down mittens, the clumsy, warm ones.

"Janine, you'd better call your cab," Signy said. "I'll make sure you don't miss out on anything. I'll stay online with you every minute while I'm traveling. You go on to Lisbon, baby. I'm going after Jared."

"When?" Paul asked.

"Now," Signy said.

"What if Tanaka pushes this incident aside, like they seem to be doing with that dead sailor?" Pilar asked.

"That's why Janine has to get to Lisbon. We need to get some pressure, some live warm human pressure, on someone to help us sort this out. I'll go down on the ice and see what I can find." Knowing that she reverted, in this stress, to the primitive, to a need for hands-on, real-time flesh-and-blood contact.

Knowing that for this, virtual was not enough.

"You have to be hired," Paul said. "No one goes there without a job."

"Tell Tanaka we don't have enough documentation to get them a product. Get me hired to finish up Jared's work."

"Sure." Paul's windowed face grinned a feral grin.

"What if Tanaka doesn't give us any help? What if Tanaka is involved in this?" Pilar asked.

"Then we'll give Tanaka a product Tanaka hasn't asked for," Paul said grimly. "We'll give them the kind of image that will sink their little business forever."

FOURTEEN

A rare sight in winter, Mount Rainier's impeccable snow-cap glinted above the city, an apparition bright enough to make Pilar squint. Clouds rolled in from the sound, predictably. The mountain would vanish in moments. Pilar was oblivious of its beauty, for somewhere in a repeating loop in the back of her mind tires howled on asphalt and metal screamed. She heard the tinkling of broken glass and the call of an owl in the sudden silence. The sound track from the night her parents died was always the same, each noise in its place, a memory track laid down in nightmare, and it ran again now, over the memory of Jared sinking into bitter cold.

Rainier vanished in fog. On a flatscreen display, White-line's translations of a night's work on a fishing ship scrolled past, the routine comments of workers at their jobs. There was no mention of Jared. Pilar watched the words go by and altered them with idle brush strokes, making them look like pagodas and flying birds. Jimmy sat quiet beside her, a stodgy lump of discomfort who obviously didn't know what to do with this situation.

"This is a bad time for you," Jimmy McKenna said. "I should go."

Janine's absence was a palpable thing in the Seattle house, a lack that made the air colder, more humid. Pilar could see, still, Janine's firm little rump marching off into the dawn, a warrior on her way to bait an Asian fox called Tanaka in his lair.

"No," Pilar said. "I don't think so."

"Jared is—special to you?"

"You mean is he my lover?"

"Yeah."

Was he? Pilar never had really thought about it that much. Jared did good stuff with his cameras, moved well. In bed, he knew the timing and the touches; he knew a woman's capacities, and his own. He was handy to have around for sex, or talk, or no sex if that's how things went. But Jared didn't wrap strings around a bed, or a friendship, or a job—

"Yes, he is. More a friend, though."

Jimmy nodded as if he understood what she meant. Maybe he did.

Paul and Signy wanted Jimmy picked over, turned inside out, wanted Pilar to find out why Jimmy McKenna existed in their space. The boy—now, why did she think of him as *boy*? In virtual, where he had insisted on staying for most of the night, Jimmy presented a deft, far-ranging mind that leaped and danced through the worlds he chose to show her; Jimmy was proving himself to be a brilliant observer of visual forms and a musical epicure of fey and eclectic tastes.

Afraid of flesh, though. Pilar hadn't pushed him. She sought Jimmy's trust; she intended to ensorcel Jimmy, more or less, for Edges' purposes. She liked him well enough to want to force him to bloom a little, too, and Pilar considered for a moment that she might be able to do it without harming him.

This could be an intriguing little game, the capture of a Jimmy. They had fallen asleep together, as chaste as children. Jimmy had offered lovemaking in virtual, with himself in the muscular persona of a prince of dreams. Pilar's refusal did not seem to surprise him.

Pilar smiled, remembering falling asleep to the sound of his soft breathing, and then a kinesic memory came to her with nauseating force, Jared struggling to reach the surface, hampered by the thick bulk of his parka. Somewhere far away, broken glass fell on frozen asphalt with a sound like crystal bells.

Pilar did not want to be alone.

"We—they, I mean Paul and Signy, want me to find out why you're here. Paul thinks you queered our transmissions with that music of yours." Pilar could see protest on Jimmy's face. "Yeah, I told him you didn't, and he knows it keyed a scrambler sequence that came from the *Siranui*, but he still thinks you knew it would fuck us over."

"No. God damn, no. I told you it came from something I got off the net. An idea for a melody—I scored it for you, Pilar, but there wasn't anything in it that could have done what you guys say it did."

"You wrote it?"

"Well, yeah."

"Good stuff, McKenna. You're a composer?"

"I mess around, yeah." Jimmy looked at his hands, palms up in his lap, as if they were alien creatures. They were soft hands, short and square, but the fingers tapered pleasantly. Jimmy's fingerpads were not the spatulate, flat sort that Pilar, for no reason she could define, disliked. Pilar reached for Jimmy's hands and drew them up to her face so he would look at her.

"Jimmy, it is beautiful work. Now. Tell me. Why did you send it to me?"

"I thought you would like it."

"Wrong answer. Why did you send it to me?" Pilar held Jimmy's palms together so that he looked as if he were praying. She stroked the backs of his hands.

"Because. Because of the 'Shelter' song."

Oh, lord, she should have known. Tongue firmly in cheek, Pilar had set the simplest of melodies against a rhythm section of Brazilian drums, and filmed herself in the most hackneyed of brass-bra fantasy costumes, a judicious scattering of amethysts, their facets reflecting chrome and washes of synchronous blue light. The song's words were easy nursery words, crooned soft and speaking of shelter, refuge, safety.

Paul always called the work "Mama Neon."

Pilar looked at Jimmy's wary eyes, so ready to be hurt, and saw in them—worship.

"I wanted to meet you. So I got your address from Whiteline. He talked about this company you had going. When he said that someone was after an avant group to do some publicity, I sent them Edges' name. Because I'd heard . . ."

"That I lost my shirt on the tour."

"Yeah," Jimmy said.

"Did you come and see me?"

"I came to the San Francisco show."

"Did you like it? The show?"

"No." Jimmy's eyes searched Pilar's face for reaction. She tried not to give one. "I didn't think it was really you," he said.

Not Mama Neon. Just a woman onstage. What had led him, then, to seek the flesh-and-blood Pilar who lived in this house? Brave man, Jimmy, to dare the imperfections of a woman live and blemished, who, at the moment, smelled of a night's hard work.

"Jimmy? Who else heard your music? Did you play it for anyone?"

"Uh, yeah. Just for one person, and she's just in the net anyway. It's not someone who would, like, know you."

"Who?" Pilar asked.

"She was in Sri Lanka, so I didn't think it would matter." Jimmy swallowed on what looked like a dry throat. Pilar thought of coffee that she hadn't yet had, that Janine usually made.

"Who?"

"Evergreen. That's the only name I know for her. She found me when I was on that job in Houston. You know, where I met Signy for the first time. Whiteline got me the job; he said Gulf Coast wanted someone who was good with tolerance-specific graphics." He paused, apparently seeing from her expression that she didn't know what he was talking about. "I can turn numbers into beautiful things, Pilar. Things to pick up and hold, and push around. Dr. James McKenna, Ph.D. in physics, but what I do is structural analysis, in virtual."

"Evergreen," Pilar said. "Where is she now, Jimmy?"

"I don't know. She's gone," Jimmy said.

"Gone? Gone where?"

"Whiteline said somewhere in Japan. He thinks."

"You miserable little shit," Pilar said. Edges had been sold. To Tanaka? To a Tanaka rival? To a competing company, one of the conglomerates who arbitrarily sent hackers searching the net to tangle new companies just for practice? Jimmy hadn't even been *paid* for messing them around, and that was the saddest thing of all. Pilar got up from her chair and walked away from him. She wanted coffee.

"I'm sorry," Jimmy said. "I'll go now."

"The hell you will," Pilar called over her shoulder. "You'll come in here, right this minute, and wash up some coffee mugs."

"Paul?" Pilar yelled at the kitchen mike.

"I'm looking for her," Paul's voice said.

FIFTEEN

Signy hunched her parka up over her shoulders and struggled down the aisle of the plane, out into the warm moist luxury of Hawaiian air and the smell of plumeria blossoms. Great heaps of them, made into leis, were held by tour guides who waited for the groups of Japanese tourists boiling out of a nearby gate. Just beyond the guides, a gaggle of bored-looking chauffeurs held up signs. Signy hurried past them, intent on remembering the route to International Departures.

"Signy Thomas? Miss Thomas, please?"

A Japanese girl in a flowing tangerine jumpsuit waved a neatly printed sign above her head. SIGNY THOMAS, it read. The jumpsuit was gauzy Milanese cotton, not the garb of a hired guide.

"Me?" Signy asked.

"Tanaka has arranged your flight to New Zealand. We must hurry."

"You managed a seat? The airline people told me there was nothing until tomorrow."

"This way, please." The girl tucked the sign under her arm and put her head down. Signy tried to match her steps to the girl's jog trot. She was a short little thing. Her straight black hair parted neatly over the nape of her neck and the triangle of skin that peeped through was pale and smooth, oddly appealing. The girl snaked her way through the crowd with the skill of a good running back. Signy wedged her way past a group of Hawaiian activists in business sarongs waiting at a departure gate. They carried bulky winter-padded raincoats over their arms and they rolled perfunctory polysyllabic curses in her direction.

A security guard lifted a velvet rope barrier and motioned Signy into a carpeted cattle chute that angled toward a plane's open door. She shifted the weight of her duffel on her shoulder and turned back to her guide.

"Thank you," Signy said.

"You are welcome." The girl looked down. "Your friend Janine Hull is very—assertive."

"Yes." Signy smiled. "I know."

Settled into a first-class seat, under one of the light blankets that airplanes always had somewhere if you asked, Signy cursed herself for a fool. Jared was dead, damn it, and his body was not Jared, was not what she sought. Or Jared lived, and she was unlikely to be able to help him survive. Anything she could accomplish in real time could be accomplished far better from home, where every mode of communication known to the civilized world waited ready. Fool, fool, why didn't someone, anyone, point that out?

Because of the primitive need to *do* something, even if it was wrong. Because that's how humans were, with their fight-or-flight reflexes that were engraved as permanent, inescapable parts of vertebrate bodies. In grief or danger, everyone was as simple as a lizard; stay warm, feed, or run. Signy sat suspended over a world of water, going nowhere at seven hundred miles per hour, because of inevitable reflex arcs in primitive hindbrains.

Signy drifted into a restless space defined by the roar of engines and the feeling of a timeless entrapment where everyone waited, forever, for the opening of a locked door.

And woke to a questioning voice, that repeated "Miss? Miss Thomas?" in tones of professional concern.

"Yes?" Signy tried not to sound as irritated as she felt.

"You seem to be blinking quite a bit. Your wrists, I mean." The woman gestured toward Signy's ready lights, two of them flashing rapidly.

"Ah. Thank you," Signy said.

The flight attendant seemed to want to hover. "I'll answer these now," Signy said. "If you'll pardon me?"

The woman frowned and found business elsewhere.

The two lights belonged to Janine and Pilar. Paul's light was dark, and Jared's. Of course, Jared's. Why had that surprised her? Signy shrugged her blanket up to form a cowl that muffled her voice somewhat and settled her headset into place.

Janine's cameras looked past pillars of yellowing stone, out to a softly lighted courtyard where a winged marble lizard coiled around a globe, his mouth pouring water into a pool surrounded by cream-colored paving.

"You're there already?" Signy asked.

"I'm in a castle," Janine said. "I get a view of a walled— garden?" Her eyes strayed across the courtyard and she focused on Moorish balustrades, on the grimace of a carved gargoyle.

"I hear you were assertive with the Tanaka people on the coast."

"No. I was an aggressive bitch." Janine investigated the bedroom, the bath, tiled in blue and white, and the writing desk, new wood that looked old. Her portable console was in place on it, up and running. The desk drawers were empty. She sat down on the bed and began to sort through her duffel. "Mr. Itano is taking me to dinner at Furasato."

"Furusato?"

"It's a chain, with good sashimi. Itano says." Janine pulled her gray tunic out of her duffel and shook it.

"No," Signy said. "Wear the pale blue, would you?"

"Okay. Signy, I'm going to need at least a rough sequence ready by tomorrow morning. Something to show Itano. Can you get Paul and Pilar in gear, for God's sake? I'll need a couple of thirty-second bits that can slant either way—something that pushes the quota system for harvesting if that's the way things go, and one that pushes high bidders if I can talk Itano into that system. High bids are the best option, as far as I can figure it."

"Then convince him. Change his mind."

"Shit. I'm a garbage engineer, not a diplomat."

"You're an environmental magician, a certified one. A highly respected role in today's dump heap of a world, kid, and don't think Itano doesn't know it."

Janine went into the bathroom. The handles on the taps were shaped like dolphins. She splashed water on her face, leaned toward the mirror, and stretched the outer corner of her eyelid. It was puffy.

"You've been crying," Signy said.

"Of course I've been crying."

"Don't cry when you're around Itano."

"Fuck you. I'll cry when and where I damned well please."

"Janine, don't blow this contract, okay? I don't think Jared's dead. I don't know why, but I don't. I think there's a chance Itano could help us get him back."

"Jared's dead," Janine said. "We took a job, it turned out to be dangerous, Jared got killed. You didn't kill him, Signy."

"If he'd dead, I killed him."

"Bull. Shit. Stop that, Signy. You didn't hear the rest of us turning this job down, did you?" Janine smoothed her tunic over her hips. "I've got to go down to the lobby. You coming to dinner?"

"I'm supposed to bug Paul for you."

"Oh, yeah."

"So I'll do it."

Signy turned Janine off and accessed New Hampshire. Paul's study was quiet, lighted only by a red glow from the fireplace. Signy made out an indefinite shape, a rumple of blankets on the floor. Paul sighed. He rolled over and settled into sleep again.

Signy left him there and called Seattle.

The studio showed the bridge on the *Siranui*. Windowed into a corner, a printout ran over a triangular sigil, a stylized two-lane blacktop painted with bright white lines. TRAWLER APPROACHING WITH FULL LOAD. PREPARE TO RECEIVE.

Pilar's man stayed on-line, it seemed. The words scrolled into storage, replaced by:

ALL SLIME LINE PERSONNEL ON P.M. SHIFT REPORT TO HOLD AT 2100.

"What's a slime line?" Signy asked anyone who might be listening in Seattle.

"Signy? That you, girl?" Pilar asked.

"Yeah."

"Do you have any idea where Janine keeps the ketjap manis? Jimmy went down to Pike Street and brought back these marvelous farm prawns and I'm trying to put together a pad thai."

"Whatever the hell that is," McKenna's voice muttered.

Pilar hadn't chased him away. What did she think she was doing? "You still around, McKenna?" Signy asked.

"He's still here," Pilar said. "He's telling me everything he knows, Signy."

"And that's useful?"

"We think we know how our system got scrambled, and we've got a good idea who might have done it. Someone named Evergreen, it seems."

"Hacker?" Signy asked.

"Sort of," Jimmy said. "I can't figure the schemata on how it worked. I've looked at it. . . . Signy, Pilar told me how you got messed up, the sensory spillover. I'm sorry. I didn't do it, but I'm sorry it happened, anyway."

"Okay. Fine," Signy said. Pilar sounded happier than she had in months. McKenna was just a kid. Signy could try to trust Pilar's instincts, just a little. Jimmy couldn't hurt any of them now; Paul was on his case. "Do you think this Evergreen works for Tanaka?" she asked.

"I don't know," Jimmy said.

"That would make it just a bit sticky, wouldn't it?" Pilar said. "Why would Tanaka be interested in sabotaging us? We're theirs, you know."

"Paul doesn't trust them," Signy said.

"Paul doesn't trust anyone," Pilar said.

True enough. "Jimmy, a pad thai is a shrimp omelet," Signy said. "More or less."

"But does it taste weird?" he asked.

"Yeah."

"Watch it, Thomas," Pilar said.

"Janine needs—"

"She told us. I can't think of anything. Not that could be ready in six hours, anyway." Pilar's voice was accompanied by scraping sounds and the tattoo of a whisk in a bowl.

"We'll have to think of *something*," Signy said. "How long has Paul been asleep?"

"Hours," Pilar said. "I'll rouse him in a bit."

"Do that." Jared, Jared, they are feeding each other and fucking like frenzied ferrets. The shits. "What have you heard from the fleet?"

"Business as usual. As absolutely usual," Pilar said.

"Right." A wave of fatigue came up from somewhere and Signy yawned.

"I'll call you when we finishing putting something together," Signy heard Pilar say, somewhere far away and unimportant.

Her mouth was dry when the alarm on her wrist woke her with its buzzing. Signy got the flight attendant to bring her a club soda. Hampered by the limitations of her little heads-up display, which gave her tiny stereo views of Seattle and New Hampshire screens, but not touch, smell, or true directional sound, Signy watched what Pilar and Jimmy had kludged together:

Gray mists swirled over a hint of water and reeds. A crane, with awkward grace, spread white wings bordered in elegant black.

A four-note motif, played pianissimo in hollow synthetic tones, cycled through random, hypnotic rhythms. It seemed to come from the edge of the water, or from beneath it.

Ripples formed and stilled again. The crane stabbed with its beak, one darting motion, and brought up wriggling silver. Bright drops fanned from the struggling fish and struck the water. Circles spread from the impact centers, rippled away their energies, and faded. The crane lifted its head to swallow in one efficient, jerky motion. And was still again, waiting.

[Paul] It's beautiful, Pilar.

Yes, it's beautiful, Signy thought. "It's too tropical," Signy said, to be contrary, because the noise of the airplane was getting into her soul, and because Jared was missing and it was *all her fault* and nobody would agree with her on that, damn them.

[Paul] Temperate, not tropical.

"I don't care," Signy said. "Everything you're probably layering in that suggests caution and careful husbandry is lost on me for the moment."

"So you're a good control," Pilar said. "You're getting what the ghettos get."

"What they get is hungry," Signy said. "Look, I just don't think this works, even as a prelim. You're aiming this first presentation to the Antarctic Treaty Commission, after a preview by Itano and his boys. That means you've got the mind-sets of diplomats and midlevel state department types to think about. The setting is Japanese, and that could ruffle some ethnic feathers. Besides, where are the penguins?"

"Everybody loves penguins," Pilar said. "They're symbolically neutral, innocent, and overused. And they're funny. No way Tanaka wants to look funny. Face, and all that."

"Tanaka execs wouldn't give a damn if you put their little executive faces on some penguins and had them waddle for the audience. Not if it sold product," Signy said. But what *did* Tanaka want? Tanaka's profit taking had been cautious, or so Janine said. And Itano talked conservation, talked the long-term view. What was long-term for these people? Twenty years? Fifty?

Paul sent voice and visuals from the New Hampshire house. "We don't *know* product," Paul said. "We have some profiles on the diplomatic paper pushers we'll be dealing with in Lisbon. We can figure the Brits and the Argentines won't basically give a damn, but the Chilean fleet wants its share and they're too broke to be competitive. Then there's Russian coalition, and they *can't* come up with a decent bid. Not enough good equipment. They'll hate it."

"They'll be for competition; at least in posture. The resurgent capitalist ethic," Pilar said.

"Anyway, we don't know what Janine is going to get Itano to agree to buy," Paul said. Paul's beard looked like it had grown another quarter of an inch. "Signy, we need to let this go and see what Janine is doing."

"We don't have time, old friend. Oh, listen in with her if you want."

"You do it," Paul countered.

"I don't want to. I'm afraid she's pushing Itano to find Jared and if she gets Itano's dander up we're likely to get fired. Then we'll never find Jared. Never find what happened to him. Never know—" Signy swallowed hard.

"Oh, why not go with this crane thingie? Work it up for aristocrats. Appeal to the innate snobbery of the well fed. I'll check in on Janine."

Signy disappeared them; Paul, Pilar, Jimmy.

Janine looked across the rim of a wineglass and watched Itano's chopsticks pluck something green and slippery from the rice bowl held at his lower lip. He put the bowl down and laid his chopsticks in their porcelain holder, ah so precisely.

Janine had placed a little notebook on the table beside her, giving Signy a way to type messages to her.

Japanese etiquette, even at dinner, found net access acceptable. Itano's business suit might have carried a set of cameras. If so, they didn't show. Maybe he wasn't recording anything. His status made such a thing possible.

"Piracy still exists," Itano said. "There are ports where one can sit in a dockside hotel and examine the ships that come and go. And make requests for their delivery dates. Oh, not highly publicized, these pirates. Even the owners of the ships that disappear do not call attention to the fact."

"Why?" Janine asked. She put her wineglass down and circled its rim with her finger.

"Such information disturbs stockholders. And the ships are seldom destroyed. Their names are changed and their registries. It is possible, on occasion, to reclaim them."

"Would one hire another set of pirates to do that?"

Itano winked and sipped his tea. Winked? U.S. born and educated, his language and gestures mixed Asian and West Coast gestures in ways that made him difficult to read. Signy wanted to send Janine a warning about that, but she didn't want to disturb Janine's concentration.

"Has Tanaka lost any ships to pirates?" Janine asked.

Itano swirled his bowl of tea in his hands. It was half

empty. He frowned at it for a moment. "I am a mediator, in this work your group brings to us. Your teacher, if you'll permit me; and it would be wise of you to permit me such a role." The epicanthic folds of his eyes contrasted with his narrow nose; damn, his face was a cultural mix, and Signy wondered about mixed blood. "You may ask me direct questions, Janine Hull, but remember, I have California sensibilities. Do not be so direct if you should speak to Mr. Tanaka himself."

"Point taken," Janine said. She picked up her tea and sipped at it. From somewhere in the background came the wailing sound of a samisen. The couple at the table next to theirs chatted in Japanese, attentive to each other. They were handsome. They were perfect. They, Signy realized, were Tanaka security.

"*Will* I speak to Mr. Tanaka himself?" Janine asked.

"I don't know," Itano said.

[Signy] Pour tea for him. Come on, be the blond geisha he's wanted all his life.

Janine picked up the teapot and, as she did so, lifted an imaginary kimono sleeve away from her arm. Now where did she learn to do that? Signy wondered. Janine tapped out a "leave me alone" signal on her wrist, flourished her phantom sleeve, and handed the cup to Itano.

"Thank you," he said.

"Piracy, theft, misleading reports on what is harvested from the sea, hunger," Janine said. "What's the answer to that hunger, Mr. Itano?"

"Why do you avoid my first name?" he asked. "I would like for you to use it. We are not adversaries, Janine."

"Because I can't say your first name, or at least I don't think I can."

"Kazuyuki," he said. "Ah. Call me Kazi. That's easier to say."

"Kazi. What's *your* answer? Not the corporate answer. You're as Yank as I am; you have lived in Palo Alto between the seawalls and the campus fences. You have seen the faces beyond those fences get thinner and thinner. How do we keep everyone fed?"

"We *won't* keep everyone fed." Kazi frowned and looked down at the table. "We can't do it now; we won't be able to do it for another twenty or thirty years. We won't be able to do it then, unless there are fewer people to feed. Janine, you know this."

He didn't mention Africa. No one did, these days. Starving bands swept across the African deserts, the remaining tribes consolidated in holy wars against outsiders. The world knew the winner's names: Yoruba, Masai, Zulu. A continent of early death and earlier breeding; the rest of the world tried to ignore Africa, to let the chaos boil undisturbed. Someday, Signy knew, that would not be possible. What New Man might arise there, to cast judgment on those who turned their backs?

"Yes," Janine said. "I know it."

"Even if the sea life survives, and it may not, there must be other resources as well. Vat foods, tailored krill, irrigation of marginal lands with seawater."

"I've seen some of that land. It's ruined forever."

"Yes. Land that will be submerged in a hundred years anyway, as the seas rise."

"*If* the seas continue to rise," Janine said.

"Saltwater irrigation of brine-tolerant plants produces biomass for the vats. In the vats, one can produce tonnes of carrot cells, corn cells." Kazi looked at Janine and answered what must have been a smile with a rueful grin of his own. "You know as many answers as I do."

"I hope for more," Janine said.

"Hope is a curse."

"Is that a Japanese proverb?"

"Perhaps," Kazi said.

Janine leaned forward across the narrow table and very, very cautiously placed her fingers on the back of Itano's hand. "I like you," Janine said.

"You are beautiful."

"I am—assertive. Help me find out what happened to Jared."

He drew his hand away. "Your missing cameraman? I'm sorry to hear that he met with misfortune, but compensation for accidental death is included in your contract. Surely it is adequate."

A payoff? A workman's comp settlement, so sorry, here's the cash. Signy found she was gripping the arms of her airline seat. Just biz, Itano seemed to be saying. But Jared wasn't just biz, Edges wasn't just a company. Edges, she realized, is family. We have each other, and that's all we have.

"Compensation? *Compensation?*" Janine asked. "Money has nothing to do with this!"

"I don't understand," Itano said.

"He is my friend," Janine whispered.

"Your lover?" Itano asked.

"My *friend*."

"I see."

Itano reached for Janine's hand and held it as if it might break. "I will try to help you, Janine Hull."

"It's not just business," Janine said. "We're a team. We're very close."

"Ah, loyalty. Yes."

"You are surprised?" Janine asked.

"I am pleased."

And he looked it. Janine had just scored points in Itano's eyes. The bastard was misty in the eye and looked ready to eat from Janine's slightly callused hand.

[Signy] So what the hell are we selling in the morning?

"Restraint," Janine said aloud. Itano looked puzzled. "Is necessary in some things and not in others." Janine finished her sentence for Itano's ears. "Let's make love, Kazi. Let's leave this restaurant and go to my little room and make love."

[Signy] !!!

Itano was on his feet in an instant. He came to Janine's side of the table and held her chair for her as she stood.

[Signy] I'll help get your presentation together. Bye.

Down to Christchurch. Signy walked across runway asphalt that was called macadam in this part of the world and smelled the same anywhere, oily old dinosaur sludge pulled up to swelter in the sun's heat. The airport put her in a van and sent her into town for a meal. Clean hills, clean streets, the buildings seemed transported whole from a London suburb to perch here, as confused about their dislocation as Signy was.

An hour later, blinking in the sunlight, she thought the Air Australis plane squatting on the runway looked rather little, the one that waited to go down toward Mc-Murdo, where, Signy was assured, someone would pick her up and carry her to the *Siranui*.

"Up here, there's a girl," the mustached pilot said as he put out an arm to help her climb the steps roughed into the top of the wing. The pilot's skin was red and freckled and blotched, a sun-damaged ruin; his eyes were faded to colorless, squinted tight and rimmed by blond lashes. He had a nice grin and Signy tried to smile at him. "No, I'll have the duffel," the pilot said. He reached out a hand for it, the duffel that Signy had tried to push through the plane's door. "Goes in the back, is how it goes."

Signy nodded and took one of the six seats. She heard thumping noises behind her. The plane rocked as the pilot stepped over her legs and into his seat. Jesus, what year was this thing built?

"You look a bit tired, if you don't mind my saying so," the pilot said.

"I am. Very tired."

"Tuck back, then." He pushed a lever and the seat back dropped to near-flat.

"Isn't there a regulation about this or something?"

"Not in my plane, love. Let's be off."

"Right," Signy said. The motors were very damned loud. She let her back relax against the seat and wiggled her stretched-out legs; oh, joy. She felt the rising plane make her heavy, and luxuriated in the feeling. Closer to Jared with every passing hour.

SIXTEEN

Pilar and Jimmy napped in shifts, collapsing on the cushions in the Seattle studio, Pilar rousing now and again to scan Whiteline's translations of talk from the *Siranui*, nothing useful. Jared had to be dead. Signy flew on toward nowhere, and would find nothing.

Pilar found an absence inside, a blank spot, where feelings of sorrow or anger or outrage might grow later, but not yet.

Late in the day, she and Jimmy, without discussing it, began to pick up the pace of work again. Pilar made a fresh pot of coffee and sent Jimmy to rummage through the kitchen for anything he could find to eat.

Whiteline's screen, empty of words, made her think he had fallen asleep.

[Pilar] Whiteline, you there, man?

[Whiteline] Nothing to say. All quiet down south.

[Pilar] You work long hours, when you work.

[Whiteline] Empress, you are so right. I gotta crash.

[Pilar] Okay. You saving?

[Whiteline] I'm saving. ZZZZ now. More later.

She let him go. Pilar sipped coffee and listened to Jimmy and Paul, who traced the available reports of diplomatic positions in Lisbon as if the Treaty Convention were a stock market. Or some sort of racing form. They sounded like bettors at some weird jockey club. They worked like demons, like business as usual. Paul seemed to be operating under the tenets of a demented solipsism: If we keep busy, last night will not have happened. Paul's manic mood seemed almost an act of faith. He laughed at something Jimmy said. The interchange sounded like old friends yucking it up.

Paul didn't bond easily with anyone; Jimmy seemed to be disarming him with quiet displays of graphic skills, with placid calm. While Jimmy worked, obsessed, he treated Paul and Pilar as if they were useful databases, nothing more. His obliviousness to the rituals of getting acquainted gave Pilar the impression that he'd been around for years. For a kid with serious social dyslexia, he was doing quite well.

Pilar looked in at their workspace:

A beam balance, the kind that blind justice usually holds, only this time a mermaid held it. Paul's crab and a frog-thing, presumably Jimmy, dumped packets of information into boxes marked with bright national flags. They stacked the boxes on one or the other pan of the balance. The boxes were familiar: the jungle-gym lattices that Edges used as personality constructs.

The crab became aware of Pilar's presence and tossed a bucket of papers in her direction.

"What's it for?" Pilar asked.

"We're simulating the vote while we're prepping cheat sheets for Tanaka's staff," Paul said.

"Sure," Pilar said. "Whatever you say." Pilar helped file diplomat's names, educational records, shopping habits, and hobbies, if known, into Paul's lattice boxes of known facts that, fitted together, gave shape and direction to the group of individuals slated to attend the Antarctic Treaty Convention. The crab picked the boxes when they were filled, turned them in his claws, and piled them on the balance pans. The pans and the mermaid who held them swayed back and forth in an unseen current, and a box that Pilar had just finished stuffing (Mexico) fell off and drifted away.

"Hey!" Pilar said.

"It's a tidal effect," Paul said. "A combination of grain

futures, currency fluctuations, newsnet stories, and a mix of other stuff that might 'sway' opinions. Nice, eh?"

"Nice."

Pilar emptied her bucket and exited. Somewhere in the distance, a crab and frog made cries of protest. Pilar ignored them. Signy was off-line, and hopefully sleeping at McMurdo by now. Janine? Pilar switched to Lisbon.

Janine's world was a view of a basket of pastries resting on white linen next to a giant cup of coffee. Janine sat at a small table in a restaurant, in a room with low ceilings, emerald green walls, and blue and white tilework, furnished with ancient heavy wood and a plethora of silver. Japanese men in black suits sat at nearby tables. In the background, black-haired waiters in ill-fitting white jackets hovered with pots of coffee.

"What's your schedule?" Pilar asked.

Janine wiped her hands on a thick white napkin and typed on her notepad.

[Janine] Meeting with Kazi's team in four hours. Then high tea with the Brits.

"What's the meeting about?"

[Janine] Prep. I'm just there to listen. Not presenting, thanks.

"Thanks, indeed," Pilar said. "Okay. Tune us in, and we'll put what you hear into the crane sequence, if we need to. I think we'll have it ready for you, hon."

[Janine] Jared?

"Nothing, Engineer. Sorry."

Kazuyuki Itano, crisp in a dark gray suit, smiled as he came to the table and sat down next to Janine.

"I have spoken with the captain of the *Siranui*," Kazi said. "He will do everything possible for your friend. But he says that recovering Dr. Balchen's body is—unlikely."

"I see. Thank you." Janine reached down and flipped the notebook closed.

Dr. Balchen's body. Corpse, cadaver, meat. Pilar lifted

her headset away and rubbed at the bridge of her nose. Jared as a corpse, dissolving into nothing; Pilar had all too clear a vision of yellowish bone showing through torn red muscle, Jared a meal for the creatures of the sea. No! The dead, *her* dead, just dissappeared; they went into a space called "nothing," where flesh was not a matter of concern. Ashes to ashes. Her own delicate bones reassured her, the texture of her skin under her fingertips, the soft downy feel of the pale hairs that grew between her eyebrows; this was her own dear and living flesh, warm and real.

Jimmy, in his skinthin and headset and gloves, looked less alive than your average cockroach. He paced around the perimeter of the holo stage, nudging invisible objects into an invisible mass. Pilar slipped back into the world behind her headset, to find the crab and the frog still swimming around their mermaid.

"Hello, Empress," Paul said. "The vote looks close."

"Close which way?" Pilar asked.

"The U.S., the E.C., and Japan can get a moratorium on fishing. If they agree to agree. The E.C. can foul us up, but they won't be able to block the moratorium unless India intervenes."

"Will they?" Pilar asked.

"No. Because India is farming her coast and isn't importing krill."

The balance pan swayed and rocked in their information currents, and the mermaid smiled. The creature had scales all over; they didn't stop at her waist. She looked sort of like Signy on a bad hair day.

"Jimmy?" Paul asked. Paul's crab grew larger, and crept into a conch where a small frog sat, blinking its huge and luminous eyes. "I have a need to persecute someone. I'm paranoid, and I've got a friend missing. I don't like that. It's time we had a little chat."

"I've told you everything I can think of about that music," Jimmy said. "Honest. Everything I know."

"Tell me again," the crab said. "Start now."

"Let us out of this aquarium, then. I need a little more reality in my space, you know?" The Jimmy-frog popped away. The Paul-crab lurched in a circle, and the holo stage darkened to black. "*You* didn't glitch the music," Paul's disembodied voice said. "This Evergreen of yours ran a key into it, one that linked Edges to her, or to whoever listened for her. The link was designed to wake up when Edges contacted the *Siranui*. So Evergreen belongs to Tanaka, we think. What do you think?"

Unadorned, Jimmy's face filled the holo stage. Paul had blocked his own from view.

"It fits," Jimmy said.

"I think I would like to talk to Evergreen," Paul said. "I truly would like to talk to her. Soon. Can you find her?"

"I can try," Jimmy said. He looked down and away.

"You do that," Paul said.

Paul let Jimmy's face fade, let the world go totally black. "Jimmy?" he asked.

"Yeah?"

"You're really good. The parameters you set up on the opinion currents are going to work like a bastard."

"Thanks," Jimmy said. "Paul, I'll do what I can. Give me a minute, okay?" In the Seattle room, Jimmy's helmeted face stared at the flatscreen in front of him; his hands worked at the keyboard.

"Jimmy?" Pilar asked. Already tracing signals from a woman he said he didn't know, he didn't seem to hear her. "Jimmy, what is it that keeps you here, catching all this shit?"

"Family," Jimmy said.

"Family?" Pilar asked. "What family?"

"Yours," Jimmy said. "The one I want to be a part of. I can *talk* here, you know?"

Because he could talk? To Edges? Could this be the structure he wanted, could this loosely knit bunch of eccentrics feel like warmth, security, *family* to Jimmy? His search implied an isolation appalling in its immensity, if he searched out *this* group to hear him.

Try as she might, and Pilar tried for a long time, staring into space, she couldn't conjure Jimmy into anything other than what he seemed to be—a lonely human, mute in most situations, trying to find a place where someone understood his individual, idiosyncratic language.

Pilar switched to the net and tried to find photos of the British delegate's wife to send to Janine. A polite glance of recognition could hardly hurt. After a time, Pilar began to hear the music she had scored to underlay her search, music called up with no conscious thought. She listened to the sound of booming surf and the cries of gulls, a basso counterpoint to the routines of her work, that filled the Seattle house with rhythms of wordless grief.

"See what I mean?" Jimmy asked her.

SEVENTEEN

"My name's Red," the pilot said.

"Signy."

"We'll be about eight hours getting there."

"That long?"

"That long."

Signy went numb and timeless in the roaring plane, feeling as tiny as a cursor on a giant screen of sky and tossing seas. Red blinked at the midnight sun and smiled at whatever music played in his headphones. The listener lights at Signy's wrist were all dark and they stayed that way. She was off-line, out of contact, lost. Recording the sky and the noise of the plane seemed a waste of time. Timeless and trapped. So slow, more than a day now since Paul woke her with his scream; if Jared lived, Signy didn't know that she would be any help at all to him. It occurred to her that she might be offering harm, not assistance, that her presence might snarl the tenuous skeins of accident or intrigue that had claimed him. Trapped and helpless.

At times Signy dozed, exhausted from playing out scenarios based on imagination, scenarios where she arrived too late, stepped in too early, said the wrong thing to the wrong person at the wrong time.

She woke as the plane began to descend, and Red seemed to notice her bemused attention to the sights outside the windows, broken stretches of water and the steaming crest of Mount Erebus. The world looked as if it had been shot in black and white. Red took the plane down past the tremendous sheer cliff that was the Ross

Ice Shelf, the cycle of the earth's weathers written in strata of pure water, immense, silent, and lethally close to the flimsy metal of the plane—but Signy arrived awake, and might have thanked him for it. They had not spoken since they left Christchurch, Signy realized, so she didn't break the silence now.

McMurdo's Tinkertoy domes looked pathetic; they were ugly blemishes scattered on the ice. The sunny air was not as cold as she'd expected, it was no colder than midday in a Rocky Mountain winter. Barren rock and windswept snow stretched to the mountainous horizon. Signy had expected silence, but the sounds that came to her were the huffing of fans and engines, the noisy exhalations of machines that kept the settlement alive. Ugly, barren, man-stained, at least outside, McMurdo's flat plain breathed indifference, an impersonal anomosity. Signy stamped snow from her boots into the grate just outside the airlock-styled double doors, ready to dislike the place before she entered it.

A simulacrum of a Mars habitat, McMurdo was open to researchers only, except for areas where personnel from supply ships could come and go. Red nodded to her, a half salute of dismissal, and headed for a prefab hut marked by a neon palm tree and a sign that read HOTEL CALIFORNIA. Nashville sounds wailed from the opened door, cut off in midphrase as the door closed behind the pilot.

Unmet, alone, Signy stood in greenish light filtered through translucent hexagons, under a Fuller dome that arched over corrugated steel buildings and wormish lengths of giant pipe. Walkways of latticed brown plastic were laid out across the snow. Moist air brought her the smell of humans and old socks. McMurdo didn't recycle air, it brought in the clear atmosphere from outside, a violation of its Mars research charter that had caused some displeasure among its U.S. and Euro sponsors. Signy looked for a YOU ARE HERE sign. She couldn't see one anywhere. Two bearded men in bright flannel shirts walked past her without a word and disappeared behind unmarked doors.

Signy waited. No one came for her.

Three bundled people came through the airlock doors. Signy couldn't tell their gender; their parkas were tied tight over their goggled faces. As she walked toward them they made a sharp right and vanished between two prefabs. Signy followed, her duffel slung over her shoulder and getting heavier by the minute. They opened a door into a long and brightly lighted hallway.

"Hey!" Signy shouted.

The third figure, male, she saw now that his parka was loosened, let the door close behind him. Signy opened it and followed him. The man walked down the hall and ducked into a room. He closed the door just as she reached it.

Signy knocked. Damn it, the man had seen her, unless she'd gone invisible and hadn't noticed. She heard him step heavily toward the door.

He opened the door a crack and frowned, a black-bearded face with the dark almond eyes of the Mideast. Behind him, an inflated plastic camel clung to a wall covered with layers of thumbtacked printouts, posters that featured plump smiling girls and palm trees, and Ziplocs filled with small nondescript rocks. A tiny desk held a welter of hammers and chisels that were bright with use, and faded rucksacks that bulged heavily.

"You're new," he said, his eyes not on Signy's face but on her duffel.

She nodded.

"The office is the door at the end of the hall." He shut his own, firmly.

Friendly place. Signy trudged toward the door at the end of the hall, marked with smeared back stencil letters at nose level. BASE OPS. She shoved it open.

The room she entered was small and filled with desks,

monitors, and wall screens, one of them dotted with tiny icons that moved slowly across a stylized map of the base and surrounding territories, if the tiny cone was Erebus and the rectangle was the airstrip.

"Hello?" Signy asked.

She heard someone sneeze. A man appeared from behind the map screen. Short, plump, and deliberate, he looked like a porcupine sans quills. He favored her with a lazy stare, waddled to a desk, and sat down.

"Thomas, is it?"

She nodded.

"You've quite the introduction." His voice was a high-pitched whine. "Tanaka rents an office and bunk here; it's yours and you don't have to share it with anyone. That's likely to cause some jealousy; don't trot around bragging about it." He rummaged through a desk drawer and came up with a dog-eared pamphlet. "You'll need to read this."

Signy took the booklet from his outstretched hand.

"Excellent," she said. "If you'll tell me how to find my quarters?"

"You'll need to read the manual before you go *anywhere*." He looked hurt, as if he were disappointed that she hadn't known.

"Sure," Signy said. "Okay." She looked around and found a chair that had only one stack of papers on it, picked them up, put them on a clear space on the gray carpet, and sat down.

Jared, Tanaka, any likelihood of doing what she had come here to do, seemed distant constructs, impossibly difficult to regain. It had been so long, so many years, since Signy had dealt with forms and rituals that could not be bypassed with a keystroke. Well, there was Edges and all of its interactions, often in real time, and the business of living that involved groceries and grounds maintenance and trips to different companies, when she couldn't talk Janine or Pilar into doing real-time liaison.

Still, bureaucrats rankled. Patience, Signy cautioned herself. She couldn't delete this man, this porcupine, and go beyond him. What would he do if she balked? Put her out in the snow and say, "Walk home?"

He just might.

Signy opened the manual and began to read. It was a survival guide, and discussed frostbite, exposure, protection from wind. It was specific about equipment needed for going out on the ice, and about hygiene. "If you can't bathe," it told her solemnly, "wipe your skin with a clean dry cloth."

Signy looked up to find Porcupine watching her intently. Signy was a speed-reader, but she dropped her eyes and stared at the pages for what she thought Porcupine would think was a long enough time to digest the manual's contents and then she nodded and stood up.

"Valuable," Signy said.

"There's a copy in your room," Porcupine told her.

But the rules wouldn't let her read it there. No, not where she might be comfortable. "Could we go there?" she asked. Please, Porky, before I lose my temper completely and flatten your pointed little nose. I'm *tired*, damn it.

He walked to the door and kept his hand on the knob. "Mess is in Orange section. Rec is in Green. Don't try to go into Yellow or Blue. Okay?"

"Okay," Signy said.

"I'll take you to your quarters." Porky opened the door and led her down the hall. "Transients usually can't find their ass with both hands for a few days down here. Are you hungry?"

"Not really," Signy said.

"Maybe I'll find you for breakfast tomorrow," Porky said.

Maybe he was trying to be friendly. Signy followed him down a maze of corridors, out across echoing spaces filled only with dome and flooring, and into another

building that Porky told her was reserved for temp offices.

"What time is it?" Signy asked.

"Nineteen hundred hours," he said. "We run on Greenwich plus twelve."

The plane had landed into the sun, in a bright midday
light. But, okay, this was dinnertime. Porky stopped before an anonymous door and handed her a keycard.

"Thank you, Mr.—"

"Snead," he said. "I'm Jim."

He turned on his heel and strode away. Signy had no
idea where she was in the maze they had just traversed,
nor had she seen anything that looked orange, green, or
any other color. She didn't for the moment, care.

The keycard let her into an entryway where a shoe
rack on a polished wooden floor announced that shoes
were not expected. Perhaps the soles of skinthins counted
as shoes, but Signy was damned if she was going to take
off her suit. The boots, though, yes, and her feet tingled
with relief as she got out of them.

The stone floor was warm as blood and she began to
shudder, suddenly chilled through, fatigue and the relaxation of privacy taking the last of her reserves and leaving her limp. But she got to the wall of screens, her feet
happy with the lush pale carpet, and opened a pathway
to Paul, to Pilar, to home. In the back of Signy's mind
was the thought of hot tea, and she felt sure she would
find a chop-chop efficient little tea maker somewhere
in here, easy to operate. She hoped that the supplies
wouldn't be limited to that thick green stuff and nothing
else. Tea, or coffee or brandy—

Paul's study was empty.

In Seattle, Pilar had left a minor production running,
fractal ferns waving over shadowed writhing shapes, all
in black greens and purples. Rough harmonics seethes
along the lower range of hearing, melodic cacophonies
that could have been the crashes and sighs of feeding

giants, and an inhuman voice called "Go?" or "Oh?" or "Woe?" Wistful, threatening, forgotten as soon as the shapes and sounds were seen or heard, Pilar's entrancements meant "go away."

Janine was off-line as well.

Signy began to search for the elusive tea maker and investigated the tied roll of a thick, black cotton futon, which looked to be the only available bed equivalent. A black lacquer screen shielded it from the rest of the room.

"Signy Thomas?"

It was a woman's voice, contralto, soft. Signy stuck her head around the screen and looked at the row of consoles.

"I'm here."

Anna de Brum's face appeared on one of the screens.

"Hello," Signy said. "Anna, isn't it?"

"Yes. I don't remember . . ."

"I've seen you with Jared."

"Right. I'm coming to McMurdo to pick up some sick-bay supplies. I've been told to bring you back with me. We'll be in to get you at about 1100 tomorrow."

That was *tomorrow.* That was forever. "It will take that long?" Signy asked.

"It will take that long. I'm sorry about Jared. We grieve for him." Anna's face showed sympathy; a warm, sorrowing mother-comfort seemed to permeate her screened face and recorded voice.

"Thank you," Signy said.

"Signy Thomas, you should rest now. You are tired, I think." Anna frowned at the screen and Signy reached a hand to touch her own face, tracing with a fingertip the hollows under her eyes, the oily travel grit on her skin.

"I think you're right," Signy said: "But what's been done? Is anyone looking for Jared? We saw a Zodiac where he went down, a face—" Anna's expression went wary. "You haven't seen it?" Signy asked. "What Jared saw, I mean?"

"No," Anna said.

"Oh, God." The recording had gone to the *Siranui's* captain; Signy was sure Paul had insisted that the captain see it. But not to Anna's eyes, perhaps not to the captain of the *Kasumi*. Actually Signy didn't *know* that Paul had sent it—

"Anna, where are you?"

"Where am I? I'm on the *Siranui*."

"Yes, but which room?"

"I'm in sick bay." And you're nuts, was what Anna's expression said.

"Can you get into the medic's cabin? Where Jared slept? I want to show you something," Signy said.

"Sure."

"Call me when you get there."

"I will," Anna said, and disappeared.

No questions, not later, Anna moved *now*, and Signy loved her for it. Jared had warmed to this woman; Signy began to understand what he had liked. Had liked. Oh, shit.

Signy turned from the blank screen and rummaged through her duffel until she found the chip copy she wanted, diddled with Tanaka's banks of equipment until she got the transmission up and ready on Kihara's cabin screen, and then paced the confines of the little suite, waiting for Anna. Impersonal, a way station, this McMurdo office. The teapot was in a cubby underneath the banks of monitors, at hand to someone working the screens, and Signy filled it and punched it on. Behind a jar of Nescafé Gold was a bottle of Glenfiddich, unopened and welcome. Signy fought with the seal and broke a thumbnail. The hell with tea. She poured a generous inch into a thick green mug and sipped. The whiskey burned a glowing line all the way down to her stomach.

"I'm in sick bay," Anna said.

"Watch this," Signy said. "And do whatever you can,

or whatever you think you should. Then come and get me. Please, come and get me." Signy keyed up Jared's walk on the *Kasumi*'s deck for Anna. "I need Jared's records, any recordings he may have made, and I can't be sure I have everything until I sort through his gear myself. Help me, Anna. Get me there."

"I'll do what I can," Anna said.

Anna would do it because Anna was one of those people who couldn't leave someone in pain. Yes, Signy felt pain. And fear, fear that someone, someone Anna probably knew, sought to hide the circumstances of Jared's disappearance, to obscure whatever discoveries Edges might make. Someone tried to slow things down and hide them away, and that knowledge hurt. Signy couldn't let herself trust Anna completely, couldn't share her fears with this woman she had just met. That hurt, too.

"You should rest now," Anna said. "I will come for you tomorrow."

"I'll rest now."

Signy set the room's system to call her for any accessor at all, tried another sip of the Scotch, and grabbed the futon from the alcove. She shoved her duffel next to it and sat cross-legged on the puffy fabric, tonguing at the Scotch and staring at the screens. Her hands moved through the jumble of clothing and cosmetics in the duffel, searching for a toothbrush and the energy to use it. Smooth and tiny in her fingers, she clutched a handful of chip copies instead, tossed in unsorted and unmarked in her rush to leave the Taos house.

Signy was not sleepy. She was exhausted, yes, but sleep seemed a ridiculous idea. The room's light was soft and there were no outside windows, so she couldn't have the confusion of constant sunlight that the manual had warned her about, not yet, anyway. Odd, this wakefulness. No, not odd. Here to work, and she couldn't work. Here to find Jared, and trapped in an ice world where transportation, even the chance of taking a walk, were in someone else's hands. The room was warm but she felt cold. She should get some food. Definitely not a good idea, her stomach told her.

Signy swallowed a good mouthful of the Scotch. Paul and Pilar were still off-line; Janine? Janine wasn't what she wanted. Idly, she slotted a chip to the small holo stage and keyed her skinthin to it. Small, yes, but the setup carried full sensory hookups and even a scent bank. The little rig was sleek and expensive. Tanaka bought good equipment. Signy scratched the itchy spot beside her left eye and turned on the rig.

A rain forest. Not *the* rain forest, but a forest fantasy out of *Green Mansions*, where birds that might have been macaws or parrots preened their psychedelic wings and screamed, discreetly, like women making love.

Pilar had recorded those screams and never said where they came from, dastardly girl.

Mists obscured and then revealed delicate traceries of leaves that massed like clouds. The setting promised utter privacy. It smelled of exotic flowers, and brown rivers, and rut. All of the flowers were white, granular white.

It was the first job Edges had taken after Jared joined them. A small botanical research firm in Surinam had wanted to buy some acres along the Rio Negro. Politics intervened; none of the principals could legally purchase Brazilian land. Paul asked Pilar about it, and Pilar knew a media madam who liked to think of herself as a Concerned Individual. Sometimes.

Edges rented a private room in an L.A. restaurant and set the forest into it. Jared invited the woman to an *intime* dinner and made the pitch. He's known about madam's penchant for aggressive execs with dominance needs and had acted precisely otherwise. He'd played her like a fish.

Jared's women came and went and stayed friends with him. He permitted? No, more than that, *facilitated*, the fulfillment of sexual fantasies, but he carried no garbage along to bed, no guilt trips or dominance games. Therefore, Susanna, who had seemed just *happy* to talk to him, and happy with Mark. Signy wondered about Jared's time with the Canadian girl. Signy wanted to ask about her; she wanted a *chance* to ask.

The tropical land purchase had gone through with no problems, except that madam insisted on keeping the land in her name and becoming a partner in the company. She'd always wanted to be a scientist, she said.

Signy pulled the chip out, remembering that somewhere, there was a recording of the dinner, one where Jared pulled off the whole business and managed never to laugh. Oh, that one was such fun.

Signy tossed the chip aside. What on earth had compelled her to bring these damn things anyway?

Lifting the bottle of Scotch to pour out a second, smallish shot, Signy rolled the chips in her hand as if they were walnuts she was thinking about cracking. She picked out another one and slotted it.

Oh, damn. Oh, not this one, Signy thought.

But Jared's shoulders were firm and cool beneath her hands and Signy's fingers felt the firm resilience of his skin, the smooth strands of Jared's thick hair, her hands working at a leather thong that knotted all that black wealth. The knot came free and he shook his head. The dark waterfall of his hair slid across his shoulders and smelled, as Jared's hair had always smelled, of forest musk.

Oh, damn.

But Jared's breath was warm and sweet against her eyelids and she looked up through the screen of his hair, sheltered and alive, feeling the weight of him, seeing firelight and shadows in the room where they lay. She held her palms against his shoulders and ran them down his arms, feeling the smooth strength of his tensed muscles as he held his weight above her.

Pilar had filmed the sequence. It started as a joke, sex encased in skinthins and no more real touch of flesh on flesh than if they were dressed in head-to-foot condoms— but Pilar had edited all the plastic away and left sensations of lovemaking as tender as the new skin under a blister.

Signy killed the sequence and looked, belatedly, for privacy guards on Tanaka's office system. She found them and sealed the stage from any watchers as best she could. The chip she held in her palm was memory, was Pilar's re-creation of something that was long behind them all; it was a fake. No, Signy decided, I won't do this.

There had been snow outside, and a full moon, that first winter in the Taos house. Pilar had bought the damned wreck of crumbling adobe, beautiful, but crumbling, and talked Jared and Signy into coming out from New Hampshire to look at it. They spent a hard summer fixing it up, and decided to winter there, leaving Paul alone in New Hampshire. They never discussed their reasons for leaving him; Paul seemed to want to be alone.

None of them had wanted sleep on that bright night. Signy made spiced wine and the three of them settled next to the *banco* that curved around the corner fireplace. They watched cinders float up to the curved adobe blackness of the little cave-shaped firebox, flare red against the soot-varnished baked clay, and fade softly to black again. Jared lay against the rabbit-skin blanket, one arm around Signy, one around Pilar. "We have to try this sometime," Pilar said.

"Not me. I'm a country boy."

Signy had her ear pressed against Jared's chest; his voice rumbled like a growly bear.

"A country Canadian. The world doesn't know how Canadians do it; you're all so reticent. Consider it a study in comparative cultural lovemaking, Jared."

"Ridiculous," Jared muttered.

Signy found a softer place on Jared's arm to rest her head. She stared up at the round bulk of the vigas above her, shadowy and dark. Jared wasn't that uninterested in the idea; she could sense an anticipation in him. "I'll film it," Signy said.

"No." Pilar reached across Jared's chest and laid her hand on Signy's breast. "No, Signy. Let's try it my way." Pilar's fingers found Signy's nipple and traced across the flesh until it tightened. "Okay?"

It started as a joke.

The hell with it, Signy decided, and punched the chip to life.

Tangled on the low bed, with Pilar's cameraed eyes next to them, and the shy awareness that something was different this time, that someone watched; Jared's kisses were hesitant, her responses guarded. Soon forgotten, the watcher became another pair of hands, another set of touches; even the numbing skinthins only a minor distraction. A log cracked in the fireplace and the shadows brightened. Signy looked up, idly and from a distance, wondering whose breath was warm on her breast, but somehow it didn't matter. Wondering whose hand was beside hers on the rigid shaft of Jared's penis, trapped in its hateful restraining Lycra, but that didn't matter, either, for he pushed the hands away, gently. "Slow," he said. "We have time."

Slow, and better because of the frustration of muted touches through fabric, better because of the heightened sense of touch that Pilar fed them through the skinthin's sensitive controls, they lay quiet, almost motionless. For a time, Signy sat astride him, feeling his hands on her back, her hands seeking between them for the promise trapped against his belly. For a time, she lay beneath his hands, his stroking, gentle hands. She watched Pilar's lenses eyes focus on her throat, vulnerable and extended, she heard her own breath, and Jared's.

Someone's warm fingers touched her thighs, tracing down an anatomic pathway that her nerves answered with a tingle that ran from the soles of her feet and back to the tensed muscles inside her belly where she wanted pressure, distension, a joining of flesh to fill the void, erase the ache, now, soon, now. The touch of fur came muted on her back, beneath her hips, beneath her heels.

She begged for Jared, silently with her mouth on his, with the arch of her pelvis that strained the skinthin's elastic fabric against tender engorged flesh. The skinthins slipped away, Pilar helping her, helping him, peel free of their sweat-slick confinement.

The transition into Pilar's reconstruction of the night, edited later, was flawless, superb. Pilar had scored the work with echoes of their breathing, with staccato pepperings of the sounds of the crackling fire, and the distant sound of a wooden flute, and later, the magnified soft silences of falling snow. Somewhere about here . . .

The room's air chilled Signy's shoulders and she reached for warmth, found it in Jared's hot skin, and pushed close against him. He nuzzled at her neck and Signy reached up to twine a hand in Pilar's hair, brought her down to lie between them, Signy's fingers finding wonder in the differences in the textures of Pilar's skin, Jared's skin, the contours of Jared's tense arms and the softness of Pilar's inner thighs. Jared's arms came seeking Signy; Pilar had moved to his side and lay pressed against his back. Signy felt the calluses on Jared's hands. He ran their roughness gently over the ridges of her ribs, her waist, reached both hands under her hips to hold her up to someone's gentle tongue. Suddenly chilled and warmed with the moisture from someone's nibbling lips, she felt silk touches slip away toward the dark deep spaces of her that ached to be filled.

Silk and slip and joy at the thrust of him, quick and deep, and she pulled him into her, deeper, lost and meeting his rapid rhythm; she found herself all too quickly at the brink of a sudden orgasm, thinking not yet, please, not yet.

"Don't wait," he whispered, and thrust again, holding still against waves of her pleasure that broke against his stillness and left her gasping, someone's cry ringing in her ears.

Signy let him leave her warmth; aware of the rigid strength of his erection as he rolled away. She lay quiet beside him, the edge off her hunger. Jared slid his hand across her belly and cupped it over the wet curls between her thighs, his palm warm and comforting. Pilar sank down on him and he pushed up his hips to meet her. Signy rolled up on her side and slipped her hand around Jared's thigh to cradle his scrotum in her hand. Wanting more, and hoping Pilar would not drain him, but Pilar arched away from him with a laughing sob. Jared sought Pilar with his arms, reaching like someone blind. Pilar guided him toward Signy's opened legs. This time, Signy let the rhythm slow, let the distance between him and her need vanish completely, lost in anticipation of stroke and thrust, closer, deeper, secure in a wild faith that this would never end, never. She pushed against him with an urgency that forgot all restraint, and tried to bring him with her to the yawning wonder she entered, a cellular unknowing where all life lived, beyond sensation, into the timeless awareness of now.

Perhaps Jared followed her. Perhaps he did, and Signy

drifted somewhere, watching the fire cast shadows on the locked figures beside her, and listened to Pilar's moans, hearing in them perhaps only the echoes of a fulfillment Signy wanted for her, for all of them. . . .

Curled on a dusty cotton futon with her fists pushed hard against her crotch. Empty and aching. She had tipped the Scotch over, and it smelled of desolation.

EIGHTEEN

Seven hours of sleep weren't going to cut it, but Signy was wide awake, alert and jittery and groggy at the edges. No messages waited on the screens. Janine was off-line. Paul and Pilar weren't answering.

Not all of the water had cooked out of the little teapot. Signy refilled it and drank two cups of instant coffee and scrubbed at the liquor stain on the carpet. She peeled out of her skinthin and found the shower to be hot, generous, and unmetered. The local time was 0700. Clean, dressed, and at loose ends, she paced the confines of the little suite, sipping at more coffee. Anna wasn't due to get here for hours. And was not on the *Siranui*, the watch officer told her, audio only.

"Where is she?" Signy asked.

"Corpsman de Brum is on her way to McMurdo."

"Thank you," Signy said. She had her finger poised over the cutoff key.

"She left a message for you," the officer said. "It says— 'Meet me at the Hotel California.' "

"I'll do that. Thanks." Signy thought she could find the place again.

There was no food in the suite. There had to be a cafeteria or something somewhere in this maze. Signy picked up her keycard and turned it over. A map of the station was printed on the back of it. Snead's forbidden sections were marked in color, three buildings away from her. The cafeteria was just past the entry doors. Fine.

The breakfast crowd buzzed with the tensions of business. The place felt like a combination of a university coffee shop and a construction-site canteen. Bearded men sat in clusters, shoveling food and talking with their heads together. Women in flannels and bulky padded clothes sat in clusters of their own, in unconscious separatism.

Signy carried her laden tray to an empty table. She felt studiously ignored, and in a fit of exasperation, pulled her camera headband into position, focused on faces, groups, framed them in an idle documentary of morning on McMurdo. Bits of conversations floated to her while she ate scrambled eggs that had traveled here in frozen cartons.

Technobabble filled the room, talk of mats of algae under the ice of freshwater lakes in the dry valleys, populations of krill that had pigmented in response to UV excess, new construction up on the slopes of Erebus.

"There's lava tubes in there, some of them big enough to be decent hallways. Makes the excavations a lot easier," someone said.

"What about stability?"

"Oh, hell, a volcano is a volcano. But if you got the sensors up all the time and don't mind moving in a hurry, it wouldn't be a bad place to live."

"Geothermal luxury, fuckin' A."

But no one was supposed to *live* here. The treaty permitted no permanent inhabitants; Signy remembered. She would ask Paul to look at lists of repeated visits—Paul liked that sort of sleuthing. No real privacy, no true sense of unlimited space existed anywhere in the world, and a presumably empty continent might appeal to some markedly weird money.

Janine's light awakened on Signy's wrist. Signy considered talking to her, right here in the middle of the feeding arena where she was already getting studied glances that quickly looked away. Signy deliberately touched the mike taped to her throat and said, "Good morning. Want some eggs?"

[Janine] Ugh.

Janine's eyes scanned a room full of Japanese sarari-men, showing Signy a meeting in progress around a long oval table, Kazi at its head. The air was thick with to-bacco smoke. Printouts competed for table space with teacups, ashtrays, and various models of notepads. The room and the faces looked late and tired. Janine's vision wandered to a steel and thermopane window that looked out at a walled stone castle, a crumbling fairy-tale build-ing set high on a rocky slope above a messy urban sprawl. Then her fingers flew on her notepad, sending typescript to the heads-up display in the corner of Signy's vision.

[Janine] Tense here. U.S. and U.K. reports came in. Not enough fish. Projections say that current harvest-ing will decrease the mature fish populations down past danger levels in five years. They're talking 5% of netted fish mature enough to reproduce—as bad as the cod stats in 1993, and that's bad.

Very bad. There were a few surviving cod, hopefully reproducing as best they could in the abandoned North Sea. Still pirated by some of the Scandinavians, but the great schools that had fed Northern Europe for centu-ries were gone and would likely never return.

In Lisbon, a bearded Anglo man spoke to a conference table surrounded by intent Japanese faces. "The gentoo penguin populations show a greater decline than the chinstraps. We have no explanation for this; their diets are much the same. It is possible that we know less of penguin population dynamics than we thought. But it seems likely that food supply is in question—penguin populations increased at the height of whaling activity and entered a status of true population explosion, then declined again when the whales began to return."

[Janine] We can do it. We can sell a moratorium on fishing in the Southern Ocean. No Fishing: Satellite monitors run by the U.N. Paul still wants it. I'll forget the low-bid system. No Fishing is the only way.

Paul had made that decision when he was ranting about sabotaging Tanaka. What the hell did he really want Janine to do? Blow the contract?

"Let me talk to Paul before you push it," Signy said. "I imagine he has some new thoughts on all this by now."

[Janine] Paul's off-line. So is Seattle. Is okay. I'm just watching, here.

"Well, don't make any moves yet. Not until we talk about it, all of us." Signy wondered if Paul had thought it over since last night and *still* wanted to push a moratorium. No way to know, right now.

Janine's cameras focused on Kazi, who sat across the table from her. Kazi cleared his throat. "The penguin specimens are healthy when sampled? This is not a disease of some sort that is decimating their populations?" he asked.

"No," the bearded man said. "The specimens we have sacrificed have been fat and healthy."

"What of the whales?" Kazi asked.

"The counts for the polar regions are not in. Preliminary reports say that calving seems to be at normal levels in the minke populations."

"Tanaka will go broke if they don't fish," Signy said to Janine. Janine shook her head slightly, causing the Japanese businessman who sat next to her to turn toward her and blink in surprise.

"Won't they?" Signy asked. A man at the next table in the McMurdo cafeteria looked up at Signy and then looked down at his plate again.

[Janine] No. Tanaka won't.

"What chance of fish population recovery if they are left alone?" Signy asked. "Do you have the stats?"

[Janine] Ozone, oceanic warming, current changes? Difficult trends to extrapolate. Chances are good. In 50 years.

And would the "recovered" populations be as poisoned as most coastal fish were now? Toxins combined, diffused, and *changed* in the sea, and climbed the food chain, altering the balance of the seas' populations in complex ways. The sea remained the Final Solution, the Universal Solvent, for Earth, at least. Difficult trends to extrapolate, indeed.

Signy stacked her dishes on her tray and carried them to the scullery window, where clatters, bangs, and mariachi music competed with pidgin chatter. A waft of steamy air carried the smell of soapsuds and roasting meat.

"What about Kazi?" Signy asked Janine. "What sort of help has he offered? About Jared?"

[Janine] Told the *Kasumi* to stay in the area. All he could do, he said.

"That's all?" Signy asked.

Janine's attention turned to Kazi, who studiously ignored her as he closed down the day's conference.

[Janine] That's all so far. Leaving now. Get Paul to tweak some of this meeting's worries into the crane sequence; I'll show it to Kazi after tea.

"What happened last night?" Signy asked.

[Janine] Politics and sex. I'll dump it to your address. It will take me a few minutes, okay?

"Okay," Signy said.

She had—three hours, the clock on the wall told her, to kill until Anna came to get her.

Aimless, Signy wandered out of the cafeteria and walked a few hallways. Politics and sex, whatever Janine had learned about Tanaka and sent unedited would be something to sort through, something to distract her for a time.

Signy turned down a walkway toward the forbidden zones, trying for a shortcut to the Tanaka office. The forbidden zones were not marked in any special way, and the buildings that Snead had said were closed to her looked no different from any other prefabs in McMurdo's maze. Signy thought about walking in, just to

see what would happen, and then decided physical access wouldn't tell her as much as her system would,
once she keyed it to search out McMurdo secrets. The
keycard she held probably recorded her attempts to
open any door; she didn't want to blow her status here,
whatever it might be.

Back in the claustrophobic Tanaka suite, Signy accessed
Janine's night, the tensions of a businesslike seduction,
ritualized compliments, Janine's quick editing, idle chatter in a bedroom.

—Janine and Kazi shared reminiscences of student days
at Stanford, of hot California wind and sun and shadowed courtyards where the bright and young gathered in
flocks, dressed in the faded cottons of that year's fashion.
Changing the world, they thought, or at least learning to
manipulate it. Signy extrapolated tensions in Kazi's voice,
picked up a faint xenophobia from him when he was con-
fronted with the reality of Janine's creamy skin, her total
blondness.

[Janine] Skilled. Thorough.

Janine had done some editing on the bed-with-Kazi
sequence, it seemed.

[Janine] Cut to payoff.

Signy smiled. Janine had planted a single mike in the
Lisbon bedroom, no camera.

New Hampshire and Seattle were still quiet; Signy
called up the empty rooms there while she listened to
Kazi follow Janine's postcoital invitation to speak of his
dreams for the future, to delineate his importance in
Tanaka's world.

"I could become the CEO," Kazi's voice said. "If things
go well, if I am cautious and efficient."

"You rank that highly?" Janine asked.

"Yoshiro Tanaka has placed all the divisions of Tanaka
in competition. For profits, of course, but also for growth.
He is getting older, and says that he wants Tanaka to
become a colossus, to be an institution that prospers for

centuries. We have a goal. We would bring the world safely through this current crisis of hunger and back into a balance of resources and demands."

The speech sounded rehearsed, a ritual recitation of a religious creed. Which, Signy figured, it was. More or less.

"Current crisis?" Janine asked. "We have centuries of exploitation and waste behind us. What's current about it?"

"We strive for a new, consciously directed exploitation. Our vision is the directed use of exploitation in the service of ecologic balance."

Kazuyuki Itano actually seemed to believe the words he'd just said. His tones were convinced, earnest, and not at all cynical. We may have done better with our careful fisherman than we thought, Signy decided.

"Who rules, in this new balance?" Janine asked.

"Ah, those who control food and access to it; they rule," Kazi said.

"Benevolently, I hope."

"Efficiently," Kazi said. "And my division, fisheries, we are very efficient."

Kazi sighed over the sound of rustling bedclothes. "Of course, there is the problem of the biomass division, vat foods. They show a larger profit margin than the fisheries this year. But we can conquer that problem, I think."

"We?" Janine asked.

The sound of ice tinkling in a glass. "I am Stanford, yes, Janine, but I am also Japanese and we work in teams in ways that are difficult for a U.S. woman to understand. We, yes, fishing and aquaculture. My team includes Tanaka's daughter, and *we* are close to our director's vision; I am sure of it."

What's her name, Signy wondered?

"Daughter?" Janine asked, but her words were muffled and Kazi laughed.

[Janine] End.

[Signy] Seattle! Hey, you guys! Is somebody working on Tanaka's daughter's name? Priority. We need to find it, okay?

No one answered. This anonymous Tanaka office irritated Signy; she felt homeless, an Antarctic bag lady with nowhere to go. There was little else she could do here.

Signy placed a few codes in the room's system, access if and when she might need it. She loaded her duffel and got her parka, and went to the Hotel California.

Plastic palms flourished in metal oilcans filled with sand. The foamed insulation on the walls was covered, here and there, with woven mats, their bright dyes faded. The mirrored bar was long and well stocked. There were no customers. No music played. A short dark man sat at one of the Formica tables. He wore a Hawaiian shirt over long-sleeved thermals. Three sets of knitted cuffs lined up over his thick wrists, gray, gray, and black. A flatscreen mounted behind the bar showed a crowd of bare-legged men chasing a soccer ball.

The bartender turned and nodded as Signy came in. Polynesian, she thought, or Filipino. He gave her a shy half-smile but he did not stand up.

"You're open?" Signy said.

"Sure I'm open. What would you like?"

Not booze, Signy thought. The salt in the eggs had made her thirsty. She had had plenty of coffee, though, enough to make her a little shaky. "Iced tea?" she asked.

"You want lemonade," he said.

"Okay."

Signy sat at one of the tables while he rummaged behind the bar and clinked ice. A coconut hung from a coat-hanger wire in one of the palm trees. It was marked with a yellow and black biohazard symbol.

The bartender sat a tall glass down in front of her.

"What's wrong with the coconut?" Signy asked.

"From Bikini," he said. "Genuine U.S.A. radioactive coconut."

"Is it going to give me cancer?" Signy asked.

"Just don't eat him," the bartender said. He looked back toward the flatscreen. "Very important game," he said. "Excuse me?"

"Sure," Signy said.

He sat down again. Signy sipped her lemonade. The bartender watched the game; Signy watched him. She had nothing to do but watch, nothing to play but the hurry-up-and-wait game that seemed normal here, the timing of this place measured by the movements of helos and ships, not by clock hours. Signy sensed the rhythms of the humans that worked here, their schedules shaped by implacable ice and the dictates of transportation, tied to the pace of machines that could go where a walking man could not. No traffic came in and out today, so this bartender rested and waited, and so must she.

"Ah!" he said as something happened onscreen. "Twenty dollars for me." The announcer chattered in Spanish. The bartender flicked a remote at the screen and turned it off. "Now you can ask questions. You're waiting for somebody?"

"Yes. Someone's coming to get me."

"Short time here, then."

"Just this morning, I think."

He nodded. "You like Antarctica?"

Jared liked it. Everything he had sent them had carried an intensity of interest, a fascination with the glimpses he had seen of the wild ice. "I don't know. I haven't seen anything but the airfield and my room."

"I think you will like it," he said. "You have that sort of face, I think. Some people can't stay here; some people can't stay away."

"What is there to like?" Signy asked.

"Penguins, seals, beautiful ice. Not the wind," the man

said. "Take off your nose, your ears, this razor wind here. But everything else is okay. You'll get pretty pictures."

He had observed her headband, the sensor hooked to her eyelid. Signy had forgotten she wore the familiar equipment. The bartender had ignored her lenses and mikes; most people got self-conscious when they thought they were being recorded.

"How long have you been here?" Signy asked.

"Nine years," he said. "I go home to Truc and see my wife, my babies, every April. Love my wife, make a new baby, come back in October."

"What happens here? What do people do?"

"Work like crazy fools, mostly. Then come here after work, or go hide out. Some people go out on the ice for a while, make up some excuse to do that. Those ones are nuts, most of them."

"What are they building on Erebus?"

"I don't know," he said. His eyes shifted around the room, as if looking for cobwebs was preferable to talking about Erebus.

Then he looked up and smiled, all sunshine and plenty of gold in his teeth, at the woman who opened the door. "Long time, de Brum," he said. He got up to greet her.

"Long time, Marty. You taking care of my friend?"

"I treat her pretty good. The usual?"

Marty grinned; Anna grinned; they stood about two feet apart, arms at their sides, not hugging, not touching. They looked like courting penguins, to Signy's eyes.

"I can't stay," Anna said. "Sorry, Marty." Anna reached for the doorknob. "The pilot's waiting."

Signy stood up and grabbed at the strap on her duffel.

"You're Signy," Anna said. "Come with me, please."

"De Brum, next time you stay and talk," the bartender said.

Anna smiled at him and hustled Signy through the

door. "Get your hood up," Anna said. "We're loaded and ready to leave."

The helo waited in a wasteland of mud and slushy snow, flimsy on its skids and tiny against a bank of clouds that barriered the—southern, of course, Signy reminded herself—southern horizon. They lifted and turned, swaying as they rose. Beyond the domes of McMurdo, the helo flew over ice-flecked seas.

"I watched Jared on the *Kasumi*," Anna said. "I think you are right. Someone else was in the water." Anna spoke into her mike, her voice muffled by the roar of the engine.

Signy looked forward to where the pilot sat, hunched forward and listening to them, she assumed.

Anna saw Signy's automatic frown and her stare in Trent's direction. "Trent flew with us to the *Kasumi*," Anna said.

"I wonder if what happened on the *Kasumi* is connected, some way, to what happened to the *Oburu?*" The pilot did not look back at the two women; he kept his attention on the skies. Signy watched his lips move and heard his voice in her earphones.

"*Oburu?*" Signy asked. OBO, OPO, her reconstruction of a life raft's faded letters; she remembered their outlines on orange fabric.

"A Tanaka trawler. That's the one that went down with all hands."

"The dead sailor," Signy said.

"You knew about that?" Trent asked.

"We watched you bring him up."

"I would not be happy to think that my ship is subject to sabotage," Anna said. "I am concerned that there has been no investigation of the *Oburu*'s loss. That I have heard about."

"Things around the fleet are as quiet as a Mafia war," Trent said. "But with the treaty under review, you'd think Tanaka would be yelling bloody murder. Asking for a U.N. escort, or some such."

The woman and the pilot shared the gossip with Signy, seemingly without concern. This must be a truly lonely place, Signy decided. A newcomer must *want* to be here, and by definition had business here. Therefore it was okay to talk to any new face, Signy guessed. "The waters have never been policed," Signy said. "Perhaps Tanaka wants them left alone." Left alone to be harvested down to the last fish, the last tonne of krill. It had nearly happened in the North Pacific, it *had* happened, for all practical purposes, in the North Atlantic. And it would happen here, the rich waters empty, even the plankton strained up as soon as it formed. The waters would go clear and sterile, the barren ice would become truly barren.

Broken ice stretched across the sea beneath her. The helo traversed a wilderness of ocean where people were fragile intruders, lethally unfit to survive. This was no place for landbased humans. The world's poverty could be measured in this, that the seas here should be stripped of their harvest.

They followed another helo down to the *Siranui*. Three figures scuttled away from it and a crew rolled it into its docking bay.

"It's Uchida," Trent said. "He's back from the *Kasumi*." He brought the helo down on the X. Signy climbed out and followed Anna to a hatch, and looked up at the man who waited there.

"Hello, Alan," she said.

His skin was tanned and dried by the sun and the cold; he looked older, and thinner, than he had in Houston. He kept his face an expressionless mask that covered a slight degree of grief, perhaps. No, she was reading too much into his apparent concern. Alan, who had hardly known Jared, would want to get back to business as usual, and was here for reasons of his own that had nothing to do with a drowned medic.

"I heard you would be here," Alan said. "I asked to come back—to meet you."

"You found nothing," she said.

"Nothing at all."

Anna herded them down a passageway. "We will go to Kihara's cabin," she said. "You wanted to look through anything Jared might have left there."

"Come with me, Alan," Signy said, aware of him close behind her, hearing the small creaks and rustles of his padded clothing and hers. Alive, so alive.

Inside the small cabin, on the tightly made bunk, Jared's personal items were laid out in neat rows. Anna's work, perhaps. The array depressed her. Jared's shaving gear and pocket clutter seemed intimately personal and at the same time anonymous, an assortment of mass-produced artifacts that meant nothing. Signy grabbed Jared's skinthin and searched for storage chips. There were none. She tossed the skinthin back on the bunk and powered up the cabin screen, New Hampshire:

Paul smiled at her, his face clean-shaven and his hair still wet from a recent shampoo. His crab sigil blinked in a corner of the screen, pincers around a folded slip of paper.

"Hello," Paul said. "Hello, Anna, Signy. Alan Campbell? Nice to meet you."

"I needed to talk to you, hours ago," Signy said. "But not now. Just wait, okay?" She started to turn Paul off. "You'd better get on-line with Janine," Signy said. "She's getting busy about now." Signy blanked the screen.

"Who's that?" Alan asked. He stood near the doorway and tossed his gloves from one hand to the other in an uneasy rhythm.

"Paul Maury," Signy said. "My partner. Anna, could we look through sick bay as well? There may be recordings there, messages only I would know to look for."

"Yes," Anna said. "Although I think there isn't anything there that belonged to Jared." She led them to sick bay. Anna watched while Signy ran checks on the screens. Alan sat on a chair in the little waiting room alcove, seeming content to wait for her all day. No one, Signy thought, but me can do a damned thing around here. She accepted that sort of internal bitching as a sign of frustration, of guilt. I got Jared into this, she remembered. My fault, it's all my fault.

"There's nothing here," Signy said. "Nothing that we haven't downloaded at home already. Thank you, Anna. Could I go back to Kihara's cabin? I would like to talk to my people in the U.S., and it's already set up for that."

"Kihara will not return today," Anna said. "Yes, go there if you like. I need to stay in sick bay. But come back when you feel hungry. I'll take you to eat and then show you whatever I can."

The passageways carried the déjà vu of Jared's remembered journeys through them, their strange familiarity altered by the presence of Alan beside her. Signy needed allies. She needed a fleshtime associate, and Alan would do if she could recruit him. Paul would hate the idea. Just us, he always said. We're all we need. "Just us" wasn't going to work anymore. Paul would have to live with a new face or two. Signy opened Kihara's cabin door, ushered Alan in, and shut the door behind her.

"I think Jared is alive," Signy said. She could see the doubt on Alan's face, the presumption that he dealt with a grief-crazed fool.

"There's some sort of sabotage going on in this fleet, in this company. You're working for them; you could possibly be in as much danger as Jared."

"Can you explain why you think this?" Campbell asked.

"Not in five words or less. I want to find Jared. If he's alive, I don't have time to censor what I tell you. I don't have time to keep secrets. I have an offer; will you listen?"

Signy realized she was speaking as if she were onscreen in a bulletin board, empowered and anonymous, forgetting all the niceties of face-to-face communication. Still, she watched Alan Campbell's face for clues, and saw a glimmer of interest, a willingness to give her the benefit of, at least, doubt.

"Let's hear it." A tall man in a low room, he stood by the silent screen, touching nothing, a visitor in someone else's territory.

"You help me. We pay with access to all our files on Tanaka. Information shared with you as soon as we get it." Not enough, his face told her. "We'll sell Tanaka on your product, if you decide to ask for a contract to make subs for them. That's what you want to do, isn't it?"

"It's a small profit we're looking at," he said. "The market for submersibles is minuscule, compared to some of the boosters Gulf Coast makes. We're more after systems comparisons—the subs are good test systems for developing long-distance vehicles—but I've seen a lot of what I wanted to see here. Why should I stay?"

"Let me try to convince you. Please. Do you have a screen in your cabin?"

"Yeah."

"Let's get out of here, then." Signy motioned to the cabin screen and Alan moved aside. "I'll need to change a few things here—what's your access number?"

Alan told her. Signy transferred Edges' codes to his terminal. "There. Let's go. This cabin bothers me." Jared's absence seemed a palpable thing in the air. Chemical traces of him teased at Signy's hindbrain, unscented pheromones spoke directly to triggers below consciousness. Her responses were chemically inevitable, a cellular uneasiness, and she wanted to be somewhere else.

"What about this stuff?" Alan motioned to the clutter on the bed.

"Bring it," she said. "Just throw it into something. Jared can sort through it when I get him back."

Alan found a sack in the tiny bathroom and loaded up the gear, obedient, perhaps responsive to Signy's sudden surge of energy. Signy felt she could conquer the world, the ice, anything. Motion and tasks, they shaped a type of confidence; Signy realized in part that she was responding to the complex nuances of real-time experience. Yes, she had traveled these passageways with Jared; yes, they were different when experienced in her own flesh. Signy walked the distance to Alan's cabin at a quick-march, slammed herself down in the only chair, and brought up New Hampshire.

Paul answered her on the instant. He'd been listening throughout the sick-bay visit, he said, and he had heard her talk with Alan. He didn't look happy.

"We're hiring Alan Campbell," Signy said. "For assistance in locating Jared. That's if we can convince him we can pay what he wants."

"I am hesitant, Signy," Paul said.

"You know I'll need help here. Alan is a Done Thing. His employment by us is not a matter for argument. I need his help."

"I understand," Paul said.

Pilar checked in, in a corner window. She sat in lotus, busy with the multiple outputs of a synthesizer. Signy nodded in her direction. "You haven't heard this, Pilar. The ship that went down was a Tanaka trawler. Named *Oburu*. Question: Was Skylochori a crewman? Also, question: Is Janine available? We need to have Janine quiz Itano about this."

Janine sent a graphic, a large ear that sported a faux diamond earring.

[Janine] All ears. Can't talk, though.

Janine was working on good old Kazi, Signy figured. Or working with him.

"Hi, Janine. I'll tag a note on the *Oburu* for you, babe. Pick it up when you can," Signy said. Alan leaned toward the screen and braced an arm on the desk. Signy shifted out of his way as best she could. "Alan, just hang on, we'll fill you in as fast as we can. For starts, Paul, outline the Master Plan for Alan's waiting ears, okay?"

"I'm not sure I have it in a brief form."

"Don't give me that."

"Yes, Lioness. The Master Plan is to arrange an international moratorium on all fishing in Antarctic waters for a minimum of thirty years. Convince Tanaka they'll make money out of that scenario, and then sell it to the Antarctic Treaty Commission. While finding Jared, of course."

"How do you figure they get more money for no fish than they're getting for fish?" Alan asked.

"Nudge them to increase aquaculture in the temperate latitudes. That would fit in with what Tanaka's daughter wants. Yeah, Signy. I found her. But the moratorium will play hob with Itano's position," Paul said.

"Anything in it for Gulf Coast? Life-support systems, subs?" Signy asked.

"Work up some fish-herding subs for them, is an offhand possibility. . . ."

Signy could almost hear the little gears spinning in Paul's head. He might explore scenarios for Gulf Coast involvement in the Tanaka empire for twenty minutes, if she didn't stop him. "Paul, fill us in on Tanaka's mysterious daughter, okay? I have a strange feeling about her." Signy got her arms out of her parka and hung it over the back of her chair, staring at the screen while she twisted out of the bulky jacket.

Paul imaged up his crab persona. The crab settled a pair of large black-rimmed spectacles on its protruding eyestalks and opened its slip of paper with a skillful claw. "The name is San-Li Tanaka. Don't look to blackmail the old man with just knowing he's got no sons, only a daughter; her status as his only get is common knowledge among the sararimen. Tanaka seems to hate her. He holds out the carrot that the company goes to the most productive manager; San-Li is in competition with every exec in the company and may not make the grade. She handles the aquaculture farms."

"I think unscrambling her importance to us is for later," Pilar said. "It's time to get a program for Janine to sell old Kazi, here." Pilar punctuated her words with a chorus of voices that argued up and down a pentatonic scale.

[Janine] Old Kazi got all choked up over the crane sequence. Music did him in.

"Congrats to McKenna," Paul said.

"I'll tell him when he gets back. Jimmy's out shopping," Pilar said.

"Janine, here's how we sell our moratorium. Have Tanaka pressure the North Pacific fisheries to let the Tanaka fleet into U.S. waters, under paper transfers of ownership to U.S. canneries—Tanaka owns a few of them, anyway." Paul set up a coastal map of the Pacific Northwest on his side of the screen, starred with tiny shore-based factories that had legal access to the limited North Pacific catch. "That would give Tanaka some slack; they could let the pressure up on Antarctic waters until the stocks recover."

On Paul's map, small black-suited men erupted from the factory roofs and stalked to the left side of the screen, to stand under a paper parasol marked with the Tanaka logo. The parasol was held by a spiny fugu fish that sported a fat-lipped grin.

Pilar had left her synthesizer. She windowed the Seattle studio into a corner, a view that showed her frowning at the flatscreen. Pilar chewed at a purple marker that left stains like bruises at the corner of her lip. She reached down and worked at the Seattle inputs. Pilar's face disappeared, and Paul's little factories erupted in flames and drifted away in smudges of black smoke. Pilar added a voice-over. "Wouldn't the U.S. canneries hate that?" Pilar asked.

"Yes." Paul replaced Pilar's smoke with a view of hot-air balloons marked with Japanese, U.S., and E.C. flags. The balloons drifted over Europe, tossing down grinning silver fish equipped with tiny parachutes. "This outcome is equally possible," Paul said.

"U.S.–Euro cooperation with Japan would take one hell of a lot of work," Signy said.

A man's hand covered the map, the balloons. "You're being monitored," Jimmy said. "In case you didn't know."

"Oh," Paul said. "Yes, I see. Hmm, let me fix this a bit. Can't get too creative, not with Signy's stuff coming in from the *Siranui*'s lines."

"Hullo, Jimmy. How was shopping?" Pilar asked.

"I got ice cream," Jimmy said. "And fudge sauce."

Jimmy appeared behind Pilar in the corner screen, Jimmy's arms filled with bulging sacks of groceries.

"McKenna?" Signy asked. "Have you found Evergreen yet?"

"Jesus. You're on my case as much as Paul—I've looked everywhere. I told you guys that," Jimmy said.

"Try to find her here—on the *Siranui*," Signy said.

Jimmy put the grocery sacks down on the floor. "Oh, shit," he said. "The one place I didn't look. . . ."

The little screen in Alan's cabin went white and blank, Paul's overrides shielding the system, for what it was worth. The audios stayed up.

"You have an address for the *Siranui*, Jimmy," Signy said. "You used it to get us on the bridge."

"Give me some time, okay?" Jimmy pleaded.

Everyone fell silent, waiting. Alan leaned away from the screen. He settled on the bunk behind Signy and rested his elbows on his knees. Signy watched Alan watching the white, empty screen.

"Jimmy's looking for our saboteur," Signy said.

"Saboteur?" Alan asked. "What's going on here?"

"Someone glitched our system. We think it was a woman called Evergreen," Signy said. "I don't know how she fits into the business with Jared, if she does. But this one random scrambling sequence is all we have. . . ."

Alan raised his eyebrows with a skeptical look. "You guys always carry on like this? Fishes and fires and stuff?"

"Pretty much," Signy said. The semblance of normalcy made her happy. In the nonsense and chatter that had filled the little screen, Signy felt at home, safe, on familiar ground. One wacko family, except for the empty space that no one but Jared would ever fill.

Signy looked down at her wrist, at the dark pip that marked Jared's absence. Jared's light suddenly blinked.

NINETEEN

Signy punched in the codes to access Jared in a frenzy of frantic caution. Her hands trembled, afraid of the idiosyncrasies of an unfamiliar system. The keys beneath her fingers were dusty. Campbell, if he had pulled any data at all, hadn't accessed it here. Faint, blurred sensations came to Signy's awareness. The screen reversed fields and went to total black.

Signy entered:

—a world with no voice, no vision. Jared's muscular body signaled to her in patterns of singular and unmistakable familiarity. Signy knew his signature in the sensations of pressure on his shoulders and in the particular spacing of the bony prominences marching down his back, the stretch of his skinthin over his thighs. He lay on his back somewhere and he seemed to be without hands.

Signy felt a knot of anger burn in her belly, outrage and fear at the partial sensations of a mutilated body, and then realized, no. Jared is sending just with his suit, he's not wearing his gloves, his mike, or his lenses.

The patterns of pressure transmitted to her skinthin's sensors told her that Jared shifted his weight to his left side and curled up in a fetal position, stretched his arm to reach for—

Gone.

Jared heard something nearby, some rhythmic sound that came from his right, muffled thuds in a walking cadence. Padded boots on thick snow? He tried shifting his weight and couldn't get his arms free of what felt like a soft straitjacket.

Irritation rose through what had been a good sleep, a deep sleep. He hated mummy bags. The damned things were well named.

Jared flexed his hands and found them wrapped in layers of soft wadding. They hurt terribly and distantly and he realized he'd been drugged, that his disinterest in the pain must be a result of some opiate or other.

His hands were frostbitten, that's what was wrong. Frostbite was so difficult to treat. He hated frostbite. He moved his clumsy, clumsy hands and found the battery pack, but he couldn't remember if he was recording. He pushed at the switches and wondered why they were made so damned small.

Signy would worry if he didn't talk to her soon. Soft Signy, she was so soft for a thin girl. She made it so hard for him to talk sometimes. Jared loved her. Love, that was a hard word to say to Signy. Love. Jared could see, so clearly, the way Signy's eyebrows arched, so that she always looked surprised; he could see the fine high lines of her cheekbones and the seashell curve of her ears. He loved Signy's ears. He wanted to tell her that, soon.

A continuous line of pressure circled Jared's eyes and traced the ridge of his frontal bone. He wore goggles, he realized; not his camera headband. The goggles were tinted for snow. Through their lenses Jared saw a series of curved arches above him and beyond that a painfully bright sky, transparent blue.

Jared closed his eyes against the glare. There were some positive things about a thick down mummy bag, warm and soft. Someone tried to help him with the battery switch. Nice of them. He thought about saying thanks.

Someone had cold hands and Jared wasn't sure if they had turned his skinthin on or off.

He slept again.

Silence, while they took a collective breath, while fingers flew over keyboards linked across three continents. Gone, couldn't reach Jared again; no combination seemed to work.

Campbell's cabin mikes erupted in babble; Janine, Paul, Pilar, all their voices tangled in feedback loops. Paul muttered repetitive curses, as if he were praying, and pounded his fist on something hollow. Pilar argued with Jimmy, her voice as shrill as razor wire in a wind. "What the hell do you mean you can't get a location from that signal?" Pilar yelled.

"I'll need more than one burst. He's wearing a battery-pack transmitter, and if he's got a GPS monitor, he didn't turn it on." Jimmy strobed through the Seattle screens, hunting God knew what, flashing through menus and accesses like a demented demon with a TV remote tuned to Fast Forward.

"I should have said something. I should have told him we picked up his signal," Signy said. But Jared couldn't have heard her without a live speaker on him somewhere, and surely whoever had grabbed him would have seen an ear speaker on him, and removed it.

"What's going on?" Alan asked.

"Jared," Signy said. No visuals of Jared had appeared on the screens. The group's sudden flurry of activity would have been completely opaque to a watcher. "We got a signal from him. Now it's gone again."

"You're sure it's him?" Alan asked.

"We know," Signy said. Those were not the random motions of a suit on a dead man. No one else moved like Jared, no one in the whole world. The certainty of Jared's life overwhelmed her, real, immediate. She felt a sudden wave of nausea; beads of chill sweat popped out on her forehead. Signy leaned forward in her chair and found a wastebasket under the desk. She hooked it close with the toe of her boot and threw up breakfast.

Behind her, she heard Alan scramble off the bunk. Signy held tight to the plastic-lined can. She never got seasick. She didn't feel seasick now. The sound of running water came from the tiny bathroom, and Alan's hurried footsteps.

Signy reached for the washcloth Alan handed her, ran the welcome wet cloth across her neck and her mouth, and smiled up at him.

"What the hell?" Alan asked. His face showed the dismay of a man confounded by a pregnant wife. Well, Signy remembered, he has a daughter. This can't look that strange to him.

"I feel better," Signy said. "I'm fine. You see, I didn't really think Jared was alive." She reached down to tie the plastic bag closed. "Where can I dump this?" she asked.

"Just sit there, okay? I've got it." Alan grabbed the can from her hands and went out the door.

He was a good man, Alan. Signy shouldn't let him clean up her messes, but she tried to stand and felt a little wobbly. Where was Jared? Where? Signy clung to the edge of the desk and took a deep breath or two. She searched out access to the bridge and sorted through the ship's operations, coded, safe, not easily accessible to manipulation, just displays. Sidetracked, damn it, Signy found herself wading through a list of readings on fuel feeds and diesel mixtures. She got out of that screen and found a list of coordinates in degrees, that ticked on and off in measured rhythm.

"Thanks," Paul's voice said.

Paul brought up a map of the Southern Ocean. A tiny ship traveled a blue, blue sea, trailed by the segmented lines of its recent path across the water. Its coordinates glowed in a corner of the screen. Paul used the same graphics Signy had seen on the map behind Snead's head at McMurdo—Huh?

"Paul?" Signy asked. She would ask if he'd been eavesdropping, silent when she needed his voice, silent when she needed his support last night.

"Got him!" Jimmy yipped. "Got him, within a hundred miles."

Jimmy graphed a blurry purple circle on Paul's map, centered over the *Siranui*'s trail in the water. The tiny ship pushed at the margin of the circle, as if it were a stylized sperm trying to exit an ovum in an odd reverse fertilization.

"How?" Paul asked. "What did you . . ."

"Jared's signal came in to the *Siranui* and got boosted from there. That puts some limits on him. Now that we've got the location on the ship, he's in here somewhere." Jimmy circled his circle with an invisible stylus that left a trail of rapidly fading red.

"Good work," Paul said.

The curved arches above Jared angled sharply and then tapered as they neared the ground. They were the craziest tent supports he'd ever seen. He stared at the one directly overhead.

"*It's a rib, specifically the sixth rib, Jared. Observe the rough line, there at the angle where the rib curves forward, for the attachment of the iliocostalis muscle.*" Professor Lachman's thick German accent cut through the music the wind made, playing through the giant harp of bone.

I beg your pardon, Professor. I do not know if whales possess an iliocostalis muscle. That is whale bone, Herr Professor. No, not baleen, a whale's bones. I am lying flat on my back in the vanished belly of a vanished leviathan in the worst virtual I've ever even thought about. The symbolism sucks. And by the way, people who have been dead for twenty years don't give anatomy lectures. You're a hallucination. You can't fool me.

> "*The ribs and terrors in the whale,*
> *Arched over me a dismal gloom.*"

That's Melville but there ain't no gloom around here. Arched over me, arched over me—

Signy heard the door open. Alan came back in and sat down. On the screen, the *Siranui* was out of the circle Jimmy had drawn, heading east.

"Now what, Paul?" Signy asked. "Jared's stationary, on land somewhere, or he's on this damned ship, within reach. Which is it?"

Paul expanded the blue map where the *Siranui* traveled. "There are islands near where you were. Islets, rather. They are quite small."

"I think Jared's on the *Siranui*. Occam's razor," Pilar said.

"Okay." Signy set Alan's cabin console to take her suit's transmissions and forward them to Paul. She spun the swivel chair and looked up at Alan Campbell. "Okay, I've got a partner who's alive and I've got a shipload of people who are telling me he's dead. I don't know whether it's a deliberate attempt to ignore what's happened to him or whether it's inertia. I don't even know whether Jared was the man who was supposed to fall off that boat, or whether it was you. Do you have any thoughts about that?"

Alan wrapped his hands around one of his knees and gave her a level, appraising look. "I can't think of any competing bidders for what I was looking at down here. So no, I don't think they were after me."

"But you're in this equation, if whoever took Jared knows you were with him."

"You just may have something there," Alan said. "The way you're putting this together makes it sound like my hide and yours may be on the market fairly cheap. But I don't know if I can buy your scenario without some—verification."

"I don't know how to get that for you," Signy said.

Alan reached behind him and fumbled with his parka. It looked like he was getting ready to leave. Signy had convinced Alan that he was dealing with a bunch of warped screenfreaks, she figured, and part of her didn't blame him for backing out.

Alan unfolded himself from the bunk and stretched. "It seems to me we should go find your man. Then we can ask him if your story fits the facts."

Just like that. Alan seemed to heading somewhere. Signy stood up, wondering what he had in mind.

"Let's go talk to the captain," Alan said.

"What if he's not any help?" Signy asked.

"Than we'll know more than we do now." Alan waited while Signy got her parka.

[Paul] Leave screen on.

Signy did.

The narrow, empty corridor looked familiar and functional, painted metal surfaces and mazes of pipes that Signy had seen through Jared's eyes. But Jared's view of the place hadn't told Signy that she would feel she stood inside the arteries and organs of some huge beast. She felt like a Jonah.

"Oh, shit," Signy said. "I don't know my etiquette. Do we just march in? Do we request the captain's permission to talk to him, or what? There are rules about all this, aren't there?"

Alan shoved his hands in the front pockets of the bulky tan parka he wore. "We'll ask the bridge for a small piece of the captain's time. He'll talk to us or he won't. That's all the etiquette there is, as long as you keep in mind that he's God, more or less. The other thing is, if somebody's doing something, don't get in their way. If he doesn't want to see us right now, well, Anna said to come back to sick bay. Maybe we'll do that."

Walking along in the cadence of Alan's steps, her three to his two, and Signy could tell Alan was slowing down for her. She found she was watching her feet. Paul and Pilar watched in real time. Signy remembered she should be eyes for them, not just stare at the floor. Jared was the cameraman; he always managed to present a total setting, always found the interesting details to highlight. There just didn't seem to be much interesting detail in the flat surfaces around here. "This is going to call for some doublespeak," Signy said. "What's the polite way to say 'I think you've got a kidnapped man on your ship and I want to look for him'?"

"Is that what you think?" Alan asked.

"Yeah."

"I guess it sounds better than saying, 'I think you kidnapped my old man and you've got him tied up somewhere.'"

Alan seemed to be looking for something at the far end of the passageway. Signy caught his eye and smiled. "I'll try to keep it civil. I guess."

"It's fine with me if you don't," Alan said. "His name's Mineta, by the way. Jiro Mineta."

Easy, lanky Alan. Signy felt, well *championed*, walking beside him. Granted, he was a little rawboned for a knight in shining armor, and Signy hated her archaic response to him—but she felt secure, with Alan at her side. In danger, seek a protector. The message was an old one, and danger cut through to the primitive, the biologic response. Signy felt like a threatened protohominid seeking out a dominant male.

Alan needed a haircut. His silky auburn hair was beginning to form curls behind his ears. It was not the sort of detail that would have interested Jared.

All sound had vanished. The world seemed very lonely. Shadows of the sheltering ribs above him moved across dirty white snow and shaded Jared's face and then did not shade his face. He licked his lips and tasted salt. His tongue explored cracks and dry textures that felt as numb and distant as if he'd been injected with lidocaine. That meant frostbite, but superimposed on the whale's ribs he remembered the intricacy of the rich red capillary networks of a human face and he knew his face would heal.

Sunburn on top of frostbite? Kihara liked to do back-woods plastic work, maybe Kihara would get a chance to play with this mess of a face. . . .

The watch had changed on the bridge. The crew's faces were all strange; no one Signy had seen from her cameras in Taos worked at the screens. Alan asked to see Captain Mineta, and one of the officers nodded and spoke rapidly into a phone.

Outside the windows, bright sky arched over brighter water and the sun danced on tiny ripples. An island appeared to starboard. It seemed to float in the sea, a mass of ice and rock. Was Jared there? Signy clenched her fists inside her pockets.

"Miss Thomas? Mr. Campbell?" Signy turned to the ladder behind her. The Japanese man who stood there had a lot of gold on his black coverall. "You will follow me, please." Captain Mineta was about forty, Signy figured. Politely stated, Mineta was portly. He was not smiling.

"Thank you, Captain," Alan said.

The room they entered was paneled in teak and furnished

in a style that Signy thought of as office anonymous, chairs upholstered in easily cleaned synthetic leather, a desk of dull finished metal. The captain motioned for them to sit.

"Welcome to the *Siranui*," Captain Mineta said. He spoke with a growling, guttural accent. "How may we assist you?" His eyes flicked to Signy and then back to Alan. Signy accepted his assumption that Alan was in charge and held her tongue. Brusque words, no courtesies, his behavior was rudely abrupt for any Asian culture. The accent was Scandinavian, she realized suddenly, and she remembered that many fishing ships carried Norwegian officers. Maybe Mineta had learned his English that way.

"Miss Thomas has just received a transmission from Dr. Balchen," Alan said. "He's alive. We would like to ask your help in locating him."

The captain's face was a stone mask. He settled back in his chair and tented his fingers together across his ample lap. His mouth tightened somewhat. "Dr. Balchen fell into waters that are known to kill in minutes. I find this news difficult to believe."

"There was a boat in the water," Signy said. "Someone pulled him out. We sent the footage; surely you've seen it."

The captain took his time before he answered.

"I have seen the film," the captain said. "I saw dark water. Somewhat blurred, as I recall. I appreciate your grief, Miss Thomas, but I fear your loss has caused you to overinterpret shadows seen by a dying man. It is our opinion, mine and my officers, that there was nothing in those waters."

Nothing? And the *Oburu*'s sinking hadn't occurred, either.

"But he was on-line, transmitting, not five minutes ago!"

"This is truly astonishing. I am happy for you. What message did he give you?" the captain asked.

"He didn't say anything. Just body motion—" Which would make no sense to anyone who didn't know Jared, in fact. Muscular sensations, isolated in a black space; that was the only proof Signy had of Jared's life. A mirage, a shared delusion, to an outsider.

And Captain Mineta must have monitored their conversations. Not an underling, the captain himself, or he could not have been so quick with his question about messages. Signy wondered if Paul had caught the inference. "Captain, Jared Balchen is alive and he is within a hundred miles of our current location."

The man raised a quizzical eyebrow at Alan. He had not made eye contact with Signy and seemed determined to respond only to the male half of this duet.

"We are in the Southern Ocean. It is uninhabited," the captain said. "I do not see how this could be."

"Perhaps he's here on the ship," Alan said.

"No one but you and Miss Thomas has arrived on this ship since the unfortunate incident with Dr. Balchen."

Wups, Signy thought, he just told us not to tell him what happens on *his* ship. Now what? Back off? There isn't time to do that. "Then perhaps he's on a nearby island," Signy said. "But I tell you again, he is alive."

Captain Mineta sat as still as a contemplative Buddha. Okay, challenge him, then.

"Edges is trying to fulfill a contract for Tanaka," Signy said. "In the process of researching our work, we study all information that comes our way, however peripheral it may seem at the time. We are aware of the loss of the *Oburu* and we fear that Jared's disappearance may be related in some way."

Signy tried to interpret the expression on Mineta's face, but she could see only a small tightening of the muscles around his eyes.

"I can see no connection," the captain said. "The *Ob-uru* sank. Investigations are under way in regards to that sinking. Nothing has been found. Nothing. No, no, there is no connection at all." Mineta lifted his hands from his lap and fluttered his fingers as if he had picked up something hot. "You are being very—speculative, Miss Thomas." He stood up, and Alan rose as well.

Mihalis Skylochori's body rested in the freezer, unless someone had moved it by now. The dead sailor was not connected to this, either.

"We will discuss this at some other time," the captain said.

Signy got up from her chair, defeated.

"Please continue with your work for Tanaka," Mineta said. "Good afternoon, Miss Thomas. Mr. Campbell."

He ushered them out the door and closed it behind them. Then he vanished up the ladder toward the bridge, dismissing them completely.

Paul and Pilar both spoke at once, creating a confusion of sound in the speaker behind Signy's ear.

"Shit," Signy said.

"Yeah." Alan saw her fingers reach up to tap at the speaker behind her ear, and he stopped talking.

"Signy, get out of there," Paul's voice said. **"Get off that ship. Come home."**

"You'll never get anywhere with him," Pilar said. **"You're just a nosy little tourist, is how I read him. Signy, unless you get some more status from somewhere, and in a hurry, Mineta's not going to listen to anything you say."**

"I gathered that," Signy said. Mineta knew something about the disappearances; Signy could *feel* that he did. He couldn't be happy about the lost trawler, no matter how it had happened to sink. "Pilar, did Janine get the files on the *Oburu*?"

"You didn't leave any," Pilar said.

"Yikes!"

"So I told Janine what I knew. I told her," Pilar said. "She'll interrogate our Mr. Itano about it."

Alan seemed to be headed for sick bay. Signy kept up with him. "Paul, I don't care if Mineta wants me out of here. I can't leave now," Signy said. "Even if I wanted to. And I don't."

"You're in danger." Paul sounded scared.

"So is Jared. Now, don't bother me for a little while, okay?"

"Right," Pilar said. Paul didn't say anything at all.

From the holds, Signy heard rumbling and mechanical growls, the *Siranui* chewing up more tons of fish. The passageways were deserted. People worked hard here; they had jobs and they did them. Signy Thomas was extraneous, in the way, a nosy intruder. The captain wasn't going to be any help.

A man gone; so sorry, on with business. Mineta's reaction was like Kazi Itano's, like Kazi's simple wonder that Edges didn't just take the hazard pay for accidental death and go about their business. People died all the time, so sorry, but it's time for the next shift now.

If you didn't love someone deeply, that was the only attitude that made sense. If you did? You struggled to keep them well, fought for them when they couldn't fight for themselves—

I love Jared, Signy thought. I'll find him.

Signy followed Alan into sick bay and shut the door behind her with a sense of relief. The tiny waiting room felt like a refuge. Anna looked up from her desk console, and she seemed not at all surprised to see them.

"Anna, we've been in contact with Jared. He's alive," Signy said.

"Your friend Pilar told me. He is nearby, she said that, too."

"Where?" Signy asked her. "Where might he be, Anna?"

"I don't know," Anna said. She shook her head from side to side, and she looked upset.

Signy slumped into one of the waiting room chairs. Alan folded himself into the chair beside her.

"I don't think he's on the ship," Anna said. "I would like to help you find him, Signy, but there is nothing I can think of except to search the nearby islands. If the captain permits. The captain called." Anna stopped, apparently distracted in mid-thought by something or other.

"Go on," Signy said.

"He said to tell you that the XO is personally inspecting every closet and drawer in the ship."

"Please give him my thanks," Signy said.

"He also said Mr. Itano in Lisbon sends his regards."

Itano had been on Mineta's case already, it seemed. That might explain some of the reaction Signy had gotten. Anna seemed to want to say more. Her expression was a puzzle. Guilt? Hope? Signy waited; for something, something complicated, seemed to be on Anna's mind.

"I know your plans for the treaty," Anna said. "Pilar told me while you were with the captain. Do you really plan to ask the Treaty Commission to shut down the fishing?"

Pilar had brought Anna into the calculations, that quickly? On what thread of trust? On Jared's response to her? No matter. "We seem to be coming to that," Signy said.

"You must try," Anna said. "You *must*. The pressures on life here are near the breaking point. I thought—we thought, many of the researchers who work here—that we were being ignored."

"Ignored?" Signy asked.

"We find so many confusing things. . . . There seems to be a pressure toward neoteny in some of the bony fishes. There are unusual shifts in the percentages of zooplankton varieties. We do not know if they are part of a long-term cycle because we do not have information that goes back more than a century, and a century can be only a short time in an ocean's system of balance. Some researchers think the populations are overstressed and on the brink of collapse. Others think the current harvests are tolerable. Those researchers seem to get more funding," Anna said.

"What are you trying to say?"

"That the sea dies around us and perhaps she cannot be healed."

Anna spoke with the conviction of grief and certain knowledge. For her, there was no uncertainty. The sea was dying. "I fear for Jared," Anna said. "I fear for you. You will make people angry; you will take away their jobs, their food, if you chase away the boats. It might not help. But I hope you can do it."

Jared and Anna had talked about the sea, now and again. Jared had envied Anna because Anna dived beneath the ice, and knew the strange world beneath it. "Did Jared know your fears about the harvesting?" Signy asked.

"I didn't tell him. No. I wish I had. Now that I know what you want to do."

"And Jared's been kidnapped because we *considered* shutting down the fishing here? Anna, we were just *thinking* about that." Thinking, speaking, together. Together, with no listeners except Jimmy's mysterious—

"Evergreen," Paul said. **"Maybe you're looking at her."**

Not Anna. Signy would have bet her life on it. There was such hope in Anna's face.

"Something's happening on the bridge," Pilar said. **"Signy, get to a screen. You'd better watch this."**

"Anna, I need the console, okay?" Signy started for it. Anna shifted out of her way as she came charging around the desk. Signy slid into the still-warm chair Anna had just vacated. The keys gave her access to the bridge speakers; a rattle of Japanese, the captain, she thought, and a woman's staccato speech.

"Pardon me," Signy muttered in Anna's direction.

Whiteline's translation, scrolling past in its implacable block letters, brought both Anna and Alan to peer over her shoulder.

THE CAPTAIN SAYS HE HAS ORDERS TO SEND MISS THOMAS ON A HELO TOUR OF NEARBY IS-LANDS.

Visuals from the bridge popped up behind the script. Captain Mineta paced back and forth, speaking to a man who stood at parade rest, his back to the bridge cameras.

CAPTAIN PISSED. WANTS ALL FOREIGNERS GONE.

Which was how Whiteline interpreted the burst of words.

"He is telling the XO that such a trip will waste fuel, but will get this gaijin witch out of his hair." Anna paused for a moment, then continued. "He wishes Itano would not instruct him on how to deal with the foreign woman. Too much interference in the harvester's schedules—he is still unhappy about the breach of usual procedures regarding Skylochori—and what?—"

PROTOCOL ERRORS WITH? SKYLO? SOME-THING

"—he is unhappy with the stories Kobe has told the families of the men who died on the *Oburu*."

SOMETHING ABOUT <u>OBURU MARU</u>

Captain Mineta left the bridge.

"I'm to be sent on a wild-goose chase, huh?" Signy asked.

"What?" Anna frowned. "Oh. Yes, it seems so. Signy, I must call Trent. I think he would wish to be our pilot."

Our pilot, was it? Signy smiled and spoke to the screen. "Get out of our way, guys. Anna needs the board."

"Damn, where's Janine?" Pilar said. Pilar's face appeared, and then the screen went blank again. Signy pushed back from the console and left the keyboard to Anna.

"I'll go with you, if Kihara gets back in time," Anna

said. "Wups, there's a message from the Old Man. The captain. I think we aren't here for a few moments. . . . I want to talk to Trent before we answer the bridge." Anna picked up a portable phone and spoke rapidly in Japanese to someone *not* onscreen.

Alan stood up and rubbed the small of his back with both hands. "I'm coming along on this tour of yours," Alan said.

"What if the bridge objects?" Signy asked.

"Then I'll be a stowaway," Alan said. "I've always wanted to be a stowaway, come to think of it."

"Hello, Trent. Could you meet us on the deck in about—fifteen minutes?" Anna waited. "Thanks."

MESSAGE WAITING, a window on the screen insisted. Anna looked up at Signy. "What do we tell Captain Mineta?"

"Tell him fine, sure, whatever he suggests," Signy said. Signy wondered if she could bribe Trent to take her where she wanted to go, once she knew where that was. She wondered what arrangements had been made for her. Would she "fall" overboard, or "fall" out of a helicopter, or would she simply end up with Jared, somewhere, somehow, both of them reported missing and a fiction developed from their records, a virtual that showed them alive and well in Paris, or some damned thing?

Anna nodded and sent an acknowledgment to the bridge.

On Signy's wrist, Paul's monitoring light glowed; a watcher, a listener, a source of security that had not protected Jared. Signy stood up and reached for Alan's hand. He accepted the contact. Signy planned never, never, to be out of Alan's reach while she remained in Antarctica.

"Are you okay?" Alan asked.

"Yes," Signy said. "I suppose I am."

"You're scheduled for a tour at 0800," Anna said. "I can go with you; Kihara's back in an hour or so. Let's go talk to Trent."

Signy and Allan followed her, up twisting metal stairways, empty and cold and ringing with memories of echoes, as if a gong had been struck in the dark spaces of the ship just moments before. Signy listened, hard, but she heard only her own breath and the soft sounds of their padded boots as they climbed. Was it day or night here? Her watch said late evening, but the bridge had carried the feel of a busy midday. Signy was not tired, not sleepy, not hungry. She felt she would never need to sleep again, not while Jared waited, somewhere. Her next breath was a deep, surprising yawn.

A sign marked the exit to the flight deck. Alan set his gloved hands on the wheel.

"No," Anna said, behind them on the stairs. "Go up."

Anna's face carried a look of grim concentration. Not from the effort of climbing stairs, surely. From something else, some internal effort. They climbed past three more landings, until the ladders ended at a small landing and a closed hatch. Anna undogged it, and they stepped out into a bitter cold that made Signy gasp. Beneath her feet, a square of open metal mesh led to ladders that zigzagged down toward the *Siranui*'s decks. They stood just above the bridge; a curve of black glass panes fanned out from the white roof directly beneath them. Three more steps led up to the base of a rotating dish, its bowl slick with ice. Steam rose from the housings at its base, from heated gears protected from the cold.

The *Siranui* dipped down into a swell and rose again, a huge thing in an immense world of leaden sky and black slick water. The light seemed to be that of evening, and Signy could not see the sun. The cold brought tears that she blinked away. Anna was busy pulling up the hood of her parka, and Signy tugged her hand away from Alan, got her own hood snugged tight, and then grabbed Alan's hand again.

The hatch opened. Trent joined them. "Hello, Signy Thomas. Hello, Alan. What are we doing?" he asked Anna.

"See if you can jockey the schedule so you get to pilot us around tomorrow," Anna said.

"Sure. Is that all you wanted?"

"I wanted to warn you that being around Miss Thomas could be dangerous," Anna said. "But I'd like you to take us around, if you would."

"You got my ass up here in the cold to ask me to fly?" Trent asked. "Anna, I *like* to fly."

"I also wanted to tell you, while your buddies aren't listening, that that the orders on hushing up the *Oburu*'s sinking came from Tanaka headquarters in Kobe."

"Did they, now?" Trent asked.

"And I wanted to tell you that Dr. Balchen is alive. Within a hundred miles of the ship, we believe."

"Son of a bitch," Trent said. "You think he's on the *Kasumi*?"

"Is it in the area?" Anna asked.

"I don't know. I'll find out," Trent said.

"It isn't," Paul said.

"Be discreet, Trent," Anna pleaded.

"I'm the epitome of discretion," Trent said. "Can we go get warm now?"

"Not yet," Anna said. She stared at the horizon, waiting for something.

Signy turned, thinking to look behind her at the great length of the ship. A whale's back, massive and glistening, cut the water about a hundred yards away. "Oh," Signy whispered.

It rose, silent and wonderful, and she heard the steam-engine hiss of its breath. The whale sank from sight.

"He is a humpback," Anna said. "He'll be up again. Wait." Anna pulled a pair of field glasses from her parka and handed them to Signy. Signy scanned the water, wondering, Where? Where will you be?

"There." Anna announced the whale's rising in a calm flat voice. Signy turned to where Anna pointed, knowing her camera headband would get an unmagnified view of what she saw through the field glasses in intimate detail.

The whale surfaced closer this time. He rolled in the water, giving them the measure of his length, the lighter colors of his belly before he puffed out his breath and sank again. Anna closed her eyes and lifted her face toward the gunmetal sky. "Three times," Anna said. "He will blow three times for us."

The whale appeared again, close enough to the ship that he could have nudged it. Defying his massive bulk and the water's pull, he lifted his impossible head from the water with the sound of a tidal wave.

As if he moved in slow motion, he gave them the view of his bulk, slowly, inch by inch; of his rheumy, dull eye, of his fissured, scarred hide, of half-healed and fresh ulcers, their red craters sticky with yellow mucus and longer than a man's thigh, running down his sides. He sank, and sank, and his dark shadow in the water disappeared.

A scent of rotting sewage rose in the air, a whiff of putrefaction and sickening decay. A sudden breeze took it away, and Signy sneezed and then breathed in clean, icy sea air, pulled it in deep and fast.

The humans waited while the ship moved up and over a huge swell, up and over another one. Anna stepped back from the rail, and the watchers accepted that the whale was truly gone.

"I've never seen one that big," Trent said, "and I've scouted a lot of whales."

"He is a visitor," Anna said, her voice certain, knowing. "An old man. Not one that we've counted before." She hugged herself tightly with her arms and looked down at the icy deck. "I think."

Anna *knew*. She knew.

"He is dying," Signy said.

Anna hunched up her shoulders and turned away from the sea. They went below.

TWENTY

Pilar marveled at the mixture of urgency and fear, apprehension and awakening, that permeated Signy's transmissions from Antarctica. Signy seemed to balance on some precarious edge of intuition, in tides of sorrow and grief, mixed with guilt when the sights around her distracted her from her goal of finding her lost lover. Signy anticipated loss with every motion.

Distilled, what would this clash of sensations bring to—a kinetic work, say? A geometry of planes of colored light for an interactor to walk through, bathe in, push against? Pilar saw a palette for a room-sized space of primary stained-glass colors, transparent, razored, angular, and brittle. Her fingers itched to begin it.

Her own emotions were less planar, more muted. What did she feel for Jared? What had she *ever* felt for him? Joy at the way his body worked, delight in the clean water-mammal lines of him; Jared the sleek. Astonishment at his naive pleasures, the Jared who would, if undisturbed, spend half an hour gazing at the intricacies of a stalk of yucca in blossom, spend half a night entranced by the patterns of flames in a well-made fire. Pilar wanted to look at him again, to trace out the textures and curves of his face—Pilar had no time for that, not now.

Jimmy worked at Janine's Seattle console, tracing out webs of probability from the transmissions to and from the *Siranui*, to and from McMurdo base. In the ordinary, workaday words that came floating to him, he sought traces of a man he didn't know. Jimmy spun his way through the nets with the frenzy of a dancing Shiva. He dances, Pilar realized, to win me. How sad.

Jimmy found his way into McMurdo's recordings of air approaches and departures, a litany of laconic comments. "Zulu Tango turning final to McMurdo," Pilar heard, and then "Roger. Cleared to land."

Jimmy's noodling around *cost;* each ticking minute charged, eventually, to Edges. Yet to be paid was Whiteline, whose fees could not be deducted on anyone's standard IRS form; yet to be totaled were the data reductions for the upcoming talks in Lisbon, the cost of Signy's tickets to McMurdo; all the busy little debits climbing, climbing. For finances, Paul was the designated worrier, but somehow, Pilar couldn't quit thinking about the bottom lines on the last statements she'd seen.

Jimmy winced at something a pilot said, far south of here and peripherally, if at all, connected to finding Jared or getting Tanaka's contract finished, paid, and banked.

"Supposed to be English," Jimmy muttered.

"Say again?" Pilar asked, but Jimmy hadn't heard her. He stayed lost in the screen over Janine's console.

Janine's console? Janine wouldn't recognize it as the one she left, and Pilar forthwith stored a macro of the way it looked last week into the Seattle outputs, to protect Janine from a sure sense of territorial violation. Jimmy had invaded, not just Janine's space, but Pilar's. Jimmy artifacts lay in rows on Janine's desk, on a bookshelf he'd confiscated to hold various Important Things. He wasn't at all messy. He just occupied a lot of volume, and Pilar itched to randomize the room back into something she could find comfortable. But she didn't.

She was thinking about anything but Jared.

"Pilar Videla, you are not dealing with the fact that Jared is alive," she said aloud. "Why is that?" Her musing gave her no answers that she wanted to hear.

Pilar turned back to her console and found Janine on-line in real time. Pilar slipped her goggles over her eyes: Portugal.

—drifting mists swirled above wet sand. A close-up of expensive black poplin, the shoulder of Kazi's raincoat. In the background; a view of a harbor, where fishing boats painted in primary colors were pulled on shore for the night.

"You convinced him. You convinced the Old Man himself. If the ban goes through, we will transfer our energies to aquaculture, and take the loss on the wild fishery," Kazi said.

"I was scared," Janine said. "I was afraid Mr. Tanaka would hang up."

"Well, he didn't." Kazi frowned at Janine. "You've caused a lot of changes, my little engineer. This will cause an upheaval in the company. Many jobs will change. It helped that you coached me to suggest transferring some of the ships to the North Pacific fisheries. The factories there will be happy to have the best of the southern ships."

"It was too easy. He's a formidable man, your Yoshiro Tanaka. Why did he go for it?" Janine asked.

"I will second-guess my company's president," Kazi said. "He thinks we will not change the Treaty Commission's position. We will gain favorable publicity for taking the ultimate conservation stance, and we will keep on fishing."

That's how Pilar figured it. In Seattle, she leaned back in her chair and crossed her arms over her chest. Janine's wet outdoor walk looked cold, and Pilar felt chilled.

"I think we will have little difficulty with the nations that have fishing fleets in other waters. They will applaud us, because their profits will be protected. The Africans will be difficult," Kazi said.

"And Pakistan," Janine said, "and Japan, and the Koreas, and the European block, and—"

"You sound as if you must approach each of these problems by yourself," Kazi said. "We have a knowledgeable staff, Janine. They are building dossiers on the representatives, tonight. Based on Mr. Maury's specifications, which we find . . . intriguing."

"Mr. Maury's specifications? Oh, how male," Pilar grumbled for the benefit of Janine's ear speaker.

Edges' dossiers were not résumés, they were models that predicted the mutability of a psyche. Put another way, Edges knew how to find buttons in people that a knowledgeable manipulator could push. What a negotiator got was a short list of quick-and-dirty suggestions. The suggestions came from the jungle-gym structure that Edges filled with all sorts of facts. The lattice was Paul's work, yes, and also it was a synthesis of Signy's knowledge of neurophysiology, Janine's working models of gates and critical pressures in systems, and Jared's feel for the reactions of an organism under stress.

"No extra charge," Janine murmured.

"I'm sorry?" Kazi asked.

"We're glad you find the dossiers useful. We try to give full value," Janine said. "But I think you know that."

They stopped at an overlook, and Janine leaned her forearms on a marble railing. She looked down at the bobbing lights in the harbor, at the colored stains they left on the smooth water.

"Tell me about the *Oburu*," Janine said.

"That's blunt enough," Pilar whispered.

"Pardon me?" Kazi asked. He gripped the rail and stared straight out at the harbor.

"The *Oburu*. A trawler that went down somewhere in the Southern Ocean. Part of your fleet."

Kazi hesitated. "It . . . sank."

"Yes, so we hear. Was Mihalis Skylochori listed as a crew member? We didn't find his name anywhere," Janine said.

Pilar heard a rustle of fabric, Kazuyuki's raincoat moving over his shoulders as he straightened his posture.

"No."

"I see," Janine said. "I asked because Edges works by collecting disparate bits of information and connecting them to other bits in unexpected ways. The game is chaotic and often unproductive, but sometimes it gets us what we need. I am collecting information for your company, Kazi. For *you*. Help me."

"I can't help you with the *Oburu*. I have told you all that I know."

"Predict for me. What will happen to *you* if there is no fishing?"

"I direct the activities of the Fishery and the Aquaculture division," Kazi said. "If there is no fishing, I will direct the Aquaculture division."

"Whose current head is San-Li Tanaka? Will she battle you to keep her position?"

"Your information is not current," Kazi said. "San-Li was transferred to the fishery two weeks ago."

"Was she?"

"Hoo-boy," Pilar said.

"Yes. Yoshiro Tanaka himself asked her to transfer. He felt it was time for her to gain experience on a working harvester."

Pilar spun in her chair. Jimmy had begun to hum the tune from "Shelter," on pitch but out of rhythm. "Jimmy, get your ass over here," Pilar said.

He stopped humming and got up from his chair without taking his eyes from his screen. "What is it?"

"San-Li Tanaka is with the fleet."

Jimmy blinked and got to Pilar's screen, fast, leaning over her shoulder.

A foghorn sounded in the Portuguese night, sad and mournful above an insect background noise that Pilar identified, for the first time, as a constant hum of traffic.

"San-Li Tanaka was sent to the *Siranui?*" Janine asked.

"Yes," Itano said.

"Two weeks ago," Pilar said. **"Just after the *Oburu* sank."**

"Thank you," Janine said to Kazi. She reached up and kissed his cheek.

"For telling you where San-Li is?" Kazi sounded puzzled.

"Yes. I would like to meet her sometime," Janine said.

"Why?" Kazi asked.

"To ask her why she sank the *Oburu*," Pilar muttered.

Janine tucked her arm into the crook of Kazi's elbow. They turned away from the harbor and walked back toward the hotel's walled courtyards. "Oh, because I've never met an heiress apparent," Janine said.

Pilar switched screens and checked in on Signy, the *Siranui:*

—sounds of clattering tableware. Signy's cameras showed Alan and Anna, seated across a table. Signy was very still, perhaps not much awake.

Pilar left her there; this news could wait for a few minutes.

Portugal: Janine lagged behind Kazi while he opened the hotel gates with a keycard.

"Hey, Pilar," Janine whispered. "Was that what you wanted?"

"You betcha," Pilar said. **"That's what I wanted. Goodnight, hon. Sleep well."**

"What about Jared?" Janine asked.

"Nothing new. Signy's going looking for him tomorrow."

"We've got the first round of talks scheduled. I'll be in meetings all day."

"So rest tonight."

"I'll try." Kazi turned, waiting for Janine. Janine walked into the quiet courtyard of the hotel, where

lighted windows marked the location of Tanka employees, working on into the night.

"Sank the *Oburu?*" Jimmy asked. "Pilar, how do you
figure that?"

"One of those connections Edges makes," Pilar said.

"She's Evergreen," Jimmy said. "Son of a bitch."
Jimmy lurched back toward Janine's console, his hands
in front of him as if he were sleepwalking. "Pilar, I'm an
idiot sometimes. Evergreen *told* me she worked in the
Seychelles. If I were going to get data out of the Seychelles, and not make it all that easy to trace—"

"If you were going to get data out of the Seychelles at
all, you'd run it from . . ." Pilar called up the netmap,
glowing lines that bound the world's cities. "Sri Lanka."

"Uh-huh. Oh, yeah. I would indeed." Jimmy began to
hum again, searching for San-Li Tanaka, known on the
net, perhaps, as Evergreen.

Signy wasn't sleepy. She wasn't hungry. Led, protesting,
to the mess by Alan and Anna, Signy knew that all she
wanted to do was to keep going, to walk the corridors
of the ship, to keep moving until something happened.
But a bowl of garnished noodles appeared in front of her,
covered with stir-fried vegetables and sautéed chicken
and spiced nuts, smoking hot, and the food was wonderful.

Anna and Alan said polite little things while they ate.
They did not discuss the whale, or Jared, or the six hours
left until the helo would rise. Signy sipped at a cup of
aromatic tea. It was too soothing, too pleasant. She wondered if the whale were still near the ship. How much
did it hurt, to be that big and that sick? Signy heard the
whale's breath, and imagined a plea in it. Her eyelids
suddenly felt sanded, and she shook her head.

"Hello?" Alan smiled at her.

"Hi. I'm back."

"Good. I wasn't looking forward to carrying you to bed. But I think that's where you should go, and soon."

"No!" Signy's voice surprised her. She sounded like a petulant child. "I mean, please, not yet. I want to look around a little."

"Signy, you won't find Jared in a broom closet. And you're about to fall over," Alan said.

"I am going to bed now." Anna stood up. "Let me show you to your cabin, Signy."

"I don't want to be alone," Signy said. "I'll stay with Alan."

Anna nodded. "I think that would be a good thing for you to do." She picked up the trays and left.

Signy watched her thread her way through the tables in the quiet room. "I like her," Signy said.

"Anna? She seems sharp enough," Alan said.

Pilar's voice came through Signy's ear patch. **"San-Li Tanaka is on board,"** she said.

"Where?" Signy asked.

"Damned if I know," Pilar said. **"No address that we can find."**

"Can you get a picture of her?" Signy asked. "Send it to Alan's cabin when you do."

"Looking," Pilar said. On Signy's wrist, Pilar's light went dull. Alan waited for Signy to explain what she'd been muttering to herself about.

"Tanaka's daughter is here, somewhere," Signy said.

"Does that mean anything?"

Signy pushed back her chair and stood up. She felt clumsy and very, very slow. "I don't know."

Jared roused from a deep sleep and found himself in the familiar confines of a man-made cave. High above his head, green fabric stretched taut on a pop-up frame. They had pitched the old tent on the banks of the Copper River and gone to bed early; all of them tired after muscling their way past some good stretches of white water. He could hear someone snoring, probably Laughlin, the fat Texan. Laughlin wasn't a man he could warm up to; but Kihara, quick with his words and wilderness-wise, Kihara he liked.

Jared's hands were on fire and his face burned. His bladder was achingly full and he was nowhere near the Copper River.

He shoved himself up on his elbows. Three men slept in the tent, dark shapes around a glowing heater. The bandages on Jared's hands made working a zipper impossible. He shrugged and kicked his way out of the sleeping bag. He crouched on his knees and bit at the bandages on his hands but they wouldn't come loose. Rucksacks and opened packs lay around the tent, over a rolled-out length of some spongy stuff, an insulating layer. It worked; the tent was steamy. He didn't see weapons. He didn't see his battery pack.

Jared could assume that these people had kept him alive for some reason. He could also assume they had trapped him in the water to begin with, or he would be back on the *Siranui* by now. He had to get outside but he needed a parka for that. Freezing to death wasn't a good idea.

Jared turned, still kneeling, and found his parka folded at the foot of his rumpled mummy bag. He grabbed the parka between his clumsy fists. It rustled damnably, but the sounds of quiet breathing behind him did not change. Still, he knew before he turned that someone watched him.

One of the sleepers was a woman. She had rolled up on her elbows and she aimed a gun at his middle. The black circle of the barrel looked as large as her head. Jared knew it wasn't, but damn it, guns pointed directly at a person tended to expand in apparent size.

"Shhh." The woman mouthed the sound and shook her head in negation.

Jared held up his bandaged hands, patted his crotch, and motioned toward the tent flap. The woman nodded and unzipped the door. No one seemed to wake. Jared got the parka over his shoulders and crawled outside.

He could hear the woman follow him, out onto packed snow, in purple twilight. Jared walked in a straight line away from the tent until he heard her steps slow behind him. If that was as far as she wanted him to go, no problem. Jared felt acutely aware of the woman's tensions; he tried to read her steps, to know her emotions from her body language in the brief, over the shoulder glimpses he caught while she walked behind him. The limits of the woman's patience were very important to him.

A glacier hung above the campsite, close, immense. The tent stood on a little island, in a canyon formed by a promontory on one side and the glacier on the other. The flat oval of the beached Zodiac lay on a pebbled beach, dwarfed by the white bones of a whale's skeleton. Likely a victim of long-gone whalers, the skeleton could have lain there since the 1800s, some part of Jared's mind told him, since before flensing became an onboard operation and the summer oil factories had gone the way of the dodo.

Jared saw these things while he wondered what he could do with his zipper. He pawed at it, helpless. The woman stepped in front of him and bent her head to inspect his fly. She had olive skin and a hawk nose and long black eyelashes. She was thirtyish and not pretty, Jared noticed, while she got the zipper undone with her cold hands and held him while he pissed. It was a hell of an introduction.

Both her hands were busy, Jared reflected, while between the two of them they got him repacked into his layers of clothing. Both her hands were free; therefore, the gun was inside the tent. Or she had stashed it in her clothes somewhere. That would be stupid, but Jared had learned, over the years, never to underestimate the power of stupidity. The woman started to step away from him. Jared hooked an elbow behind her neck and clamped his other hand over her nose and mouth. His knee slammed into the bend of her knee and they went down together.

She twisted like a cat, but he got his weight stretched out on top of her in a strange parody of a missionary position. Jared kept the woman's mouth covered with one bandaged hand while he pawed and patted at her, but he could find nothing that felt like a gun. He sat up astride her and pushed the gauzy bandaged wad of his hand up against her nose to extend her neck, forcing the back of her head into the packed snow. He put the heel of his other hand directly on her trachea, and pushed, gently. The woman grabbed at his forearms.

"Don't scream," Jared whispered. He pushed at her throat just a little more, for emphasis. "Don't scream. Reach up, slow now, and undo the bandages on *this* hand." He rocked the cartilage of her windpipe back and forth with his left hand, to help her understand. "*This* hand, okay?"

She blinked rapidly and tried to nod.

The bandages were fastened with clear tape. Jared kept an eye on the silent tent while the woman unwrapped lengths of stretch gauze. Glacier, beach, the sea; they were camped on a small island, somewhere near the continent in the empty, frozen south. The diffuse light gave no directional clues. He saw no seals or penguins. Did that mean anything?

The air struck Jared's hand, and he examined it. The damage was nasty, an observation that he made with clinical detachment. The skin over the distal phalanx on his left fifth finger had turned dead white. Blisters had formed on the finger pads, but the thumb had been spared.

Jared flexed his hand and watched the woman until she inhaled. He switched hands, and felt the blister on his index finger break as his bare hand clamped across her face.

"Now the other one," he said.

The sensory functions of his index finger had survived. The texture of her cheek under his exposed raw finger pad felt like acid sandpaper. She got the second bandage off. His right hand appeared to be no more damaged than his left, and the fifth finger wasn't blistered.

The woman stared up at him, her pupils dilated wide in her brown eyes, and the indelibly imprinted physician inside Jared noted those wide pupils, an effect of catecholamines on the woman's central nervous system. He could feel a small branch of her facial artery throb at the edge of her jaw. Her pulse rate was nicely elevated.

He might have to kill this woman and he couldn't quite see himself doing it. Then he remembered a hand on his collar and how he had tried to relax in the water, and how this woman, *this* woman, had forced him under again. Bitch.

Jared reached up and put the heel of his free hand on the woman's forehead, so that his fingers rested over her eyes. Just beneath the ridge of her eyebrows, his tender fingers sought the notches where tiny nerve bundles curved upward to send sensory branches across the forehead. Jared put pressure there. The woman tried to push the back of her head deeper into the snow. Fine.

Jared stretched out on top of her, carefully, pushing his legs between hers and letting his weight settle against her chest. Her arms pounded at his sides and her heels kicked at his thighs. These motions were a minor annoyance. Jared let go of her throat and covered her mouth with his. His damaged lip cracked when he opened his mouth and clamped it on hers. It hurt.

Jared grabbed the wad of soiled gauze and shook loose a free end. When the gag was in place, he checked the knots with a certain degree of satisfaction and gently wiped a smear of his blood away from the woman's temple.

"We will get up now," Jared said. "We will walk close

together, like lovers." He kept his voice low, but it shook with rage. He took a deep breath. Rage would not serve him well, just now. He spoke with his mouth close to her ear. "We will go down to the beach. We will take the Zodiac. Yes, you can try to make noise when we are working with the boat, because I plan to let you loose then. I will stay close to you. You can hope that your friends can wake, get out of the tent, and kill me before I kill you, if you hit something or drop anything. You can hope that, but you will be wrong. You see, I will kill you if you make noise. I will kill you if you run. I will kill you if you do anything that alarms me in any way. I would very much like for one of these things to happen. Do you understand me?"

The woman kept her dilated eyes on him and nodded.

Jared rolled off of her and they struggled to their feet. He twisted her arms up behind her and held them there. He kept the pace slow, because they were clumsy, walking together like this. Even if he didn't kill her, he planned to let her feel that icy water, at least once. He hoped the Zodiac's motor held gas. He hoped it was equipped with emergency flares, or a radio, or some such.

They walked down toward the beach, circling away from the tent, their steps bringing up soft whispers from the summer snow.

TWENTY-ONE

There were two bunks in Alan's cabin, stacked atop each other, their fittings made of a reddish wood glazed with many coats of varnish. Lying down would feel so good. But the console pulled at Signy's attention. She sat down in front of it.

Alan sighed and stretched out on the lower bunk.

Pilar had sent no pictures of the Tanaka heiress.

Signy called Seattle, called Pilar. Pilar answered slowly, distracted by some conversation she was having with Jimmy.

"You're too spaced to do much good there," Alan said.

Signy heard the bunk creak behind her. She ignored Alan and spoke to the console. "Where's San-Li's picture?" Signy asked.

"Girl, there aren't any to be found," Pilar said. "Jimmy hacked some medical records from somewhere while you were stuffing your face. Prescription records. San-Li's on chronic doses of human growth hormone. Maybe she's a dwarf or something; I dunno."

"That's rare as hen's feathers," Signy grumbled. She found herself yawning. "I mean teeth."

"Will you get the hell off-line? You're too tired to make sense," Pilar said.

"I want to talk to Paul."

Paul appeared on the little flatscreen, a haggard Paul with a frown. "No, you don't," Paul said. "Goodnight, Signy."

Paul's face vanished.

"Wait!"

The console refused to give her pictures of anything. Voice only, Paul said, "We're watching. We're guarding both of you, in our limited fashion. Someone's going to baby-sit your terminal all night, okay? We'll hear you if you so much as fart, darling. But enough's enough. Get some rest."

Alan reached down over her shoulders and lifted Signy's hands away from the keyboard. "I'll keep her in reach," he told Paul.

"Don't!" Signy jerked her hands away from Alan's grip. Alan had been on the boat with Jared. Alan might have arranged the accident; he could have called the kidnappers to the *Kasumi*. Signy was afraid of him. Go to Anna? She didn't know Anna. Anna had left Jared on the *Kasumi*. Maybe Anna was involved.

"Don't what?" Alan let her push his hands away.

"I—"

"You're afraid of me."

"Yes."

"You need to trust somebody. You don't know if I'm the right person to trust. We have a business agreement, remember? If you knew me better, you'd know that means something. And what I haven't told you is that I need to come back with business for Gulf Coast. Gulf Coast is having just a few problems these days. I'm old. I bring some bacon home, or I take an early retirement."

"And you don't want to do that."

"No way," Alan said.

That made sense. Nothing else much did, as tired as she was.

Alan turned away from her and pulled a terry robe out of a cabinet. "Now that we've got that straight, you get first dibs on the shower. Then we're going to bed. Paul, is that all right with you?" Alan asked the blank screen.

"Oh, yes," Paul said.

"Okay," Signy said. "Okay, okay. I'm going."

She emerged from the steamy shower to find Alan sitting on the bunk, his hands held together between his knees.

"It was a good night, back in Houston," he said. "Signy, I haven't forgotten it."

"Neither have I."

He got up and headed for the shower. "I'll take the top bunk."

"Nope. I need something warm to hang on to. If you don't mind being crowded."

"I don't mind," Alan said.

Wavelets lapped at the shore. Brash ice and small bergs slid down the little channel, riding a current toward a looming wall of ice and vanishing around it toward territory unknown. Twilight dulled the shadows of the glacier, of the shore, of the bergs slipping their way through black water. The camp sheltered between giant walls of ice that seemed designed to produce echoes. Clouds rolled past the narrow wedge of sky between the glacier wall and the ice cliff that jutted into the sea. The clouds rode high and fast. There seemed to be little chance of the Antarctic fogs that were said to rise at a moment's notice. The islet seemed to be in a strait, or perhaps in the twisting recesses of a canyon that might dead-end at some unexpected cul-de-sac.

The tent's small dome looked tiny, scaled next to the amazing wall of glacier, but Jared found it difficult to tear his eyes away from it. The zippered closure of the tent remained motionless, but he imagined someone inside, rousing now with the sleepy awareness that the woman and her prisoner had been gone too long.

Salt-soaked pebbles crunched under their feet as they left the snow. Jared pressed his lips together at the noise. The Zodiac was beached well above the high-tide mark, and it contained tarp-wrapped bundles that looked heavy. Three oars lay loose in it, short stubby ones that were never meant to get the craft any great distance. The apparent weight of the bundles convinced him that two people wouldn't be able to lift the boat off the noisy rocks and carry it into the water. Jared pushed the woman toward one side of the Zodiac and grabbed the other. He heaved, and the friction of the thing, sliding across the scruff of the little beach, made a racket that scared the hell out of him. So he pushed harder, and as the Zodiac began to lift into the silent water, he realized that the noise of the pebbles was scarcely louder than that of his own breathing. Jared motioned the woman into the boat and clambered inside as it came free of the shore.

He stood facing the shore and poled the boat with one of the oars until the shore fell away and he couldn't reach bottom. He motioned toward the two remaining oars. The woman, her eyes dark wounds in the half-light, fastened the oars to the oarlocks and began to back away from shore with strong, sure strokes. The boat turned broadside into an incoming wavelet and Jared ruddered the damned thing around to follow the berg's path in the unseen current. He stepped toward the stern and pushed the woman away from the seat, grabbing the oars from her so he could row and keep an eye on the tent. She crouched near his feet and stared up at him. Her nostrils flared as she fought for breath against the gag. The veins on her throat bulged with her exertions, but she wasn't retching. He would have to get her gag off if she did, or she could aspirate, strangle on her own stomach juices. Aware that he needed her alive, not dead, Jared accepted that he had never wanted to kill her in the first place.

The tent, even at this slight distance, seemed much smaller than before. Jared's shoulders and back delighted in the pull against the oars, the solid feel of them against his burning hands. The smears of blood his hands left on the shafts seemed to help his grip, and he didn't take time to fish in his jacket for his gloves.

The woman shifted her knees and got them beneath her. Her hand began to move toward the gag on her face. Jared kicked at her without breaking his stroke at the oars, and she let her hands fall into her lap. She twisted her head so she could see the tent.

Again, and again, Jared drove the oars against the inertia of the heavy water, aiming for a smallish floe about a hundred meters offshore, wanting to get it between their silhouette and the tent. Brash ice brushed against the Zodiac and parted before it. In this sea, they would not die of thirst, not with this much fresh water floating in chunks beside them. Not of thirst. Hypothermia and starvation would be sufficient to do them in. Jared glanced behind him at the floe, which seemed to be farther away than he'd thought at first.

When he looked back, the mouth of the tent was open. Puffs of fog swirled from the black opening, the tent breathing its trapped heat into the cold air.

He pulled again, watching the two parkaed men crawl from the tent, watching them look about to where the Zodiac no longer lay.

He pulled again. The taller man scuttled back into the tent and the shorter one squatted beside the opening.

He pulled again. A hand clutching a rifle emerged from the tent mouth. Damn, not a hand gun. The rifle carried a bulky telescopic sight. Infrared? Probably.

He pulled again. With slow, deliberate motions, the squatting man reached for the gun, broke it, loaded it, and scouted the sea.

The floe was too far away. The water was filled with broken ice chips and lumps of bergy bits, all too small to hide the silhouette of the boat and its two passengers. Jared tried to look like an ice floe, but he didn't think he was going to be able to fool the rifleman. The man stood and fitted his eye to the flange of the scope.

Jared shipped the oars. He grabbed the woman beneath her armpits and lifted her to his lap. She was a dead weight, not fighting him. He turned her so that she faced shore. Jared hugged her, nestling his chin against her shoulder and holding her arms tight to her sides. The rifle wavered slightly. The second man scrambled out of the tent and looked toward the sea.

Even with the scope, the Zodiac was far enough from shore to make missing it possible. But it wasn't far enough away from the gun that Jared dared let go of the woman and grab for the outboard engine, which was still tilted up on the stern with its prop above the water. The engine was an unfamiliar make. Jared reached for the oars again, gripping the woman's hips between his thighs. The rifle steadied.

A swell rose beneath the Zodiac, tilting its port side toward the sky on a wall of water. A smell of rotting fish, foul breath, and musty cellars rose from somewhere deep. Jared fought the balance of the little boat, trying to turn its nose into the wave, fighting with the oars.

The shore vanished. Jared struggled for a glimpse of it, seeing instead a moving wall of gray-black, mottled flesh, the charcoal bulk of a humpback whale. The giant surfaced inches away from the Zodiac, between it and the shore.

Jared threw the woman out of his way and lunged for the motor. He wrestled its mounts until something clicked and the prop sank toward the water. A keychain swung from the ignition. He grabbed for the key and twisted it. The motor whined, coughed, and roared to life.

"Psyche!" someone shouted.

The gunshot that followed echoed off the glacier, the promontory, the waves. The whale sank as Jared fishtailed the Zodiac toward the lee side of the little floe.

In the narrow lower bunk, in the dim cabin, Signy lifted her head and looked over Alan's chest to the screen. It showed the Seattle studio:

—Pilar sat on the floor, cross-legged, a keyboard and flat-screen in front of her. Beside her, lying on his belly, Jimmy spoke to her as he worked. They had the sound off.

Signy drifted away again, and dreamed of rows of paper-doll Japanese children, tiny ones linked arm to arm. One end of the paper strip was fastened to a staff, and an unseen dancer waved it back and forth, making spirals and swirls in the dark air. The dolls seemed patient and resigned. Signy thought she would try to graph it and show it to Pilar; there was something very important in the pattern, somewhere.

"Mmph," Alan muttered, and turned over.

Signy nestled against Alan's bony back, secure between his warmth and the bulkhead, and watched the lights from the cabin screen change the colors of the varnished wood above her in the dark.

TWENTY-TWO

From Lisbon, Pilar let Janine's images run unedited and real-time: Janine working at a frenzied pace and seldom saying anything except to give instructions to the techs who surrounded her. The hotel suite Tanaka had rented became a wonderland, a place to influence visitors who might be persuaded to change one vote, or part of an opinion.

On a normal job, in a normal time, Edges would be hovering over the screens right now, chewing on nuances and fine-tuning the presentations, with Signy worrying, Jared reassuring her and everyone else, and Paul pulling new information out of nanoland and tossing it in at seeming random. Paul tossed, usually, while Janine sorted Paul's information into neat, usable piles. Not now, not with Jared gone, Signy off in a futile chase, and Paul revising delegate profiles and sending updates to Lisbon as they came in.

"What are you doing, Pilar?" Jimmy asked.

"Worrying."

"About what?"

"About this contract. The lineup on votes is so damned close."

"I wish I could help," Jimmy said, "but I don't do politics."

"Everyone does politics," Pilar said. In fact, Jimmy wouldn't be much help right now. Signy would be, but she was asleep. Paul always had the eye for this stuff, if Jared was around to keep him from careening off at some oblique angle. Jared would say, "There, there," and listen, and things would get *clear*.

Janine finished a lighting check in the Lisbon hotel, put her hands on her hips, and turned in a circle.

"How's it look?" Janine asked.

The anonymous rented rooms held a fortune in virtual equipment, and a fortune in the presence of a pair of sleek Tanaka security guards, a carefully bland man and a muscular woman, unobtrusive. The guards, and Pilar couldn't figure out how many there actually were, worked rotating shifts, around the clock.

Waiting, in stored sequences of light and sound, waiting to go onstage, vistas of clean mosaic ice impeded the progress of a masted ship, ice whose patterns became infinity, ice that covered and obscured the horizons of rooms filled with the scent of clean brine and the tang of sea air. Seals played there, and birds flew, and an offstage sun slanted the light into kaleidoscopes of pristine colors.

Janine had set the heating on the warm side, after one of the techs, a dark-eyed and rather plump person from Milan, had come on shift wearing a thick sweater.

Conversation areas with chairs and hassocks upholstered in hot, campfire colors offered shelter from the vast, cold surroundings.

"Beautiful," Pilar said. "Sound?"

"You won't get all the harmonics. Not on remote," Janine said. "But here goes."

The Lisbon room filled with music, low volume, but pervasive. Pilar had used a few motifs from Williams' *Sinfonia Antarctica*, some of the choral sections. She had worked them into Jimmy's music, deep whispers of melody that underlay the scenes, caressed them, the music Jimmy said he had learned from a woman, or a dream.

Paul sent an intruder to the Seattle screens, a crab that scuttled back and forth across Pilar's synthesizer keyboard and sat down firmly on a C chord. The crab wiped drops of sweat from its nonexistent forehead. "The E.C. is going to ask for a fishing ban," Paul said.

"Are you sure?" Pilar asked.

"Yes. I got the word from an open transmission to the *Journal of Aquaculture;* the British delegate is friends with the editor. Britain wants it leaked before morning, from the timing." Paul sent his words over text, scrolling past Pilar's eyes toward a Save function. Pilar bit at her lip as she read. She forwarded the text to Janine.

In Tanaka's Lisbon suite, Janine sat curled in an orange armchair. She had her notebook propped on her knees. She accepted a cup of something from an offscreen arm, and muttered, "Thanks."

Pilar windowed Janine away and looked at Paul's text—

The E.C. planned to introduce a proposal for a ban. Britain had pushed hard for it, for reasons that had much to do with sentiment, and much to do with its subsidies of aquaculture in the Indian Ocean.

"I hoped the E.C. would do this," Paul said.

Most of the krill harvest went to the Third World, anyhow, although significant quantities showed up, disguised and flavorless, in protein supplements. Soy could be used in its place, and purchasing it from water-thrifty countries would be a neutral factor in Euro trade.

"We've got the E.C., it sounds like. The trick is to swing the Mideastern votes," Paul said.

"What's our plan for that?" Pilar asked.

"We don't have one," Paul said.

No one had ever figured out the Mideast, no one could predict if its countries were in mortal opposition to each other this week, or bosom partners in a new coalition since yesterday. Edges couldn't figure them, but losing the vote on a new Mideast configuration was a no-fault situation.

"Plan? The plan is, for better or worse, we go with

what we have. This is done." Janine waved her arm, vaguely, at the Tanaka suite. "We've got a little time. All night, anyway, if Britain pulls its little surprise in today's session. They may wait until Monday, but that's asking for a miracle, I guess. Paul, Pilar, get lost for a while. I'm going to shower and change for breakfast." Janine turned them off, firmly.

"Me, too," Paul said. "The shower, I mean."

They were gone. Pilar sipped cold coffee and looked in on Alan Campbell's cabin on the *Siranui*.

Signy, crowded in a narrow bunk next to Alan, murmured something in her sleep, now, which was last night to her, and Gods knew what here—

Pilar left that place. The yellowish glare of a night city came through her bare Seattle window. Pilar wished she had time to tweak the sets in the Lisbon room. She wished the contract's success was built on stronger foundations, that the secret key to making the ban a reality was in her hand. Search, Pilar told herself, go freewheel and find a lever.

Tanaka, lost ships, sabotage that didn't make sense, a daughter that figured in here somewhere. San-Li, a daughter with a name that wasn't Japanese. Pilar searched for a bio on San-Li's mother, and didn't find one.

Why would San-Li Tanaka have a jones for growth hormone? Why would anyone? Jared was the medic; he would know.

Pilar started to access Jared, and stopped herself with a nervous little laugh. Wrong move of the fingers, but she found herself in Signy's old files:

Tucked away under Stuff, a topic that Signy filled with things that didn't fit anywhere—Pilar found a view of herself, a couple of days ago, staring out the Seattle window.

Garbage.

Pilar set a search function for "growth hormone":

More or less in reverse order, images scrolled past, younger Pilars and Janines, some views of the Taos house and Jared up to his elbows in mud plaster, and then New Hampshire, bright foliage, a leaf-peeping tour of the lakeside, and Jared's voice.

Pilar settled into her headset, and accepted Signy's experience of the day, the feel of Signy's angular body, the pleasure Signy had felt, walking between her two lovers through the blatant colors of a New England autumn morning.

"Longevity," Signy said, years before today, over the crunch of fallen leaves. "Ah, Jared, you know as much about that as I do."

"Starvation's one way," Jared said.

"Yeah. Paul's a candidate."

Signy's imaged hands felt cold and Signy/Pilar stuffed them in her pockets. Shadows dappled Jared's shoulders; he squinted up at the sun. Paul made a hrummphing noise and kicked at a drift of crimson.

"Then there's the little nanomachines to trot around and clean out free radicals," Jared said.

"I'm still waiting for those to get built," Signy said. "Until then, there's keeping slightly under lean body weight. Get yourself a perfect blood chemistry by fair means or foul . . ."

"Signy's advocating drugs, Paul," Jared said.

"Again?" Paul asked.

". . . and some of the anabolic steroids have been tried. Growth hormone, too."

"You did some work on that, didn't you?" Paul asked her.

Pilar could feel the tension rise in Signy's shoulders, in the back of her neck, the muscles of her jaw.

"In Atlanta. Yeah." Signy walked on for a while, staring down at granite and dying leaves. "We got some good results, too. We built some really fucking *geriatric* rats."

Signy reached down and picked up a rock, and flung it side-armed toward the lake with all the energy of sudden rage. It skipped once and sank.

Pilar, in the quiet hours of a foggy Seattle night, sighed and tried to call up Signy's old research papers. Either Signy hadn't bothered to save them, or she had them locked away under some obscure title.

A knot burned in its familiar place between Pilar's shoulders. She leaned back, stretched, and whimpered.

"Is something wrong?" Jimmy asked.

"I could use a neck rub," Pilar said.

Jimmy's hands lifted from his keyboard. He let them settle back again and ducked his chin. "I—in a little while, okay? I thought you wanted me to look for Jared."

The concept of fleshtime touch seemed to threaten him. Pilar considered pushing him and decided against it. "I *do* want you to find Jared. I want *somebody* to find Jared. And I want you to find this Tanaka bitch." Pilar looked at her hands, her thin brown fingers. They reminded her of talons; they were designed to grasp and tear. Jared had seen them that way; he had seen her as a bird of prey and imaged her, once, in plumage and steel.

Jared's description had been fair. Pilar was not kind, in her own eyes. Or if she was, she knew her kindness as a measured thing, calculated for response and gain.

"If she's on that ship, she hides real well," Jimmy said.

"Kazi's her boss. She's got to call him sometime or the other. She's got to call Papa."

"The old man is guarded, max. I've tried him," Jimmy said.

"Good man," Pilar said, and she let her pleasure ride in her voice. A measured, calculated pleasure. Jimmy grinned. Stimulus: response. Pilar regretted how predictable it was.

* * *

And looked at Lisbon, where the sun was up. If there had been roosters, they would be crowing now.

Janine and Kazi walked toward the Palacio. Janine, scrubbed and shiny clean, seemed bemused by crowds of morning workers, people with thick white skins and dank black hair that marked a population whose faces did not look Spanish. The crowded streets could have been in any city, but for those faces. In late January, the land and the wan light hinted of autumn and the sea. Ancient rococo archways led into mazed streets of decaying stone.

There was little, in Lisbon, left from the days of sea rovers and gold bullion, the days of the rape of the New World. An earthquake had destroyed it, and started some sort of religious rebellion. So many innocents had died, and the question rose—Where was God?

Pilar smelled fresh coffee. Jimmy put a cup down beside her.

"Thanks," Pilar said.

Jimmy laid his palms against her neck and kneaded her tight muscles. He was good at it.

"Really, thanks." Jimmy's fingers worked at Pilar's temples, tilting her headset, and her view of Lisbon. Pilar batted at his hands. "No, no. You're messing the focus."

"Sorry," Jimmy said. He pulled his hands away.

Lisbon:

Itano's face looked closed and grim. The Tanaka delegation, with blond Janine in their midst, climbed the steps into the new Palacio, which had been designed to keep every stone-carver in Europe busy for a decade. It had.

"Jimmy, the meeting starts now," Pilar said. "I'll be with Janine. I'm going to stay with her for a while."

Pilar dismissed Jimmy from her reality, Jimmy's fears, his earnest, sincere presence.

A helo chukkered somewhere high above the ship. Signy squinted up through the too-bright light and saw it coming down. She found a spot in the sun outside the hangar doors where she thought she wouldn't be in the way. Her layers of parka and coveralls should have kept the cold from her, but it seeped in anyhow, a pervasive wet reality breathed into the air from land and water that never warmed. Signy turned her back toward the sun, hoping for some solar gain.

The helo rocked itself onto the deck like a big-bellied bug. Signy watched the landing through her headset, which gave her a heads-up display from home as well, a small square screen in her peripheral vision.

Trent, Anna, and Alan were the only humans Signy expected to deal with today. They were familiar with camera gear, and not likely to ask for privacy clauses or recording contracts. Signy wanted the visuals, and access to printscreens if she needed them, so she stood there looking as much like a bug as the helo did, she figured.

Trent and Alan waited near the coffeepot in the hangar. Alan a murderer? A saboteur? Anna? The concepts didn't fit. Staying alive and unmaimed in the thin shell of a helo, or dealing with the growling machinery that ground up the sea harvest, damn it, just *working* here should provide enough stress to keep life precious, to keep some tone in anyone's neurotransmitters. Jared's disappearance could be, in this sane and busy setting, just a glitch. A fixable glitch.

Pilar, riding Janine's senses, entered a cavernous auditorium, an oval amphitheater. Broad terraces held ranks of padded conference chairs that looked down into a center arena. Polished marble walls and hangings in dark reds and ambers sought to produce a climate for stately deliberation and the enactment of noble deeds. In the great hall in Lisbon, the world's movers and shakers gathered to discuss the health and well-being of a community of crustaceans, a citizenry whose members were the size of jelly beans.

The delegates to the Antarctic Treaty Convention sat at a long oval table, whose central holo stage was currently filled with a model of a fine specimen of *Euphasia superba*. The room was designed like a stadium, and Janine sat in a cheering section, a wedge formation of black suits ranked behind the Japanese delegate. Half of the section wore headsets. Janine looked right at home.

"What's doing?" Pilar asked.

[Janine] Zzz.

Janine fed the hall's audio to Seattle. A man with a proper British voice described pigment variations in krill. He reported that he didn't know what the new pigments *meant*, just that they had *changed*. Janine looked at the speaker, who was somewhat colorless in hair, eyes, and voice.

"What, no pretty costumes?" Pilar asked.

Janine circled the arena with her eyes. Behind placards that listed name and nation, the delegates wore Western business suits; the women wore tunics in primary colors. Not a single caftan, sari, or fez relieved the monotony.

[Janine] Conformity is in, this year.

The krill vanished from the stage. France, a muscular and totally bald gentleman who was the designated chairperson for this meeting of the august Antarctic Treaty Commission, rapped his gavel. *En Français*, he declared the preliminary reports on the health of the ecosystem *fini*, with no time for *commentaire*. Janine ran the translator's voice in tandem with his. English and

French words clashed and combined. Pilar liked the effect. It was time, France said, to discuss changes in the treaty. France hoped there would be none.

Pilar approved his futile plea for brevity, and wondered if he suffered a slight and patriotic indisposition of the liver. It would explain his desire for haste, and be a sufficient cause for a wish for miracles.

With due deliberation, the Commission decided to consider new motions. Colorless Britain took the floor and requested a ban on fishing in Antarctica.

[Janine] Here we go.

Delegates rumbled as they heard what Britain asked. A second wave of grumbling followed the first, as those few who needed, or pretended to need, translation, responded to the words.

"... for a period of time to be not less than the next scheduled meeting of this august body thirty years from this date, that no marine life of any kind whatsoever be removed from the waters southerly of fifty-five degrees," Britain said.

[Janine] That cuts off a lot of home water from Chile and Argentina. They're bound to bitch.

They didn't, not immediately. Chile got up from his chair and went to Argentina, who was a solid-looking woman with glossy black hair. She wore it in a dancer's knot at the back of her neck. Chile bent over and spoke rapidly in the woman's ear. She said something that Janine's mikes didn't pick up.

Chile stood up and backed away. The man from Chile and the Argentine woman gestured at each other with much nodding and waving of hands. Chile returned to his chair.

Australia gave the U.K. a second. France opened the floor for discussion. The Japanese delegate was on his feet in the instant. He was a ramrod straight, very small man. Pilar couldn't get a look at his face.

In English, he said, "Mr. Chairman, such a proposal is

unconscionable. World hunger demands the use of available resources, including those of Antarctica. Japan, as a member of the Treaty Commission, opposes any change in the current apportionment of the valuable harvest from the Southern Ocean."

"Huh?" Pilar asked.

Janine looked from face to impassive face, scanning the Japanese delegation. Tanaka's men did not seem surprised. Kazi crossed his arms and would not look at her.

The Japanese delegate spoke on, with a formal and passionate anger. He finished his initial barrage of objections, and did not bow as he sat down.

[Janine] Oh, shit. Now what?

"You didn't have a clue?" Pilar asked.

[Janine] Zero, zilch clues. Kazi=Bastard.

"Amen."

[Janine] SHIT!

"Just sit there, okay? Kazi has to explain this. I hope," Pilar said.

[Janine] He'd better.

There went the contract.

Failure, failure, Pilar was getting fucking tired of failure. First the damned tour, and then Jared, who, alive or dead, was damaging them all so painfully. Now this. Pilar bent forward as if her stomach hurt. It didn't.

One of the houses would have to be sold. Not this one, Pilar hoped. But Paul wouldn't let go of the family place in New Hampshire without a fight. The house in Taos was the least expensive to maintain, and it was the biggest. Paul wouldn't sell, he would cash out before he would let that old colonial go. If he left, quit, said goodbye? Paul wouldn't, he couldn't.

Paul might.

Then what happens to the rest of us?

Pilar found herself wondering about Jimmy's income, his resources, and hated herself for it. But she *liked* Jimmy. Pilar was growing fond of him, in a mild way.

Now she would never know if she would ever see a true Jimmy, a person of his own. Jimmy had become a construct defined by the shapes of his potential uses.

[Janine] I'm scared.

"Me, too," Pilar said.

Anna went out to meet Kihara, who hustled toward her, a bouncy, quick man. Kihara looked happy. No reason he wouldn't; he had had a couple of days of R&R, and the news of Jared's disappearance would have meant little to him. Unfortunate, an inconvenience; no more than that. Jared and Kihara had been casual buddies, not close friends. And anyway, he wouldn't recognize Signy Thomas, a bundled woman in a parka; Kihara wouldn't know that Signy was Jared's worried masked lover. Why did Signy think everyone's routines would change for one missing man?

Through the glare of the helo's windscreen, Signy could make out the shape of the pilot's mustache and the line of his jaw. Signy watched him talk into his mike, impatient. It was Cordova, and he didn't shut the helo down. The helo whined with increased revs, lifted again, and turned away from the ship, rising toward the sun. Signy looked away, blinking from the bright light, and sneezed.

"Bless you," Jimmy said.

"It's Cordova," Signy told her throat mike. "Jared's pilot."

"Is it? He just told the flight officer he was in a hurry. Had some business, he said."

Signy pulled back the cuff of her parka and looked at her wrist. Jimmy was her only observer.

"Where's Pilar?" Signy asked.

"With Janine. The conference has gotten weird."

"Weird how?" Signy asked.

"Japan is opposing a fishing ban."

"Huh?" Signy asked. "That isn't the plan. Japan is supposed to push *for* a ban. Everything we've done is tailored to sell a goddamned ban. . . ." Did this mean Edges was fired? If that happened, what would happen to her? Tanaka would get her home, away from here, maybe at her own expense, and it wouldn't be Tanaka's money that continued a search for a man overboard. Edges' line of credit—the last time Signy had checked, there had been enough left to buy her a search of her own. Maybe.

What was Janine going to do? Signy started to ask Jimmy to hook into Lisbon real-time. So that she could—could do absolutely nothing helpful. Pilar would have to help handle the problem, whatever it was. Pilar could do it. Pilar *had* to.

Signy wished that the crew would hurry and get the *Siranui*'s helo into the air, before it was called back.

Anna left Kihara at the hangar door. Signy waved at her.

"Jimmy, Pilar and Paul can deal with Lisbon. They'll figure something out." Pilar and Paul could blow Lisbon to hell and gone, and they probably would. Janine was obviously in deep shit, and so was everything else. The contract? Gone, probably. "I want to help. But I'll be looking only for Jared, and I can't do any research for them, not from the helo. Just feed me the high points of all this, would you?"

"At your service," Jimmy said.

Anna waited beside Signy while the flight crew moved Trent's helo out to the deck. Somewhere, in the process of getting clearance to follow Cordova's helo up and away from the ship, Signy lost Jimmy, lost contact with home. She felt an emotional lurch, cut off for what seemed like a long, blank time, but Jimmy's light came back on, and his voice in her ear. **"Gotcha,"** he said. **"Had to run through McMurdo. You know somebody named Marty?"**

"Marty? He's a bartender."

"He's also got a real fine setup for monitoring damned near anything. He says 'Hi, Anna.'"

"I'll tell her," Signy said. What the hell was going on in Lisbon? In the turmoil, the group hadn't done an in-depth analysis of Tanaka corporation, of the personalities involved in it. No funny stuff on Tanaka's part had been assumed, so Signy's preliminary scan on the company men had been all that Edges had looked at. And when the funny stuff had come along, Signy, and Janine and Pilar too, had chosen to ignore it, over Jared's insistence that something was wrong. But no one had listened to Jared, or Paul, and therefore, there was no inhouse simulation against which to play this puzzling scenario. Damn, there hadn't been *time* to make one.

Worried, distracted, Signy watched the *Siranui* grow smaller as the helo rose. A trawler approached it, ready to unload another few tons of fish. The helo's noise, that the people beside her endured in silence, the sense of watchful waiting inside this flimsy flying bubble, brought her back to current concerns. Jared lived. Signy planned to find him.

Trent turned the helo away from the ship, on a path Signy could see in her mind, a grid on the waters where the *Kasumi* had fished for submarines. She remembered it well.

Jimmy wanted Pilar's attention. Pilar ignored him, and stayed in the drama playing itself out in Lisbon.

The Third World nations aligned themselves, predictably, on the lines of hunger. Famines were mentioned. Subsidies were suggested for landlocked countries who were willing to support the ban. Britain pointed out that food distribution was a U.N. function. The U.S. hadn't said a word yet. Janine sat frozen, listening to the arguments back and forth, back and forth. Pilar let Lisbon fade away.

"I'm listening," Pilar said.

"Signy's out on her search. I'm following her through McMurdo. That means I can't watch the *Siranui* at the same time, so I'm saving the stuff from there."

"Yeah. Do that."

Jimmy went back to his console; Pilar spoke to Janine.

"Babe, I'm going to get Paul in on this, now," Pilar said.

[Janine] Please. Do it.

Pilar stripped off her headset and wandered around the Seattle room for a minute, trying to get the world back into place. All of the presentations would need to be changed if Japan stuck with its position, and Pilar wasn't sure Paul was going to be any help getting the works retuned. Choreographed for the joy of solitude, for half-forgotten luxuries of time and distance, the set pieces were designed to say, This is ours, this is our heritage, Earth has grandeur and can survive.

To change the sets, the sounds, the slants? Hours of work, days, would be needed, even if the work was still wanted. Had Edges been fired last night at some wee-hour meeting? Wouldn't Kazi have said something, if that's what had happened?

Pilar pulled her headset back on and called New Hampshire:

Paul's crab climbed through the lattices of an amoeboid, strangely soft-edged *thing*. The interior of the construct seemed to be a cavern, braced with struts of curved elastic bars that looked like steel and had the sueded feel of latex.

"What the . . . ?" Pilar asked.

"I can't make it linear, Empress. There's too much coming in."

The space went *tilt*. Pilar grabbed for a rope that writhed, blood-warm and resilient, in her hands.

"Reductions of English-language newspapers in Chile and Argentina; you'd be amazed at some of the battles that go on in the fishing grounds. They have territorial boundaries as clearly marked as those of wolf packs, and devil take anyone who puts their nets in the wrong waters on the wrong day."

Moist veils of some pinkish membrane drifted across Pilar's shoulders. Pilar struggled, suddenly tiny, trying to reach the Paul-crab.

"The fishing packs are multinational, multicompany, Pilar, did you know that? They group up on friendship and superstition, once they're out of port." The crab flung itself to another strut in the half-formed maze, and the angle of the construct rotated bottoms up or inside out, Pilar couldn't tell which. She felt *everted*, and she didn't like the feeling at all.

"And to make it more fun, over here we've got maritime insurance company reports from last year. A whole subculture I never suspected. There are pirates in the world, Pilar; they work out of the Malacca straits; that's one place, but the companies don't turn in loss reports from piracy. It makes the stockholders nervous. Didn't you hear Itano talk about them?" The crab extruded a human hand from inside a claw and adjusted a knot of sticky caramel-colored optic cable that hung from a curving bar above its head.

Balanced, teetering, on the support Pilar's feet found beneath her, she backed away from an endless drop into a whirlpool. The whirlpool was green and sucked away anything nearby, sheets of printout, translucent fish bones, camo uniforms that spread into parodies of soldiers as they fell.

Pilar looked away, fast, catching a glimpse of rigid brocade skirts done in bas-relief. Paul had dressed her as a Chinese empress carved out of ivory. Pilar could see tiny gold nails in the joints of her fingers.

Paul's words tumbled out, staccato, rapid.

"... Of course, the vector analysis of the geometry of interpersonal space has not yet been defined in this way, but sooner or later, Empress, it leads back to us. To Jared, if we stretch the strings in the proper way."

Pilar had seen Paul Maury wired, but not like this, had not seen him, ever, lost in a frantic jumble of images like these, whose speed, tumbling across the construct she had entered, frightened her.

The crab bounced in place, like a kid with a full bladder. "And there, there in the distance is the German company that sells explosives to a mining company in Zaire that get black-marketed as fertilizer to an export dealer in Taiwan, that get packaged as XO brandy and sold to the store in Ushuaia. See? That's what Skylochori bought. The dead, dead man. He blew something up, ka-boom!"

Paul had gone spla. Loony. Mentally ill. Someone had to do something about this. Signy? Signy was busy. Pilar couldn't deal with crazy; Pilar heard a little voice in her head saying, Poor baby, poor baby, get someone to help him.

"Paul! Paul, stop it!" Pilar yelled.

Paul sent silence that burned in her ears. A lump formed in Pilar's throat, a big hot lump with sharp edges.

"What's the matter?" He sounded so calm, so reasonable.

"You sound crazy." Pilar untangled herself from the tendrils of the construct and ripped her headset away from her face.

"Oh, sorry," Paul's voice said, blessedly otherwhere, now that Pilar was safe again, in her own body, in her own head. "This isn't quite together yet, is it?"

Paul seemed contrite, apologetic, and sane.

"No."

"What's the matter, Empress?"

Paul wasn't totally nuts. Frightened, Pilar sought for a rationalization, for any thread of reasoning to explain what the hell was happening to him, and she knew, while her mind built frames around this, walled it off, that she was lying to herself.

Paul needed what Jared gave him, chiding hints that kept him sane. Pilar didn't often see Paul's work this raw, this unfinished. *Her* stuff looked fairly bizarre while she was actually getting it together. This weird? Yeah, probably. But Paul—this was different, and Pilar knew it, and Paul's craziness scared her. Pilar didn't want to think about what might happen if Paul lost it completely.

She shoved her fear deep into the background and said, "Japan is objecting to the fishing ban. They want the present quotas, they say."

Silence.

"Paul?"

"I'm sure they have their reasons, Empress."

"But what can we *do?*"

"I think, my dear, that we can wait. At least until lunch."

"You'll watch Janine with me?"

"Oh, yes," Paul said. "Yes, indeed."

Five meters high, about twenty meters long, the floe was scant shelter. It was an undistinguished, smallish, frozen lump of a floe, but shelter it was, and therefore beautiful. Jared cut the throttle back as the floe hid the Zodiac from shore. He didn't want to get back into open water, just yet. The channel curved ahead and lost itself between glacier and promontory. A smallish berg ahead looked promising as the potential next hiding place. But which way was out? Ahead? Back past the tent?

In rapid succession, three shots echoed off the ice cliffs. Shouts carried from the men onshore, echoed and multiplied so that they sounded like a company of infantry.

Even with the throttle kicked back to almost idle, the Zodiac was running out of iceberg. The range of a good hunting rifle, its accuracy if properly sighted, left Jared in danger of a careful shot. The Zodiac was a bigger, easier target.

Presumably, rafts had safety features. Jared doubted a rifle could sink this little toy tub, but losing air from a compartment or two could make the Zodiac list. Sloshing around in liquid ice seemed an unfortunate idea.

The echoes of the rifles died away, leaving only the sounds of the Zodiac's motor, a dead certain indicator of Jared's location, except that, like the rifle shots, the sound of it bounced off the glacier in confusing ways. Around him, a magic beauty existed, a panorama of ice and shadows stained in colors of burnt oranges, ambers, deep greens.

Jared figured he would like to head in the direction of McMurdo, if he knew which way that was. Where had the *Kasumi* been and how far might these people have carried him, drugged and unconscious?

The floe traveled in a patch of open water. Ahead, a small berg waited, across an empty expanse that would silhouette the Zodiac against the background of the promontory's white, white ice. Jared was aware of how soft he was, far too aware of the potential damage that could be created by a high-velocity missile driving its shock wave through human flesh. He thought of trying to stay here, behind this friendly little floe.

Out in the open water, the whale rose just under the surface and rolled on its side without raising a ripple on the water. It didn't seem to be injured. Without warning, it broached, rising half out of the water and falling back with a crash. By then, Jared had the Zodiac halfway to the iceberg. He heard a rifle crack; once, twice.

When he reached the shelter of the berg, Jared twisted

so that he could see the water behind him, deep green and not stained with the whale's blood. The tent was hidden behind a curve in the channel. Jared couldn't see any pursuers, and he sped along beside the berg until he passed its sheltering bulk. An abrupt twist in the channel carried the Zodiac out past the cove, or passage, or whatever the hell it was. Behind him were men with guns, ahead was broken ice and a sea running high. An offshore wind bit at his ears and his bare hands. The clouds were lowering and they had taken all the colors away.

The woman grabbed for a handhold as the Zodiac sank down over the first big roller. Jared reached with one hand and pulled at the ties of her gag.

"Get that damned thing off!" he shouted.

The woman pulled it loose and hurled herself toward the edge of the boat. Jared thought for a minute she was going overboard, but she retched, repeatedly, instead. She took a deep breath, spat, wiped her mouth, and sank back into the Zodiac as it rode another wave.

Jared kept the shore to starboard and cut the Zodiac's speed back. The glacier, a sheer wall of layered ice, its seaward face kilometers wide, emptied itself into the sea. The Zodiac's little motor hummed along, steady. It had been kept well tuned, a fact for which Jared was deeply grateful. The motor had no fuel gauge, and Jared spent some long minutes wondering if one of the tarps hid a can of gasoline.

Distance didn't calm him. Jared felt irritable; he wanted—drugs, of course. He wanted the nice smooth feeling he'd had for three or four days, according to the length of his beard, which had gotten past the stubbly stage and felt soft to his fingers.

Past the glacier, the sea butted against overhangs of pack ice. Jared watched the shore for potential landing spots. The swells were getting too high for his liking, and the clouds lowered themselves toward the sea. The light faded as he watched. Now that Jared no longer dreaded the tearing agony of a bullet in his back, he remembered that he didn't know if the Zodiac carried food, or flares, or anything that could be used as a shelter. Seals could legally be killed to feed man or dog, except dogs had been banned here for thirty years. Even without weapons, he could probably batter one to death with an oar if he had to do it. They probably tasted fishy. Jared didn't want to kill a seal, and he didn't know where the hell he was.

The woman might know. She hadn't said anything. She watched the shore, not him, but she hadn't tried to fight him.

Jared mused on stupidity and wondered why he'd been so hell-bent to leave the nice warm tent, where the only danger was immediate death. He'd only wanted to escape, waking helpless and trapped, a feeling made worse because of his bound hands.

He'd been an idiot. His captors could have killed him at any time, and they hadn't.

The shoreline curved inward, and gave a faint hope of shelter. A sudden break in the clouds showed a glimpse of high, distant mountain peaks above the shore, blinding white. The water brightened from gray to green and went back to gray as the clouds settled on the water again, close and low.

Snow began to fall, pellets driven by the wind to pepper Jared's face. He blinked sleety water away from his eyes, and hoped he could get the Zodiac to shore before shore disappeared.

Something black broke the monotony of the ice, and Jared aimed for it. Closer in, he saw it for what it was, a leopard seal hauled out on the ice. If a seal could get onshore, Jared figured he could.

He surfed the Zodiac shoreward, intent on watching the waves form offshore, waiting, waiting. Not this one, not yet; now. Here we go.

Jared gunned the motor to catch the wave he wanted. It carried the Zodiac onshore with a satisfying rush.

All that was needed, Jared figured, as the inflatable skidded onto a patch of bare rock, was a palm tree or two, and a girl in a bikini.

TWENTY-THREE

The inside of the helo was a warm shell, an enclosed timeless bubble of white noise that rose and fell over vistas of cloud and ice. Ice with all the names of ice that Signy had ever heard—brash, bergy bits, firn, a stretch of iron-hard sastrugi carved by time and wind into Zen sculptures, seen when the helo went overland across the snowpack to reach another part of the sea—Signy wanted more names than English knew for the shapes, colors, forms of it. The day was overcast, the light soft and foggy. Inland, mountains rose high and desolate, sharp-peaked shapes of raw power.

Trent muttered about the weather as the helo skimmed across waves and islets, searching for potential harbors near the coast.

Signy had told Trent to watch for a small craft, a raft, a Zodiac. She looked for anything black, and found instead the backs of seals, dark shadows, sunstruck phosphenes from her own blinking.

Trent's terse comments to the *Siranui*, to McMurdo, assumed strange imports in Signy's ears; Trent's "Rogers," and "Say agains?" becoming codes for storms, floating corpses, disasters.

Signy closed her aching eyes and let them focus on nothing, a nothing colored with amorphous cloud shapes in yellows and dull reds, with tiny imploding dots formed of visual fatigue. She had this one flight, a foolish visual search for someone lost, and then she would have to seek for Jared in other ways.

Jared could be on the *Siranui*. Signy could be leaving

him behind, helpless, hurt or tied up somewhere. One transmission burst, twelve hours ago, was all she had to give her hope. Why hadn't there been more?

Signy had this flight, with three people who might simply be decent humans with no ulterior motives, but decent humans could serve so many indecent purposes—and say, later, to themselves, to any accuser, I was only doing my job.

If this visual search failed, as it was far too likely to do? Anna might know someone here who would take a helo up, take a boat out. Right now, Signy could fantasize that Jared was healthy, well fed, warm, that he would find a way free of whatever bonds held him.

"There's a hell of a lot of weather, folks," Trent said. "McMurdo's tracking a storm for us, and we're skirting its edges. There's sections of the grid that we won't get a look at today."

"Well, maybe this inconvenient friend of Signy's is in the right part of the grid," Alan said.

"Let's hope so." Trent lowered the helo to look at something, but Signy saw only more water and more ice. Anna kept her face turned to the window, watching, watching. Anna had been quiet for a long time.

"How long can we keep looking?" Signy asked.

"A while," Trent said.

In Lisbon, the Palacio's techs had suspended a holo of the southern latitudes above center stage. A huge bowl of a contour map hung over the delegates' heads like the bottom half of a cut melon. The fifty-degree line sliced off the southern tip of South America. The blurry line of the Antarctic convergence circled the outer limits of the winter ice, a boundary that marked the turmoil of the meeting place of sun-heated and ice-chilled waters, an area of rich nutrients to feed sea creatures.

Pilar decided the effect was okay, the same sort of view

people in the space station got of Earth hanging above
them.

Far away on the cold southern seas, in real time, fishing fleets trawled back and forth across the Antarctic
convergence, searching for the sweet spots, wherever the
krill thought they were in any given season. On the projection above the delegates' heads, suspended and slowly
turning, last year's thickest krill concentrations were
marked in translucent squares of coral red, the color of
well-cooked lobsters.

Beneath the holo, alliances formed and broke. Watching, Pilar could pick out the delegates who had known
about the U.K.'s proposal in advance. They had their positions thought out, their statements ready, pro and con,
and their behaviors showed no surprise. Others kept
their eyes glued on their notebooks while they tapped
out requests for instructions, data, potential strategies.

Janine's muscles sent sensations of tight knots, perceptible monitors of anxiety. Pilar damped down Janine's
kinesics signals and keyed up a white-noise series of controlled breaths, a repeated series of calm, counted exhalations. Janine's fingers tapped entries on her keyboard
that she deleted, unsent.

"Sweetheart," Pilar said, "are you rehearsing what
you're going to ask Kazi, or what?"

[Janine] I hate him.

"No, you don't. It's biz, Janine. Just ask him, at lunch,
what the hell is going on."

[Janine] Kazi, are we fired? How's that?

"Not subtle," Pilar said.

[Janine] I'll find out what happened. Idiots here
talk forever, ever, ever.

**"The Tanaka contingent is still carrying our
prompts."** Paul's voice seemed to come from a space
over Janine's head. **"Do you think they've built an alternate program to sell?"**

"How the hell should I know, Paul? You're the

strategist." Pilar snapped the words out. Then she feared she might have pushed Paul too far, that he would withdraw again.

"They have," Paul said. **"Damn them. It's the only thing that makes sense."**

Paul sounded so certain. Give him a few minutes, and he would have an entire alternate scenario planned, ready for Edges to put together to Tanaka specs. In only a few hundred impossible man-hours. Pilar had to believe that Paul could do it, that he wouldn't space out and add to everyone's problems. Jared could have teased Paul along, kept him calm. Jared wasn't here.

God, kowtowing to these Tanaka people was going to be a royal pain. Yes, boss; we deeply regret that you didn't tell us what was really happening, yes, sir; we'll fix it, so sorry. If we could just dump the contract and tell Janine it was okay to march out in a huff and get on a plane for home—but there's Jared, if he's not dead by now, and there's money. We can't quit, Pilar thought. We have to wait and be fired, if we aren't already.

At breakfast, Kazi had passed out crib sheets to his team. Laid out for the Tanaka crew were the voting records and political leanings of most of the attending delegates. Personal foibles, passions, and quirks rounded out many of the profiles. In their notebooks, Kazi's people carried prompts from the work Signy had done in Houston, revised and condensed and weighted with changes from trends that Paul and Jimmy had reviewed last night.

Talk about new varieties of trees designed for rapid growth, the prompts advised. Mention ermine, sandalwood, and ivory to the Europeans. Do not say the word "green," or "thirst," or "rain forest" to anyone. Say "toxin," if you can. Speak of contaminants, in art, music, food, if you can.

The ban had a decent chance, still, in this group of conservation-minded Antarctic buffs. How their individual governments saw the proposal was a different can of worms. And now, Pilar mourned, we'll never know if it could have worked.

[Janine] France looks hungry. Maybe here comes lunch.

France, at the head of the oval table, rapped the gavel and stood. The room erupted in babble. Janine, hampered by a moving barricade of suits, tried to get close to Kazi. She dodged and nudged and said "Pardon me," working her way through the Japanese delegation that crowded up the stairs and toward the foyer.

Pilar tuned Janine's kinesics back in, prepared to monitor Janine's tension, wanting the feeling of action, however distant it might be.

"Stay with him, kid," Pilar urged. "Get what you can. It's Friday; we've got all weekend to sort this out."

Pilar could see Kazi nodding to a man whose words were full of gutturals and excitement. Janine dodged around someone with a large set of shoulders and gained a position next to Kazi. Kazi smiled at her.

"What's going on?" Janine asked.

"We are scheduled for luncheon with the Portuguese delegate," Kazi said. "He is serving a national dish. Pork cooked with clams?"

A wall of smiling Japanese faces surrounded Itano. Pilar felt, through the sensors, Janine's right foot hit the marble floor with a discreet, but definite—stamp.

"*Amêijoas com carne,*" Janine said. Janine's voice was light and lovely. The rest of her was a solid knot of anger. She reached for Kazi's proffered arm and held it so that it brushed her breast. Kazi smiled down at her, a tall man protecting a tender blonde.

Janine's fingers dug into Kazi's arm, hard. Kazi reached over and patted her hand, and leaned close, his lips close to her ear. "*Remain calm,*" Kazi whispered. He smiled at the woman from Argentina, who had shouldered her way to the center of the crowd.

"That's Isabel Sarmiento," Pilar said.

"Kazi!" the woman said. "You are looking so well!"

"And you, Bella. May I present Dr. Hull?"

"Hello," Janine said. "Pleased to—"

"Dr. Hull, so nice to meet you. Kazi and I were classmates at Stanford. You're lunching with Portugal? I hope you like cilantro," Sarmiento said to Kazi, adding, sotto voce, "Chile plans to bring up the sinking of the *Noche Blanca*. And the *Oburu*." She winked. "You owe me, Kazito."

Señora Sarmiento let the crowd take her out of the range of a reply.

Janine focused on the woman's thick knot of black hair, as glossy as if it had been varnished. "Kazi, what the hell are you *doing*?" she hissed.

"Later, dear," he whispered. "Smile, please?"

The woman scrambled forward and helped Jared pull the raft up the beach, into the roaring wind. There was nothing on this stretch of land to break it, and it whistled and threw handfuls of snow into his face and down the neck of his parka. The leopard seal had disappeared. The snow fell white and the air was darker.

Jared tried to unwrap one of the tarps that covered a bundle in the raft.

"Help me with this!" Jared shouted. The wind whipped his words away, and he wasn't sure the woman would understand them, anyway. But she grabbed a corner of the tarp and held it while the wind unfolded it for them. They ducked beneath the tarp and pulled it over them, tying it down where they could and tucking it under boxes. They ended up with a draft-free shelter, walled by the containers the raft carried, where they sat knee to knee, huddled in the dark. A place where they might get a little rest before they worked on building something that would keep them from freezing if they slept.

Jared's hands and feet had been cold forever, and now he felt the cold climbing his arms and legs, although his middle still felt warm. Waves of fiery pain throbbed in his hands once the wind stopped chilling them. His fingers felt huge, clumsy, like balloons filled with scalding liquid. The rest of him didn't feel slow or stupid, not yet. That would happen if his core temperature began to fall. Would he notice?

"Thanks," Jared said. "Psyche? Is that your name?"

The woman stared at him.

"You have killed us," she said.

Her English was thickly accented and carefully enunciated. She spoke to him as if he were somewhat simple and might have difficulty understanding her.

"Perhaps I have," Jared said. "In any case, I think we have time enough to talk. Talk to me, Psyche. Tell me why you tried to kill me."

"No. We did not."

"Then *why* did you knock me off that boat? What the hell were you doing?"

The whites of Psyche's eyes were lustrous in the dusk. She looked away from him, at the tarp that sheltered them from the wind, which had begun to die down.

"I am the wife of Mihalis Skylochori," she said.

"So you kidnapped me? I had nothing to do with his drowning."

"He was a bastard, Mihalis."

"But yours."

"Yes."

"Why have you taken me, Psyche?"

"Because of money." Psyche turned her head and spat. Her chapped lips were more pale than her face. She wiped her mouth with her hand.

"Whose money, Psyche?"

"Mihalis—my Mihalis, and his friends. They were good boys, once. But times are bad. The seas—"

Psyche paused. Jared waited. He found his gloves in

his pocket, and drew them over his injured hands. The salt and the bugs from his own skin were going to cause infection. He thought, distantly, that he was going to lose part of a finger or two. He thought he was trapped with an actress, and he wished he could tell her she was playing for the most attentive audience she would ever have.

"The seas are dying," Jared said.

"We live where Odysseus wandered, barbarian. Do not think to tell us what we know."

Psyche rubbed at her forehead and shifted so that her body was closer to him, not farther away. We are cold, Jared thought, we are so cold, that whatever our hatreds are, they cannot last. In a minute, I will reach for her, and hug her close to me, because we need each other's warmth.

"A woman hired us. To make trouble in the seas, she said. The catch—too many people fight over the catch. The wealth of the seas. Pfah. The wealth of the seas is smelly little bugs. They are all we have left now." Psyche shifted her shoulders against the box behind her. "This woman—a Tanaka woman—she asked us to do a job for her and then she would not pay us."

"So you came after me?"

"You show the world many things, you rich American camera people. You are not so rich as you were, and we are glad."

"You kidnapped me because of the cameras?"

"No. You were a man on a Tanaka deck, that's all we knew. We wanted our money," Psyche said. She twisted to reach for the latch of the box behind her. "We thought that the woman would not want her story told to the world. And we would get our money."

"Don't pull a gun out of there," Jared said. He had begun to shiver, and he hoped Psyche wouldn't notice. Jared feared that his reflexes were slowing down, and he wasn't sure he could grab her in time to stop her.

"A gun? If I had one, I would kill you. I don't."

Psyche lifted the lid of the box and rummaged in it without looking inside. She kept her eyes on Jared's face.

"Here," she said. "Will this help us now, Jared Balchen?"

She tossed him his battery pack.

TWENTY-FOUR

Trent's silence and his concentration on his flying led Signy to believe that he really was concerned about the weather. Alan sighed, once, and his hand crept up to grip the shoulder strap of his harness and stayed there. It wasn't a bumpy ride. Signy wondered what Alan knew that she didn't. The helo's speed seemed to vary a lot, at times seeming to cruise over the terrain, at times almost standing still in the air. Signy didn't think Trent was finding any reason to slow down when that happened, so it must be the winds that did it. Signy didn't like that, either. Patches of sunlight were getting more scarce as the minutes passed.

"Sorry," Trent said, as they turned away from a wall of solid cloud. "Our corridor is shrinking. We may need to set down at McMurdo rather than back on ship. It's thick over the *Siranui* about now."

"Should we head there? To McMurdo?" Signy asked.

Trent sighed and wiggled his shoulders. "Nah," he said. "We've got a little more light to use up before we have to quit. I hate to waste it."

Trent wouldn't put them all at risk; Signy had to believe that. And anyway, she didn't want to land and find a "Game Over" message from Tanaka.

Icy shores, glaciers forcing the land down as they made their way to the sea, glimpses of high mountains; what had been beautiful just hours ago now looked terrible, merciless; the land sent a monotonous message of barren danger. The rich life of the southern seas? How could anything live here? Jared, unless someone sheltered him, had to be dead by now. It would be easy to say—I give up. Let's go back. It would be so easy to say that, and end this noisy, fearful journey into nowhere.

Unsought, a construct made of her wishes and terrors, Signy felt a heavy pressure against her left side, the bulk and weight of a human form with the knob of a sharp elbow against her/his ribs, and the sensation of her/his muscles tensed and shuddering.

It couldn't be. Signy was dreaming this, bringing Jared's presence alive out of wishes and desperation.

"Jared?" Signy whispered.

"Anybody home?" Jared asked. **"Thought I'd check in."**

"Where? Where are you?" Signy yelled the words over the noise of the helo, forgetting that she was hooked into the cabin's mikes. "I got him! I got him, he's on-line; he's out here!"

Anna tugged her earphones away from her ears with a wince, but it was followed by a grin.

"All right!" Trent bellowed. Alan whooped. She shushed them with a frantic wave of her hands.

"Where are we, Psyche?"

"Backdoor Bay," a woman's voice said. **"We are near the Erebus glacier tongue."**

Signy could see Jared's cameras focused on a human face, a blurred outline that appeared in an everyday, nothing-special view on her tiny heads-up screen. She switched the visuals to cover the full screen of her headset, letting Jared's perceptions fill her world, letting the helo's cabin become a distant thing, a secondary concern, accepting Jared's motions, the feel of him, the strange absence of sensations from his hands. Jared watched the woman tucked against his side, her shadowed face, her cracked, pale lips.

"Backdoor Bay?" Signy asked. "Trent, can we get there?"

Signy's body grew heavy against the seat as Trent torqued the helo around and headed inland toward a thick wall of cloud. "It's pretty sloppy over there," Trent said. "We'll see."

"Pilar? You want to come in with me, I think. We got a transmission here," Jimmy's voice said. Signy heard him, and she heard Pilar's voice yelling for Janine.

"We're on our way, Jared," Signy said.

"Who's we?"

"Me, Anna, Alan. And Trent."

"Okay. You came south, Signy?"

"Jared? Jared, is it really you?" Paul asked.

"Yes, it's really me, you skinny-assed shyster."

"Trent, how far is it? How long will it take?" Signy asked.

"Twenty minutes if the weather holds. If this cloud cover gets too thick out here we'll have to go into Mc-Murdo, refuel, and sit it out," he said over Paul's **"You bastard. You asinine overmuscled mock-up of an . . ."**

"Jared, did you hear that?" Signy asked.

". . . overgrown Canuck jock."

"Paul! Shut up!" Signy hissed.

"I love you, too, Paul," Jared said. **"Yeah, Signy. I heard you say you're on your way. I'm just sitting here, girl. Take your time."**

Sometimes it seemed that Kaziyuki Itano knew everyone in Lisbon. Kazi had managed to get Janine seated next to him, but then he chatted with the woman at his left, deliberately keeping his conversation directed away from Janine's questions.

Janine toyed with her appetizer plate, an arrangement of pastries and pickled things. The pastries smelled of butter.

"Janine! Jared's on-line." Pilar's shout in Janine's

ear speaker startled her; she jumped. Kazi looked up, frowning. Janine pushed her chair away from the table and threw her napkin onto her oily plate. She needed a full rig; a notebook wouldn't do for this—

Janine, running, zigzagged through the tables. A waiter carrying a fat silver tureen dodged out of her way, hissing as hot soup stung his fingers. Janine's boots clattered on the stone floors and disapproving faces turned to look as she passed. She skidded around a corner and ran down the long hallway, past blue and white tile inlays that featured innocent scenes of sea creatures and fruit.

Jared kept the bitter away; that was what he did. Janine was the newcomer in Edges, the youngest, but Jared had always smoothed the rough spots, told her what she needed to know before she made some horrid gaffe. For a while, she'd been afraid to speak up. Jared had nudged her into interactions, and Pilar was less aloof when Jared was around. He had a way of defusing Pilar's fear of love, somehow.

When Jared got home, the world would feel normal again. To see him, to get as close as virtual would let her get—to tell him he was missed—

Three more doors—Janine searched in her pockets for her headset. Her headband rig wouldn't give her a full visual and she wanted one. Behind the control booth's door, the tech from Milan munched on salted nuts and watched the empty stage. He turned in his chair and raised an eyebrow as she came through the door at full speed.

"I need a link," Janine said. She had her headset in place before she sat down.

Surrounding Janine's visual field, blessedly present in sound, touch, and light, Janine saw and felt the thin woman cradled in the curve of Jared's arm. Wind howled in the background. The scene was dusky.

"We've got company. Someone's tapped in with us," she heard Jimmy say.

"Umm, nice work." Real time in the Lisbon control booth, startling, the tech's words intruded. Janine lifted her headset. The tech stared down at the center stage of the great hall, his chin propped in one hand.

—a woman's face appeared to float above the stage of the Palacio. Jared's headband cameras panned the interior of a sort of tent, giving the watchers a view of the interior of his little shelter of stretched fabric. He was nested in boxes and clutter piled on the bottom of a beached Zodiac.

Sitting beside Janine in Lisbon, the tech filled in macros, humming while he worked, and framed Jared's face in shadows.

"Do you have a face shot on this guy? I could add it in," the tech said.

"Shit!" Janine whispered. "Shut that off!"

—Jared and the unknown woman huddled center stage. Jared's gloved hand lifted a corner of the fabric that sheltered them. He looked out at a blinding white expanse of snow, at a dark sea where ice tossed on giant waves.

The tech projected the landscape to the walls, a full 360 degrees of storm in blue-grays and cold whites. "I'm using some of the stuff you put in the Tanaka suite," he said. "It fits right in."

—The roar of an Antarctic wind filled the hall in Lisbon. It boomed out over the room's ranks of seats, empty except for a few stray delegates who had wandered in. They were the quick eaters, maybe, or the ones who were not interested in lunch. They looked up, idle watchers at a drama that could have made little sense to them.

"Turn it off. The projection, please, turn it off," Janine begged.

"No, let it run," the tech said. "It's from Antarctica, isn't it? That's why we're here, after all."

Signy could hear the whining of the wind outside the flimsy shelter where Jared and the woman named Psyche huddled, their backs against a gray plastic crate marked with serial numbers and cyrillic characters in black. The woman twisted around and rummaged inside it. She brought out a quilted felt mat, the kind movers used to protect furniture for storage. Jared and Psyche shifted in the small space, making a cocoon of the thing. Psyche hugged Jared tight and pressed her lean frame against his side.

Jared had stopped shivering. He wasn't moving much at all. He held Psyche, his hands locked together across her back. She jerked, and Signy could see Jared's hands pat her, as if she were a baby. Psyche sobbed once more and then held him tighter.

"My friends are coming," Jared said. **"Psyche, we'll be out of here in a little while."**

"What of Nikos? Of Mus?"

"Your two buddies?"

"The woman wants to know if we can pick up her friends," Signy said.

"We can't carry everybody," Trent said. "If we can sight 'em, we'll tell McMurdo where they are."

The helo rose over a ridge and flew along a wall of glacier.

"Hi, Jared," Janine's voice said.

"Hello, engineer. Now we're all here, right? Psyche, don't worry; somebody will pick up your buddies."

Signy listened to Jared's breathing. She heard Janine enter the virtual, but Janine didn't say anything after her first hello. Janine waited to catch up, and apparently sensed from the silences, the tensions, that things were moving fast. Quick reflexes, Janine had.

"Are you hurt? Are you injured, either one of you?"
Signy asked.

"My hands are frostbitten," Jared said. **"Psyche's
okay; no injuries."**

Signy looked out of the helo's windows at the glacier
rolling past, its heights hidden in thick cloud cover. Seaward, broken ice rolled on whitecaps. The helo passed
through a wisp of cloud.

"Are you cold?" Signy asked.

"Hell, yes, I'm cold," Jared said. **"We're cold. Yes."**

"I'm sorry. I don't want you to be cold; I don't want
anyone to be cold, ever."

"Signy, you're burbling," Pilar said.

"I love it when you burble," Jared said. **"Pilar?
Janine? I love you, too."**

The helo crossed a ridge. Beyond the ice wall, sheltered by a tongue of rock that jutted into the sea, a small
islet held a battered-looking green tent, a banal man-
made intrusion in the day's silent vistas of ice.

"There's somebody," Trent said.

"They aren't ours," Signy said. "Trent, go on. Jared's
not with them."

Two men erupted from the tent. They stretched out
their arms and waved frantically. Their opened mouths
shouted unheard dark pleas from the sunburned ovals of
their faces.

"They'll just have to worry for a while, then. We're
close now, Signy." Trent dipped the helo and waved at
the men, and then pulled up again, while he spoke to
McMurdo, giving the location and landmarks of the little
island.

"Sorry, guys," Trent said.

The men ran after the rising helo for a few desperate
steps. Then they stopped and walked back toward the
tent.

"Those idiots have a support vessel somewhere. They

didn't just cruise to Antarctica in a Zodiac," Trent said. "Maybe their boat could pick them up."

"Jared, did you hear?" Signy asked.

For an answer, Jared hugged Psyche a little tighter to his chest. **"You had a story to tell, Psyche,"** Jared said. **"You haven't told me all of it. Where is your ship? You have one, don't you?"**

"The *Sirena*," Psyche said. **"It belongs to Mihalis and his brothers. It waits, near the glacier."**

"How did you get into this mess?"

"We fished with the Chilean fleet last season. Another trawler—the *Noche Blanca*—we partnered up with her. We had friends on that boat."

Jared rocked the woman in his arms, waiting.

"They are dead now," Psyche said. **"We found a good spot; we were pulling up krill faster than we could let them fall into the hold. We got too close to the Japanese trawlers. They were already there in that place but we hadn't seen them. We didn't know. . . .**

"The Japanese shot the *Noche Blanca* out of the water."

Pilar opened a window to Janine. "Wasn't that what Argentina told Kazi about?"

"Yep," Janine said. "Shh."

They both switched their attention back to Jared, to the woman in the tent.

"You aren't saboteurs," Jared said.

"No. At McMurdo, at the Hotel California, we were offered a job," Psyche said. **"To cripple a Japanese boat. To show that all the fleets harass each other, they said to us. The woman—the Tanaka**

woman—said this would help stop the shooting. That the publicity would make the seas safer, that if the treaty countries had to stop turning their eyes away from these violences, then they would become too expensive to continue, and the shooting would stop."

"Sweet Jesus," Signy said. "They actually planned a media event? Lots of smoke and thunder, and plenty of camera angles?"

"Sounds like it," Paul said.

"Mihalis convinced the woman that we could do this thing. He was good with women, Mihalis," Psyche said. "We waited in Ushuaia. The woman sent us credit, and Mihalis bought *plastique*. It was—potent? Is that what you say?"

"Yes," Jared said. "Potent."

"When the fleets came back in October, we slipped up to the *Oburu* in the night. You must remember, these people had killed our friends." Psyche looked up at Jared's face.

Jared smiled at her, or nodded; Signy could feel his head move. The woman blinked and continued. "Mihalis made charges to set at the waterline. The trawler sank."

Signy, in real time, caught a view of a solid wall of cloud. The helo buzzed its way toward it. We shouldn't go in there, Signy thought. If we were sane, we would not fly into those clouds.

"That's how your husband died?" Jared asked.

Psyche's hands tightened their grip on Jared's arm. She had her head tucked down against his chest and she did not look up. "We searched. We did not find him. We did not find anyone alive."

Paul's voice came through Signy's mike, an unwelcome intrusion. "No interview potential without survivors. No wonder they got stiffed on the bill."

"It comes from hiring amateurs," Pilar said. "Stick with pros, I always say."

"Hush," Signy said. They hushed.

"Did you know her name?" Jared asked. "Who was she, Psyche?" Jared's voice faded. A whine of feedback obliterated the woman's answer.

"Trouble," Jimmy McKenna said. "We've got heavy shit line noise here. . . ."

Trent's voice intruded, talking to McMurdo. "Roger," he said. "We are advised."

"What?" Signy yelled. She heard static in her ears and her visuals gave her a mosaic of broken points of light, Jared's face vanishing in their dancing complexities.

"McMurdo says the storm is going to hang here for three—four days. Can your boy last that long?" Trent asked.

"Jared, do you have food? Any heaters?" Signy asked. There was no answer.

"Jimmy, get him back!" Signy pleaded.

"I'm trying. I'm trying, okay?"

Signy ripped her headset away from her face. The bubble of the helo floated in a gray nowhere. She felt it tilt. A quick blur of black broke the colorless expanse around the helo, a line of boulders between sea and sky, and then the sight of solid ground vanished again.

"Jared?" she asked.

"No food. No heat."

"Trent, they won't last. The support boat is called the *Sirena*. It's near the glacier. Tell them to try and pick them up. Jared, or those men, whoever they can reach. Tell them to try." Signy shoved her headset back over her eyes.

Trent spoke to his mike, asking McMurdo to send a message to the trawler.

"Jared? We'll be there as soon as we can. Jared, can you hear me?" Signy asked.

"Yeah," he said.

Signy couldn't see him; the view in her headset was an array of shattered colors. The colors swirled and coalesced, following complicated rules Signy could not define.

—A woman's face formed from the chaos; not Psyche's.

She is starving, Signy thought. She is very young, in late adolescence at most, but her eyes look much older than her face. Asian, but a strange mixture; her features are not classic Japanese. I know her name. . . .

"Signy Thomas, your pilot is very brave and very foolish. You are flying into an area of high winds and poor visibility. You should have turned back by now."

"San-Li," Signy said.

"Evergreen," she heard Jimmy whisper.

"Cordova is in the air and very close to Psyche Skylochori and Dr. Balchen. Cordova will pick them up and take them to the *Kasumi*. They will not be harmed." The thin girl-child formed her words carefully, her lips moving as if she were lip-synching—moving before Signy heard the words. As if she were a simulacrum.

"Paul?" Signy asked.

"Let her do it, Signy."

"She's not lying about the storm," Jimmy said. **"McMurdo's calling everyone in."**

The San-Li figure broke and faded, replaced by a crystalline input from Jared, a clear view of the interior of his little shelter and an increase in his muscular tension, an awakening to some stimulus or other.

"Jared, did you see her?" Signy asked.

"I heard her. Signy, I'll take *any* ride out of here. We'll sort it out later." Jared stood up. Signy felt the sure motions of his body as he reached for the tarp and threw it aside. He tilted his head back, seeking the location of the buzzing sound of an incoming helo. Signy felt him relax when its outline appeared. Its dragonfly shape swooped toward the Zodiac, coming in from the sea.

"EEE-HAH!" Jared yelled. He leaned back on his heels and waved with both arms. Beside him, the woman stretched her arms up as if she would pull the helo out of the sky. She was very short, Signy realized; she was a tiny little thing.

The helo flew overhead and landed about fifty meters from the Zodiac. Jared and the woman ran for it. The pilot was Cordova, recognizable from the droop of his mustache. He cut the rotors, held up his palm to ward them back, and frowned until the speed had died down. Then he motioned them forward to the open door.

"Hello! Hello, my friend. It's damned good to see you!" Jared yelled over the engine noise. He grabbed Psyche by the waist and heaved, lifting her from the snow to the helo's safety in one motion. Psyche scrambled for the backseat and Jared hauled himself into the helo, his hand outstretched for Cordova's. They punched at each other for a grinning minute, even while Jared settled into the upholstered seat, into the warm, intimate safety of the helo's cabin.

Janine heard scattered applause. She looked down into the Palacio's dusky ranks of seats. More stray people had gathered. Some of them munched at sandwiches.

Above them:

Cordova's white teeth gleamed in a monstrous grin, and the noise of the helo, at a painfully loud volume, rose even higher as the stage became the interior of the helo, rocking up and away from the ice.

Signy leaned forward against the harness straps. Trent aimed for a tiny rift in the clouds and the helo broke through into an area of lighter gray. Anna watched the sea, watched for something out there in the brash and bergs. Anna pursed her lips and turned to look forward, intent on the shore.

Signy stretched, grabbed the back of Alan's seat, and looked over his shoulder, to better see—

The shore making a shallow curve, a flat sheet of ice that had sagged down and wedged tight on its way into the sea. The raft, a tiny oval pulled up on the tilted slab, a black punctuation mark on an expanse of white, and Cordova's helo lifting.

Inside the helo's bubble, Jared reveled in the secure pressure of the belt harness against his chest, the sight of the ranks of instruments gleaming and blinking across the cockpit, the feel of increased weight as the helo rose and Cordova pushed them forward and low, over a tossing sea. Far to his left, another helo approached. Signy was in there. She had come so far. And found him, although in some ways, Jared had never expected that she wouldn't; he had never doubted that someone would come for him.

Some people lived all their lives without ever trusting that they were loved. Jared felt immense sorrow for people like that. Poor bastards. How did they live through any day?

Jared had always been loved. He had never questioned it; he would not question it now.

He sank into the seat, pressing his back against its padding; he stretched his legs and pulled back the cuff of his parka. Signy, Paul, Pilar, Janine—all the indicator lights glowed; everyone here. His own familiar slot in the ranks was lighted as well. There was a guy named Jimmy, he'd heard Signy talking to him. Jared didn't know him, but what the hell—the more the merrier. He felt a sweet euphoria, a sense of well-being that flooded over him and made even the throbbing in his hands an indicator of continued life; the pain of healing. Hunger chewed at his empty belly; his face hurt. How wonderful that his face hurt! Jared laughed aloud with the giddy joy of escape.

Cordova would land somewhere, and Signy would be there. Maybe she had a sandwich or something with her.

"Signy?" Jared asked. "Do you . . ."

The helo's engine coughed. Cordova cursed and his hands flew over his controls. The engine caught, coughed, coughed again and died. The helo flew just above the water. The cabin tilted and Jared felt his weight sag against the shoulder harness as the helo began to heel over toward the waves that reached up for them, too close, too close. Spinning, the horizon came up to cross the cockpit, dividing it vertically into water and sky. Metal screamed. The rotor blades cut into the sea. Jared saw, distantly, Cordova's face, distorted into a rictus of terror. Cordova fought the controls, struggled with—

The water struck the side of the helo with a flat, jarring slap. Water rose up the cabin's sides. The fuselage might float. Or maybe parts of it would. Jared felt the water slew the craft to starboard, felt the fuselage begin a slow spin, seeking a balance of buoyancy between the weight of the blades and the motor. His hands, his damaged hands, found the release button on his harness. It snapped away. Jared reached for the woman in the seat behind him. Psyche sat frozen, staring straight ahead. Jared punched at the buckles on her harness and grabbed for her. The helo rolled up on its side, its door coming completely free of the water. Jared twisted so that his back rested on Cordova's shoulder, braced his feet against the door and kicked hard.

Fresh clean wind broke into the cabin. Hampered, for Cordova and the woman struggled beneath him, Jared found a grip on the edge of the cabin door and hoisted himself up. The helo settled into a smooth place in the water, a smooth glossy place. The smell of fuel reached up, rich in the air, slick on the water. On the horizon, Jared saw a whale breaking the surface of the waves.

An alarm beeped in the interior of the helo. Its stupidity amused Jared somewhat. The emergency locator would be sending out pulses now, would do so for hours unless the salt water shorted it out, and those transmitters were well shielded.

Where now? Into the water? Unless the cabin sank, even with the risk of the spilled fuel, they had to stay with the helo, stay on something that floated.

Jared grabbed Cordova and pulled him up through the door. Cordova's flailing hands found a hold on the helo's side. Jared hauled himself out and clung flat-bellied, his fingers seeking for holds on the slick surface. Psyche struggled to the opening and raised her arms. Jared reached for her. Someone was screaming, but it wasn't Psyche; someone screamed and Jared thought it might be Signy, or Paul. The noise was a nuisance Jared didn't need, over the beep of the alarm, the sucking sound of water. Psyche's shoulders came free of the door, fast, almost knocking him away from his perch. The helo seemed to be staying afloat. This was good. Jared grabbed Psyche's arm and held her tight while she scrambled up and grabbed him, and Cordova, wedging herself between them. The helo listed, settling toward a new balance.

Jared heard a soft *whump*, like the rush of air around a closing door. Flames rose from the sea, as high as city walls. The helo rolled bottom up as the sea ignited. Jared clung to it until the water closed over his head, clung to Psyche until she broke free of his grip. The buoyancy of his clothing lifted him up into a pocket of blazing fuel. He let go of the helo and ducked, proud that he hadn't tried to inhale the burning gases. The undersurface of the water was lighted neon orange. Below him, the sea reflected the colors, fractured them into reds and greens, a wondrous fan of colors, and he searched for Psyche, for Cordova, for human shapes in the depths. He struck out into the sea, fighting to clear the edge of the flames, hanging on to his breath until he had to clench his jaws tight with the effort. Ahead of him, and above, he saw the woman's legs, kicking in panic. He reached her and let himself rise, hoping there would be breathable air around her.

His hand broke the surface of the water. Heat enveloped it, a heat that was cold and yellow and roared in his ears. Helpless in the grip of a breathing reflex, he lifted his head. His lungs pulled in the nothingness of great pain, of roaring flame. He heard the sound of a helo's rotors, so close above him, but Cordova's helo had crashed, hadn't it?

Shove the woman, push her free of the fire. Jared could feel his arms move, and his legs, trying to swim, as if they were on autopilot. The light around him existed in all the names of colors Pilar had tried to teach him, and he remembered how Signy had chanted them once, laughing with Pilar and setting a virtual for him, a virtual filled with washes of pure light—emerald, celadon, citrine, cobalt yellow, but this yellow was filled with transcendent white, the white of metal glowing under an oxyacetylene torch—topaz, aquamarine, sapphire, moonstone seen in moonlight, all the colors of Signy's eyes.

TWENTY-FIVE

Trent circled the perimeter of the flames, darting in too close for any safety limits Signy could imagine. The helo tossed in updrafts. Nothing appeared on the surface of the water, no wreckage, no tattered scrap of clothing, nothing.

Sobs came to Signy's ears, and a high-pitched keening. None of the shouted curses or the terrible howls were identifiable to her except that one voice did not cry out, did not speak, and that voice was Jared's.

Jared's cameras functioned, his sensors. His arm remained extended toward Psyche, to lift her head? To clutch at her? Psyche's face gaped blind at a holocaust she could no longer see; she sank away. Jared's hand, stretched forward, opened in the flames, relaxed into the burning sea, floated on the water, his hand's shape as innocent as a fallen leaf. Signy drifted, down, as Jared drifted, down, in colors of greens and grays that deepened, deepened.

The cacophony of sounds, the textures of what she twisted in her hands, the awareness that she breathed; Signy's consciousness stalled at the complexity of inputs and sent: Does not compute. She heard Alan's voice, remembered the concept "Alan," the concept—words—

"Nothing! Trent, there's nothing here! Get us the hell away!"

Signy heard Alan yelling in the noise of motors and flames and wind. She realized she held Anna's sleeve, its puffy fabric crushed and compacted in her hands.

—the soft, relaxed motions of Jared's body drifted her

down; smooth, slow. She should tell them not to die here. No one else needed to die here.

"He's dead," Signy said. "Psyche is dead. Cordova—"

—turned in the water, his limp body spread in a starfish shape as he spiraled past her—

"—is dead."

Jared/she rolled over, in a languorous twisting turn, while from the depths, the whale rose, and nudged, nudged her/his body toward the surface.

"Whale, this will do no good," Signy whispered.

She felt thick strong arms around her, a warm persistent presence. Anna held her. Anna, who reached out and held tight.

The fleshtime touch meant so little; Signy drifted down again, down, away from the whale, who turned and vanished.

Anna shook her. Signy tried to get away from Anna; Anna's earthbound, fleshbound persistence; why did she interrupt?

Reflected, redoubled, a seascape filled the hall in Lisbon, an intimate world of watered, shimmering details placed in scale by a drifting hand, by a tangle of Jared's hair crossing a lens like a frond of seaweed.

The watchers below looked up, idly, at the bulk of a whale's flank, at scars and disease laid out before them on an immense gray hide, at the blunted snout of a leviathan that nosed at a limp human arm and then turned away. Silence and gentle motions rocked away into gray, faded. . . .

Janine heard someone shouting at Signy. Jimmy's voice, harsh, cut through the babble from Trent's helo.

"Paul's off-line," Jimmy said. **"I can't access him."**

"He's cut himself out of the system. Let him be. It's grief," Pilar said.

Beside her, Janine heard the tech sigh. He took the

lighting down to black, then brought it back up, lighting an empty stage, bringing workplace illumination to the returning delegates as they began to file in and sit down with their cups of coffee and their notebooks. The room filled with the buzz of quiet conversations.

Janine closed her eyes.

—In black, she felt the sway of currents, a sensual, utterly relaxed drifting—

This had to stop. Now. This was beyond reason; this was sick.

"Jimmy, run Jared's inputs to save, would you?" Janine asked.

"Working," Jimmy said.

The motion from Jared's drifting body stopped. Janine lifted her headset off and stared at its complex lenses, blind eyes that saw too much. She let her head sink forward, onto the cool surface of the console in front of her.

Pilar felt the absence of sensation envelop her like cotton. It was good of Jimmy to shut down the inputs from Jared's suit. Jared wasn't *there*, anymore. He just wasn't there. Pilar wondered if her parents had felt the sense of calm she had sensed in Jared's dying, or if they had suffered agonies in those moments when the car crushed itself around them. Pilar knew they had died hearing shrieks of tortured metal. Hearing was the last sense to go, so it was said. Had the sounds become unearthly music in those last instants? She would never know.

Outside the Seattle window, a dull January rain fell. Slow cold droplets streaked down the glass. Fog, and rain. So dull, such an ordinary rain. Pilar turned away and watched, over and over, the dazzle of colors, the secret, silent heart of a firestorm. She wanted to set it in stone. There were jeweler's tools somewhere in the house, there were lumps of coral and amber, agate the color of caramels. . . . Cool and smooth, Pilar wanted the feel of polished stone under her hands. A segmented form . . . somewhere something wonderful lurked in this maelstrom.

"Pilar? Pilar?" Jimmy's voice was as irritating as the whine of a fly in a winter kitchen.

"Leave me alone." Pilar wondered why her voice sounded so flat, so bored. "I'm working." Magic words. I'm working, she always told them, when something lurked at the edge of vision, when she listened to sounds that might fit together into melodies and rhythms. All of them left her alone when she said that, as if her musings were sacred things that wouldn't bear disturbance. When sometimes, her silence was simply a way to withdraw, to be elsewhere for a little time. Someone would have to explain the code to Jimmy someday. Janine would take care of it; Janine watched out for her like a mother hen.

"Janine needs you," Jimmy said. "So does Signy. Pilar, you have to help them."

Pilar sighed. "Okay. Okay."

Fleeing a storm. Signy watched the terrible Antarctic skies, the quiet figures of the humans around her. She made no plans. This flight, this warm bubble of life suspended above the sea would continue in its own time, its own way. Or the helo would tumble and spin and crash. That could happen. "*Life is generally fatal, Signy.*" Jared used to say that. It came to her that Jared was the one who had spooked her virtuals, had sent the image of the waxy hand adrift in the flames, that night in Taos when Signy had felt so alone, so lost. Had he known he'd done it?

Yes. Yes, he must have known. Jared had seen, somehow, a part of his dying; he had sent her a warning.

Bullshit. That was spook stuff, that was crystals and mystic nonsense. And yet—did he know I was sending him to die?

"I'm so tired," Signy said.

"We're close," Trent told her. Alan twisted in his harness and reached back for her hand. Signy let him take it, her wrist with its band of lights—Pilar, Janine, Jimmy. In Jared's place; Jimmy. Ah, shit.

Signy heard Janine talking to someone.

"I'd better look at Lisbon," Signy told the quiet people in the helo. Her headset was wearing a bruise into her cheekbone. She rubbed at the sore spot while she watched.

Janine heard the speaker's gavel. The afternoon session was opening ten minutes late. Janine stared daggers at the tech sitting beside her. He looked worried.

"I'm sorry," he said. "I'm sorry it went like that."

Janine hated him. A man Janine didn't know, an uninvited intruder who had just shared Jared's personal, private death with anyone who wanted to look up and see it. What did he think he had done? Did it matter?

He seemed so mundane, so unremarkable. He seemed like someone who would dream of a better flat, many children, perhaps a little boat to take out in the harbor on Sundays. The flesh of his neck bulged out over the collar of his pink shirt. Janine wondered why he didn't unbutton it.

The door opened. Janine heard the rustle of expensive silk; Kazi. She saw a glint of tears in his eyes.

"Janine, poor child." Kazi's arms reached around her.

"You saw?" Janine let him hold her. She didn't plan to cry.

"Yes. The crash at sea, yes. A courageous death; bravely met."

Courage? Jared had just kept working, doing the next thing. That wasn't *courage*; that was just Jared.

"You need tea. Or brandy. I'll take you to your room.

You will want privacy," Kazi said. "Come, Janine, come; let's go."

Privacy was not what Janine wanted. She stood, Kazi's arms helping lift her, as if she were very old.

"I'll get some brandy," the tech said. He scrambled to his feet and opened the door, wafting a trace of cologne to mark his path, a cologne with one of those macho names. Matador, or Dork, or something like that.

"Thank you. I'm Kazuyuki Itano. We haven't met . . ."

"Gianni."

Gianni was anything but macho, and Janine smiled, watching his plump little behind disappear down the stairwell. Gianni. John. John Dork. Now she had a name for him.

Janine laughed, a short painful sound that hurt her throat. She held on to the door. Her eyes blurred. Damn tears anyway. A sob broke through her control. Kazi's arms reached around her in a clumsy, gentle hug. Janine pushed him aside, reached for the chair, and sank into it.

"It's not worth it," Janine said. "Jared's dead. I'm leaving. I've got to get home."

Kazi knelt beside her and held both her hands in his.

"Don't go. Don't go, Janine. This is a tragedy, yes. But please, you can't leave now."

Janine's nose was dripping. She twisted a hand free and reached for the carefully folded handkerchief peeping out of Kazi's breast pocket. The hanky was silky cotton, full sized, luxurious. Janine shook it out and honked into it.

"The hell I can't. They need me." Signy wouldn't be home for days. Pilar had Jimmy. Paul? Had disappeared off-line. Janine didn't want to try to fit into Seattle right now, and the Taos house would be empty. So empty. "Yoshiro's daughter decides to play politics and kills off my man, along with a lot of other people. You ask us to do a job for you, and then you change the goddamned rules and don't tell us. You're crazy. Old Man Tanaka is crazy. His daughter is crazy."

"His daughter? If she hired those people, she was ill advised in her choice of mercenaries. You seem convinced that she ordered Cordova to kill himself."

"She sabotaged him," Janine said.

"I cannot accept your accusation."

"I'm not accusing you. I plan to accuse *her*."

"San-Li, if she truly hired the people who sank the *Oburu*, acted foolishly but honorably in seeking to—balance—the hostilities in the Southern Ocean. Tanaka did not sink the *Noche Blanca*."

"Who did?" Janine asked.

"Tanaka is not the only fishing fleet. We don't know, yet."

"You're making excuses for her, Kazi. Did she get permission from anyone before she pulled this shit?"

Kazi looked down at his hands, locked together in his lap.

"It's your company; I know," Janine said. "So you have to defend it. But I had expected more of you."

That hurt him. Janine watched his eyes narrow, his face smooth into an expressionless mask.

"I would not expect you to accept the words of the Greek woman without confirmation, Itano-san." San-Li Tanaka's face appeared on a flatscreen.

Kazi blinked once; he did not answer.

"Seek it, if you will. I am shamed by your assumptions. I trust you will verify them before your unkind thoughts punish me further."

The young woman lowered her eyes. She had sent only a view of her face, in close-up, with a background of a shoji screen.

"Got her," Jimmy whispered. **"She's in the Tanaka office at McMurdo."**

Signy, watching as the helo sped there under gray

skies, asked, **"Will she greet me, do you think? Will she offer her condolences in person?"**

San-Li swallowed, her throat moving as if her mouth were very, very dry. **"Janine Hull, I am sorry that Cordova was not able to return your friend to safety. I sent Cordova to rescue him, once we had located Dr. Balchen's position from the transmissions he was able to send.**

"I failed. I have sent a copy of the events of the crash to Kobe. Our technicians will analyze the motions of the helo. They suspect a fuel failure of some sort."

"Holy shit," Jimmy whispered.

The transmission from the office at McMurdo switched to a more distant camera, showing San-Li's head and shoulders, her hands, short unpolished nails and chapped, reddened knuckles, one of them scabbed like a child's knee. San-Li toyed with a silver letter opener, an ornate dragon with a sharp blade of a tail. Someone reached from offscreen and laid a finger on San-Li's wrist. She put the letter opener down.

"Some alternatives are closed to her," Kazi said.

San-Li raised her head and looked at Kazi. **"I must go now. Señor Abeyta, the delegate from Chile? Watched the scenes in the raft. And the rest. You may need to change your strategy with him."**

San-Li disappeared.

Kazi shrugged. "But I think she would not suicide if her guardians left her. She is a fighter, San-Li."

Gianni appeared, panting, with a huge snifter and a dusty bottle. Kazi took it from him and observed the label. "Thank you," he said to Gianni. "Could you leave us for a little while?"

Gianni ducked his head and left.

Kazi closed the door and sat down, his fingers working at the cork on the dusty bottle. "This will help, Janine."

He sniffed at the bottle's neck and poured out a good inch of dark amber fluid. "You will not need to come to the assembly this afternoon."

Janine sat very still, waiting, and heard Pilar's voice in her ear speaker, a whisper, **"Let's hear it, Kazi old boy."**

"There will be little new business. The delegates must assimilate some new material that is just now being circulated on the mineral-rights section of the treaty."

"Something you knew about?" Janine asked.

"Yes. It's not important right now."

Janine frowned at him.

"Yes, Janine, you can see this material when you are ready," Kazi said.

"More stuff? Babe, I don't think any of us can handle treaty language right now," Pilar said.

"This was not how or when I planned to tell you why we have opposed the ban. This is not a good time. You see, Janine, Tanaka has other interests in the Southern Ocean. The fishing is profitable, yes, and for now, we must ask that it continue." Kazi handed her the snifter.

Brandy fumes rose from it, warming and rich. Little beads formed in the condensation and rolled back down the sides of the glass; it seemed to be an excellent brandy. Janine cupped her hands around the bowl of the snifter and stared into its tawny depths. Waiting Kazi out. She sipped, a tiny mouthful, then a swallow.

"We must oppose the fishing ban," Kazi said. "At the same time, we must present the possibility that the harvest could fall to nothing if the seas are not carefully managed. For this, your work is excellent. We have faith that it will do what we want it to do. It does not need to be changed."

"It's designed to help sell a ban, Kazi. We believe in such a ban, my friends and I."

"Yes. Your work is passionate. Because of it, the motion to stop fishing the Antarctic may pass. If it does, we will make a loud outcry, but we will be pleased.

"But you have done enough, today. As have I. You should lie down, Janine. You should not try to think."

Not think? Janine listened to Pilar's hoarse, flat voice. **"We *shouldn't* try to deal with this now, he's right about that. But he ain't telling the whole story. Be careful, kid."** Janine watched Pilar's light go dark on her wrist.

"Do what he says, Janine." Signy, sounding so detached, so numb.

"I don't want to be alone," Janine said.

"No one does," Kazi said.

"Bring the brandy?"

"Of course."

Janine let Kazi lead her away. Back toward her room, its blue and white tiles, its blank console tuned to nothing.

Fresh tracks from a vacuum cleaner marked the surface of the carpet in the Tanaka suite at McMurdo. San-Li and her escort had left no sense of presence; not a damp towel in the bathroom, not a trace of human heat in the air. Console and sleeping alcove, two chairs; Signy worried that there were only two chairs for four people. Hostess, was she?

The absurdity of it made her smile. She sat down on the carpet and braced her back against the wall. The little room was crowded, filled with parkas and big clumsy boots tracking back and forth to obliterate the cleaner's tracks. Shoes on this carpet seemed strange.

Signy felt invisible sitting there, sheltered by a little cave she made of her parka thrown over her shoulders, motionless while the others shifted and circled, sorting themselves into activities, plans, the business of what came next. Her plans? She must trace how and when Cordova had been sabotaged. She must do that, soon. Cordova had been sabotaged; Signy was sure of it. Someone had fucked over that helo of his. When? When Cordova came to the *Siranui*, when Signy and Anna had watched the whale rising? The timing, the timing, someone had to know Cordova would pick up Jared. Or did they care? Was Cordova a target and Jared's death truly only an accident?

Jared's death was Signy's fault. *She* had killed Jared, killed him by sending him into some stupid business intrigue.

A different part of her mind went—Oh, yeah? Jared got a chance to come to the ice, to the last true wilderness. Do you really think you could have stopped him?

Did San-Li have an agent on the *Sirena*? Cordova had gone somewhere in a hurry, maybe to Psyche's boat, to wait until he was called to his "rescue" mission.

Anna handed a mug of coffee to Signy. "We'll get you home. You need to be home."

Signy nodded and held the mug.

Trent woke the console and talked to the *Siranui*. Signy couldn't hear the replies. Alan sat down beside her. Signy leaned against him, watching the blank holo stage, watching how Trent and Anna stepped around it, coming and going, and then Anna called a view of the Hotel California.

—Marty, the bartender, sloshed soapy water over the floor. He wore a different shirt this time, reef fish swimming into and out of giant pink orchids.

"Hello, Marty. Get me to New Hampshire," Signy said.

"Hello, camera lady." Marty propped the mop in a bucket and wiped his hands on the thighs of his khakis. "East Coast U.S., right?"

"Yes."

"New Hampshire," Alan said.

"Yes," Signy said.

Marty and Anna discussed flights and pilots with Base

Ops. A charter plane was coming in. There was room on it, yes, for a return passenger. A few hours, yes.

Paul's light had stayed aggressively off, for hours now.

Pilar drifted through the streets, carried by eddies and currents in the patterns of passing strangers, clumps and knots and shifting single-file formations. She walked.

And walked, listening to the cadence of her heels on pavement, on old brick, on patches of soggy grass. Time to go. New places, new faces; begin again. Jared died, her fault; Jared died trying to make back money Pilar had blown. Jared died; but he would have gone to that miserable expanse of sea and ice anyway, intrigued by a chance to see something he hadn't seen before, do something he hadn't done. Too confusing, too complex, time to go.

Pilar thought of hotel lobbies, of airport shuttles weaving nets that entangled cities, fates, destinations, picking up and spitting out interchangeable faces, interchangeable tasks, futile, futile. Yeah. Fly, get gone. Pilar fingered the credit chip in her pocket. Kazi said Edges still had a job. She didn't believe it for a minute.

Hungry, cold, Pilar followed the path of least resistance: down. Looking out at sea wrack crusted on the bases of the old logs under the empty piers, from where her feet had brought her, the little park on a spit of land that jutted out into the harbor just beyond the Pike Street Market.

Glowing space heaters stood on pedestals set in concrete, a city's afterthought designed to comfort tourists. The heaters cast globes of red light into the fog. Motionless figures stood around them, solid obelisks in a liquid landscape of silence and shadow. Under the curve of an amphitheater designed to suggest a seashell, three tall men played—steel drums, steel drums, and a flute, its keys worn down to base metal that gleamed yellow through the silver. Pilar could see the pink pads of the flutist's fingers through the holes he'd cut in the fingertips of his gloves. The flutist capered as he played, a thin Kokopelli with no hunch to his back. The band played to pass the time, or to keep warm, listlessly waiting for an occasional tossed and crumpled dollar. Pilar swayed with the music, her motions muffled under her parka. One of the drummers smiled at her, a tired, reluctant smile in a face that made her think Masai.

The drummer appraised her, her face? A question rose in his eyes; Pilar nodded.

"Pilar," she mouthed, soundlessly. The drummer smiled again, not so tired-looking this time. Pilar's braid had fallen forward over her shoulder. She loosened it and shook out her hair and dropped her parka beside the drums. The sea air chilled the warm spots on her skin-thin, the creases between thigh and pelvis, the back of her neck, the soft skin under her arms and between her breasts. Pilar kicked off her shoes and began to dance.

No lights, no staging, costumed in her wired skinthin of flesh-colored Lycra, Pilar danced. Tried, feeling the drummers' eyes on her, to pull the little band to her rhythms; yes. They picked up her changes, responsive, resilient, oh, yes. Dancing for pennies; Pilar Videla belonged here. Here, not in the mazes of finance and intrigue where she had never belonged, where *coyotes* from Nambe had no business trying to compete.

The flute rose above basso drumtalk, trilling a descant, and Pilar scribed out arcs of implied geometries, sang, in the silent voices of muscle and sweat, a language of her own devising. . . .

Of the flight of austral birds, of sea creatures suspended in liquid grace, of simple trusts and the rhythms of surf and breath. Of nights where hunters waited in the grass, where blood and fire were fated, inevitable, redeeming.

Melody, rhythm, motion; Pilar and the drums and the flute rode each other's energies, shifting seamless from rhythm to rhythm, from transition to transition, and a wall formed around her now, watchers, a solid wall; some of them smiled. Riding the necessities of breath and melody, triumphant. Tonic minor chord, glissando on the drums, major. Enough. . . .

Breathless, Pilar spun outside the circle she had created, out of the applause and into the shadows.

Redlighted by the glow of the heaters, Jimmy's soft and earnest face, worried, frowned at her. Jimmy tilted his head toward home.

"Must I?" Pilar asked.

"I guess not. You were going to leave, right?"

"Right."

"Well. I'll come with you."

They wandered through the interstices of the crowd, where tropisms of warmth and cold moved the watchers like a disturbed school of fish; the process reestablished positions at the heaters.

A man in purposeful motion intersected their path. Street person? Mugger? Jimmy half-turned as the man approached, shifting to put his bulk between Pilar and a possible threat.

"Dancer?" His gloved hands full of bills, the tall drummer held them out to her. "Your share. Pilar." The drummer said her name as if he believed it was really her for the first time, now that he was close enough to touch her.

"I—"

"Thanks," Jimmy said. He took the sheaf of bills and tucked them in the pocket of her parka. "Thanks, man." Jimmy's hand on Pilar's elbow steered her out of the crowd, away from the drummer. Pilar smiled over her shoulder at the man's dark face.

Away from noise, until the streets were empty around them; they walked uphill.

Jimmy was out of shape. Pilar could hear him breathe hard, climbing the steep pavement, both of them leaning forward against the slope.

Pilar stopped at an empty corner, thinking to turn down the street, away. To leave him.

"I don't need the money," Pilar said.

"Yes, you do. It's pride."

"I have no pride."

"Yeah, I know. But *he* does."

Rain began to fall, the cold, quiet rain of winter. Her feet hurt. Jimmy reached out his hand, and she took it, their netted fingers touching, mesh on mesh. His hand was warm.

"Let's go, Jimmy."

TWENTY-SIX

When they were gone, Anna back to the *Siranui* with Trent, Alan out to scrounge up food that Signy didn't want, Signy was left alone with the neat little holo stage and console in the Tanaka suite.

Signy clutched her parka over her shoulders and powered up the console. No one's signal showed on her wrist. Not Jimmy or Pilar, certainly not Paul. Paul had shut down all of his lines. Signy even tried the public access number, and frowned at Paul's smiling, younger face on the answering machine.

In Lisbon, Signy found Janine sitting with her notebook in her room, the camera showing Janine's face, tearless and intent, and the empty room behind her.

"Where's Kazi?" Signy asked.

"Gone," Janine said. "For the weekend. He was called back to headquarters, or so he said."

"What are you going to do, kid?"

"Stay."

"You don't have to."

"Yeah. I don't have to." Janine did not say, There's nobody home, nobody—"Have *you* heard from Pilar?" Janine stuck out her jaw, defiant, waiting.

"No, babe. I guess she's out walking. Or something. Do you know any way we can get into Paul's system?"

"No—Signy, I'm okay. There's this mineral-rights stuff; I haven't looked at it yet. I'm staying. I want to. There's not much going on until the Monday session."

Signy imagined Janine drifting around the emptying hotel, wandering the mazes of Lisbon streets.

"It's not like Jared and I were lovers, Signy. I loved him, yes. But I can handle it. And if someone needs to find me, I'll be here."

Someone, meaning Pilar, or Paul. Paul wasn't going to come on-line.

"Okay. I'll let them know, if they check in."

"Have a good flight, Signy."

"Right."

Janine vanished.

Signy heard a knock, and she jumped, thinking, That's Alan, thinking, It sounds like there's solid steel behind that wood paneling. The security camera showed a view of Alan, alone, holding foam containers and spoons. Signy keyed the door open.

Alan brought the containers to the desk, pulled off a lid, and released the scent of—chile. Chile con carne.

"I found this, poking around. A Filipino guy makes it. He says it's too hot. It isn't."

Because Alan looked so worried, Signy tried a spoonful. It wasn't too hot. It wasn't half bad, either. Signy dug under the counter for the Glenfiddich. The bottle she pulled out was new, its seals intact. She handed it to Alan.

"Am I still on the job?" Alan asked.

"I don't know. It looks like we don't have much to offer. We said we'd open our files on Tanaka to you. We'll do that." If she could get Paul's system up and running, she'd get the files. Most of Paul's files were duplicated in Taos, automatic download, but Signy didn't know what Paul might have deleted. Paul's withdrawal spoke of depression, or worse. Reclusive, dependent on Jared and the rest of the motile members of the organism that was Edges for input from the outside world, when had they last seen him in fleshtime? It had been at least a year. At least two years.

"I doubt as I'd much want to work with Tanaka myself, or let any of my people loose in one of their ships.

But we could still sell them a few things, I guess. Do you have another job in mind for me? Somehow you look like you do."

"We could be monitored." Signy tilted her head toward the screen.

"Likely." Alan poured Scotch for both of them and they sipped it. Signy closed her eyes and let the burn of the liquor slide down her throat. It hurt her raw stomach. Fine. Signy wasn't at all sure that Alan would be wise to keep working with Edges, even if that's what he wanted to do. If the company still existed. What was Edges now? A loose coalition between a psychotic recluse lawyer, a woman who had once done some fair neurochemical research, one dead doc, a media has-been, and a little blond girl who loved her.

God, what were we when we were good? As soon as I nail San-Li on this murder, I'm going to—I sent Jared to his death.

I can't live with that.

"What are you thinking, lady?" Alan asked.

"I'm worried about Janine. I hate to leave her alone. But there's nothing to be done about it. There's something I'd like to show you. When I can."

"Something that happened today. Yeah. Shame that chopper went down when it did. Damned shame."

The look in Alan's eyes said that he didn't think the helo crash was pure accident.

"I just might go to Lisbon," Alan said.

"Huh?"

"You stretch out on this futon, here, and I'll call Gulf Coast. They can have me a rig set up in Lisbon by the time I get there. There may be something in this aquaculture business for Gulf Coast to look at."

Signy hoped Alan would find something. It seemed he had friends that he cared about. Alan was another loyalty addict, like Signy. The poor bastard.

"Thanks. For the chile." Thansh, Signy heard herself

say. The Scotch was getting to her tongue. The futon felt very soft. Signy let it take her weight, surprised by how many of her joints ached. Cold and tension had been at them. Sleep here, in the enemy's lair? Yeah. Where else could she be safe? Here, even her sleep was recorded and transmitted to the Taos house, so that even if Signy Thomas died, the how and why would be documented. If anyone cared to look.

"You'll watch out for Janine?" Signy enunciated the words carefully, carefully.

"Janine is my daughter's age," Alan said. "She only knows what she's seen of me in the last few days, but she's an engineer. I imagine we speak the same language, at least sometimes."

You can help her research some background about helicopters. About why they crash. Janine is so alone and Pilar could help but she won't, but I have to explain that to you, don't I, and I don't think I . . .

Sleep came up like black mist.

Alan was shaking her shoulder.

"Signy? Signy, the plane is here. Time to wake up, hon."

Alan walked with her across the plastic matting, past the locked door of the Hotel California.

The limbs of the bare trees looked like screams. Charcoal screams, scratched across the geometries of white painted church steeples; the little hills rolled on forever. Signy had always felt claustrophobic in New England. She wanted horizons, distance. The sky was too low here, had always been too low.

Brown grass lay naked on the lawns, freeze-drying in wan morning sunlight. Cruel land, to be so cold with no snow; Signy huddled inside her parka, climbing down the steep grade to the door of the house, hoping Paul hadn't changed the locks.

Hushed, dark, a feeling of nobody home. The smell of old garbage reached her on a wave of stifling heat.

Signy heard, with a dull sense of inevitability, Jared's voice, a quiet conversation, and Paul answering him.

Jared spoke of Chaco Canyon, of a crumbling stone city and the quiet peace of a dry forgotten valley. Signy remembered when it was, Jared talking to Paul on an October evening when they had still lived in this house, a conversation in flesh-time and long past. Jared had described a network of ancient roads, and parrot feathers, bright against the sand, the living birds traded up from Central America to the high desert.

Signy had listened from the kitchen; she was the cook for the week. The hell with cholesterol, she had marinated a good hunk of sauerbraten and it simmered, happily, while she made thin, lacy potato pancakes. There was applesauce from Macs Jared had picked, his face dappled in the leaf-shadow, climbing trees like an idiot adolescent. Throwing apples. Signy had rummaged around the kitchen until she found gingersnaps to blend into the spiced gravy.

We all ate too much, Signy remembered.

Feeling muscles bunch up in her shoulders, Signy opened the door into the study.

A skeletal figure in skinthins and headset lay in a fetal curl beside the holo stage. Paul's knees, his elbows, looked swollen and huge. He looked like a victim of some terrible arthritis—no, this was starvation, there was just so little flesh on his bones; the joints in his thin, thin hands were not swollen.

Even while Signy watched, Paul's fingers danced, quick as spiders, on the keyboard that he held between his knees. His chest moved in a placid, everyday rhythm. Paul wore about three days' worth of beard, and that was oddly reassuring. It meant he'd been able to get up and walk, at least within the past week.

Jared's dead and it's my fault. Is Paul going to die, too?

We knew this was happening, Signy told herself. We knew it, all of us, and denied it; Paul has been alone here and we just wouldn't interfere with him, because . . . because we needed to believe he was okay.

The impulse to grab Paul, shake him, hold him, was almost overwhelming. Signy was afraid the shock of real-time touch would stop his heart.

Paul was oblivious of her presence. Signy walked around him, considering. She pulled on her headset and entered the space that was Paul's present reality.

"Hello," Signy said.

"Signy! What the hell are you doing?"

"Say hello, Paul. I'm home."

—Signy appeared from the kitchen, dressed in a red flannel shirt that she had forgotten she had ever owned. Younger; as he had made her, Signy could see her supple hands, the smooth flesh over her knuckles as she wiped them on a dishtowel. She looked up, not wanting to, at Jared, sprawled in one of the dark leather Queen Annes Paul kept near the fireplace. Jared's shoulders, his heavy hair tied in its familiar knot, the cuff of his chamois shirt turned back on his wrist. Jared twisted to look at her and he grinned.

Signy tried to find anger. Tried to find it in the stretch of Jared's shirt across his shoulders, in his smile of amazement, as if he had never seen her before.

Wanting to beg, Help me with Paul. Help me, Jared.

Knowing she couldn't ask that, not ever again.

"Is dinner ready?" Jared asked.

Paul could work so damned fast. He'd built this simulacrum in two days.

Jared got up from the chair, kicked out his right knee, the one that tended to bother him, and was there, close to Signy as she stood frozen, her hands trapped in a virtual dishtowel so that she couldn't reach Paul's controls. Warm, solid, Jared's arms around her, the soft feel of his chamois shirt against her cheek. Signy smelled his living scent, earthy loam, healthy male, musk.

"Stop it, Paul!"

"Paul needs this, Signy. For a while," Jared said. Jared's wistful look, his shy grin. "Death is a concept." His voice made slight vibrations in his chest; Signy could sense them. Perfect. "Entropy, seen in the right perspective, is only a set of equations. My continued presence wouldn't be to everyone's taste, I know. The aesthetics might prove bothersome to timid souls. But you aren't timid. And I miss you."

Paul's words. These were Paul's words, mouthed in Jared's voice, but Jared's touch felt real, was unmistakable, Jared's touch that she wanted so desperately.

Ugly, ugly. Signy jerked her head back and fought her hands out of their imagined restraints. She found the controls, the reassuring touch of plastic keys, frantic, shuddering as she hurried through sequences, shutting down.

Jared vanished, the virtual study vanished, leaving the real-time, dusty room, and Paul, sitting up now, his face still hidden behind his headset.

Paul sniffed and wiped his nose with the back of his hand.

He sat there, unresisting, while Signy lifted his headset away. His bloodshot eyes looked through her, looked past her.

"Oh, Paul. It's a bit sick, you know?"

Paul blinked, and Signy left him there while she got to the bathroom, yanked back the slimy white plastic of the shower curtain, found a clean towel buried in the linen closet. She turned on the shower, hot, and went back to the study. She tugged Paul to his feet and helped him peel out of his skinthins.

Paul had hollows between every rib, but there was

some flesh on him, a little muscle, and his hands, holding Signy's shoulders, were strong.

He didn't protest. He even tried to help, a little. Signy shoved him into the shower.

"There isn't any soap," Paul said.

In the medicine chest, Signy found a hotel bar wrapped in yellowed paper.

"Here." She tossed it over the shower curtain, into the steam. "I'll pack for you. We need to hurry, Paul."

She left him, listening to make sure that the shower still ran, that she could hear him. Signy plugged in the public line to Seattle.

[Signy] I need help with Paul. I need you in Taos. Now.

She sent the message and got back to the bathroom. Paul rolled a towel under his scrotum, standing full-faced to her, as unaware of her real presence as if she had been blind to him, as if she had been in virtual and far away.

"You're taking me to Taos." Paul raised his arm and dried the dripping tangle of black hair under his armpit.

"You got that right, buddy."

"I need . . ."

"Whatever it is you need, you can pull it off the net."

Not half as resistant as Signy had feared, even with a sort of bemused docility, Paul tolerated her leading him onto the flights west. He walked well enough. Signy had thought she might have to carry him. Paul followed her, meekly, through the crowds of vacant-faced travelers in the terminals. They didn't seem to exist for him.

Coming north from Albuquerque, Paul actually smiled, seeing for the first time in fleshtime the curve of the Rio Grande gorge, the gentle bulk of Taos Mountain sheltering the little town, chalky sunset pastels staining the wind-drifted snow on the mesa.

* * *

Signy got a couple of vitamin pills and a cup of sugared tea into Paul before he turned on the console, the one Jared usually used, and settled his headset on. Signy didn't fight him about it.

The house still felt like no one was home. Even with the fires lighted, the house was shadows, was empty space. Signy paced back and forth, searching aimlessly. She straightened the rumpled bedding in the big bedroom. The room smelled stale, old. Signy left it and closed the door.

Just watching, Signy sprawled on the banco in the virtual room, her hands around a cup of tea that grew cold. Just watching. Paul worked, his thin shoulders jerking as he fought some construct. He could tear down the whole edifice, destroy the Lisbon productions, bring up multiple ghosts of Jared to walk through this house. Join Paul, that was one answer. Climb in, create a Jared to please them both, a personality less frustrating than the living one had ever been. Signy could damned sure do a better job with Jared's dialogue; Paul wasn't half close to accuracy in phrasing or rhythm. Paul didn't have the lilt of Jared's voice quite right, the minute hesitations Jared used when he wanted to say something he thought was important. Signy *knew* she could make Jared's speech get up and walk.

Why the hell not?

TWENTY-SEVEN

Pilar and Jimmy walked past canyons of closed office buildings; they passed through the lighted spaces that marked the façades of bars, hotels, the faint stirs of nightlife in a city that had little use for it.

A cabbie drowsed at his station in front of the Mariott, under a covered archway, the clean paving damp in spite of its shelter. Jimmy stood hunched against the cold, his hands stuffed deep in the pockets of his parka. Pilar's hand on the wet pocked chrome of the cab's door handle, the cabbie lifting his head, waiting.

"Are you coming?" Pilar asked.

Jimmy said nothing.

"You're sure about this? Leaving with me, I mean?"

Jimmy shook his head, once.

Pilar opened the door. "Seatac?"

The cabbie nodded, secure behind his armored windows.

Pilar let her hand fall away from the door handle. "Neither am I."

Jimmy shrugged. The cabbie leaned back against his headrest again.

"I'm cold," Pilar said.

"Let's go home. Let's go home, Pilar. I'll warm you. If I can."

She was so sleepy, so tired, so tired. Pilar climbed into the cab, ran her credit card across the waiting slot and typed in her address. Jimmy settled in beside her. The cab pulled away, as silent as its driver, moving uphill on wet streets that shimmered with rare streaks of color in the gently lighted night city.

Walking into the dark, quiet house, Pilar realized the cabbie wouldn't need a recharge when he got back to the hotel. The route was all downhill from here. At least she had given him a good fare. It was the only thing she could think of that had come out right for a long, long time.

They dropped their wet parkas in the hall. They didn't look into the studio as they went past. Jimmy helped Pilar out of her boots, her skinthin. She stumbled into the shower and let it run hot. It wasn't enough to warm her.

Half-wet, in the chill room, Pilar sat on the side of the bed, amazed, for Jimmy stripped out of his skinthin, truly naked, his white, white skin nubbly with goose bumps. Jimmy sat down on the floor and matter-of-factly picked up one of Pilar's bare feet. He kneaded it thoroughly. Then the other.

Pilar sighed with the pleasure/pain of it, bones and tendons pressed, released, throbbed, a process that left relaxation and fatigue competing in odd ways.

"Thank you," Pilar said.

Jimmy lifted her feet to the bed, smoothed the comforter around her, and padded away. Pilar heard water running in the bathroom; Jimmy washing up.

She wasn't that surprised when he slipped into bed beside her, moving cautiously, as if he feared to wake her. Pilar was far from sleep. She wasn't that surprised that the gentle, skilled moves Jimmy had learned in porno virtuals served him well in fleshtime.

Janine sprawled on her hotel bed in Lisbon and traced the pattern of its brocade bedspread with her fingers. Her eyes felt sanded. Dry and sanded.

"It wasn't as if we were lovers, Signy."

Janine hadn't said the rest of the words, the ones that she had wanted to say and didn't because they choked in her throat, words with fangs and claws. She couldn't let the hurt out even now, not with Signy as shook as she'd ever be likely to get, and off-line anyway on some commercial flight back toward home. There just wasn't any reason to yell at Signy, no reason to start a fight.

It wasn't as if *Janine* had ever been Jared's lover, damn it. Signy and Jared were a closed community when it came to lust. Signy and Jared. Signy and Paul. Pilar and Paul. Even though Jared wouldn't leave anyone *out*, you know? So, yeah, he was good in bed, we'll all of us miss that. He was gentle and rough, and *polite*. A fucking *generous* man, sharing the wealth, damn him anyway.

But Pilar would disappear with Jared whenever he came to the house, and Janine always heard them, tried not to hear them, laughing and groaning and screaming for what seemed like hours.

On the rough plaster ceiling, a fly traced a tiny pattern, circular, endless. The room was stifling, airless, sterile.

Janine got up and checked, once again, that her notebook was ready to pick up any message from anyone. Then she grabbed her headset and lay back on the bed.

—enclosed in white space, white noise. White, that after a time began to glow with colors, to whisper in busy small tongues. I am going home, Janine heard, a rolling whisper, a repeated loop. I am going home.

Don't know where that is, voice. You got any ideas?

—Home, homes. Homesss. Sss. Sssss. Snow. Know.

What the hell was Kazi planning, huddled with Tanaka in security Janine couldn't break? What was Kazi hearing now from his quiet, thin boss in Kobe who said so little? A minimalist plan, maybe. We will all eat salt.

—salt, tuh, tuh, tuh.

The sound was the throbbing in Janine's temples, the rush of blood in her ears.

After a time, Janine got up and called up a view of the hotel lobby. Curled up on her side on the bed, she watched the living, the busy:

The hotel began to fill again, with hurried, isolated, quiet people, who didn't want to be seen talking to each other. They wore closed faces and found excuses to be elsewhere, when on Friday they had been all smiles and chitchat. Some of the better-funded carried overnight luggage, coming back from quick trips for further instructions. Some of the delegates kept their gaze on the carpet, their pace determined, and Janine imagined them sitting in their locked rooms, transmitting information back to their respective countries and waiting until their bosses returned from weekend privacies, from days of rest.

His shoulders hunched, wearing his silk raincoat and for God's sake, *shades*, Kazi crossed the center carpets and turned behind one of the pillars. Two of his security people followed him, the woman with the big thighs and the man who doubled as an electronics tech, a muscular, fast-moving electronics tech.

Sheesh, the guy looked like a chop-sockey hero. The woman acted like a mute.

The woman had never said anything at all, not when Janine had been in the room with her. Janine wanted to hate her, hate both of them. They were typecast and far too *predictable*. Janine wanted to bug their rooms, if they had rooms, and see what they were like behind their smooth faces. Perhaps they had names, families, losses of their own.

Kazi stopped and said something. The two guards left him.

Coming here, was he? Janine wanted to see him, oh, yes, indeed. She wanted to punch Kazi in his nice hard middle, hard enough to hurt him, bad. And she wanted to hug him, and feel how warm he was. She had to talk to him, had to find out something, anything, had to learn where to go next.

Janine climbed off the bed, pulled off her headset, and and jerked the door open, just as Kazi raised his hand to knock. Without makeup, her hair a tangle, wearing a skinthin and that was all. Kazi's eyes widened.

"Kazi, where do I go next?"

"Pardon me?"

"What happens to me?" Janine waved her hand to invite him in.

Kazi walked to the center of the room, frowning at her. He looked older. His cheeks were shadowed and gaunt, as if he'd been fasting. "You remain as you are," Kazi said. "We are happy with your work. I told you that."

"Then *why* didn't you tell us what you were going to do?"

"It's difficult to explain."

"I'm listening."

Janine shifted on her feet and crossed her arms over her chest. She did not invite Kazi to sit down. In the lenses of his sunglasses, she saw twin reflections of her face. Her topknot was standing straight up, and Kazi seemed to be focusing on that and nothing else.

This is me. This is how I look when I'm hurting, Janine wanted to say, and didn't.

"There has been much I have not been free to tell you," Kazi said.

"Tell me now. I don't want any more surprises. Throw me one more curve and I'll be out of here on the next flight."

"We learned—the morning of the opening session, only then, I promise you—that the Arab states plan to support the ban. Their votes should insure that it passes. But they oppose a new Japanese-Israeli project in Ethiopia. We're are working there on a project, a project that has not yet been publicly announced. Tanaka will provide the tech for vat biomass production, a joint venture for us with the Israelis and with a U.S. company, Pacific Biosystems. If Japan votes for the ban, the Arabs will vote against it."

"They can't be that naive. *You* can't be that naive."

"We think it will work."

"You're crazy. You could have told me," Janine said. Stepping from side to side, so that she could watch her twin reflections move back and forth in Kazi's stupid mirrorshades.

"We had no time. And there were listeners."

"You are sure we aren't bugged right now?"

"No. But I am telling you everything I know. As fast as you will let me. You are important to me, more important than the risk of losing this vote." Kazi looked worried. He looked like he meant what he said.

"It's too late for us to change anything," Janine said. "You know that. My people . . . are distracted."

Make that nonfunctional. Make that: My people are gone, destroyed, off-line, and in several major ways, nonexistent. Unless they get their act back together in a hurry—

"It's primitive, this gamble of yours," Janine said. "We might have helped you, run some projections to see if this childish gambit has a chance of flying."

And Jared is dead. Killed by what seems to have been a childish gambit.

"You've killed one of us, remember?" Janine turned her back on Kazi and walked to the blank, blank screen at the desk. "You let it happen. That was an error, Kazuyuki Itano. That was a fucking error. For all you know, we've spent the last two days altering the parameters on every bit of virtual you've paid for, in ways too subtle for you to figure out. Think about it."

Janine sat down and slapped at her notebook. It responded with random flashes of light. She lifted her hands away. Behind her, she heard a rustle of silk, a thud.

Janine spun around in her chair and found Kazi kneeling at her feet, his hands clasped. He looked like a Victorian suitor about to propose marriage.

"What?" Janine tried not to smile. "What the hell?"

"Janine. Janine, I think you have not done this."

"I haven't. Yet."

"Listen to me. There is something behind what we are doing, something you should know. The fishing ban means so little compared to this. I have been honest when I told you we have little concern for it. We want something else from Antarctica."

"Not fish?"

"Janine, we want the ice. We want to harvest the ice. You see, if we lose the ban proposal, we can accept a modification, with good grace, of the minerals provisions in the treaty. A modification that will seem to be only theoretical, you see? Ninety percent of the Earth's fresh water is frozen in Antarctica. Pure and cold, and great chunks of it are calved from the glaciers every year and wasted. It's impossible to harvest, people think. The difficulties—are enormous. But the need is great."

"You want to harvest *icebergs?*"

Kazi bowed his head over his clasped hands, a Buddhist monk in tailored silk.

"I think you mean it," Janine said.

"We do."

Ho, damn, when Pilar heard about this one . . .

Kazi meant it. God, the engineering it would take.

Signy? Paul? Janine looked behind her at the notebook's blank, blank screen.

"Kazi?"

"Yes?" He was still on his knees.

"Are you drunk?"

"No."

"You should be." Janine tapped room service and ordered champagne. "Come and sit on the bed. Come tell me *all* about this, would you?"

All day, the air lay gray and heavy around the Taos house, velvet quiet. Banks of cloud moved in from the west, with no wind to drive them. Signy sprawled on the big bed, watching Paul, who sometimes slept and sometimes did not. Paul would wake near dusk, when the storm came.

Signy drowsed beside him, not touching him, and she idly listed what food was in the house—likely the storm would pass with only a foot or so of snow, but sometimes a big one rolled up out of Baja and left drifts that lasted for days—plenty in the freezer, and tea and coffee, enough, yes. There was nothing fresh, but Signy doubted Paul would notice.

When Paul stretched and woke, Signy was ready for him, ready with an idle distraction that had crossed her mind while she drifted, drifted, in and out of dazed, calm, numb daytime sleep.

Quick, quick, padding lightfooted across the chilly floors, Signy found a sequence and sent it to Paul just as he sat down at Jared's console.

—the coughing sounds of the engine, the helo slewing sideways into the sea, the world going tilt. Signy added a pastiche of San-Li's words and her own sleepy conversation with Alan, set them to loop.

"I have sent a recording of the events of the crash to Kobe." San-Li, her precise soprano voice.

Alan's Southwestern drawl: "It's a shame that chopper went down when it did."

Paul shook his goggled head.

"Find all the little parts. Piece them together," Signy whispered. "San-Li killed Jared. Get her, Paul."

Paul didn't answer, lost, his fingers searching, bringing up screens.

Signy brought tea to him and put it down near his left hand, where he could reach it if he would.

Janine waited, still, for some support, some direction, poor baby. Signy found the Lisbon screens dark, set to transmit only audio, to accept only messages from Edges.

—In the dark hotel room, Janine giggled. The deep baritone of Kazi's voice said something Japanese or incoherent, or both.

Seattle showed this message:

[Jimmy] I'll bring her.

The Seattle house was closed, quiet, shut down.

Signy called up the Tokyo market reports, set them running in a sidebar, and sent them to Paul's screen.

"Thanks," Paul said.

Just as if he were going to look at them. Signy grinned to herself, all cheered up as if the worst were over, and she didn't think it was. Get Paul healed, and then she could die. Signy got up and walked around, pacing the house in a habitual way, watching the evening. Outside, snow began to fall, solid and flakily determined.

This looked like an all-night storm. Signy wondered when Jimmy and Pilar would get to Taos. She wondered if Jimmy could really convince Pilar to make the trip.

"This could be quite a storm," Jared said. He stood beside Signy at the window.

"How did you get here so quietly?" Signy asked.

Jared looked down at the wool socks on his feet.

"I see." Signy twitched the corner of her left eye, to signal her headset to give her back real-time vision. Jared vanished. The snow-streaked window began to swirl with colors, Signy's headset confused by the signals her salt tears left, running down her cheeks.

TWENTY-EIGHT

Before she pulled Kazi into bed, Janine set her console to tell any callers to keep quiet, do not disturb. The silence at home disgusted her. Signy was back in Taos, she knew that much, and the Seattle house was locked tight and empty. The console saved Kazi's chatter; Janine planned to get him talking.

Janine pushed Kazi's hands away from her breasts. "You have to promise me you'll do something about San-Li."

Kazi rolled onto his back and locked his hands behind his head. "You believe she killed your friend."

"Even if she didn't. Convince me *you* had nothing to do with it."

"Convince you?"

Naked, both of them, in some ways vulnerable. And Kazi's guards, if they waited in the hall, might not get to him in time if Janine did something violent and swift. She wished, sort of, that she had thought in advance about something she *could* do.

"Let me try." Kazi blinked at the ceiling. "You must find your own answers to your questions, I think. You will look at every record available, or your friends will. I do *not* have any information that says San-Li damaged the helicopter that crashed."

"What if we find out that she did? What will happen to San-Li?"

Kazi reached for Janine's hand, very hesitant in the way he moved. "Nothing good," Kazi whispered.

They nuzzled for a while, and began to talk—of ice,

and engineers, and Kazi's weekend work. Janine found herself intrigued, awakened, by the gonzo energy of Tanaka's plans for the ice. Beautiful, crazy plans. The hell with home.

Kazi talked, under the stimulus of Janine's questions, until he was hoarse.

Janine was rough with him, demanding and directive, while they made love. Kazi liked that. So did she. Janine didn't let him rest, not until she was tired herself. They talked until they fell asleep.

When morning was upon them, Janine ordered coffee and juices brought to her room. Across the tiny table, Kazi sat rumpled in his shirt, taking his coffee with tiny, whispering sips.

"When you come to Kobe," Kazi said, "I will find a nice apartment for you."

"What do you mean, when I come to Kobe?"

"You must. You can continue your work with your company after this treaty is settled, of course. But you can do that in virtual. And I will be very attentive. We have many holidays, you know."

"Yes. Where will you be living, while I'm waiting for your holidays?"

"In my own house. It is a very nice house."

"Of course."

Janine steered the conversation back to the ice. Kazi didn't seem to notice.

Alone in the shower, after Kazi had gone to his room to change for the day's work, it occurred to Janine that someone might be awake in Taos. Wet and dripping, she checked the console. Signy had called in, but she'd left no message. Janine was running late.

[Janine] NEWS. DAMN IT, I HAVE NEWS.

Janine sent the message to Taos and left it flashing while she got her makeup on. Her eyes looked more tired than she felt. Kazi knocked at her door, to escort her to the day's work.

In the wan Lisbon morning, light from narrow windows cut slanting stripes across the dull florals of the carpets as they walked toward the conference hall. Kazi's twin guards appeared in the hallway and followed them at a discreet but obvious distance. On duty, Monday morning, they looked sleek, efficient, and quietly pleased, as if they knew the boss had enjoyed his night with the gaijin woman. Perhaps they figured Kazi would be calm, and their day would go well.

Janine felt Kazi stiffen and looked up to see Señor Abeyta, the delegate from Chile, approaching with definite plans for eye contact and an agenda on his face.

The language of diplomacy suddenly appalled Janine, the pirouettes and sidesteps, the dance itself. It was only money. Money, an abstract, drove real forces of hunger and starvation and death, forces that these two idiots wanted to discuss so delicately. In their own terms. Of course. It was time to change a few rules around here. As Pilar would say, let's fucking cut to the chase.

Janine stepped in front of Kazi, between him and the diplomat from Chile.

"Good morning, Mr. Abeyta."

Abeyta drew back slightly. He hadn't expected a subordinate to be the initiator of this conversation. Good. "You planned to use the sinking of the *Noche Blanca* as a lever to keep Tanaka quiet about your rather lax reporting of the tonnage you've been pulling out of the water. Tanaka planned to cooperate, because they've been a little lax themselves. Between you, you could have traded off damage for damage, and kept the whole thing quiet.

"But the *Sirena* went down and the Skylochori woman gave the straight story to anyone who's here. So you're both looking pretty dumb."

Abeyta opened his mouth to reply but Janine didn't give him time.

"Whether or not this ban goes through, there are going to be spy-eyes all over the Southern Ocean from now on. So if you're still fishing, you're going to have to behave when you do."

"Janine!" Kazi growled her name, a warning. Kazi Itano stood as rigid as a tin soldier, and his lips did not move.

"Remain calm, Kazi." Janine smiled at Señor Abeyta. "My friend Itano, here, has an offer for you. If you help the ban get into operation, you get aquaculture tech and loans. You can get quite a few tubes of anchovy paste out of vat cultures, and Tanaka's wizards can show you how to do it. That way you both come out all right. Or you can fish for what's left, both of you. And you know the bucket's almost empty. Think about it."

Abeyta looked tempted. "But—"

"But this isn't how it's done. I know. Chile, do we have a deal?"

"I . . ."

"Work it out with Kazi," Janine said. And walked on down the hall, leaving them staring after her. The stripes of light from the windows cut across their startled faces, shadows of bars on a cage.

In the great hall, Alan Campbell paced back and forth behind Janine's chair, waiting. Alan was a reminder, sudden and unexpected, of cold and terror and inexplicable death. And he was supposed to be in Antarctica, not here. Janine really thought someone might have told her. Damn.

"Good morning," Alan said.

"What the hell are you doing here?" Janine asked.

"Didn't anyone say?"

"Nobody's saying a goddamned thing. Nobody!"

"Then there's probably a lot to talk about. Want some coffee?"

"Uh—I just had some."

"Watch me drink mine, then?"

"I should . . ."

"Nothing's going to be happening on that stage for a few hours. Come with me, Janine."

Janine wasn't sure how Alan did it, but he got her turned for the door. Alan offered his elbow for her to hold, as if she were very old, or very young. Alan nodded to Kazi, who was coming down the steps in a rush. Behind Kazi's shoulder, the Tanaka security guards chattered out the morning's store of information. They watched the crowd as they talked, their alert eyes marking them for what they were in spite of the camouflage of their discreet business suits.

Kazi, looking startled, bowed to Alan.

There were tasks, social tasks. Signy didn't have to do them, didn't have to act as if things were in any way, shape, or form anywhere near normal. But she found herself staring at the list of messages that had made their way to the house. If she weren't so numb, she might have screamed to all of the waiting world to fuck off, leave us alone, get lost. She might have screamed, "*Hate me, for God's sake! I killed him!*"

No, that would be mean. Act as if decency exists, Signy told herself. Don't be mean.

There were messages in the house files from people Signy didn't know, people she vaguely knew. Signy fiddled with the phrasing on a recorded message that would respond to condolence calls, and then tagged them all with a bland, generic "Thank you. Jared's friends deeply appreciate your concern."

Unviewed, Signy filed the calls away. Later, later, she would try to get up the strength to talk to the ones who mattered—to her? No, that would be too selfish. The ones who mattered to Jared, but not yet, not just yet.

We have no rituals for this, Signy realized. No set tribal ceremonies to mark a passage; our lack of procedural certainties is part of our determination not to follow our parents' ways of dealing with life. We are not a part of any tradition but our own; we carry little scraps of societal courtesies that we have hauled along with us from our childhoods, things like thankyous and table manners. The rest of our rituals have come from business codes, ways to get jobs done.

There was a poverty in it. If Signy were to light candles, turn mirrors to the wall, or set a vigil by an empty coffin and sing and tell stories, she would feel like a liar. Fasting, ashes, black crepe? How ridiculous. But they had been real symbols, once.

One call had to be made. Signy phrased the message in her mind, and called Mark.

—The Ottawa address gave her a background of a plain-Jane office; Signy thought manufacturing, or shipping or some such. It was late, well after office hours. Signy hoped to get an answering machine, but Mark, in a plaid flannel shirt, looked up at her from behind a battered wooden desk. His face was like and unlike Jared's. A little brother's face, so young.

"Mark?" Signy asked.

"Hello, Signy." Jared's eyes were like his. "What's wrong?"

There was no way to say this, no words that would ever be right. "Jared's dead. Drowned, in a helicopter crash in the sea off Antarctica. There's no way to recover the body. I'm sorry."

Pain and confusion and anger were what Signy read in Mark's face, the anger extrapolated from what she knew of Jared's facial muscles, a subtle change in the muscles of the jaw.

"I see." And then Mark's face showed concern, concern for *her*. "This must be terrible for you. Is there anything I can do to help you? Anything you need?"

"No," Signy said. Jared's brother, yeah.

"I'll take care of things here. There are some papers, and things. In some ways, this will make things simpler for Kelan."

"Kelan?"

"Jared's daughter."

Oh, Lord.

"I didn't know he had a daughter," Signy said.

"Neither did Jared. Sue didn't want to tell him yet." Mark's wry little smile was the same, exactly the same, as Jared's. "We haven't been able to figure out how to work this. Sue wants Kelan to know her father, but I'm her father too. We wouldn't be happy changing that."

Oh, Lord. We'll have to deal with this.

"We'll work on it. Sue likes large families. It seems Kelan is part of one."

Signy nodded at Jared's brother. The child would be beautiful. Jared's daughter would be so very beautiful. If the little girl learned who her father was, it must be in a good way, a sound and complete way. She must learn how much Jared would have loved her. If he'd known.

"Oh, God, I wish he could have seen her," Signy said.

"So do I." Mark turned and rubbed his hands across his face like a man waking. Then he shook his head, as if he'd been startled.

"We saw part of it, some of how Jared . . . I'll send you the records of what happened. If you want," Signy said.

"Not now. I'll want to know, but not now. I'll have to tell Sue, first."

Jared had a *child?* The bastard, how could he have a daughter and not tell anyone? Mark said Jared didn't know about her, but surely, surely, he must have.

"How old is Kelan?" Signy asked.

"Nine months," Mark Balchen said. "She took her first step yesterday. Take care, Signy."

Nine *months?*

The screen went blank, the air around Signy's face shifted, she heard the stamp of boots in the hallway. Pilar called to her. They collided in the hallway in a tangle of arms and hugs and snow-laden parkas.

"God, it's cold," Pilar said.

"Yeah. Come in, come to the fire. Paul's here."

"You dug him out of his lair? Good work, girl. It must have taken a backhoe—" Pilar stopped, her arms falling limp to her sides, as she looked in through the doorway and saw Paul in the studio.

The knobs of the vertebrae on Paul's back tented up the fabric of his skinthin. He sat crouched and bent in his chair, his head bobbing up and down as he watched something on the screen.

"Ah, shit," Pilar whispered. "Nightmare in Starvation Alley. That's cruel, that's what it is." Pilar tiptoed closer to Paul. She stretched her hand toward him, but she didn't touch him. Paul's screen cast its light on Pilar's furious, still face.

"Do you have any idea what's he working on?" Jimmy asked.

"I asked him to search out San-Li's part in the helo crash," Signy said. "But I don't know. I've been afraid to look."

"He doesn't look like he's altogether . . . together," Jimmy said. "Will he eat?"

"He sipped at a mug of soup last night. He drinks tea."

Pilar turned away from Paul, shaking her head.

Jimmy shrugged. "Okay. I'll just slip in beside him, here. Some pancakes or scrambled eggs or something would go real well, in just a little while."

"You act like you've seen this before," Signy said.

"Signy. I've *been* this before. Probably why I stay so fat, is, I'm afraid I could get like this again. Paul's better off than you think, is what I think."

"Do you really think he'll eat?" Signy asked.

"If he doesn't, Pilar probably will. And me. It was a long damned walk out from town." Jimmy brushed snow away from the thighs of his corduroy trousers.

Pilar's nose was red beneath the cheekpieces of her headset. Jimmy's cheeks looked scalded, like a sunburn.

"You walked?" Signy asked.

"There's about three feet of snow outside," Jimmy said. "We couldn't get here any other way."

"Oh, damn. I hadn't looked outside since—I'll get you something hot," Signy said.

Pilar followed Signy to the kitchen. She watched while Signy rummaged through the cupboards, and Signy couldn't figure out what to say, or how to say it. Tinned milk, frozen whipped cream.

"Chocolate?" Signy asked.

Pilar got up, slowly. "I'll fix it," Pilar said.

There were cinnamon sticks in the spice cabinet somewhere; Signy remembered buying them. Pilar's hand reached over her shoulder and plucked the canister off the shelf.

"It's okay, *jita*," Pilar said, but Pilar was crying, too, both of them crying and holding each other's shoulders.

"Oh, God. I killed him, Pilar."

"No, you didn't. Shut up." Pilar drew away.

"I sent him down there."

"Live with it or die," Pilar said.

"I—"

"I shocked you, did I? Listen, sweetheart, we've all got guilt here. We needed some money, didn't we? Where's the stirring thingie?"

We've all got guilt here—Signy found the whisk in the drawer and handed it to Pilar. We've all got guilt. But while Pilar whisked grated chocolate into hot milk, Signy found herself blurting out—

"The bastard has a kid."

"Huh?" Pilar asked.

"Jared. Has a daughter. Nine. Months. Old."

Pilar added a tiny dash of black pepper to the pot and poured the chocolate into mugs. It smelled wonderful. "You're kidding."

"No, I'm not."

"Oh, the *cabron!*" Pilar handed two of the mugs to Signy and began to laugh. "Oh, wonderful!"

Signy just stared at her.

"So those *were* good *huevos* he had between his legs. I guess I always wondered."

"But a *baby?* Not a year old yet?"

"Busy boy, wasn't he? Well, it happens. Don't wave those cups around, you'll spill them. Does Paul know?"

"I just found out," Signy said, trailing Pilar down the hall.

"Paul!" Pilar called out. But Paul shushed her with an idle finger.

—On the holo stage, Janine and Alan Campbell sat side by side in one of the bright, hot-colored conversation nooks in the Tanaka entertainment suite. They had filled most of the space around them with diagrams and charts and strange cartoon graphics, changing the carefully orchestrated icescapes to hell and gone.

At her station, Signy vanished the Taos room and entered Janine's world, but she entered it, on a whimsy, through Alan's inputs.

—Alan's body language carried a unique set of tensions; bemused interest, a tolerance of human cantankerousness, a quirky optimism. In all those close hours, in all they had survived together, Signy had not met him in virtual, had not donned his tensions and reflexes or looked out through his eyes. The experience was a different sort of awareness of him, miles from sex, in some ways more intimate. Alan was a calm day in Indian summer, a comfortable, tolerant set of energies.

Alan's cameras showed the Tanaka courtesy suite in Lisbon.

"Hi there, Signy," Alan said.

Wups. Alan had sensors that told him who was riding on his muscles. Signy backed away, quickly, feeling like a Peeping Tom, or some such. "Hi."

In a sidebar, outlined in glowing turquoise to show the information was guarded in the files of the home system, Signy read:

[Paul] Tanaka wants to harvest icebergs, sell fresh water.

"What?" Pilar asked.

Signy grabbed for her notepad.

[Signy] You're kidding.

[Paul] No.

[Signy] Sell fresh water <u>where?</u>

[Paul] Everywhere.

Janine looked up when she heard Pilar's voice. Signy, viewing Janine from Alan's cameras, watched a flash of hurt cross Janine's face, a quickly hidden grimace of pain.

"Oh, damn," Pilar whispered.

Signy heard Pilar's quick footsteps running from the studio.

"They're in the backpack," Jimmy called, somewhere in the real world.

"I know," Pilar said. "Shit!"

"Look at this," Janine said.

The Lisbon hotel suite vanished, replaced by a ridiculous model, a giant curving chain of icebergs linked by cables, with tender ships escorting them north. A segmented, headless ice-worm.

"Nukes for power," Janine said. "The engines drilled into the bergs themselves. It would take a lot of number crunching to keep everything going the same way, what with breakups and reconfigurations, and tides. . . ."

"Indeed it would. Yes, ma'am." Alan's voice, intrigued; amused.

Signy panned the ice-train model, rotated it to view it

as if she approached it from the sea, came in closer. She spied a human figure on top of one of the bergs, a figure the size of an ant, and suddenly the scale of the thing came home to her. The berg was kilometers long.

"That one's average size for what they want to haul," Alan said. "Ain't small, is it?"

Signy switched her viewpoint to one of the Lisbon room's security cameras. Alan and Janine sat in their chairs beside the model of the ice train and talked about thin mylar wraps and reflective surfaces and ice melt as insulators, and Signy got the idea that the curve of the chain was a result of Coriolis forces, the energies of the spinning earth. Now, that was *big*.

"Well, the Russkies have a lot of power plants from the old sub fleet. No need to waste 'em, I guess," Alan said.

Signy started to say something, but stopped at a flash of motion. Pilar had found her portable rig.

Pilar popped into Lisbon, as her thin, unadorned self. She bent over like a crane and smacked a kiss on Janine's cheek. "Hiya, sweet. I'm sorry I left you with all this."

"Yeah." Janine's voice came tiny, a child's voice. "Yeah, you did. But that's you, Pilar. Now back off, okay? We've got some work to do."

"Work? What sort of work?" Pilar asked.

"Just settle down, here. The scam is, the fishing ban goes through or it doesn't, but Japan gets a tiny wrinkle written in to the mineral-rights provisions, a word or two. And then Tanaka negotiates with the Antarctic Treaty Commission and buys bergs. The free ones, the calves from the glaciers, out to two hundred miles, of course, but that's a whole 'nother kettle of fish, whether you go with the permanent summer boundaries of the ice pack, or of the continent itself."

Paul's crab sigil appeared in Lisbon, a crab that danced its way from graph to graph. Signy pulled away from the virtual to look at Paul in real time. He seemed interested and alert, and he'd finished his mug of chocolate. Jimmy and Pilar sat cross-legged on the floor beside him, working with portable consoles and goggles.

"The Commission would get fees for the ice," Paul said. "They might just like that."

Somebody needed to feed these people. Signy guessed that meant it was time for her to cook.

Their voices followed her down the hallway and came to her through the kitchen speaker. Signy pulled her headset out of her way and rested it on her forehead. Flicking in and out of virtual had left her with burned fingers and burned food more than once.

She rummaged through supplies: pancakes, a canned ham, some frozen OJ; the kitchen speakers brought Edges' conversation to her while she worked.

"There's places you probably can't drive the bergs." Janine's voice. "Even with nukes, you need enough mass to make the operation worthwhile on a cost basis. So you've gotta push a lot of ice, and you've gotta push it where it has a mind to go anyway. Japan is a good market, and the west side of the Americas and the west coast of Africa. You can't turn the suckers in to the Mediterreanean; they won't make the curve with any technology Alan or I can think of. So the Mideast doesn't get much out of this, I guess."

"What about temperature changes? Wouldn't the bergs cool things off, when you got them wherever they're going?" Paul asked.

"Yeah," Janine said. "The melt would make for cold surfing outside L.A. What you do is you harvest the water out of the bottom, out of their wrappers, see, and you've got a long, long time to do the work. Thaw as needed, almost."

"You just park them in somebody's harbor?" Pilar asked.

"Tether one or two offshore," Alan said.

Signy heard laughter. She pulled the headset over her face to see what was so funny.

—Someone had modeled a skier, in swim trunks and a scuba mask, and sent him schussing down the sides of an iceberg.

"Theme parks? Recreation?" Jimmy asked.

"That's one idea. To offset the cost and the bitching, you charge people to play on them. The answer on local cooling effects and their impact on the sea is that nobody knows the answer," Janine said.

"Ski Ensenada," Pilar said.

Signy pushed her headset out of the way and flicked a drop of water on the griddle. It danced and popped. She poured out six circles of cream-colored batter. They hissed comfortably as they spread.

The ham, sliced, brushed with honey and mustard and a sprinkle of ground cloves, sent a nice smell from the oven.

"Paul, we'll need some words," Janine said. "Before lunch, here, a couple of hours. Okay?"

"Jiggle the treaty language?" Paul asked.

"Tanaka's legal staff has come up with an alternate phrase, somewhere in here," Janine said.

"Okay," Paul said. "I'll look at it."

"Right. Now all we need to do is sell it. Got any ideas?" Janine asked.

"Jesus," Pilar said. "Put those icescapes we made back up, would you, sweet? We can't possibly do a whole new setting in two hours. Let's see what we've got to work with."

Signy flipped the pancakes, got the OJ ready while their top sides browned, made six more, and figured she'd just carry everything in to the studio. Something in there had made them all go quiet.

What about Jared? What about the fact that they were working for a company that used murder as one of its tools? That half-starved crazy daughter of Tanaka's did, anyway. But Paul would find a way to trap her.

Where did vengeance belong? Where was rage best spent?

Mihalis, who had tried to cripple a fishing boat for money, had died as quickly as his victims. Psyche, who had been a hesitant participant in his scam, had drowned with Jared. San-Li, it seemed, had not planned for anyone to die. She'd just known it could happen. Sabotaging Cordova's helo had been a risky business. If San-Li Tanaka had wanted to get rid of *all* the witnesses and the records they might have kept, she would have blown the Skylochori ship, the *Sirena*, clean out of the water, long before Jared's rescue call came in.

To kill all of them, San-Li would have needed to get rid of the brothers on the ice, along with Psyche and the escaped Jared, and the ship. That would have been a complicated business. San-Li must have been aiming for the ship. Or maybe just for the woman and her brothers. Jared's call for help was the unplanned thing.

Kazi had found San-Li's mistakes to be shameful. There was an implication, in the way he'd talked in those awful moments after she'd appeared on the Lisbon screens, that the girl would be punished, probably in very unpleasant ways, for her mistakes.

Jared, damn it, was *dead* behind that child's "mistakes." But San-Li *was* a child. A murderous one. Is that what we must do in response to her, become amoral children, careless of other lives? Signy wondered.

Where does the rage go?

A slice of ham slid too far toward the edge of one of the plates. Signy pushed it back into position, and licked salty-sweet juice from her finger.

Balancing plates on her forearms in imitation of a hash-house waitress, she made it to the studio without dropping them. Hell, she was only carrying three this trip.

—Signy found the Lisbon icescapes restored, unchanged, the Taos humans speaking with disembodied voices, watching and listening.

"This is good stuff," Pilar said. "I can't see what needs changing."

"Beautiful. Beautiful. I didn't have time enough there. I didn't get to look around," Alan said.

Signy put a plate down next to Paul, and found spaces for plates on the floor next to Pilar's and Jimmy's knees.

Baked ham and hot honey smells wafted along her path. Signy wondered if they would notice.

"Food," Jimmy said. "I smell food."

"Uh, huh," Signy said. While headsets came off and plates began to get shifted to laps, Paul set projections of Alan and Janine on the Taos holo stage, visitors at the party, but they couldn't eat the food.

"Make them thirsty," Signy said.

"Feed them salt," Janine whispered.

"Salt. Smoked fish, salt-sweet nuts, pickled things. Do you think Tanaka would spring for caviar?" Signy asked.

"We didn't budget for caviar," Janine said.

"Tanaka can't bitch. They—ran some changes in the specs, after all," Signy said.

"Didn't they just?" Janine giggled. "Good, pure water. No fizzies. Water in those clear glass carafes that look like lab containers. Tall, tall glasses, yeah."

Pilar, who sat with her headset off, forking up ham and pancakes, said, "That would work."

"That's all we need?" Janine asked.

"Yeah. Get pure water ice to float in the pitchers. Transparent. The best ice in Lisbon." Pilar shifted her plate from her lap to the floor, wiped her fingers on her thighs, and grabbed her headset again.

"Jimmy?" Paul asked. "Come help me with some stuff. And Janine, you'd better get back to the conference. We don't have a mike down there, just what the news services will feed us."

The Lisbon room vanished in a slow dissolve. The watchers waited while shadows grew large in Taos, in the evening hours of a winter storm. Alan, invisible, murmured something Taos couldn't hear.

"I don't think I will do that," Janine said. "I don't think I will go down to the conference."

"Huh?" Paul asked.

"I'm coming home."

Signy got into her own chair and her headset.

"Just like that?" Pilar asked.

"I've . . . had enough." Janine sent voice only, and her voice trembled. "Please."

"You can't—" Pilar said.

Janine had been left alone with all the Lisbon work. Janine needed comforting, as best as could happen with Pilar and Jimmy as close as they seemed to be getting. "Oh, yes, she can," Signy said. "It's okay, Janine." Who the hell cared about Tanaka's contract, anyway? "Come home. We want you."

"But who runs Lisbon?" Paul asked.

"Alan," Signy said.

"Me?" Alan's voice asked.

"You're staying in Lisbon, aren't you?"

"Yeah. Sure."

"Well, the vote goes or it doesn't. Tanaka has their sales pitch. The room will run itself, unless a sequence crashes, and we can work on that from here." Jimmy could, anyway. "We'll help, Alan. We'll help—we're right here."

Alan didn't say anything. Signy heard him take in a breath.

"Fine, then," Paul said. "I'll send you a contract."

"I don't recall saying yes to all this," Alan said.

"You—" Something caught Signy's eye. "You haven't said no," Signy said. In the Taos shadows, Jared sprawled on the *banco* by the fireplace, his arms folded. The glow from the embers highlighted his cheekbones, the Zuni ring of turquoise and coral on his left hand. He winked at Signy.

Jimmy watched Paul's screen, unaware; Pilar was stretched out on her back, looking up at the *vigas*. They didn't see him. Not yet.

"Janine?" Signy asked. "Hurry, babe."

TWENTY-NINE

"If you're going to stick around here, you've got to keep up with what's happening," Signy whispered to the ghost in the corner. "So file this in your memory. You have a daughter."

She blinked the ghost away. Jared didn't flinch when Signy spoke to him, didn't seem to register what she'd said. But Paul, later, would replay her words.

Jared had a daughter. The child's existence created uncharted territories, changed the architecture of future spaces. And areas of legal responses surrounded the little girl named Kelan. Paul would explore them, when he heard of her.

Pilar, sprawled on the floor next to Paul's console, heard Signy's whisper. "What?" Pilar asked.

"Nothing," Signy said.

Pilar rolled on her side and stared at her empty plate. She stood, bent to pick up the plate, got Jimmy's as well, and went off toward the kitchen. Signy retrieved Paul's dishes from beside his elbow.

On Paul's flatscreen, the interior of the *Siranui*'s hangar ran herky-jerky, stopped and then speeded up, the space draped with arcs of chain and the angular geometries of tools. Standing near the sheet metal of the wall, an imaged Alan drew coffee from a dull steel urn. Flick: The scene switched to a pan of the deck, a view from Signy's cameras as she looked around for Anna.

"It doesn't look like Cordova's helo ever came inside the *Siranui*'s hangar. Not while Signy was looking." Jimmy had propped his feet up on the desk next to Paul's flatscreen. He'd found an improbable point of balance with his butt at the edge of a rolling chair, his notepad on his lap, and his chin resting on his parka, which Jimmy had rolled around his neck like some sort of pillow. It kept his head from dropping too far forward, Signy guessed.

"It didn't," Signy said. "Cordova came in and left that morning without leaving the pad."

"San-Li would have hired somebody to louse up his helo," Paul said. "What do you think, Jimmy?"

"I think if I go crawling around the *Siranui*'s personnel records one more time, alarms are going to go off clear to Kobe."

"Let 'em," Paul said.

Pilar came back from the kitchen, picked up her backpack from the floor, and wandered toward the workroom off the kitchen. Signy heard a click as the lights went on, the hiss of closing draperies. Still holding Paul's plate—he'd eaten most of the food—Signy followed her.

Pilar dug lumps of colored stone, an assortment of hammers, and sharp steel tools from the depths of her backpack. She scattered them on the scarred wooden table where Jared used to putter. Pilar's face had that oblivious, faraway look of hers, spaced out and elsewhere.

Wanting comfort, wanting talk, just talk, but Signy said nothing. Shouldn't it be enough that Pilar had come here, where she didn't like to be?

Pilar pulled a bubblewrapped cylinder from her backpack and unwrapped a votive candle, one of the fat yellow ones in a glass. This one had a picture of the Virgin on it, done in bright blues and reds. Pilar set it upright and lighted it.

Signy stood in the doorway, quiet. Surprised? Yes, for Pilar never mentioned church when she talked of her childhood. Pilar never went to mass, certainly, and she had a fine cutting skepticism about religion in general.

Pilar's candle-lighting seemed a fumbling, clumsy thing, a return to the half-remembered comforts or pains of childhood.

The tiny light wavered, then steadied. Pilar sat down with her hammers and her stones. The heavy weight of her hair covered her shoulders and veiled her face.

Signy twitched the corner of her eye, looking away from real time and into virtual, hoping Paul had set up a Jared to follow her motions through the house—but she saw only lists of names, the work of Paul's real time.

Jared wasn't where Signy needed him to be. Not when she needed him. Jared's ghost offered no presence, no answers.

The challenge, Signy supposed, was to deal with what was possible. Things To Do; she stacked Paul's plate in the sink while she began a list—Janine would get here by dusk tomorrow. Jimmy seemed to be taking over the job of interacting with Paul. That would make things better, or worse. For the moment, Signy didn't give a damn. And what was *she* supposed to do, for now? Wash dishes?

Fuck that. Signy went back to her own console. To build a structure of a San-Li, to understand her, to know her intimately, for only then could Signy find the special pleasures that would trap San-Li, the private pains.

Staccato glimpses of Edge's archives returned Signy to a familiar, timeless state, a place in her body called work, a pleasant, righteous measuring out of energy that distanced her from the welter of emotions around her. Here, in the world defined by Signy's fingers, her eyes, Jared existed as he ever was, in every damned nook and cranny. Of course Jared was here, no ghost, nothing Paul had made to haunt her. Jared was simply *here*.

These were not photo albums, not flat, static images, not diaries whose words, edited even as they were written, created frames for memory and wishes to alter. Damn it, the spaces Signy entered gave her the breathing, laughing presence of the man himself. Ghost? Jared seemed no more a ghost than—than she was, a younger Signy who lumbered her way through the past, grumbling and worrying. Jared was no more a ghost than Pilar, and perhaps less of one than Paul. The Paul who walked through Signy's private world seemed more real than the man who sat beside her.

In fleshtime and not three feet away, Paul mumbled something to Jimmy, and they both chuckled.

All of them had accepted Paul as a virtual these past few years, a construct Paul had altered to suit himself, one made to please them. The imagined Paul was a much healthier persona to deal with than the real one, and he was a lot more likable.

What the hell was real around here, what was alive? Signy planned to construct a San-Li Tanaka, a San-Li existent in pixels and bytes, and build her to walk in the Taos house. But would she recognize the girl herself, if San-Li came to the door tonight and asked shelter from the storm?

San-Li, San-Li, where art thou?

—Signy searched for her, found a dull hive of business as usual at Jimmy's old address for her in the Seychelles, backed up from there to a Tanaka payroll that listed San-Li's name in Kobe, last year, and dead-ended.

Paul and Jimmy made a lot of noise, getting up for a break. The sound of their steps went toward the kitchen. Cabinet doors opened and closed, chairs scraped.

Where to go from here? Signy could ask Jimmy to upload his interchanges with Evergreen, if he'd saved them. Word frequencies might indicate what bothered San-Li, some hints of her fleshtime life might be buried in there somewhere.

Signy got up and followed the men. Paul, holding a mug of tea in both hands, leaned against the refrigerator. Jimmy sat on the countertop next to the sink. He nodded to Signy and thumped his heels against the cabinets in a slow blues rhythm.

"We've got San-Li's face," Jimmy said. "Her speech patterns, such as they were when she talked to Janine and Kazi in Lisbon. The little bit of history Paul found, about how her dad doesn't seem to like her much. There's the two guys on the *Sirena*, but they're scooting north as fast as they can, and they just aren't taking calls. I tried 'em."

"What about Cordova?" Signy asked.

"Cordova was in and out everywhere, and the guy worked cash only, as far as I can tell. He's got relatives, a big, big family. Checking through them would be a fleshtime job, it looks like. Cordova may not have known *anything*. What we're looking for could have happened on that Greek boat, or back in Chile."

"We may just have to fake it," Paul said.

"Fake what?" Signy asked.

"A fabricated presentation, a simulation of a crime. I'd rather use the real thing, of course." Paul looked sad and completely serious.

"This San-Li didn't give us much to work with," Jimmy said. "Not good hard copy, anyway. She keeps real quiet, old Evergreen."

"It wasn't that I expected her to be running her cameras when she got someone to mess over that helicopter," Paul said. "But she's difficult to trace, even on the *Siranui*. You'd think the ship would run monitors on people, time clocks or something."

"She said she cleaned fish. . . ." Something nudged at Signy's memory, Jared's walk above the *Siranui*'s hold, a masked face that looked up to stare at him. San-Li? "Paul? When San-Li called into Lisbon, that's the only time we've seen her, right?"

"Yeah."

"I think I've seen her somewhere else."

Signy went back to the studio, Paul and Jimmy behind her. Jimmy carried a bag of trail mix. Well, Signy figured, any calorie is a good calorie right now, I suppose.

—Signy called back the scenes of the *Siranui*'s hold, the rows of workers, the woman who had stared up at Jared. The eyes might be San-Li's. Signy splitscreened that face next to the view of San-Li that had appeared on the Lisbon screens after Jared's death. In the green hood of the protective suit the woman wore, it was so hard to tell if the faces matched.

Signy faded them away and switched to a close-up view of San-Li's chapped knuckles, the silver letter opener. There. A round red burn on her ring finger, raw and ugly.

"Her hands. She's hurt her hands. Do you think she could have done the sabotage herself?" Signy asked.

The mark on her finger was a burn, definitely. Signy vanished the hands.

"No." The fleshtime Paul put his cup down on top of a stack of printout. "We'll look."

"Your San-Li may be a little different from the one we're building," Jimmy said.

A model, a personality simulacrum to fit into one of Paul's clever little matrices. "We'll meld them later," Signy said. "If we don't have the real woman, we'll need a model to predict her reactions, her behaviors. It seems we plan to use her against herself."

"You got that straight," Jimmy said.

"I don't have much to work with. I don't know her lovers, or how she spends her money. I don't know what turns her on. Did you save your conversations with Evergreen?" Signy asked.

"Yeah, I did," Jimmy said. "She was just somebody on the boards, someone friendly. We didn't talk that much, and it's all script, anyway. I'll pull the files for you."

Jimmy sat at Signy's console and tapped through old type-screens. "You might want to look at some stuff Pilar found, while I fix a file on Evergreen for you."

"What stuff?" Signy asked.

"Medical records and stuff." Jimmy got out of the chair as Signy dived for it.

Medical records. Well, they hadn't had time to tell her everything. Before Signy left fleshtime, she saw Jimmy settle the bag of trail mix on the desk, close to Paul's hand. Good work, that.

Medical records and stuff, yeah. What Jimmy sent to Signy's screen was a list of orders from a pharmacy. No discount house, this; the markup on the drugs was a substantial one.

Human growth hormone, esoteric estrogen analogues; Signy puzzled her way down the list and found antiseptics, heparin. Heparin? To keep a medication port from clogging. And there, orders for replacement catheters.

Intravenous medications, adjusted by daily monitoring of blood levels, this little girl was finely tuned. Growth hormone in chronic doses, her thin, thin face. They— they? Somebody, or San-Li herself, was following a shifting set of longevity regimes that Signy knew *quite* well; this mix of medications implied a program very similar to the one Signy had researched back in Atlanta. But the regime they'd used had been for *lab animals*, damn it. Nobody had even *thought* about testing it on humans.

Semistarvation was part of the routine. The child's gaunt face suddenly made sense. San-Li was anorexic, or close to it. Had she chosen to starve herself? Or was her hunger a discipline imposed on her from outside?

Other drugs had been ordered at various times, even occasional small doses of amphetamines and antidepressants. So San-Li did get hungry, or wakefulness was needed for long periods, and the tranks suggested temper outbreaks, or anxiety attacks, or other, more subtle manipulations of mood. Signy ran a quick correlation, and yes, the tranks, when they had been used, matched up with increases in circulating progestins. Finely tuned, finely tuned.

Some hospital or research lab had to be doing the blood work to keep this pharmaceutical jigsaw puzzle together. Try private, discreet, try research clinics first—

Try the *Index Medicus* for longevity research in the past, make it—ten—years, flag it for Japanese researchers, again for Kobe. Go, go, go.

Signy waited, tapping her virtual toes, and found— Well. Stupid (image of heel of hand striking forehead, so Signy did that, thumped herself on the head and groaned), if she'd looked in Tanaka's home turf first, she might have gotten here a little sooner. The researcher was a D.V.M. What else would she be, working the aquaculture division of Tanaka's own labs? And there, carefully dated and timed in to the minute, a log, a graph that listed daily weights, blood glucose levels, painstaking measurements of free radicals (that list dropped after a five-year run), circulating steroids of all varieties and fractions. Filed as *Cyprinus carpio* #14, heaven help us, a carp. A forty-kilo carp.

Well, what the hell? Fish had this funny tendency to be functional immortals.

Functional immortals. This San-Li was no unplanned child. Somewhere, somewhere, there would be records of careful embryo selection, of genetic screenings, primitive though they may have been when this child had been designed.

A little wave of pity bubbled up from somewhere, a small voice that said *poor baby*. Its echoes vanished in a greater pool of speculations, fear, and a puzzled feeling of envy.

A thirty-year treaty, to such a woman, would seem so short. Poor fool, did San-Li think to live until the seas restocked themselves, the species changed to thrive on toxins and oil sludge? Did she plan to set up great, slow engines in the seas to cleanse them?

How much would San-Li fear injury, accident, death by violence? The imminent chances of sudden death on that harvester ship must have terrified her beyond all reason. But San-Li was young. She was human, mostly, and still adolescent, therefore reckless. San-Li would be incapable of believing that she could ever die.

Paul and Jimmy were close enough to touch, and worlds away.

[Signy] Paul?

"What?" Paul answered in an ordinary way, in his ordinary voice in the fleshtime present.

"She's an immortal. I mean, San-Li's got a chance at a long, long life."

"Don't we all?" Paul asked.

"Oh, shit. I mean, San-Li's been altered in major ways. Aging is going to be a long, slow process. I'm talking a really good chance for two hundred years, here. Maybe longer. Maybe longer."

"Really?" Paul folded his arms and nodded. "If this is so—if San-Li lives far beyond our deaths, she will have many, many years in which to remember us." The smile on Paul's face was a ugly thing, a primate threat.

"What are you planning?"

"I would like for her to know her victims. Better than she's ever known a lover, or ever will."

"Jared . . ."

"Jared what?"

"He wouldn't like it, Paul."

"Don't speak for him, Signy."

Jimmy, make him stop. But Jimmy was elsewhere, goggled and remote. "Pilar?" Signy whispered. Interrupt this, Pilar, distract Paul, find a way to call back the sane parts of him.

—Signy entered Pilar's vision, Pilar in Jared's Taos workshop. Pilar scrutinized the lump of red, rough coral she held and turned in her hands. She had shaped a claw, roughly carved, incomplete. Its talons splayed wide, grasping for something just out of reach.

"My feelings for Janine are far more complex than

even you might have imagined," Pilar said, speaking to someone else. "There exist some forms of love that physical intimacy can destroy. Such a love is mine for Janine." Pilar's voice pleaded with her listener.

"I know," Jared said. Jared sat at the scarred, battered pine worktable. Pilar gazed at the smooth strong veins tracing their outlines on the backs of his hands. The votive light's yellow flame wavered, flickered, steadied. Pilar reached to touch Jared. His hands, their warmth, their strength, encircled hers; Signy felt their touch when Pilar did. Signy wanted to draw away, to vanish the sensations, but Pilar's calm repose stayed safe in Jared's touch, yes.

El Dia de los Muertos. The altars would be draped in marigolds, bright gold to honor the dead. Pilar's yellow candle glowed with a paler light. It was not a tradition Signy knew, and she doubted Pilar knew or cared to know its origins. Pilar was Anglo, and Pilar carried genes from the Pueblos and from the Spaniards that had come north out of Mexico, fleeing the Inquisition or seeking land and wealth.

Rituals overlap, resonate; genes, even in those isolated early centuries in the New World, always managed to mingle. Far to the south, in a day of bright and pleasant sunshine and on through a torchlit night in November, the descendants of the Aztecs still went out to picnic at gravesides. Bakers made sweet pastries to honor the dead, colored with happy pinks and bright oranges, gay little creations with explicit ribs and skeletal grins made of sugar frosting. In that worldview, some people of one's acquaintance happened to be alive, some happened to be dead. All of them enjoyed company. *Es verdad*.

"Pilar? Signy is here," Jared said.

"Why do you hide?" Pilar asked, looking up toward the studio speaker. "It's only Jared—"

Signy drew away, leaving Pilar's presence, Pilar's world of malleable gems and waking dreams. Signy closed down her console and fled from the familiar touch of its keys.

She was left with the fleshtime studio, the eerie stillness of predawn, the quiet, fidgety realities of Jimmy and Paul. Their company was that of zombies; they had gone away into their separate and shared closed worlds again, back into places Signy couldn't bear to enter.

She had to get away. Why had she wanted to bring these strangers here? Signy wanted, very much, to go home. Home?

Signy pulled her headset over her eyes.

—Signy paced the familiar corridors that spanned the world and listened to androgynous, calm voices listing the day's events. The world went about the business of murders, brush-fire wars, and water riots. Same as it ever was.

THIRTY

In the emptiness, icescapes formed, perfect, pristine.

Signy fought for balance. Bitter snow found the top of her boot and melted, burning, against her ankle.

Signy was utterly alone. Her huddled, tiny shape marked a central point in an infinity of windswept snow and howling winds. Above her arched a dome of hazy sky that diffused a sourceless, abrasive light.

Somewhere, far away, Signy could hear the sea.

She could die here. No outcrop of stone, no wind-carved drift offered shelter from the cold. Crevasses waited beneath the blurred white contours under Signy's feet. If she took a single step, any step, her weight would break through the crusted snow. She would fall, fall forever, past walls of eternal ice. Signy sank to her knees, slowly, afraid to move.

"Signy? Signy Thomas?"

The girl's face was so close that Signy could see the perfect texture of her soft, ivory skin. Warm in a black room, San-Li wore black brocade, draped high against her long, narrow throat.

"Hello, San-Li."

San-Li gripped the arms of a narrow, highbacked chair carved from a rich reddish wood. She held herself rigidly upright.

"The events in Antarctica have been unfortunate for you. I extend my deepest sympathy, and my regrets."

"Do you?" Looking at the child's gaunt, immobile face, Signy said, "I think you believe what you say. Did you kill them, San-Li? Jared, and the others?"

As if she hadn't heard, San-Li said, "There will be a time of mourning. But when it is over, growth must continue. I would offer you—not your Jared, who is lost, but something to meet the challenge of your talents."

Did this little monster have any concept of the utter outrageousness of her intrusion? Signy told herself she wasn't on her knees, that she wasn't cold. She was sitting at a desk in Taos, New Mexico, and she shifted in her skinthin so that her image stood with folded arms, looking down at San-Li.

"*Don't* push me, infant!" Signy said.

San-Li lifted her hand, palm forward, and spoke with a staccato rapidity. "Our plans to acquire the Antarctic ice have a high probability of success. The intricacies of transporting it will be very great, but those are engineering problems only. I should like to circumvent some of the environmentalists' alarms, their innate conservatism. You could be of great assistance to me."

"You're offering me a job."

"Yes."

"The others?"

"No. Only you, Signy Thomas. You have welded a group together from individuals with many weaknesses. Without your skills, they would have flung themselves into chaotic pursuits long ago. You could correlate, and disarm, the myriad warring interests a new water source will represent. The others could not."

"You think that my loyalty is easily transferred," Signy said.

"You have an elastic sense of boundaries. The boy Jimmy now holds your loyalty as well, and a man named Alan Campbell. Was it not easy to include them in your mosaic?"

It had *not* been easy. It had been *necessary*. Child, you have built a simulacrum of me that shows me much about myself.

"Come work with me," San-Li said.

Paul had said those same words, so many years ago, with that same pleading tone, with that same underlying assurance.

"Wrong words, San-Li." Feeling burning tears across her cheeks.

"Come and work with me."

Signy could. The concept tempted her. Leave these imperfect souls, this morass of cross-purposed desires and needs. Abandon Paul to his introspective, gleeful madness, Pilar to her restless pursuit of tomorrow. Leave them, they would hardly notice.

A multiple series of futures tumbled through Signy's mind; she walked the boundaries of a grim room tinted in sepia, alone with a doddering Paul and his ravings. Janine, in another set of possibilities, had gone off to find yet another unapproachable personage to reject her. Or Jimmy remained with her and Paul, a Jimmy isolated in his static, frozen timescapes of old art and new music.

"No," Signy said. I have built the foundations of my possible futures with my own hands. Whatever they might become, they are mine. In time, San-Li, what you offer would be the same as what I have now. Only different.

Signy's fingers knew the way to disappear the room, the girl, the sense of presence. She hesitated.

"San-Li? Be wary of us. If we find a way to charge you with murder, we will. We do not wish you well."

Signy forced herself into real time. She spun in her chair and grabbed at the arm next to her, plump soft skin—Jimmy's arm.

"Shit!" Jimmy jerked, forcibly pulled into fleshtime.

"San-Li's—" Signy stabbed at an override button on her console, giving her system a faked power surge, a burst of static that she doubted would fool San-Li.

"—in here with me."

"Why didn't you say so? Let's just run a little tracer

here, shall we?" Jimmy's fingers sped on his keyboard and he began to hum a little tune.

Signy released the override.

—San-Li's face returned, perhaps puzzled, perhaps aware that someone nudged at her privacy.

"She's still at McMurdo," Jimmy whispered.

Signy permitted the flick of her fingers' motion, vanishing the warm room, the girl's dark eyes, her pale, vulnerable throat.

"When she was Evergreen, she was so sweet. She used to ask about my music. She sent me haiku," Jimmy said.

"She did it," Signy said. "San-Li killed them all. But nobody's got evidence."

"I found this old geezer on the net," Jimmy said. "He says that all you have to do is put a condom full of Drano in a gas tank, or anyhow, that used to happen in 'Nam. The lye dissolves the condom, and sooner or later it corrodes through a fuel line. Out of gas. Just like that."

The technique wouldn't guarantee spectacular, flaming crashes. Over deadly cold water, a forced landing would be all that was needed. "What's the timing?" Signy asked.

"Six, eight hours."

"So that's how it was. If San-Li killed Psyche and her boys, then nobody could ever trace Miss Tanaka back to the sinking of the *Oburu*. They could wonder, but that's all they could do."

"Lemme get Paul out here." Jimmy took Pilar's console and eased his way into Paul's world. "Fleshtime break," Jimmy whispered, and Paul nodded.

"I was listening," Paul said. "From the top, here's how it goes. San-Li hired Skylochori and company to attack the *Oburu*. They blew the job. We know that much."

"Then San-Li backed off," Signy said. "Either Papa

got wind of what happened and cut off her allowance so she couldn't pay up, or San-Li just wasn't going to pay Psyche for a bad job. My vote is Papa was nosing around San-Li's accounts. San-Li knew about this iceberg scam and I'll bet she wanted a part of it. I'll theorize that Papa found out she'd been interested in the harassment going on in the fishing fleets. That's when he sent her to clean fish."

"Sounds good," Jimmy said.

"After San-Li didn't pay up, Psyche and the brothers started lurking around the outskirts of the Tanaka fleet. Somehow they faked a distress signal and the sub carrier went out to look for it. The Skylochoris came in close, saw somebody on deck, and hooked Jared overboard. Then they told San-Li they had a hostage," Paul said. He leaned back in his chair and laced his hands beside his head. "Good heavens. I don't do criminal law. This is so *juvenile.*"

"San-Li is seventeen," Signy said. "She heard, because she was listening to us, that *Jared* was the hostage. She knew we were looking for him. Shit, the whole *world* knew we were looking for him."

"Not quite," Paul said. "But go on."

"San-Li was already close to real trouble with Papa, or maybe Papa knew about the whole thing and was planning to keep San-Li in that fish hold until she grew scales. She had to try to fix things, so she got in touch with Psyche. San-Li couldn't have known what documentation Psyche had of the *Oburu*'s sinking—film? Audio? Psyche would have told San-Li she had it all recorded, even if she didn't. San-Li wanted Psyche's recordings, bad. So she hired Cordova at McMurdo. Cordova was supposed to bring Psyche in, and San-Li would have promised payment. I don't know what San-Li thought she would do with Jared."

"She thought he was with the brothers. He was supposed to climb in Cordova's helo with everybody else when Cordova went to pick them up," Jimmy said. "They would have made one nice neat disposable package, Psyche and the two men and Jared. It would have taken Cordova four hours to fly from the *Siranui* to the *Sirena* and two hours to get back to the *Siranui* again. There was the risk that the helo would poop out on the *Sirena*'s deck, but it was a risk San-Li had to take."

"Well," Paul said. "Well, then."

"You don't have any hard copy of any of this," Signy said.

"Oh, that's hardly needed." Paul turned back to his console. Signy jumped for her keyboard.

"What are you going to *do?*"

"I am going to stage the sabotage," Paul said.

—a sleek, immaculate Paul sat in the New Hampshire library. A grinning shark appeared near Paul's shoulder. The creature swam through the air, circling Paul's chair with lazy interest.

"Can't we just subpoena the Skylochori brothers or something?" Signy asked.

Jimmy popped his image into one of the Queen Annes. "Signy, I can figure what they know. They know somebody hired their brother to try to blow up a ship, but they don't know who; I'd bet on it. They kidnapped a guy, but a good lawyer could coach them to say they picked up a man overboard and were just trying to get somebody to come after him."

"They're no help, then."

"Nope," Jimmy said.

Edges could get the Skylochoris harassed, maybe get them jailed. Why bother? Let them have their *Sirena* and the labor that went with her. Let them worry for the rest of their lives about every stranger's knock at their doors, wonder if this time the man with the warrant had found them. Let them wonder every day if this was their last day of freedom.

Jimmy vanished, and Paul, replaced by a view of

McMurdo's sloppy, muddy landing field, a view Signy had seen on her way into the domes.

Paul could use McMurdo as a background and land Cordova's helo on it. He could image a San-Li beside the helo. Cut and paste. Make it real. To what purpose?

Because it was doing something, and doing something, right now, seemed to be good for Paul, and if that's how the thinking was going around here it was time to call the boys in white coats to come and pick up everybody.

Signy left them at it and went to the kitchen. The dishes hadn't moved themselves out of the sink. Shit. Signy turned on the water and began to rinse plates. At least an apparition of Jared wasn't standing around trying to help her.

THIRTY-ONE

Muffled thuds came through the house speakers. Janine's voice yelled, "Let me the fuck in!"

Signy opened the front door on fresh, wet air while Janine was still giant-stepping through drifts.

"You made it." Signy hugged her, and they spun around in the doorway. Janine brought motion with her, struggles with time and distance, and impatient, electric energy.

"What the fuck have you been doing?" Janine backed away and shook her head. Snow, flung from her hair, turned to tiny dots of wet mist on Signy's face.

Jimmy got himself behind Janine's shoulders in a maneuver that avoided eye contact. He held Janine's parka while she twisted out of it. Janine ignored him. Jimmy brushed snow away from the sleeves of the parka and hung it on a peg.

"I was washing dishes. My hands were wet so it took me a minute to get the door," Signy said. "Oh, babe. I'm glad you're here."

"We were working, idiot." Pilar came out of the studio and grabbed Janine in a rough hug.

"Yeah, right. My God, I'm wired." Janine closed her eyes and butted her head against Pilar's shoulder.

"Hello, engineer," Paul said.

Janine looked up at him. "Uh, hello."

"I know. I look like shit."

"Yeah, you do. You really do." Janine drew away from Pilar, stood on tiptoes, and kissed Paul's cheek, gently.

Janine, Pilar, motionless and wary, assessed each other as wrestlers might.

"Come in here a minute," Pilar said. "I want to know what you think about this." Pilar grabbed Janine's hand and led her into the workshop.

Jimmy, watching them go, looked like he was going to cry. Paul went away as well, back to his console and his headset.

Signy leaned against the wall and folded her arms. "You won't lose Pilar. Or, when you do, I promise you it won't be this easy. They'll be out in a while."

"I'm not worried," Jimmy said.

"I think you are. A little."

Jimmy grinned and shook his head. "Yeah." He looked at the closed workshop door. "I'll make coffee," Jimmy said.

"I just did," Signy said. "It's probably ready by now."

"Oh, rats, I forgot the groceries." Janine reappeared, at a trot, and grabbed her parka from its hook.

"How were the roads?" Signy asked.

"I followed the snowplow in. I rented a runabout; we'll have to take it back. Somebody help me get the groceries, okay?" Janine slammed the door behind her, letting in a swirl of cold wind and the neutral, soft light of a late, cloudy afternoon.

Jimmy shrugged and got his coat.

"Peace offerings of brute labor are often effective. Also, she likes flowers, sparklies, and good neck rubs," Signy said.

"I'll remember that." Jimmy followed Janine out the door.

Signy spooned up the remnants of her bowl of buffalo chile and had a last bite of *sopapilla* dipped in honey.

The group had settled where they could in the clutter

of equipment near the holo stage, their tropisms leading them to find space close to the warmth of the corner fireplace. This used to be called a "living room," Signy remembered. A place to rest and socialize.

Jimmy guarded the fire. He was pleased with it, it seemed; he'd been intrigued by the art of making fires vertically, with three pine splits stacked like a teepee.

Huddled in the early evening, they ate and rested. Paul sat on the floor, spooning up chile from his bowl. There had been some bickering over whose duty it was to chop onions (Jimmy had, while Janine and Pilar argued about it), and there had been a studied lack of interest in Paul's appetite. (It was ravenous.)

Signy braced her back against the *banco* where Jared was wont to sprawl and watch the fire. She pulled a knee up to her chest and rested her chin on it.

Begin. Somebody, begin, she pleaded silently. For I can't.

They had no words.

It had been *Signy*'s needs that brought them here. They had traveled here in their flesh because of her urging, because she said she'd needed help with Paul. And now they seemed more isolated, more distant from each other than they had ever been in the safe intimacy of the net. Where the blows they gave each other were cushioned, where the hurtful words they spoke—could be deleted, or explained away.

They were all so quiet. Jared was not here. Jared, if he were here, could get them talking. Jared could let them sort out what Paul might need and how they might help him find it. They would begin to deal with hurt, with grief, with what came next. Jared could *do* that and the talk was never clumsy or stilted, it just happened.

"I—" Janine said; a word that trailed off while Pilar said, "Impossible. We're so impossible."

In a rush of motion, Pilar left them, to wall them away

behind whatever she did in the workshop. Paul put down his bowl. Blind to them, he went back to Jared's console.

Their flight left cold, empty spaces in the room.

"I don't mean to interrupt," Alan's voice said. The lights on Signy's flatscreen threw red and blue swirls onto the empty holo stage. **"But if anybody's interested in what I've been doing in this icehouse you left me in, I'd be glad to tell you."**

Signy got to her feet, to her chair, to her headset. "We're here," she said.

—Alan in a business suit was a changed Alan, a polished Alan. He was, Signy decided, beautiful. Behind him, the Tanaka suite lay deserted, cluttered with empty dishes and crumpled napkins.

"They went through a lot of food last night." Alan waved his hand at the disordered tables. "We had to send a runner for more water, though, and I threw in an order for a couple of cases of champagne. So if you wanted to make 'em thirsty, you managed just real well."

"Did people stay around?" Janine asked. She snuggled close to Signy, a warm presence, a voice coming from close by.

In the distance, Pilar said, "You can set up your rig in the workroom. Come on, Jimmy. There's no *room* in the studio."

"They stayed *late*," Alan said. "The vote on the fishing ban has been moved up in the schedule. As in, this morning. I don't know if that throws you a curve. I hope not."

"It doesn't matter," Paul said, Paul in Jared's chair. "I'll window in the newsnet feeds and we'll get the vote as it comes in. What we need you to do is, you get in range of our friend Abeyta, the proud gentleman from Chile. If anyone is going to mount an opposition to the minerals provision as written, they'll come to him. While the vote is going on."

"You know that?" Alan asked.

"I know it," Paul aid. "Kazi talked with Abeyta last night. He's all for the ice. After the offer Kazi made him, he would have to be."

"Who did the listening?" Janine asked.

"Jimmy listened," Paul said.

And Paul had spent his time staging a scenario to punish San-Li; he'd been at it most of the day. But he'd made sure that Jimmy kept in touch with Lisbon. At least he'd done that.

"Good for Kazi," Janine said. "I thought I'd messed him up with Abeyta for sure."

"You tried hard enough," Pilar said, sotto voce, over a background rumble of stones tumbling in a polisher.

"Go on down to the voting, Alan," Paul said. "Call us when you're there."

Alan vanished.

So simply, so quietly, the delegates made their choice. Edges watched the newsnet, on flatscreen. The sober, proper gentle-persons voted to leave the world's last wild fishery alone for a time.

Japan made its plea—The world needs the protein now. From the nations near the world's thirsty waist, the cry rose—We cannot wait. We are starving.

The countries who were not starving, not yet, sent expressions of tired sympathy, and voted for the ban.

Leave the southern ocean alone; let it survive and heal if that is possible, Europe said, and Russia agreed. The empty Arctic helped the Russians in their moral stance, perhaps. Don't eat the fish, the Americas said, and China. Leave the deeps to Leviathan and the will of Allah, the bitter Mideast said, voting, with grim distaste, in uneasy agreement with Britain, Australia, and Israel.

With stoic faces, Japan's delegation accepted the verdict.

* * *

"Well, that's done," Janine said.

"It didn't seem like such a big deal." Alan's words, transmitted from the Palacio, mingled with the babble that followed the vote count, the Brownian movement of the crowd as people planned their next moves in Lisbon. Alan moved with the crowd, keeping Abeyta in sight ahead of him.

Paul sent a virtual crab to scuttle down the hallway, two steps ahead of Alan's feet. "Don't celebrate just yet," Paul said. "There's the little matter of the ice."

"Anna will celebrate," Alan said.

Alan had a gift for anonymity, it seemed. Taller by a head than the people around him, but he looked like he belonged where he was, in the center of a group that collected around a long table and braced themselves to begin the wordy, lengthy business of ratifying the Antarctic Treaty for yet another thirty years.

"Has anyone heard from her?" Signy asked.

"I haven't," Alan said. He looked toward the head of the table, where France cleared his throat, picked up a sheaf of papers, and began to read.

—Fading in, replacing Alan's view of the delegates, a desolation of ice and glory formed, ominous, powerful, and silent. Jared's hands hurt. He stood on packed snow, under a stormy sky. Broken ice floated in the sea. He/she was cold, and tired, and hopeful.

Egoless, engulfed, Signy was *there* with Jared, the knowledge of his/her strength welcome, comfortable, comforting.

"Is Paul doing this?" Janine asked. "Paul? What the shit are you *doing?*"

Signy shook her head, unable to speak. She didn't know. She truly didn't know.

"Paul, she's here." Jimmy spoke, his calm, soft presence smoothing away some of Paul's angular tensions, dulling the edge of Signy's fear.

"I hardly thought she'd manage to stay away," Paul said. "She'll join us when she's ready."

"Who?" Janine asked.

"San-Li," Signy said.

"No way," Janine whispered.

A pebble rattled on the beach. Jared/they, alerted by the sound, saw the girl's thinness, became aware of her terrible, constant hunger. San-Li wore a blue coverall from the *Siranui*'s stockroom, and a wool watch cap. The coverall hung loose around her. San-Li walked toward Jared/the watchers with hesitant steps, as if she were, as yet, unaware of them.

"Join us," Paul said.

The girl blinked at the light. She turned her head from side to side.

"You're in the right place. Signy's here."

"Paul!" Signy's shout echoed in the Taos studio. She grabbed for Paul's shoulder. (The ice tilted.) Paul twisted away from Signy's touch.

Somewhere, Pilar laughed.

Jared stepped aside, making room for another figure. Paul, dressed in the most impeccable of dark gray business suits, appeared on the ice. He bowed to San-Li and offered his arm.

"You can't keep me here," San-Li said.

"Force was never what we had in mind. You've come to us in our sorrow, and we would like you to stay with us for a time. To honor Jared," Paul said.

"It is not appropriate," San-Li said.

"Oh, but it is. Don't be frightened. We respect your need for privacy. To many of the visitors here, you are simply not present."

Paul brought San-Li to sit beside him on a Victorian love-seat that appeared on the sunstruck ice. "Nor is this." He/they (but Jared was gone, now) stroked the back of San-Li's hand, the rough knuckles, the spot of raw burn on San-Li's finger.

Visitors? Signy felt their attention, their blurred, mingled interests, gathered in the background. Waiting.

"Who are these people?" Signy asked.

"The lurkers? Whiteline is here; and a lot of people who seem to know Jared," Pilar said. "Paul's set this up on open lines; San-Li's screened away, but the rest of this is on the net."

San-Li's hand, seen against a background of black, toyed with a silver letter opener shaped like a dragon. San-Li's hand picked up a limp sausage made from a condom filled with white powder and slipped it in the pocket of her parka.

Cut: Cordova's helo waited on McMurdo's landing strip. A small figure in black trudged toward it.

Cut: Small chapped hands unscrewed a fuel cap and fed the condom inside.

"It wasn't like that!" San-Li said. "It wasn't like that at all," while the helo rose above the sea. San-Li's injured hand, now a giant's, reached up for the helo and plucked it from the air like a daisy.

"Perhaps not," Paul said.

Caught in the spinning blades, San-Li's hand shredded into bloody fragments that stank of brine and rotting kelp. San-Li whimpered.

"But we . . ." Pilar's voice paused, while it seemed she examined something nearby and of extreme interest. ". . . could convince people that it was. Like that."

Torn metal shrieked like a woman. A claw of red coral, carved and polished, coalesced from the drops of San-Li's blood.

"Signy, who's doing this?" Janine asked.

"Janine, baby," Pilar said, "all of us are. It's a requiem, that's what it is. Performance Art. Real." A hammer fell and something shattered. "Time."

"Pilar, must you?" Signy whispered.

"She killed my brother." Mark spoke, his angry voice much like Jared's. "Let her learn how we feel about that."

"Is Susanna with you?" Signy asked.

"Oh, yes." Susanna was a soft voice, a soft presence, one of the many disembodied observers hovering near the lonely slab of ice where San-Li stood.

San-Li's fear, her rage, ran like a current through the shared awareness. San-Li braced against terror and terror became purpose. As it had always, in San-Li's life, become purpose. Signy *knew* her, now. San-Li existed, glittering and complete, built of facets made of grueling physical and mental disciplines, Yoshiro Tanaka's calculated, calculated scorn of the female he had chosen to create as heir, San-Li's hatred of, and love for, her father, and San-Li's yearning for unfettered years of power. That hope lent Tanaka's daughter an unflinching willingness to survive.

"Signy, what do they want? What price do I pay?" San-Li asked.

Debits, credits. Signy could imagine the columns adding up in San-Li's mind, this much to squelch a nasty rumor, this much to replace a lost ship. "Money can't buy you out of this. Money, spent freely, could buy you simulations better than ours, simulations that would show you innocent, but we don't give a damn about that."

Acceptance came to Signy, resignation of a sort. It seemed that Pilar and Paul and Jimmy had spent the day's energies on creating a rite of passage, however strange it might be. Perhaps it would serve their needs, Signy's needs. What it might mean to San-Li was another question. "Cash won't be enough, San-Li. I think that all we want you to do is stay with us, for a while."

"I don't want . . ."

"The discomfort will be acute, I assure you. Sharing this with us is, however, a matter of honor." Signy waited, feeling the sense of held breath surrounding the Tanaka daughter, the mixed sensations of anger and bemused anticipation. Honor, my ass, Signy thought. This will be such an *inexpensive* ordeal. Think about it, kid.

San-Li melded into their awarenesses, determinedly among them. Jared sat down on the loveseat next to San-Li. He held San-Li's hand and patted it.

Suddenly in Lisbon, they saw bent heads, an array of notepads. They heard rapid French, creaking chairs, and Alan.

"Son of a bitch," Alan said. **"I think they're going to get to the minerals section of the treaty this afternoon."**

"Our best shot is they just run right past it," Paul said.

"There may be a studious lack of attention," Alan said. **"If Kazi and Abeyta have done their homework. These people look disinterested enough to make a person *tense*."**

"Hang in there," Janine said.

"I will do that. I truly will." Alan disappeared.

—The world, the green world, rippled. With Jared, weightless and relaxed, Signy looked up through iridescent water at a ceiling of ice carved into cathedral arches. She/they wondered at the effortless grace of a swimming bird, watched a dance between a woman and a huge and curious seal.

Rising with Jared, toward the surface, toward air and light, Signy listened. *They* listened; Signy could feel the observers close to her in nonspace.

Hammers striking stone. Deep, freight-train sound of a whale taking a measured breath. Whalesong.

An oboe sang a counterpoint to the whale's melody.

Time spun, and place, and images that Jared, bemused, seemed to explore with them. Jared watched with them as Pilar danced grief in a cold Seattle fog.

"Jimmy, you brought this?" Pilar asked.

"Yes."

—Paul followed Jared along a high sun-dappled trail in southern Colorado. The Spanish Peaks lay beyond the ridge. Listening to Paul's labored panting, Jared halted. Paul turned around and frowned at him.

"You're resting because I'm tired?" Paul asked.

"Yes."

"Don't *do* that," Paul said.

"Okay."

They walked on, until Paul sat down, bang, in the middle of the trail, and began to laugh.

—walking, in easy strides, Jared/they felt the solid ir-regularity of brick paving beneath their feet. Jared whis-tled, tuneless, as he walked along Beacon Street, the weight of a worsted jacket over his shoulder. Infant spring leaves danced in the wind, and his eyes appraised that sweet young thing as she walked by, and left her unresponsive face to watch another, taller girl, who winked at him.

Startled, momentarily, delighted, yes, he/they turned to watch her walk past. Signy had never seen that jacket, that Boston spring.

Another watcher entered the nonspace where Jared walked.

"Alan," Paul said. "When did you get here?"

"I've been checking in and out," Alan said. Yes, Signy realized, I sensed you, subtle and complicated, and won-dered who you were. Stay.

They watched the girl; Alan and Jimmy now overlaid their particular tensions of responses, pro and con, re-garding that particular, momentary girl possibility.

"He is (we, Jared and I, are) not simply a collection of memories!" Signy heard her voice grate out the words, strident, dismayed.

Jared the student, Jared the lover, Jared who tried to stop pain, images rushed by, tumbled across Signy's eyes and her memory.

They/we know, someone said.

Jared/they brushed gentle fingers across Signy's cheek.

"I sent you away and you died," Signy said.

"*We* sent him, Signy."

Whose voices? Janine's voice, Paul's, Pilar's.

"You couldn't have held me back," Jared said.

Alto voices swelled into a wordless chord. Red light defined the countours of bulky, modeled muscles, gliding under metal-smooth skin. Inhuman arms, not Jared's, held Signy, held all of them, in security and iron strength. This was not Jared, this synthesis of awareness. Jared existed in it, but not alone. So many strengths were here.

"Forgive yourself," Signy heard Jared whisper. "Or, as Pilar would put it; live with it or die."

Could she?

I've never been held like that. San-Li's chapped hand wrote the wistful words in tiny, cramped letters that twisted and vanished, whirled away on the wind.

A tenor, impossibly true in pitch and timbre, called out an eleison.

"Alan," Paul said. "What you're looking at. Show us."

Paul, the multitracked bastard, remembered real time.

Alan picked the hard copy he held, murmured apologies, went out into the halls and found a scanner.

Paul, murmuring phrases from the document Alan sent to Paul's screen, stepped back on the imaged ice. In the distance of that space, Paul set up an Escheresque infinity, pale blue and diamond white, a lattice of three-atomed, crystalline water. Ice.

Paul reached out and folded the scene into a sheet of thick paper.

"Hold this for us, would you, San-Li?" Paul asked. "Thank you, dear."

* * *

Signy/they walked with Jared, past rows of cots where the hungry, the ill, the poisoned, lay in eternal boredom, exhausted by the work of living. When Jared looked up, the corridor stretched forever, the lines of cots vanishing in the distance.

Jared left that pathetic reality, its unending, numbing repetitions, left it for the day. It would be there in the morning. It would always be there.

On a powder morning in Taos, Jared embraced gravity and motion in an exuberant, masterful rush of skis down Al's Run. He shouted at the top of his lungs.

Twinned sprays of snow flew, followed his skis, and formed a giant prismed wake.

A head turned, slowly, its weight borne on a heavy neck of beaten silver. Pilar incised faint spokes of color into the iris of the beast's eye with a scalpel of titanium steel. The tiny sounds it made creaked and scraped above a rumbling bass rhythm at the lower range of human hearing, the pulsing of a giant heart.

"You hurt," Jimmy said. "That hurts us."

"Creation hurts." Pilar stood with her head tilted, her eyes on—

Susanna, laughing, a tall girl in khaki shorts. Susanna knelt by a midsummer stream, cupping handfuls of water over her long black hair, her neck, washing away trail sweat.

Had Mark captured Susanna's summer laugh? Had Jared? Did it matter?

"Paul, Janine; Jared has a daughter," Signy said. "She's learning to walk."

Paul's startle, Janine's rush of warm delight, Jimmy's somewhat dismayed interest in the possibility, Pilar's acceptance; Signy embraced them all. She wanted to see Kelan, to hold her.

"A baby?" Janine asked. "A *baby?*"

"Well," Paul said. "Well."

"Kelan looks like her father," Susanna said. "Thank goodness."

"When can we see her?" Signy asked.

"Soon," Susanna said. "Soon, and often. You'll love her."

"Yes," Signy said. "I will."

Jared? Part of this, yes. The multiple, overlaid inputs of touches, tensions, angles of vision included Jared's reality, his delight in the physical, intricate world. Signy could sense him, amused, interested. His alert attention watched with them, the body she/they wore now was a part of every observer. And their eyes created—

A single drop of water falling into the sea. It tolled like a giant bell and they looked up toward a distant surface. As the drop fell, it was, had always been, a claw, grasping for something just out of reach. The color of red coral, taking shape as it fell beneath them.

Shapes, translucent, mutable, that might have been a rounded, massive belly, a heavy head, limbs supple and more massive than a dragon's haunches, flailed and sank in a collage of textures and struggle. The light from a beating heart pulsed with the color of marigolds, the wavering reflection of the sun. Swirling downward in a great eddy, separate, separate and lonely, segments made of loves and losses formed and vanished and formed again as they fell.

A monstrous concern circled the circling, sinking shapes of love and power.

The undersurface of the water was lighted neon orange. A great presence circled and nudged, nudged upward, the embryonic creature forming itself from the sea, a creature that pulled its substance from the swirling waters and centered itself around its beating heart. Midwife on a whale's back, it rose toward air and light.

Toward light, flames, a wondrous fan of colors. A thigh flexed, a claw tightened and clung and vaulted into the air, into washes of pure light—emerald, celadon, citrine, cobalt yellow, but this yellow was filled with transcendent white, the white of metal glowing in flame.

Topaz, aquamarine, sapphire blue, moonstone seen in moonlight.

Laughing, the salamander gulped flame. The creature examined, in motions that wrote unknown scripts and soundless words, the newborn, terrible power of its burnished limbs. Living, elemental, and joyous, it existed.

Pilar stood on the empty ice next to San-Li. Pilar held a little figure in her hand, a salamander made of stones and metal.

"It's beautiful," San-Li said.

"It's a symbol. A salamander can be torn apart, but it is reborn in flame. We survive, San-Li. Will you?"

After a time, bright letters took shape in the darkness.

the exploitation of minerals
is forbidden
on the Antarctic continent and its continental shelf
for a period of thirty years from the date of ratification
of this treaty

"Very good!" Paul said. "That little segment of the treaty leaves a hole for Tanaka's water buyers to slip through. The Commission won't vote on it until October or so. People, we have lots of work to do before then."

Paul sounded happy.

The copy of the treaty faded and vanished.

"Thank you, San-Li," Paul said. "You may go."

San-Li was left alone on the ice. Her dismay spoke to them from the signals of her tight, quick muscles.

"Thanks, Evergreen," Jimmy said.

San-Li and the ice disappeared.

Jared walked on the mesa. He looked up at Taos Mountain's snowcap, stained red in sunset colors. The air smelled of recent rain and wet sage.

Jared snapped his fingers and the watchers, obedient, vanished.

THIRTY-TWO

The newsnets gave full coverage to the funeral of Yoshiro Tanaka. Signy, in Taos, watched a flatscreen view of wall-to-wall black umbrellas crowding a rainy Kobe street.

"Paul, we should never have let her go. We had a monster in our grasp and we turned her loose."

"Is San-Li Tanaka a monster?" Paul stayed in New Hampshire most of the time, but he was in Taos now, he came to Taos when Kelan did. Paul had taught Jared's daughter to read. Kelan used to sit on his lap and listen to the same stories over and over again. Paul, helpfully, made mistakes for Kelan to correct. By the time Kelan was four, she could read on her own. Now she was ten and she read legal briefs to Paul.

"Yes, San-Li is a monster," Signy said. "She's become second-in-command at Tanaka Pacific, formerly Tanaka Company and Pacific Biosystems, through an *extremely* clever series of career moves. Make that woman-in-charge of Tanaka Pacific, now that Yoshiro is dead, and she's never made a mistake yet. That's monstrous."

"She made *one* mistake," Paul said.

"Yes."

On the flatscreen, priests in yellow robes preceded a coffin draped in wet flowers. Surrounded by a phalanx of bodyguards, a slender woman walked behind the coffin.

"Good and evil can be measured on many scales," Paul said. "San-Li began the rescue of the ecosystem of the Southern Ocean. That's probably good. Tanaka's water is keeping part of the U.S. West Coast alive for a few more miserable years. That's probably evil. Balance her actions, Signy, and give me your judgment."

"No," Signy said. "That's not my job."

"Do you still talk to her?" Paul asked.

"Pilar does." Pilar and Jimmy and Janine were on the Station, doing in-depth interviews with a crew outbound for Saturn. Signy hoped Janine wouldn't sign on for the trip, but you never knew.

"What's Alan doing?" Paul asked.

"He's out teaching Kelan how to split wood. Or she's teaching him, I don't know which. Enough of this funeral, Paul. Susanna and Mark are coming in from the airport to pick up their child in *one hour*. I have things to do. I guess our fun's over for the summer."

Kelan would go back to Canada, to school and winter. During the winter, Kelan popped in and out of the studios in Taos and New Hampshire and Seattle. Sometimes she spent time walking beside Jared, sharing things he'd done years ago, asking interminable questions of the rest of them.

"*I'm a lot like Jared, aren't I, Signy?*" Kelan had asked Signy once.

"*You're like him. You're like Mark and Susanna, too.*"

"*And Paul.*"

"*Yes. But you're more like Kelan than anyone else.*"

"Signy, there's a contract proposal I want to show you," Paul said.

"After dinner," Signy said. "Please?"

EPILOGUE

Anna's little sloop flanked the ice train as it moved north. Anna usually ran a zigzag course, crossing and recrossing the boundaries of the band of cool water the ice left in its invisible, slow wake. The changes in the seas's tiny creatures were more easily measured there. Anna couldn't be sure yet, wouldn't know for years, but it seemed the cooler water caused no harm.

The ice train had left the Ross Ice Shelf fourteen months ago and it would cross the equator today.

Anna thought she would tell Kelan to come up to the deck to get her earring. That old, old ceremony always pleased the young.

But Kelan left her studies, the summer coursework that had sent her here to work with gray-haired Anna, and came topside without prompting. For a haole, she was gorgeous, Kelan with her dark curls and her brown eyes, the vibrant energy of her newly ripened body.

"We're almost at the equator, aren't we?" Kelan asked.

"It's not a line painted on the water," Anna said. On the horizon, Anna spied what she had hoped to see. She laughed.

"What?" Kelan asked. She squinted as she stared out at the fractured sunlight on the water. "Oh. I see it!"

The whale broached, sped toward the sloop, and rose again. She slapped her tail on the water and blew a mighty plume for Anna and Kelan to watch. Her arrival announced, the young humpback came alongside and rolled her length for their scrutiny. She looked healthy and unscarred, still, but she was very young.

Kelan leaned over the rail at a precarious angle. A pendant hung from a chain around her neck. It looked heavy. It swung back and forth with the tilt of the waves.

The whale vanished as if she had never been. Kelan stood upright again.

"Will she be back?" Kelan asked.

"Humpbacks like to blow three times," Anna said. "That's a pretty necklace, Kelan."

The girl's hand reached to enclose it. The length of her hand, it was an intricately carved salamander, a graceful little creature of red coral, amber, and agate, set in beaten silver.

"Thank you," Kelan said. "Pilar made it for me." Kelan searched the empty water for the whale. "I wish the whale would stay with us. Do you think she might?"

"I think she might." The young humpback had always visited Anna, these past years. The whale would continue to leave her herd and visit Anna until she calved. Then she would stay with her sisters, and her sisters were shy.

"You know her, don't you, Anna?"

"I knew her father."

"How old is she?"

"Twenty. Like you."

The young humpback showed no signs of illness as yet, and she had bred. Anna worried for her, and for her unborn calf, and guarded them as best she could.

The whale saluted them with ritual solemnity, sending up a flawless plume of breath, and later, another, while the little sloop sailed north with the ice.

■ READ ON FOR A PREVIEW OF ■

THE MAN IN THE TREE

SAGE

WALKER

Available now from Tom Doherty Associates

TOR A TOR HARDCOVER

ONE

Pleasure Centers

The sun in the hollow center of *Kybele* is supported by six Eiffel Towers.

In daylight, the clusters of petals near the top of the towers, closed, look like bulbous minarets. As they unfold, black shadows strike the fields and forests below. Kaleidoscopic patterns of ever-increasing darkness spread over the landscape until the edges of the petals almost touch each other and the day-bright interior of the asteroid is dimmed for night.

Kybele was Earth's first, perhaps Earth's *only*, seedship, and she existed because there was a chance, a statistically infinitesimal chance, that someday she or a daughter ship of hers might return, headed back toward Earth with hope and life. *Kybele*'s singular existence was possible because of asteroid mining, hope, and diverted resources from an Earth that said it couldn't afford her. The Mars colony, small and underground, was only viable because of money from asteroid mining. The time frame for terraforming Mars, a planet with no seas and no magnetic core, was centuries longer than *Kybele*'s voyage.

Earth's humans were in a battle for survival that constantly teetered near disaster. *Kybele* was a long-shot insurance policy of sorts. Some very good minds had run the numbers and found an intersection, a window, between dwindling resources and increasing technical ability where a seedship could be built. *Kybele* was that intersection.

Helt Borresen, Incident Analyst for the seedship, walked spinward from the base of Athens tower on a path he knew well. He sat down beside a creek and fitted his back against the trunk of an aspen. The creek talked a little of this and that.

This was a private place, one he liked. He came here for solitude, but last night and the night before he'd caught glimpses of an interesting woman, barely seen in the shadows, a woman who moved quickly and quietly, as if she were watching something but didn't want to be seen.

Downhill from the aspen, a marshy meadow flanked the creek. Tall grasses grew there, late summer yellow, some of them seeding for next year. Cattails marked soggy ground. Beyond the meadow, anti-spinward, the deep gash of Petra canyon was darker than the forest that grew to its rim. Beyond it, up the curved inner surface of *Kybele*'s hollow interior, the forest ended abruptly at the edge of croplands, squares of plowed black soil and yellow stubble, striped by shadows from the legs of the towers and going monochrome in the fading light. The warmth of an October day began to fade and a cool breeze came up to rustle the cattails. *Kybele*'s night was programmed to replicate the twenty-eight-day cycles of Earth's moon, and as Helt sat, half-dozing, the light dimmed toward quarter moonlight, dark enough to silver the grass and turn the shadows black.

A flicker of white brought his focus back to the meadow. White-tailed deer, a dozen or so, appeared in the tall grass, as quickly and quietly as if they had been popped into place by a special-effects team. Two yearling bucks, their antlers only brave stubs, were with the females, but none of the big guys. The herd was close enough that Helt heard grass tear as they munched their way toward the water. He had never been able to see a herd of deer, or elk, or reindeer, without counting them. Fourteen. The herd went downhill in the tall grass and vanished.

The show was over. He thought about getting up.

And then he didn't, for the pair of young bucks reappeared at the edge of the meadow. The woman he had seen here briefly last night stepped out of the pines on the far side of the clearing. She had a bottle tied to her belt and something small gripped in her right hand.

The deer came to her. She was on the far side of the deer from Helt, so he couldn't see what she did to the neck of one and then the other. Whatever it was, when she finished, she shoved at the neck of the deer she had just handled. It didn't move away. The little buck lowered his head to have the skin around the nubs of his antlers scratched. His buddy decided he needed some attention, too.

The woman groomed both of them for a little while. Then she laughed, low and soft, and clapped her hands. The deer bounced away. She unhooked a bottle from her belt, put things in it, and screwed down the lid. The motions caused the interlocked squares of her plaid shirt to tighten and loosen over her breasts in pleasant ways.

She turned and walked toward Helt's aspen. He supposed she saw him. He was visible enough against the white trunk of the tree, so he stood up. She was a tall woman. The top of her head would have fit comfortably just under his chin. She had dark hair, tied back. The faux moonlight made it shine.

She stopped walking.

"Hi," Helt said.

She gave a little shrug. It looked liked resigned acceptance of his presence. "Hello," she said aloud. "I disturbed you."

"I enjoyed watching you. I'm only a little disturbed."

"About what?"

"About what you did to call them in."

"Oh." She reached in her shirt pocket and pulled out a little control box. She stepped closer to Helt, to show him. "They have electrodes in their pleasure centers, and the buzz they get gets stronger the closer they come to this. The guys you saw were numbers thirty-three and thirty-five. I pushed their buttons. They came running."

She was close enough that he could smell her hair, her skin. He didn't smell perfume, just clean healthy human, and whatever scent there is that tells a hindbrain a woman is nearby. She was maybe ten years younger than Helt and her eyebrows were dark wings above her large eyes. In the moonlight, he thought her eyes were gray.

Helt felt lonely. He was lonely. He had no one special right now, and hadn't for a couple of years. Well, four, actually.

"I'm disappointed."

"Why?"

"It's just tech. I wanted to think it was magic."

"It's sufficiently advanced to seem so. To a deer."

"Clarke's third law. Advanced technology looks like magic. Did you ever read any of his novels?" Helt asked.

"No. I came across that quote once and liked it."

The novels had been written in the twentieth century. The 2209 Helt lived in was very different from the future the old dreamer had imagined. Humanity had stayed at the edge of disaster, as ever, and survived some of its own failings—so far.

"I'm Elena," she said. "Biosystems."

"Helt. Systems Support." He wondered why he'd never met her. He wondered how long she'd been on board.

They started walking toward Athens tower.

"Thirty-three and thirty-five will be leaving the herd soon, out for a tour of enforced bachelorhood," Elena said. "The stags will see to that. I needed some blood from them. We monitor hormone levels, nutrition, muscle mass, many other things." She spoke standard Omaha English, but there was a touch of hesitation, of indrawn breath, before some of her words. "These yearling bucks have stayed with their moms a bit longer than we expected," Elena said. "If they're developing normally, their testosterone levels should be lower than they were a few weeks ago. Rutting season is almost over."

Helt didn't mind a discussion of testosterone levels at all. His were rising a little, and he decided to take her willingness to play biology teacher as a positive sign.

Beneath the support pillars of the towers, the ground was in permanent shadow. People walked there because it was easy. Nothing much grew underfoot. Helt thought of giant mushrooms, blind insects, cave-adapted species, spooky creatures made of old fantasy. Perhaps he would avoid mentioning them to the SysSu techs. They might manufacture some displays to jump out and go "Boo!" Just because they could.

"Are you worried that the deer won't be guy enough for their jobs?" Helt asked.

"That's what I'm checking. They have a lot of adapting to do," Elena said. "They seem to be thriving at half-g. They love to jump, but we've seen no broken legs yet, so they've sorted that out. They can't be really wild with this much human contact; there's taming, of sorts. They don't get shot at, so they don't flee us the way their cousins back home do. And there aren't any large predators to give their adrenals a workout."

No large predators, except for humans. When it came time to thin the herd, to harvest venison, would Biosystems establish a hunt? Would running the deer become a sport on *Kybele*, good for working off human frustrations and sharpening the survival skills of the herd? Surely Biosystems had thought of this, and had made a list of pros and cons. Helt would look to see what they were, later. "Do you think the fear of getting eaten would keep them healthier?" he asked.

"Perhaps. They are active without that, so far. They play. The males battle each other. But there's so much to think about. Maybe they're missing mosquito bites, or something," Elena said.

"You're teasing me," Helt said.

"Yes."

"Please tell me you won't put mosquitoes up here."

The woman named Elena looked up at him and smiled. He still couldn't tell exactly what color her eyes were. The lights near the elevator door made them look sort of hazel, maybe. Her plaid shirt was black and white and gray.

He hoped she liked men who were sort of sand-colored all over. He hoped she didn't mind a five o'clock shadow with a few white whiskers in it. He hoped she didn't mind that his hair looked like someone had cut it with a pair of office scissors, for that's what he had done four days ago when he'd noticed it was falling in his eyes.

Helt wished the walk had been longer. He liked Elena. Walking with a woman beside him felt good.

The elevator was large enough for twenty. There was no good reason for him to stand really close to her as it took them down from Center, so he didn't.

The doors began to slide open on Level One. "Could we keep talking?" Helt asked.

"I really have to get back to my lab before my blood gets hot," Elena said. She looked down at the thermos bottle clipped to her belt, tapped it, and walked away. She was going toward the train station that would take her back to Stonehenge, he supposed.

But he'd seen a little smile at the corner of her mouth.

His interface gave him her name; Elena, Biosystems, was Elena Maury, MD, PhD. He found a headshot that gave him a good look at her huge eyes, her high cheekbones. Her eyes, in the photo, looked more hazel than the gray he'd seen in moonlight and in the elevator lighting.

That was enough to know for now.

TWO

The Man in the Tree

It was Wednesday evening, and Helt Borresen wasn't up in Center for the sunset. He was beneath Center on Level One, eating supper in the Frontier Diner. The diner was a mundane place of stone-topped tables and bamboo chairs. The air held a reassuring hint of French fries and coffee, and because it served a 24/7 clientele, you could get breakfast at any hour. Helt liked breakfast for supper, so he was having a spinach omelet with a side Caprese salad.

If Elena followed a daily schedule, she would be back in Center about now. He could go up there. She might not be there. She might be looking at her deer and think he was pushy or weird, or, worse, if he went up there she might think Helt Borresen had come hunting for her.

Yeah, it was time and past time to look for a love that would last a lifetime. So he really was hunting and he might as well admit it.

He was afraid, and he might as well admit that, too. His mother had been injured when he was young, and the injury had left scars on her brain. He knew, intellectually, that it was nothing he had done, yet he was still afraid that anyone he loved would get hurt. It was an irrational fear and he knew it.

Admit it, sure. Change it? Not so easy.

Helt scooped up the last bite of the nutmeg-laced spinach with a piece of toast and looked up at the man approaching his table. Navigation coveralls, dark five o'clock stubble on his chin and his shaved head, a lot of muscle in neck and shoulders, and the brown eyes of a puppy who had just been yelled at and didn't understand why.

"Helt Borresen?"

"That's me. I'm Helt."

"Yves Copani. I went to your office but you weren't there. I apologize for coming after hours, but—" Copani pulled his interface out of a pocket and gripped it tightly.

"But you just got off work and there's something you want me to see," Helt said. "It's okay. I'm still working, actually." A moonlit walk wasn't going to happen tonight. Fine. Now he wouldn't have to worry that seeing Elena again so soon would make him seem like a pest. "Sit down. Send your file to IA Helt." Helt reached for the folded screen next to his coffee cup and popped it open. "Want some coffee?"

This evening's waitperson approached and filled Helt's cup. Copani waved him away. "No, no thank you."

What came to Helt's screen was the Curriculum Vitae of Yves Copani, welder, whose engineering doctorate had been earned in Milan. He was overeducated for the job of tunneling out nickel-iron from *Kybele*'s Level Three. That he was overeducated was no surprise; most contract workers held doctorates in something or other. Helt scanned the rest of the info as well.

"I want to stay here," Copani said. "I want to spend my life here."

A lot of dreamers on Earth below wanted to come here, live here, take the risk that their descendants, seven generations down the line, would reach a new planet and be able to live on it. Only a few of the rich, a few of the lucky, made it past the barrier of requirements and became outbound colonists.

A lot of realists on Earth below thought they were crazy to take the chance. Earth was a sad and damaged place, but parts of her still functioned, and that she could support human life was a given. No one knew if the new planet could do that.

"Is it still possible?" Yves asked.

"Barely. There's still some shuffle room on the passenger list for the last shuttle, but there isn't much. You've asked David II for a colonist slot, I'm guessing."

"I'm not sure he's looked at the request," Copani said.

David Luo II was the Engineering boss on *Kybele*, a busy, busy man.

"So you came to me."

"I hoped you could help," Copani said.

"I may not be able to. I'm the Incident Analyst. My job is to arbitrate conflicts between Navigation, Bioscience, and Systems Support if and when they come up. I do some intramural work in the divisions when I'm called in, but it's only advisory." Helt permitted his overdeveloped sense of fairness to come forward and ask questions. Why me and not him? Why don't I get sent off so he gets to stay? Not fun. Why not him and me both stay? "Yves, it's true that in extraordinary circumstances I can make upgrades to colonist status, if there are no objections from the division chiefs. For me to sponsor you, I'd need to show you would be of extraordinary benefit to the ship. Are you extraordinary?"

"I don't know. I don't think so."

"You aren't grandiose, anyway. That's good, but humility isn't something I can sell to David II or his boss. Your CV says you have a job waiting in Cape Town for three times the amount of money you're making here."

Salaries on *Kybele* were high. Contract workers usually drew enough AUs, Access Units, *Kybele* currency, to meet expenses, and converted the rest to euros in Earth-based accounts. The AU was a sound currency. The conversion rate was, as of last week, something like 1 AU to 2.3 euros.

AUs, like any currency, were tokens for barter, their value based on energy expenditure, physical or mental, and traded for other energies or material things. For now, they could be converted back to euros for Earth-based transactions.

The lottery for colonist selection and funds from supporting nations had given *Kybele* a fat bank balance. She spent like a sailor on shore leave, but she also exported tech advances and media to Earth below and was making money from them.

"You're telling me you are willing to give that up, to stay here as a flunky welding steel rods to keep tunnels from collapsing, for the rest of your life. Why?"

"I'm in love," Copani said. "She's in Biosystems, a colonist. She doesn't want to leave."

Oh. "I see." Elena's name was a version of Helen, and a Helen in a time long past had launched a thousand ships and a war. Helt was screwing up his courage to go to war with himself, his old fears, his new ones, over the Helen he had met last night. Love, the possibility of love, counted, damn it.

"That's an honest reason to want to stay," Helt said. "In that case, why don't you order some dinner and we'll figure out a narrative I can use to bring you to David II's attention. That would be the place for you to start."

Helt signaled the waiter.

Back in his office, Helt promised himself he would only work one more hour and then go home.

Because linear information, lists, two-dimensional graphs got too visually busy too fast for him, Helt looked at the humans on *Kybele* as bubbles of information. He liked Venn diagrams, spherical ones. His programs rendered facts and factoids about a particular individual into colors, shapes, and varying degrees of opacity. In the past ten years, some of the bubbles had acquired accumulations of biography, work history, friendships, frictions. Over time, as events, likes, and dislikes pushed and pulled, aggregates formed. Attractive traits drew other bubbles closer. Givers and team players attracted other souls; takers and users were often, but not always, repelled.

Sometimes he displayed the ever-shifting groups as a coalescence of wrinkled balloons, sometimes as clusters of spiky morningstars, ferocious weapons. Over time, they had formed ameboid blobs that corresponded pretty well with the three working departments on *Kybele*, Navigation, Systems Support, Biosystems.

Take thirty thousand people and create a framework of habitats, interactions, and work that will let their descendants survive and reproduce for two hundred years, while keeping the skills needed to live on a new world. The population will live in isolation. No one gets to go outside and play. There will be no visitors.

It was a prison or a paradise, depending on your philosophy. The people in Helt's new world, his fellow passengers, were prisoners of nothing but their own hopes and dreams. They had chosen to live in this enclosure, a hollow asteroid on a one-way journey to a relatively nearby star. They knew the risks.

They knew the risks of staying on Earth as well. Wars were continuous, but entire civilizations sustained themselves on arable land at the poles. The population was down to three billion and might have stabilized there. It would be centuries before the planet's oceans, her basic life-cycle drivers, recovered from the acid the Anthropocene era had dumped in them. Maybe old Gaia could heal herself. Maybe not.

Odds were, this worldlet named *Kybele* would get where it was going. It would reach a new world, a full-sized one, a planet with liquid water and all the building blocks of life. That the new planet would sustain human life was not a given. Even so, a lot of people were willing to take the gamble.

Odds were, the only thing that could make *Kybele* herself uninhabitable were the people inside it.

The hollow rock that was *Kybele*, once thrown toward its new star, would get where it was going, but by design and necessity, its air and water and food supplies would fail without the constant input of skilled human hands and human minds. That reality, hopefully, imposed a social contract of mutual tolerance that would survive the stresses and conflicts humans make for themselves. Maybe. If everyone worked at it.

Helt was daydreaming himself into the what and how of scenarios he could not, on his own, control. The broad-spectrum lights on the west wall of his office had gone dark so the greenery could rest. A bot searched for leaves on the floor. Helt searched for a pear in yellowing leaves, but all of his were gone. He got out of his chair, walked out into the hall, stretched out his arms, remembered a plaid shirt worn by a beautiful woman, and went back to his desk.

A lot of people weren't entered in his State of *Kybele* construct. Only the ones who had been players in inter-departmental disagreements of one flavor or another interacted in Helt's spheres of data. The three divisions on *Kybele* handled their own internal affairs when they could, and those interactions didn't usually come to Helt's attention.

Yves Copani wasn't in there.

Only one more hour's work, Helt had told himself, but he really wanted to find an excuse to let Yves Copani stay on *Kybele*. He liked the man.

Yves Copani was trained as an architect, but he'd hired on as a welder. He loved his quarters in Petra, and music, and his buddies, and hard work, and his girl. Oh, he loved his girl. She worked in Stonehenge and her name was Susanna, not Elena. Yes, he checked, and felt a little embarrassed about it.

In short, Yves loved everything he saw or touched or ate, unless he hated it, and if he hated something he wanted to make it beautiful so he could love it. He wanted the stars, and he wanted to stay with his true love.

True loves seldom lasted, but Helt liked the simplicity of the man's outlook. He liked it, but he wouldn't let it change the multiple factors in his off-list protocol, the one designed to sort out who went back to Earth and who stayed aboard.

The protocol was used to sort through nets of relationships and interactions if the three division chiefs disagreed about who should go and who should stay, and no one was disagreeing about Yves Copani. He was just a contract worker who had never come to their attention or given them a problem. But Helt was sifting the files all the same.

Yves had worked some off-shift hours in the vineyards in Center. Helt wondered if that's how he'd met his true love, or if he worked there to please her. Yves's grandfather had worked for Ferrari, certainly not a sound reason to want to keep him aboard.

Helt was admiring a Ferrari in one corner of his screen when Severo Mares's face took over the other. The chief of Navigation Security Services, *Kybele*'s euphemism for cops, was in uniform, well past time to be off-shift.

"Why do you look so happy?" Severo asked.

"Because you reminded me it's time for me to go home three hours ago."

"It's about a man in a tree," Severo said.

"Tell me."

"At twenty forty-four we got a call from a couple who were out, uh, hiking. They saw something in a tree, and it scared them. We went up and found a man in a tree, and blood everywhere. We just got him down. He's dead."

Location coordinates flashed across the screen. The tree, and the EMTs who surrounded it, were half a kilometer spinward from the base of Athens tower, in wilderness. "We think he jumped. There are broken limbs on some of the trees around. He must have tried to glide down."

"What the hell? Did he hallucinate a hang glider or something?"

Hang gliding in *Kybele*'s half-g and strong Corolis force was fun, the survivors of the sport had said—before Navigation started giving stiff fines for trying it.

"Damned if I know," Severo said.

TOR

Award-winning authors
Compelling stories

Please join us at the website
below for more information
about this author and other great
Tor selections, and to sign up for
our monthly newsletter!